A
GATHERING
STORM

A NOVEL

LYNN MASON

Book Cover by Damonza

ISBN 978-1-7373422-8-1 (paperback)

ISBN 979-8-2276448-6-2 (second edition print)

ISBN 978-1-7373422-9-8 (ebook)

Visit the author at lynnmason.com

A GATHERING STORM

1

THE THREE PARTNERS AT Sandstorm International had just finished a teleconference with Oman-based clients, a U.S. shipping company seeking to augment training for their security personnel stationed at the port of Muscat, and now debated a walk to their favorite bistro for a late breakfast.

"We know where Kate stands," Jake said.

"For the record, I made Kate an omelet the size of a large pizza this morning, and with about as much cheese," Nick said.

"That was hours ago, and I always have room for second breakfast," Kate replied.

Jake stood and stretched. "Shall we? I'm starving."

An email popped into Kate's inbox, with only a subject line: *Let me know when call is over.* "Hang on. Margaret needs us."

Jake opened the door and stood aside for Margaret to enter Kate and Nick's shared office.

"What's up?" Kate asked.

"Do you remember that woman who visited twice last year? Leslie Vincent?"

"Oh no," Nick said, before Kate could respond. "Absolutely not."

"Hush," Kate told him.

"She's on the phone requesting a meeting with you."

"No," Nick said.

"At least she called this time," Kate said. "When does she want to meet?"

"This afternoon at one o'clock."

"No," Nick said.

"She indicated there would be others joining her."

"Oh my God, how many times do I have to say no?"

Jake snorted. Margaret waited for Kate, who gnawed her bottom lip. She picked up her iPhone, then set it back on her desk.

"Fine," she said. "One o'clock."

"Damn it, Kate."

Margaret smiled. "Main conference room at one."

"Let Leslie know that she's going to get a nasty text message from me," Kate called after Margaret's retreating figure.

"I can't believe this is happening," Nick muttered.

"Come on, aren't you even a little bit curious?" Kate stood, grabbed her phone and purse, and motioned the two men toward the door. "We can argue about it over second breakfast."

Ω

As usual, Nick lost the argument to his wife over second breakfast. Kate sent a WhatsApp message to the woman calling herself Leslie Vincent, but all she received in return were not-so-cryptic emojis of poop and fire.

"I'm not sure that bodes well," Kate commented over her Belgian waffle smothered in butter, whipped cream, and fresh fruit.

Nick ordered a pitcher of Bloody Mary and drank most of it himself.

A few minutes before one, the partners arrayed themselves at the conference room table, with Kate at the head flanked by Nick and Jake. Sandstorm International, a Boston-based boutique security consultancy, was no longer able to accommodate same-day meeting requests except from their most important clients or most important potential clients, but Kate was willing to make an exception for Leslie Vincent. If she were a cat, curiosity would have cost her all nine lives, in quick succession.

"I don't deserve this," Nick said to Kate.

"You're right, darling, you deserve much worse." Kate smiled sweetly at him as the frosted-glass door swung open and Margaret showed in their guests.

The partners stood. Kate managed to conceal a smile, Nick barely stifled a sigh, and Jake coughed to muffle a snicker.

Diana Fraser, who was known to call herself Leslie Vincent on occasion, entered first, followed by a thin, fit man with stylishly mussed hair wearing a tailored suit. Two men followed him, and then a fifth individual burst through the door and beelined for Kate, a huge grin on his face.

"Charlie!"

Kate hugged Charlie Rodriguez, whose tight embrace lifted her off the ground a couple of inches. Charlie slapped Nick on the back and reached across the table to fist-bump Jake before taking up position at Diana's side.

"Please, sit," Kate said.

Their five visitors had separated themselves, Diana and Charlie on one side, the three men on the other. The fit man with the tailored suit caught Kate's eye and gave her the quickest of winks. Kate gestured for Diana to begin.

"Kate, Nick, Jake, I'd like to introduce you to our partners from *la Direction Générale de la Sécurité Extérieure*, the French external security service. Laurent Dubois, the director-general; Henri Ardouin, the chief of protocol; and Emmanuel Giraud, their top Sahel analyst."

"A pleasure to meet you," Kate replied. She saw in her peripheral vision that Nick and Jake gave no indication that they knew anyone on the French side.

"Gentlemen, Kate Cavanaugh, Nick Cavanaugh, and Jake Gillespie of Sandstorm International."

"*Enchanté*, madame, messieurs," said Dubois. "Diana has told us much about you."

"What can Sandstorm do for the CIA and the DGSE?" Kate asked.

Diana Fraser, the CIA's station chief in Paris, smiled apologetically at Kate, her former subordinate. "I'm not sure where to start."

"Maybe I should save you the trouble and tell you we're not taking on new clients," Nick said.

Fraser smirked at him. Charlie snickered. Ardouin, the DGSE's chief of protocol, hissed at Dubois in French. Dubois waved away the concern.

"Ignore him," Kate said. "We're all ears."

"How familiar are you with the Sahel?"

"We do some work in West Africa, but mostly Senegal, Ghana, and Nigeria."

"Nothing in Mali?"

"Not directly. Our NGO clients push into Mali, Niger, and Burkina Faso from their home base in Senegal. We advise them on best practices, but Sandstorm hasn't put boots on the ground. Even for the locals it's exceptionally dangerous, especially if they don't have the right tribal or ethnic background."

"Then you know for a Westerner it's downright suicidal to leave the confines of Bamako or the other regional capitals," Diana said.

Kate had an inkling of where this was headed. "Have people made some bad life choices?"

"Spectacularly bad."

Nick sighed. "Look, we have a lot going on. Whatever you want from us, just say it. Please."

Ardouin again hissed at Dubois. "*Juste écoute*," Dubois responded. Just listen.

Fraser continued. "Between our two countries, we have at least five known hostages held by al-Qaeda's affiliate, the Islamic Emirate of the Maghreb, in northern Mali. Two Americans and three French nationals."

Nick raised his eyebrows. "And?"

Fraser cringed. "We don't know where they are."

The partners exchanged glances. Kate frowned. "I'm sorry to hear that."

"We want you to find them."

"Let me get this straight. You'd like us to do what the most powerful intelligence agency in the world, and a partner service that once controlled the country in question, can't do?" Nick gestured to Kate and Jake. "The three of us?"

"Yes."

"*C'est complètement absurde*," Ardouin said to Dubois.

Nick looked curiously at Fraser. "You seem so...I don't know...together. But then you speak."

Charlie covered his face, laughing.

Kate shot Nick a look. "That's a pretty big ask," she said.

"I know. And we're not here on a lark. We've tried everything. All available resources on both sides have been directed against this problem for the past six months."

"Six months really isn't that long," Kate said.

"We're under a lot of pressure," Fraser said.

"From whom? The families?"

"No, the families are the FBI's problem."

"Then..."

Fraser sighed. "Perhaps you're aware that the new administration is eager for a foreign policy win? And that the vice president himself has taken a keen interest in the plight of American missionaries overseas?"

Kate held up a hand. "Now that I'm no longer an underpaid, underappreciated government employee, I don't have to care about a politician's priorities."

Fraser smiled tightly. "I don't have that luxury. The director is up everyone's ass on this. Africa Division is throwing everything they have, which isn't much, at the problem. After ignoring the issue for years, the Counterterrorism Center's leaders decided they want in on the action and have started calling the shots, but they're late to the game and offering edicts disguised as suggestions that aren't terribly helpful."

"Shocking," Kate said dryly.

"It's fallen to the field, specifically Laurent and me, to develop a coherent strategy and direct collection."

"But?"

"It turns out that northern Mali is a black hole for both services. It's too big, too vast, and everyone has an agenda and constantly shifting loyalties. We haven't been able to establish a foothold or determine whom we should actually be engaging for actionable information on the hostages."

"You know, I'm willing to give the Agency a pass on this failure, but what's your excuse, Monsieur Dubois? No one keen to help the former colonial overlord?" Nick asked.

Ardouin bristled, but the corners of Dubois's mouth twitched in amusement. "I'm told you are well-versed in history, Mr. Cavanaugh, so I will not attempt to justify our current struggles in Mali or her neighbors."

Nick looked disappointed that Dubois didn't take the bait.

"Back to why you're here," Kate said. "You want us to find the hostages. And then what?"

"Just find them."

"You're looking at a military rescue?" Jake asked.

"It's a possibility, but a lot depends on where they are. The goal is not to get anyone killed, obviously."

Kate cocked her head. "Why the rush? I understand you're being pressured, but this is hardly the first time that politicians have pressured the Agency."

"I'll let Charlie and Emmanuel explain."

Charlie led off. "As Diana said, there are at least five in custody. The two Americans are a married couple, evangelicals who were 'divinely called' to the Sahel. They were nabbed in backwoods Niger in late 2015 and immediately spirited over the border into Mali, where we believe they were handed over to IEM, who has held them ever since. They're older, the husband in his mid-seventies, the wife a couple years younger. Our most recent reporting indicates that the husband is in poor health."

Jake, the combat medic, leaned forward. "What's the problem?"

"His kids said he had a pretty severe heart attack about a decade ago and has been on a boatload of meds to keep him stable. He's been in custody for over eighteen months at this point, almost certainly without medication and under tremendous stress."

"Proof of life?" Nick asked.

"Not since early 2016. We're fairly confident they're still alive, but for how much longer?" Charlie tossed up his hands.

"Al-Qaeda and friends, at least in that part of the world, have been far more interested in kidnapping-for-ransom as opposed to kidnapping-for-beheading, à la ISIS," Kate said. "Correct?"

"Correct."

"So, the fear is that an elderly evangelical couple will succumb to difficult conditions in captivity as opposed to dying gruesomely?"

"Yes...and no." Charlie glanced at Diana. She nodded. "We've had some intermittent coverage of the bad guys' phones, Arabs with known links to IEM. The nerds at NSA think there's mounting frustration over the U.S.'s refusal to pay a ransom."

"What are they asking?"

"Eight million dollars for the couple."

Jake whistled. "I know the government can't pay, but any hope of the family coming up with that kind of cash?"

"Not a prayer. The concern is that the Americans might be made an example of, especially if the husband is on his last legs, anyway."

"And *les français*? Don't you people pay ransoms? Keep those terrorist coffers full?" Nick said.

Dubois smiled patiently. "I cannot discuss our past actions, but our president, like yours, prefers to see our hostages liberated without payment of ransom."

"Tell us about your citizens," Kate said.

Giraud, the analyst, cleared his throat. "The first to be taken were the two sisters, volunteers with an NGO, in the summer of 2014. They had been providing aid to vulnerable populations in Timbuktu in the aftermath of the jihadists' takeover of the city two years prior. They're in their early sixties, unmarried and childless, both former teachers. They have one brother, who has been vocal about his displeasure with the government for failing to get them back."

"And the third?"

"A businessman with wide-ranging interests in the region. He was visiting a mining project in Burkina Faso, in 2016, when gunmen attacked. Like your citizens, he was then handed over to IEM in Mali."

"Asking price?"

"Three million euros for each."

"Almost twenty million dollars in total." Nick shook his head. "We're in the wrong line of work."

Jake smirked. "For real."

"You're sure your citizens are alive?" Kate asked.

"*Oui.* We received a video of the sisters approximately eight months ago. Both appeared in decent health, although clearly under duress. A video of the businessman followed, approximately three months ago. Our technicians believe they're authentic."

"How confident are you that the five are held together?"

"Pretty confident," Charlie replied. "The challenge for us has been how frequently they move, and how well the camps are concealed. Like Diana said, it's a wasteland in the north of the country. They could be anywhere."

"And all you want us to do is find them?" Nick said.

"Yes," Fraser replied.

"Well, I've heard enough," Nick said. He looked across the table at Jake, who nodded. "We're in."

Giraud leaned toward Dubois and Ardouin and spoke excitedly. Diana and Charlie remained quiet. Dubois shushed Giraud.

"But he said—"

"It is not yet decided until Madame Cavanaugh says it is so."

Jake laughed. Nick smirked and shook his head in resignation. Kate drummed her fingers on the table and stared at Fraser, who shifted in her seat.

"What aren't you telling us?"

Diana waited a moment before answering, searching for the right words. "There are some...personalities involved."

"Such as?"

"Look, we'd try to limit your exposure to—"

"Diana. Who?"

Fraser sighed. "Neil Weiss."

Kate felt her left eyelid twitch. "And?"

"Van Pelt."

Nick and Jake watched Kate, but she kept her gaze on Fraser, hoping to appear impassive. Charlie looked like he might put his fist through the wall.

"I thought he was banished to meaningless jobs."

"Six months ago, the Hostage Task Force *was* a meaningless job. Then the new leadership rolled in and overnight Van Pelt went from a staff of a few fellow rejects and a nonexistent budget to an influx of personnel, real money, and biweekly briefings with the director."

"Weiss's people?"

Fraser nodded. "The Sahel is Weiss's new playground. He's convinced Mali will spawn the next great threat to America."

"Rational people find that assertion a bit hyperbolic," Charlie said. "But he figured out that if he pretends to care about the hostages, he may generate some incidental reporting on his IEM targets. That's all he really cares about."

"Do they know you're here?"

"They do," Fraser replied.

"And?"

"*Unsupportive* is the politest way I can phrase it. However, we have the director's approval to seek outside assistance. He's not happy with the task force's progress so far."

Kate leaned back in her chair and crossed her arms. "Thanks for coming by. We'll let you know our decision."

"Any thoughts on when that might be?"

Kate shrugged. "We'll call you when we call you."

Fraser opened her mouth to respond, then thought better of it. "I understand. We appreciate your time. Charlie and I can extend here in Boston until the end of the week, but then I have to head back to Paris. As for our French colleagues..."

"We will remain until you make your decision, Madame Cavanaugh. We look forward to your response."

Kate smiled tightly. "Margaret will show you out."

Ʊ

"Dude, you thinking what I'm thinking?" Jake asked once they had adjourned to Kate and Nick's office.

"Oh yeah. Tuareg militia."

"Hell yeah, Tuareg militia."

"And we can be French Foreign Legionnaires!"

"You know what that means," Jake said.

"Tattoos," they said in unison.

Kate sat on the couch and kicked off her heels. It never failed, her and Nick supportive of or opposed to different projects. The last time Fraser and Dubois had walked through Sandstorm's doors, a mere ten months ago, it had taken all of Kate's considerable powers of persuasion to convince Nick to take the job. Now, he was ready to jet off to Mali and raise a Tuareg militia. For what reason they needed a Tuareg militia was unclear, but that was immaterial at the moment.

Their excitement calmed to a dull roar after a detailed discussion of their planned temporary tattoos—Nick and Jake were the only Marines that Kate knew who did not have tattoos of any kind—and Nick dropped to the couch beside Kate.

"What's up, babe? You want in on the tattoo action?"

"She could rock a sleeve," Jake said, stroking his chin and evaluating Kate's toned arms, highlighted by her sleeveless dress.

"You really want to take this job?"

Nick grinned. "Surprised? Thought you'd have to use your Jedi mind tricks to convince me?"

"Not exactly."

Nick twisted to face her. "Wait, you don't want the job?"

"I'm not sure it's a good idea."

"Not a good idea? This is right up your alley. We bum around the desert for a few weeks, find the hostages, let the SEALs be heroes, and make bank. Plus, we'll make the CIA and the DGSE look like fools, which is priceless."

Jake nodded enthusiastically.

Kate shook her head as if to clear it. "You think we—the three of us—will find hostages held by terrorists roaming around a vast wilderness in a few weeks? The same hostages that powerful governments with nearly bottomless resources can't find over the course of years?"

"Not a doubt in my mind. And I know there's not a doubt in yours, either. 'We'll call you when we call you.' Loved the power play. Let them sweat, then we roll in and save the day."

Kate stared at him. "I don't understand what's happening here. This is the CIA and French DGSE we're talking about. The very same intelligence services that literally sent us to therapy."

Nick reached for Kate's hand. "And I like to think that you and I and all our crazy stories have enriched Dr. Larson's professional life. But we're talking hostages and terrorist assholes. Black and white, good and evil."

"Not some dumb kid who needs to be saved from herself?" Kate's thoughts flashed to Camille Dubois, the daughter of the DGSE director-general, whom they had persuaded from traveling to Syria and joining the Islamic State last year.

"I'll always be grateful we took that job. It was the right thing to do, and you saw that long before I did. I think this job is worth considering, too, for the same reasons."

Kate wrinkled her nose. "You just want tattoos and a Tuareg militia."

Nick smiled and squeezed her hand. "I'm a simple man."

Ω

Nick held Kate close, running his hands up and down her back and sides. She had collapsed against his chest and now her lips pressed kisses against his neck. He nuzzled her forehead, breathing in her scent.

"I'm sorry about earlier today," he said.

She lifted her head to look at him. "Why are you sorry?"

"I really thought you'd be all for this. When I said we were in..."

"Sweetie, we both know that no matter who says what, we're always going to talk about it and figure out what works best for us. Right?"

"Right."

"And besides, no one takes you seriously, anyway." She grinned and kissed him.

"Madame Cavanaugh is zee boss," he said in his best, worst French accent.

"If nothing else, I'm glad that's what Dubois took away from his last experience with us."

Nick's fingers traced her spine. "Who's Neil Weiss?"

"He's no one."

"Your left eyelid twitched when Fraser mentioned him. Usually, it does that only when I really, really annoy you. Kind of seems like he's someone."

"Just a name I'd hoped never to hear again."

"Worse than Van Pelt?"

"Different. More competent, therefore more dangerous."

Nick was vaguely aware of her sliding south, trailing kisses down his chest and abdomen. The mention of Stan Van Pelt had put every American in the room on edge, and although Nick and Jake's unfortunate experiences with the man had been limited, they despised him just the same. But it was nothing compared to Kate's hatred. As Kate nibbled at his abs, he rested a hand on her head and absently twirled a lock of her hair around his finger. He realized what was about to happen a moment before it did, and cupped her chin.

"Kate Devlin, are you trying to distract me?"

"If you'll let me." Her striking hazel eyes, flecked with green and gold, locked onto his, daring him to let her.

"We need to talk."

"You can talk. I'll listen."

"No. This is important."

She pulled away and gestured for him to continue. "As you wish."

"If this Weiss character and Van Pelt weren't involved, would you be more interested in the job?"

"I don't know. It's complicated."

"Last year—"

"Last year Diana brought a desperate father to our door. Today she brought the CIA, all its vicious politics, and a prickly allied service with its own goals and politics into that conference room. I'm not terribly keen to reenter that world. I didn't leave it on the best of terms, if you'll recall."

"Fuck Van Pelt for that."

"Yes, but he wasn't the only reason."

"Weiss?"

"Among others. But please don't forget that I didn't leave the CIA just because of a few bullies. I left because I was tired of that life, and working with you and Jake seemed like it would be a lot more fun and rewarding."

"Is it?"

"Infinitely. Especially because I'm the boss." She smiled and patted his hip.

"Whether we take the job or not, I'm good with whatever you want. No Sandstorm assignment should ever make you miserable."

"It's not a no, it's just not a yes yet, either."

"I understand. We'll take as much time as you need to decide." Nick ran his fingers through her hair, gazing at her. "I love you."

"I love you, too."

"Okay," he said.

"Okay what?"

"I'm ready."

Kate arched a slender brow and kissed the palm of the hand that tried to gently guide her head back to where he wanted it. "Oh, sweetie, too much talking. That ship has sailed."

Nick sighed. "I knew I'd regret that."

But then she did something to his thumb that made him think that not all hope was lost. He held his breath. He saw the laughter in her eyes just before the pleasure overtook him.

2

THE NEXT THREE DAYS saw the Sandstorm partners busy with an array of projects in far-flung lands. They had begun to transfer day-to-day management of well-established jobs to their project managers, freeing them to focus on the most complicated ventures and high-priority clients. Like their prince in Dubai.

"He's building a new waterfront compound and wants us to trick it out like his desert hunting lodge," Nick announced to Kate and Jake.

"Done and done," Jake said. "Our easiest money comes from that guy."

"He's insisting that I bring Kate on my next trip. Time for another debrief."

"I'm always up for receiving state secrets in Dubai," Kate said. "And seeing old friends, of course."

"All right, we'll set aside some time for a quick visit, maybe next month. He hasn't broken ground on whatever obscenity he plans to build, but it can't hurt to scope out the area and attend one of his soirées with a hot chick on my arm."

"You ought to hit Oman while you're there. Press the flesh with the new clients," Jake said.

"Good call. I was thinking, we should see if our subcontractors in the Philippines have ever done work in the Gulf. They did a nice job with the facilities in Mindanao. We might be able to talk these guys into an upgrade."

"Agreed. We could also consider—"

"Why would we need a Tuareg militia?" Kate asked without warning.

Nick and Jake glanced at each other. They hadn't spoken of the potential job in Mali since the day it was offered, but it hadn't been far from Kate's mind. She noodled over it at the office, during workouts, while walking their dog, and during evenings with Nick, who seemed content to give her time and space to come to a decision. It was Thursday, and though Kate was still undecided, she knew they owed Fraser and Dubois an answer.

"You want to tell her?" Jake asked Nick.

"Truthfully?" Nick said to Kate.

"No, definitely lie to me."

"We just want a Tuareg militia."

"You know, sort of a 'when in Mali' deal," Jake offered.

"Why Legionnaires?"

"Because it sounded cool?" Nick grimaced and then said to Jake, "I hate when she makes us explain our terrible ideas."

"I didn't say they were terrible," Kate said. She twirled her pen and gnawed on her bottom lip, running through a scenario in her head. She saw a glimmer of excitement reach Nick's eyes.

"Do *you* have an idea?" he asked her.

"I might. *Might*," she emphasized, as they both leaned forward in anticipation.

"Tuareg militias? Legionnaires? Tattoos?" Nick said eagerly.

"No tattoos."

"Aw, babe."

"All right," she said. "Here's what I'm thinking."

ʊ

Nick and Jake listened intently to Kate. She talked without interruption, feeling more than slightly insane as she outlined her idea for how Sandstorm might find unfindable hostages in the wasteland that was northern Mali without any existing sources or infrastructure. Her rational brain knew it was an exercise in futility—Mali was almost twice the size of Texas and one of the least-developed countries on the planet, riven by terrorism and ethnic violence, plagued by disease and famine, and ravaged by climate change and the resulting mass migration toward already-overburdened cities and towns. Much of the population lived in grinding poverty and under the heel of extremists or insurgents or armed factions. Kate had trouble seeing how they would succeed where the CIA had failed, but those failures made more sense after a few days of research.

The idealist in her believed that anything was possible, believed that maybe it was worth a shot. What harm could there be in bumming around the desert for a few weeks?

She tossed up her hands. "That's what I've got so far. Tear it apart."

They stared at her. Then they high-fived. "We're going to Mali!" Nick said.

"This doesn't stand a chance of working," Kate said.

"Strongly disagree."

"Fraser and Dubois won't like it," she mused.

"Then they can take their business elsewhere."

"You really want to try this?" she asked.

"Absolutely," Nick said. Jake nodded.

"We'll see what the others say." Kate sent an encrypted email that she had written yesterday to critical members of the team. "I also took the liberty of drawing up detailed contracts that differ from our normal paperwork. I won't move forward unless they agree to our terms." She handed copies to both men. "Let me know if you want any changes made."

As they skimmed the contracts, Kate received the first reply to her email. *Holy shit, count me in.* She smiled. Minutes later, another email arrived. *My goodness, love, this might be your craziest plan yet. We are with you.*

"The gang's all in," she said.

"Goddamn, Kate," Jake said, his eyes bugging out at the financials. "This makes Dubai prince money look like pocket change. You really think they'll pay this?"

"They will if they want our services. Desperate government agencies are willing to spend a lot of money, right?"

"I like this section," Nick said, pointing.

Kate didn't have to look to know which section he liked. She had spent hours focused on the wording, leaving no room for interpretation. "That especially is non-negotiable."

"Your wife drives a hard bargain," Jake said to Nick. "She's gonna clean you out in the divorce."

Nick sighed. "Don't I know it."

"Well?" Kate asked.

They grinned. "Let's go take the CIA and their frog friends for a ride," Nick said.

Kate picked up her phone and tapped out a message to Diana Fraser, telling her to come to Sandstorm tomorrow at nine a.m. Fraser responded immediately, and Kate felt her relief through the phone.

"All right," she said. "Let's get ready for tomorrow."

Ω

The CIA and the DGSE arrived promptly at nine. The partners were already settled in the conference room, and Kate forced herself to refrain from attacking the platter of breakfast pastries in the center of the table. She intended to make this as painful as possible for her ex-employer, but they could at least be good hosts.

Margaret showed in their guests and they took opposite sides of the table, as they had earlier in the week. Their receptionist collected coffee requests as everyone settled into their seats. Charlie immediately reached for the pastries and Kate followed his lead, grabbing a flaky croissant. He winked at her as he bit into a Danish. Ardouin, the DGSE chief of protocol, looked critically at the platter.

"These are from a patisserie," Kate said. "The owner is French."

"I am fine with just coffee," he said with a sniff.

Kate shrugged. "Suit yourself."

The coffees arrived and they got down to business. Kate passed out copies of Sandstorm's contract. Dubois accepted his eagerly, but Fraser looked nervous.

"First things first. Nothing moves forward without your signatures on this document. And I suggest you read the fine print carefully," Kate said.

For several minutes the only sound was the rustling of papers and the clink of cups on saucers. Then the Americans, ahead of their French counterparts, reached Kate's addendum. Fraser paused to rub her eyes and take a fortifying sip of espresso. Charlie munched on his Danish and nodded along in agreement as he read. He shot her a surreptitious thumbs-up and waited for Fraser to react. Fraser then turned the page to Sandstorm's financial terms. Her head dropped.

"Something wrong?" Kate asked innocently.

"I guess no friends-and-family discount," Fraser said weakly.

Ardouin adjusted his tie. "Madame Fraser, surely you understand that this is merely their opening gambit. The negotiations—"

"There will be no negotiations. These are our terms. Take them or leave them," Kate said.

"We will need time to consider our options and—"

"You have until the moment you walk out of this office. Should you return at a later date to secure our services, assuming our services are still available, you will find that we have become exponentially more expensive and possibly more draconian."

You are so hot, Nick mouthed to Kate.

She smiled at him and reached for another pastry, a *pain au chocolat*, perfectly baked by the far less obnoxious Frenchman who greeted Kate personally every time he saw her.

Ardouin ranted at Dubois in French. "These people are immature, incompetent, and overpriced. We would be better off hiring actual criminals to find our citizens, not these highway robbers."

Kate spoke sharply in French, a rather colorful epithet directed at the chief of protocol and a pointed suggestion that he excuse himself from the proceedings if he couldn't be professional. Ardouin jerked in surprise and stared at her. Emmanuel Giraud's eyes widened. Fraser tried to disguise her laugh with a cough.

"Did I forget to mention that Madame Cavanaugh speaks perfect French?" Dubois asked mildly. "My mistake."

Nick spoke in Arabic to Kate. "What's the frog's problem?"

"Something about you being immature and incompetent," Kate responded, also in Arabic.

"He's an excellent judge of character."

"She's also fluent in Arabic. As is the monsieur," Dubois noted. "And that only begins to scratch the surface of their unique talents. I ask that you set aside your assumptions about our hosts until after we've talked through the matter at hand."

Ardouin took a slug of his coffee and averted his eyes from Kate.

"Now, I fully expect that you have questions. Let's discuss," Kate said.

Dubois gestured to Fraser. "*Mesdames d'abord.*"

"I think most of this is doable. We'll fast-track the paperwork for your clearances. You'll have access to everything we know. Four of you?"

"Let's make it five. We need to loop in our tech expert. And we want approval to share whatever we think is necessary with the foreign nationals on the team."

"Seeing as I know those foreign nationals, I'll be happy to vouch for them. Now, the matter of operational funds."

"Thirty million, in clean bills, no funny business, to be spent as we see fit, no questions asked. All under our control."

"That'll be a tough sell."

"Don't worry, the cash will be accounted for according to Agency standards."

"Should I even bother to ask why you want that much money?"

"No."

Fraser studied Kate. "You absolutely cannot pay a ransom with U.S. government funds."

"We know."

"The thirty million is in addition to your fee and expenses?"

"Yes. You'll pay our full fee up front and we'll bill for expenses at the conclusion of the operation. We commit to thirty days, then reevaluate where we stand. If both sides agree that the operation should continue, we'll present new terms at that time."

"When you say that you maintain full operational control..."

"You're free to offer input, and we're free to ignore it."

Fraser tapped a specific paragraph in the contract, the one Kate knew would cause the most heartburn. "This right here, this clause that gives you an out for any reason you deem necessary at any time, no questions asked, no refunds given."

"My favorite part," Nick said.

Fraser looked at Kate with tired eyes. "People will lose their minds."

"Undoubtedly."

"Look, I understand why."

Kate waited, but Diana chose not to elaborate. "You have two options. Don't sign, and seek assistance elsewhere. Or, sign and keep your 'personalities' under control so I don't walk away with all your money before the job is done." Kate offered her former boss an equanimous shrug.

Fraser picked up her pen and stared at the contract.

Ardouin was aghast. "Madame Fraser, you cannot possibly consider signing this document. Thirty days with no guarantees? Full payment before a single action is taken? Complete operational control? Thirty million dollars *plus* their fees and expenses? Nothing to stop them from walking away at any time? It is madness!"

Dubois reached into his jacket and extracted a Mont Blanc fountain pen from his inner pocket. He scrawled his signature on the document, committing the French external security service to Sandstorm's terms.

"Laurent!"

"I am the director-general, Henri. It is my prerogative."

"I cannot support this."

"I absolve you of all responsibility, my friend." Dubois looked to his American counterpart. "Madame Fraser? Shall we make your last year in Paris a memorable one?"

Diana signed with a flourish. "What could possibly go wrong?"

"Would you like a list?" Nick asked her.

She sighed. "Dear God, no."

Kate took the signed contracts and she, Nick, and Jake added their own signatures. She then summoned Margaret, who would organize account information and ensure each party received hard and soft copies of the paperwork.

"Okay, let's talk details." Kate turned to Dubois. "We'd like to make use of the French military base in Timbuktu. We need a secure facility to hold the money."

"Our service has a presence on a restricted section of the base. I'll ensure that you and your team have access. Will you operate from the base?"

"No. But we need a fallback point should things go south. Also, I assume that both the CIA and the DGSE will want to station people at the base to annoy us?" Kate raised an inquiring eyebrow at both chiefs.

Dubois smiled. "We've offered our hospitality to your Hostage Task Force, and I understand they've accepted."

Fraser nodded. "I'll be there for the duration. Trying to keep the Hostage Task Force out of your hair."

"Me too," Charlie said.

"As will we," Dubois said. "You should have no question as to the importance our government places on the hostages' safe return."

"Given the risks we are taking by allowing you access to our facility and our intelligence, you must sign a nondisclosure agreement," Ardouin said.

"Absolutely not," Kate replied. Dubois's lips twitched in a smile.

"We should decide who plays us in the movie," Nick said to Jake. "I'm definitely one of the Chrises. Either *Captain America* Chris or *Thor* Chris."

"Madame Cavanaugh."

"He's going to keep pushing your buttons until you lighten up," Kate told Ardouin in French.

"I know it's hard to believe, but we really are discreet," Jake said. "We're not in this for glory."

"Speak for yourself," Nick said.

"You really must ignore him," Kate said to Ardouin before he could sputter another protest.

The chief of protocol made a show of washing his hands of the matter. "I have registered my objections. I defer to the director-general. Bad decisions are, as he said, his prerogative."

Dubois sighed. "Henri, Madame Cavanaugh is a former intelligence officer and her partners are former United States Marines. I believe they can keep a secret."

"One more thing. We want Charlie," Kate said.

Charlie nearly leaped from his chair in excitement. He leaned toward Fraser, begging her with puppy eyes.

"His safety is paramount."

"Of course."

"And under no circumstances is he to participate in anything illegal."

Nick laughed. "I'm pretty sure everything we do will be illegal. And with your money."

Fraser shot Nick a warning look. "You have no idea how far up my ass the lawyers will be when I show them this contract. Please don't compound my pain by making a CIA officer an accessory to your crimes."

"He'll be there to turn information into intel gold," Kate said. "We just need him to do his real job."

Fraser looked like she was about to regret her next words. "Fine. Consider Charlie seconded to you for the duration of this operation."

Charlie tossed up his arms and signaled a touchdown. "*Vive le Mali!*"

♌

When the meeting finally wrapped up at six p.m., about two hours later than it should have, mostly thanks to Ardouin, Kate made straight for the couch in their office and collapsed, pulling a blanket over her head. Nick moved her legs, sat, and then situated her feet in his lap. He tossed aside her ballet flats and began massaging her left foot.

"It's only going to get worse," she said from under the blanket.

"I know."

"Would you be upset if I pulled the plug now?"

"Nope."

He ran his thumb over her arch, easing up on the pressure as he neared her heel, which acted up when she ran too much. She tended to run too much when she was stressed. She had logged a lot of miles over the last few days, Shadow their Yemeni rescue dog with boundless energy at her side. It would be a yoga weekend.

She emerged from under the blanket. "I assumed Van Pelt would be the first person I killed, but Ardouin is making a serious play to be number one."

Nick smirked and moved to her right foot. "It's a master class in condescension, that's for sure. But, to be fair, he doesn't know us. I'm sure he thinks this is some grand American plot to embarrass his country."

"It's about to become that if he doesn't lose the attitude," Kate grumbled.

"Dubois needs to be careful. He's not supposed to know anything about us either, yet he seems remarkably trusting of our unconventional ways and unbothered by my incompetence and immaturity."

"Yeah, I'll tell Fraser to rein him in. Can you imagine what Ardouin would do with that information?"

"I think he'd reach a new level of insufferable."

Kate reluctantly extricated her feet from his hands. "Come on, let's go home. Shadow is probably beside himself that we're late."

Ω

On Monday, Kate summoned George, Sandstorm's blue-haired hacker on retainer, to the office. Charlie, now living in a downtown Boston hotel with a secure computer and a head full of critical intel that would shape the group's plans, had commandeered the consultancy's smaller back conference room and set up his command center. He eagerly awaited George's arrival, knowing her only as the hacker who had broken into the DGSE's secure network last year during Sandstorm's Operation Grenouille.

Margaret escorted George to the conference room, giving the hacker's hoodie, torn jeans, and red Converse All-Stars a reproving look as she allowed the convicted criminal to join her employers and their polite, clean-cut friend. George dumped her backpack on the table, pulled out her laptop, and cracked her knuckles.

"Who are we hacking today?"

"She's so the part," Charlie said in awe.

George looked at him, noticing him for the first time. "Who's the Boy Scout?"

"George, this is Charlie, a former colleague of mine," Kate said.

"Damn, what is it with the CIA? You people are nothing like the movies."

"Mild-mannered bureaucrat is only my cover," Charlie said. "I spend my evenings breaking into the embassies of our enemies and stealing their most valuable secrets."

"And what was she?" George asked, gesturing to Kate. "A stone-cold assassin, all eighty-two pounds of her?"

"Have you seen how she eats? She weighs at least eighty-five pounds."

"If we could focus on something besides my weight, that'd be super." Kate then reached for the box of doughnuts Charlie had brought, choosing a Boston cream.

Nick and Jake walked in, fist-bumped George, and took seats at the table. Jake rooted through the doughnuts for a glazed, which he dunked in his coffee.

"Central casting did much better with your Devil Dogs," George said, pointing at the two Marines.

"Today, we're central casting, and we need to create a terrorist," Kate said.

George grinned. "Now this is some CIA shit right here. You have someone in mind, or are we starting from scratch?"

Kate opened a photo file on her laptop, which was connected to the conference room's television. A familiar face filled the flatscreen, a green-eyed, white-bearded tribesman from Yemen's Al Jawf Governorate.

"Who's this handsome gentleman?"

"A blank canvas in terms of his electronic and social media footprint. We need him to have an opaque past with some shady business dealings in the Middle East. I'm thinking import-export, with a base of operations in Mukalla, Yemen. Weapons and matériel and khat in addition to legal goods. He should also be a devout Sunni Muslim who supports al-Qaeda."

George cocked her head. "I can work with that."

"But his overt online presence should be relatively benign. Just a company website in Arabic and English, nothing too slick. Social media isn't his scene, and we don't have enough time to teach this old dog new tricks. I want him to be a member of some very specific WhatsApp and Telegram groups, though, which Charlie will provide."

"Easy."

"He can be a loiterer in the big groups, but I want to create historical chats between him and ostensibly certain individuals on his phone. One-on-one and small-group conversations."

"If you have phones and SIM cards, I can mess around to adjust the dates so the messages will appear to have been exchanged at a time of your choosing."

Kate reached down and retrieved a bag of new Samsung smartphones. "We've got everything."

�⛉

A special delivery for Nick and Jake arrived later that week from Paris: sets of French Foreign Legion desert-camouflage uniforms, identical to those worn by Legionnaires who served as part of Operation Serval, the French military's antiterrorism campaign in northern Mali from January 2013 to July 2014.

Nick modeled his fatigues for Kate that night. His uniform bore captain's bars, his rank at time of discharge from the Marine Corps. Jake's bore sergeant's stripes, the closest to his Marine discharge rank of staff sergeant.

"Très sexy, Capitaine Cavanaugh," she said, lounging on their bed.

He set his new green beret on his head at a jaunty angle and appraised his look in the full-length mirror on the back of their open closet door. "Nothing beats Marine digicam, but this has its Saharan charms."

"You know, every Legionnaire is supposed to learn at least some French. It's part of their basic training."

"Coincidentally, like me, my alter ego does not care for our Gallic friends. He skated by in basic with the occasional *bonjour* and *merci* and 'I like your *derrière*' when he hooked up with a Legion groupie. And there were a lot of Legion groupies," he said with a sly look in Kate's direction.

"Hard to understand why Ardouin was so opposed to letting you play dress-up," Kate said dryly.

Nick touched the *Légion étrangère* patch on his shoulder, then removed the beret and fingered the insignia of the First Foreign Cavalry Regiment. "Legionnaires have fought by America's side in a number of wars, including in Afghanistan. My alter ego might have sold his services to the highest bidder, but I would never make light of their sacrifices or disrespect the uniform."

"I know. And Dubois knows that, too."

"Besides, Ardouin was far more opposed to *your* request than mine. I thought he was going to have an aneurysm when Dubois agreed to it."

"It's so tempting to abuse their trust."

Nick shed the uniform and folded it neatly, setting it atop two other sets on a shelf in the walk-in closet. He approached the bed wearing nothing but the green beret, his cobalt eyes burning holes through her silk negligée. Kate gave her nightie a fifty-percent chance of surviving the next few minutes. One of his big hands traveled from her knee up her thigh and under the silk, cupping her bottom.

"Have I told you lately how much I like your *derrière?*"

3

THE NEXT TWO WEEKS flew by in a blur of activity. Kate, with help from Charlie and George, had created online profiles and histories to her satisfaction. Their Dubai-based team had made only minor revisions, mostly helping Kate phrase certain thoughts or ostensible conversations in Arabic to match the style of the original source material. Kate had then put George in touch with Amy Kowalski, who was champing at the bit to develop her character's history and online presence. Judging by the gales of laughter that Kate heard from George and Charlie in the conference room during their video calls with Amy, she knew her best friend and former colleague had cranked up the crazy to eleven and broken off the knob.

Nick and Jake were busy with preparations specific to their roles as Legionnaires and maintaining security for the Sandstorm team. As excited as they were about bumming around the desert, both men were stressed over the enormity of the task. The former Marines, who had fought seven combat tours together in Iraq and Afghanistan, recognized the challenges and had gotten impressively creative with ideas to mitigate at least some of the threats they would face.

But they knew that there was no possible way they could account for all the conceivable threats in a place like northern Mali, which was either lawless or ruled by the iron fist of the terrorists.

"It's different than Iraq or Afghanistan," Nick said. "It's so big. And it's just us."

"That does beg an interesting question. Do we trust anyone to come for us if shit goes sideways?" Jake asked.

"The French have thousands of troops in country, including special forces. We have a small presence in Niger," Nick said, scratching at his beard stubble.

"That doesn't answer my question."

Both men looked at Kate. She tossed up her hands.

"I honestly don't know," she said. "This is a black op. I'm confident that Fraser would fight like hell to send the cavalry, but she doesn't control military assets and no one will want to own this if we run into real trouble."

"Black ops are super cool until they're not," Nick said.

"It's a no-go unless you both are comfortable with what we can control and, perhaps more importantly, what we can't control," Kate reminded them.

"I like the plan. I think it's solid," Jake said.

"We're putting an awful lot of faith into people's acting skills," Nick said. "And the one it all rides on has been the wallflower during our past shenanigans."

Jake cocked his head thoughtfully. "I think he'll surprise us."

"I've talked to him every day since we started this. He's a quick learner and he understands what's at stake," Kate said. "Plus, Fatima would never let this go forward if she had doubts."

Nick nodded. "Okay. We'll take it a day at a time, like always. I do wish we had an air asset that we could control, though. Just in case."

"Remember Colonel Patterson?" Jake asked.

Nick brightened. "Of course."

"I had the same concern so I tracked him down. He's contracting for a transportation company that provides helicopter medevacs for the military." He paused for effect. "In Niger."

Nick grinned. "I bet we can make it worth his while to hang out in Timbuktu for a month with his helo."

"I'll make the call."

Nick looked at Kate. "You ready to make our call?"

"You're sure you want a Tuareg militia?"

"Babe, the only thing I'm more sure about is my undying love for you."

Kate good-naturedly rolled her eyes. "I suppose I should take what I can get."

☊

Kate used a clean Samsung smartphone to make the call to a Malian employed by U.S. Embassy Bamako's political section. Diana Fraser had provided the man's mobile phone number with strict instructions that Sandstorm was never to tell anyone, especially the Malian, where they obtained it.

The Malian was a Tuareg from Kidal, a small city in the north of the country near the Algerian border. He was invaluable to the political section for his wide-ranging contacts in the north, especially throughout the regions of Kidal, Gao, and Timbuktu, and his good relationships with Tuaregs and Arabs on all sides of the numerous political divides.

Kate called in the evening, Mali time. He answered on the first ring. Kate exchanged pleasantries in French, explained what she wanted, and never once identified herself or Nick, who was seated at her side on the couch in their office. The Malian listened, asked a few questions, and gave her a name and a phone number. Kate thanked him and told him a token of their appreciation would be sent to a bank or less formal financial institution of his choosing.

Then Kate punched in the number he had given her and set it to speaker-phone. Nick crossed his fingers. A man answered in Tamashek, the language of the Tuaregs. Kate spoke in French.

"*Bon soir*, Cherif. My name is Kate. I'm told you control a militia near Timbuktu."

☊

Dubois's people met the Sandstorm crew at their arrival gate at Charles de Gaulle International Airport, spiriting Kate, Nick, Jake, Amy, and Charlie through passport control and to a waiting van outside the terminal. DGSE officers collected their luggage and drove them to a small airport outside of Paris, where a Gulfstream jet awaited them for the flight to the French military base in Timbuktu, Mali.

Diana Fraser, Laurent Dubois, Henri Ardouin, and Emmanuel Giraud were already on board the plane, chatting and sipping champagne.

"I will hit that," said Amy, shrugging out of her backpack and making straight for the bottle of champagne.

The flight attendant poured her a flute. Amy reached over and clinked glasses with Fraser, who looked genuinely happy to see her other former subordinate. Amy still referred to their old boss as "that skinny bitch" in conversations with Kate, but now with a hint of warmth in her voice. Kate and Amy hadn't gotten off to the best of starts with Fraser during their final CIA assignment in Yemen, but Fraser had come through for them when it mattered.

"Good flight?" Fraser asked.

Nick took a gulp of champagne. "Air France maintains a passable business-class cabin. I prefer warmer nuts, though." He grinned at Ardouin, who rolled his eyes.

Dubois signaled the flight attendant, who picked up the phone and spoke to the pilots. The engines powered up.

"We have all our gear?" Jake asked.

"Everything you sent has been loaded," Dubois said. "Please relax and help yourself to any amenities. The flight to Timbuktu will take approximately six hours."

Ω

A second Gulfstream that originated in Dubai made excellent time and arrived an hour ahead of schedule and thirty minutes in advance of the Gulfstream out of Paris. The DGSE plane offloaded its passengers first; the group stepped into shimmering heat waves over the tarmac.

"Love that Third World stench," Amy murmured, wrinkling her nose at air thick with diesel fumes, brown dust, and a hint of raw sewage, carried on the breeze from the city.

"Oh my God, this is the desert. Why is it so humid?" Charlie asked, pulling at his shirt that was already sticking to him.

"Rainy season," Kate replied. She set her sunglasses, which had fogged immediately upon exposure to the wall of humidity, atop her head.

"Maybe summer was not the ideal timeframe in which to bum around the desert," Nick said.

"Too late!" Fraser said brightly.

"Shall we welcome the rest of our motley crew?" Kate asked.

They dumped their bags into waiting French military vehicles and faced the second plane. The door opened and the stairwell descended, lowered by an attractive male flight attendant. A tornado of black robes appeared at the top of the stairs and glided down, clicking across the weathered tarmac in stiletto heels. Kate approached Fatima al-Maqdisi and hugged her friend and former Arabic-language teacher.

"How are you, love?" Fatima adjusted the loose hijab around her head and waved to Nick, Jake, and Amy.

"Eagerly awaiting the appearance of our sheikh."

As if on cue, a green-eyed, white-bearded tribesman from Yemen's north materialized in the doorway and imperiously surveyed the scene on the tarmac before him. A flick of his hand sent the flight attendant scuttling toward the back of the plane. He reappeared with a wide belt holding a jambiya, the broad, curved ceremonial dagger sported by Yemeni tribesmen across that broken land. The sheikh allowed the young man to help him fasten the belt at the small of his back. Then the tribesman, dressed in a spotless white thobe and a red-and-white kaffiyeh, joined them on the tarmac.

"*Marhaba*, Kate," said Sharaf al-Jawfi, his eyes twinkling in the bright after-noon sun.

Kate offered formal greetings in Arabic and a slight bow, as befitting a man of rank. Fatima snorted.

"Don't encourage him. He's been insufferable for weeks."

Kate laughed and hugged their ersatz sheikh. They joined the others, and Nick and Jake teased Sharaf in a mix of English and Arabic. He gave it right back to his former employers from their time in Yemen. Fatima joined Amy and Charlie and Fraser, the latter admiring Fatima's shoes and Gucci handbag.

Kate's sunglasses were no longer fogged, so she covered her eyes and took a moment to study the group. The three Frenchmen watched the reunion with curiosity. She didn't need psychic powers to read Ardouin's mind; the chief of protocol no longer bothered to hide his disdain for whatever Sandstorm had planned, and the unexpected appearance of two Yemenis didn't assuage his concerns. Giraud was like most CIA analysts Kate knew, just happy to be there watching the operational sausage get made. And Dubois was putting the pieces together in his mind, never before having met the people he knew only as Umm Ali and Natasha. He looked at her, his head tilted thoughtfully, and Kate grinned at him. He returned the smile.

"Come," he said. "We'll take you to our section of the base."

♌

The DGSE section of camp was a mishmash of CONEX boxes and other temporary structures that had become semi-permanent, typical of military ac-tions in foreign lands that last years beyond their optimistically anticipated end date. In France's case, their intervention in Mali after the jihadist takeover of Timbuktu in 2012 began with Operation Serval in early 2013; Operation

Barkhane, a joint effort with the G-5 Sahel forces comprised of former French colonies—Mali, Mauritania, Niger, Chad, and Burkina Faso—to reestablish Malian government control over its northern territory followed in August 2014, and remained ongoing. Barkhane greatly expanded upon Serval's reach in the country, but the French military's success had been limited following the initial expulsion of jihadists from the major cities, as the terrorists melted into the hinterlands and rallied—or shanghaied—rural populations to their cause, and now controlled significant territory in the center and north of the country.

Nick and Jake likened France's challenges in Mali to the U.S.'s challenges in Afghanistan. Entrenched incompetence and endemic corruption on a staggering scale would always trump military prowess and the best of intentions. Nick, a voracious consumer of military histories, had added several tomes on the French Foreign Legion and France's colonial history in Africa to their bookshelves and then talked Kate's ear off as he finished each in quick succession. The definitive account of operations Serval and Barkhane hadn't yet been written, but he found enough information online via reputable news and academic sources to fill his quiver with metaphorical arrows that he intended to sling at Dubois and Ardouin, should the situation call for American wit and unhelpful commentary on another country's military quagmires.

Dubois led the group into the largest building and brought them to the conference room. Several individuals sat clustered around the far side of the long table, talking amongst themselves. Kate took a deep yoga breath, hoping to calm her roiling gut.

Fraser, the most senior American representative, took charge and motioned for everyone to sit. The Sandstorm team took positions as far from Kate's former colleagues as they could. Nick watched Kate with concern, and she shot him a tight smile.

"Okay, folks, we all know why we're here. This joint CIA-DSGE effort will hopefully result in intel on our hostages' location and facilitate a rescue. Given the challenges we face, we've outsourced some of the collection going forward to

Sandstorm International, a security consultancy. I know there are some familiar faces here—Kate Cavanaugh and Amy Kowalski are former Agency officers. We need to get them up to speed on the most recent developments and then turn them loose. Their entire team has been cleared for this classified briefing. Hostage Task Force, you're up," Fraser said, and then sat beside Dubois.

Stan Van Pelt, the former chief of the CIA's station in Sanaa, Yemen, rose from the head of the table opposite Kate and straightened his red tie. Inexplicably, he was dressed in a suit, although Kate saw that it was not a bespoke suit of the fashion that he wore in Yemen. The finer things in life were harder to afford on a Washington-based civil servant's salary.

"The Hostage Task Force was created in order to respond to a number of terrorist kidnapping incidents around the world. Our highest priority is the rescue of our hostages here in the Sahel, and the director himself has taken a keen interest in our work. I'd like to note that we've made outstanding progress in the last few months under my command and—"

"Stan, just focus on the facts, please."

Amy snickered. "There's the Limp Dick we know and despise," she whispered to Kate.

"Yes, well, I'll allow the experts to speak to the specifics."

Van Pelt ceded the floor to a stooped, sinewy man with a shock of wild gray hair and a bushy gray beard that put most terrorist beards to shame. He held a clicker in his right hand and waited for a young woman to load a PowerPoint presentation onto the room's television. His beady eyes swept over the Sandstorm crew with undisguised contempt, lingering on Kate.

"Neil Weiss, chief of CT operations in the Sahel," he said. "Our priority target is Islamic Emirate of the Maghreb emir Khalifa al-Ghazawi, a longtime member of al-Qaeda's shura. Khalifa is Libyan, half Arab and half Tuareg, giving him a unique place in the Malian terrorist ecosystem. He's number eight on the U.S. government's list of most-wanted terrorists, but I consider him number three, behind the top two al-Qaeda leaders in Pakistan. IEM has been incredibly profitable under his leadership, keeping greater AQ afloat in lean times."

Weiss clicked to a grainy photo of a bearded, turbaned man surrounded by other bearded, turbaned men. "This is Khalifa about fifteen years ago, in Afghanistan. We assess that he escaped from Tora Bora with Bin Laden and helped the group reconstitute in Pakistan. Then Bin Laden appointed him emir of IEM and dispatched him back to Libya. He's been living in northern Mali amongst the Arabs and Tuaregs friendly to IEM since the onset of civil war in Libya in 2011."

As Weiss continued his history lesson on Khalifa al-Ghazawi, Nick leaned close to Kate. "What died on his face?"

Amy leaned in from Kate's other side. "I've long suspected an opossum, and probably a rabid one, given his behavior over the years."

"I always thought he looked like an unkempt crotch," Kate observed quietly, keeping her gaze straight ahead.

Both Nick and Amy guffawed, causing Weiss to pause his presentation and the rest of the audience to turn and look at them.

"May I?" Nick asked Kate.

"Have at it," Kate said.

"Neil, question," Nick said before Weiss restarted his monologue. "I thought we were here to find hostages."

"You are," Fraser replied immediately.

"Then why the hard-on for this one doofus?"

Fraser sat back to watch the show. Van Pelt pulled at his shirt cuffs, exposing onyx cuff links that Kate recognized from Yemen. His eyes darted around the room, looking everywhere except her. The young woman behind the laptop had been staring at Nick since they entered the room, moving her gaze only when the PowerPoint required her attention, and now she licked her lips.

Weiss glowered at Nick. "As I said, Khalifa should be as high as number three on our list of terrorists to capture or kill. He presents an existential threat to the United States."

"Sounds like your problem. We're here to find the hostages you *can't* find. How does this history lesson help us do that?"

"We assess with high confidence that Khalifa's network holds the hostages."

"And?"

"We assess with even higher confidence that you will not get anywhere near that network or the hostages."

An uncomfortable silence hung over the table. "For the sake of the American taxpayer, I hope you're wrong," Nick said.

"Khalifa al-Ghazawi has spent the last two decades outrunning—"

"Outwitting," Amy corrected.

"—counterterrorism pressure from us, the French, and now us *and* the French. He's one of al-Qaeda's top operatives, with counterintelligence experience across an array of operating environments. He's in his element here in Mali. He'll know your moves before you know your moves."

"We take great pride in being insanely unpredictable," Amy said.

"We've had the finest operational minds pursuing Khalifa since 9/11. We've never gotten close. And you think you can just drive into the desert and break bread with the man?"

"Sure, why not?" Nick said.

Weiss and Van Pelt shared an amused look. "Mr. Cavanaugh, I can't blame you for seizing an opportunity to cash in on certain individuals' misplaced faith in your abilities, but I'm sure you understand how this looks to those of us with long, successful careers against top terrorist targets," Van Pelt said.

Kate laid a hand on Nick's forearm to prevent him from launching himself across the table and throttling Van Pelt. "Please, continue your presentation."

Weiss clicked to another slide, one with a list of names that Charlie had already shared and whom Sandstorm had no intention of engaging. "The most you can hope for is contact with the hangers-on, those allowed to loiter around Khalifa's outermost circle. These are the people with whom a conversation, or even a face-to-face meeting, is possible. He uses at least a dozen businessmen and brokers, both Arab and Tuareg, to pass messages and set terms, which seem to change by the day. Our sources report that Khalifa never gets near the hostages, and none of our middlemen have ever been permitted contact with either him or the hostages. However, some of the more careless brokers occasionally let an interesting nugget of information slip. We would appreciate you sharing the details of any calls or meetings you have. We may be able to corroborate our previous and ongoing collection, and further refine our efforts."

"Of course," Kate replied. "We'll funnel any reporting through Charlie."

"Chief, may I?" asked the young woman at the laptop.

"This is Lacey Simms, my top targeter in the Sahel Department. She's been hot on Khalifa's trail since she joined us a couple of years ago. She's spearheading our current lines of collection and helped get us past the outer ring very recently."

"This is the letter I wrote with the help of our interpreters that one of our sources passed to a Kidal-based Tuareg with known connections to Khalifa's military advisers." She handed some papers down the table.

Fraser and Dubois each took a copy of the translated version. Kate, Nick, Fatima, and Sharaf shared copies of the Arabic version. The letter was written in formal Modern Standard Arabic and purported to be from an Algeria-based businessman who wanted to expand his smuggling routes through northern Mali. The letter requested a meeting to discuss mutually beneficial business opportunities. Kate knew from the body of reporting that Charlie had shared that Khalifa communicated in Maghrebi Arabic with his regional cohorts, and expected them to do the same. He saved his prowess in Modern Standard for formal correspondence with al-Qaeda leadership or contacts from outside the region.

"The goal is to prompt movement, or communication, which we're poised to pick up through coverage of the outer ring's phones," Lacey continued.

"Your agency needs new interpreters," Fatima commented in Arabic. "The only thing your eavesdroppers will hear is the sound of Khalifa's laughter. Assuming this letter wasn't destroyed on the spot."

"I'm sure the interpreters just translated what they were told to translate," Kate replied, also in Arabic. "Not to mention this went through several hundred layers of bureaucracy before it got out the door."

"It misses the point completely. I am not privy to all your intelligence, but even I know from a casual perusal of what you have shared that this is not who Khalifa is."

"It also reads exactly like something the U.S. government would write to try to lure out a target."

"Could work to our advantage," Nick said.

Kate returned to English. "Thank you for sharing this, Lacey. I'm sure it will spur a response in no time."

"What's your plan?" Weiss asked.

Kate looked at her team, a motley crew if ever there was one. She shrugged. "Pray for a miracle, I guess. Based on your assessment, those hostages seem screwed."

Van Pelt drew back his shoulders. "As the director's representative to this operation, it's my responsibility to coordinate all collection. That means full knowledge of your plans and intentions, and my approval to proceed."

"No."

"But—"

"No. Should we deign to inform you of our plans and intentions, it will be done through Diana and Director-General Dubois." Kate stood, and her motley crew stood with her. "We'd like to see the rest of the facility, if you wouldn't mind, Monsieur Dubois."

"*Bien sûr*, Madame Cavanaugh."

"Fuck me," Amy muttered once they departed the conference room. "Limp Dick and Crotch Face, now there's a pair."

"Sorry," Fraser said with a sigh. "The more things change, the more they stay the same."

The wall of heat hit them like a sledgehammer as they exited the building and followed Dubois toward another hardened structure. He paused at a keypad on the door.

"This is the armory. We have your operational funds, all thirty million dollars, inside here, as well as your weaponry, ammunition, and requested supplies. We've arranged for your full access to the building, sans escort. Your code is as follows: 0-6-0-6-1-9-4-4."

"Nice," Nick said. Everyone looked at him. "D-Day. Come on, guys."

"Who else has access to this building?" Kate asked.

"My officers at base, of course, each with their own unique passcode. We have also given access to Diana, as the senior CIA representative, and your two paramilitary officers who accompanied the Hostage Task Force. They have some gear stored here as well."

Dubois led them into the dim interior. He flipped on the overhead lights, illuminating two sets of side-by-side cages. The two nearest cages stored shelves piled high with ammunition and racks of sidearms, rifles, and light machine guns, plus body armor and other tactical gear. Dubois stopped between the second set of cages and faced the one on the left.

"Your gear. You're free to keep it here, or we will help you load it onto your trucks."

Nick and Jake stepped inside to take a quick inventory of their Pelican cases and the store of ammo for their rifles and pistols, and the three M249 light machine guns on loan from the CIA. They had enough firepower to conquer northern Mali themselves.

"Looks good," Jake said.

"And here we have your funds. We can provide bill counters, should you wish to verify."

Kate looked inside the cage at the pallet on which shrink-wrapped blocks of U.S. currency rested. She counted thirty blocks of cash, each containing a million dollars in hundred-dollar bills.

"We'll trust that Agency bean counters did their jobs. And that no one has tampered with it." She looked at Diana.

"I checked it personally before it was loaded onto the plane."

"Good enough for me." Kate tugged at the heavy chain, fastened by a padlock, that secured the cage door. "I'm a little concerned about this, though."

"It's not ideal," Dubois agreed. "However, Diana and I discussed this at length. Sometimes high-tech solutions, in a place like Mali, cause more problems than they prevent. The power here is extremely unstable, and—"

Just then, the electricity cut out, plunging the group into darkness. A minute later, generators hummed to life and restored power to the armory.

"As I was saying, that is a frequent occurrence. Our diesel generators can power the entire base, but we do have shorts if a surge is particularly strong. We didn't want to find ourselves in a situation where a damaged electrical system prevented access to the funds." He handed out keys to Kate, Nick and Jake. "These are keys to the padlock. Diana has the fourth."

"Can we trust her?" Nick stage-whispered to Kate.

"It's her ass on the line once we pay that ransom."

"How many of your fancy shoes could thirty million buy?" Amy asked Fraser.

The CIA's chief of Paris Station looked longingly at the pallet of cash. "Forget shoes. I'd retire to the French countryside and never speak to another soul as long as I lived."

Dubois's mobile phone rang. He listened and confirmed his understanding, then ended the call. "I'm told there are some people waiting for you outside the gates." A smiled played on his lips. "They caused some consternation for base security, but all is calm."

"We want to move to our compound before sunset," Jake said, checking his watch. "We still have time if there's anything we need to wrap up here, but we ought to get moving within the hour."

"We need to gear up and load everything," Nick said. "We'll take as much ammo as we can. Pixie, how much money do you want on hand?"

"Five million," Kate replied.

Fraser put a hand to her heart and closed her eyes.

"Ladies, gentlemen, if you'll excuse me, I need to brief the general on the military side regarding your arrival and assure him that your small army poses no threat to the base. Diana, it would be good for you to meet the general."

"Lead the way."

As soon as the door closed behind Fraser and Dubois, Kate tested all three keys in the padlock securing the chain. Then she unwound the chain and handed it to Nick, who examined the links for any weakness. Kate, Amy, and Charlie entered the cage and surveyed each block of currency, ensuring that all were tightly shrink-wrapped.

"We do trust Fraser, right?" Charlie said.

"One hundred percent," Kate said without hesitation.

"We just don't trust anyone else," Amy said. "I know it would be a hassle to wire up a new security system just for us, but any asshole with a pair of bolt cutters could have a field day in here."

"Chain appears strong," Nick said. "Everything as it should be in there?"

"Looks good. Let's move five blocks."

Nick, Jake, and Charlie carried five million dollars out of the cage and set the money beside the array of Pelican cases. Then Jake rooted through one case for a black pouch, which he opened to reveal several items. Nick pulled forth a black electrical box, an uninterrupted power supply, essentially a large battery that could consistently power small electronics when the power cut out.

"Can you find an outlet?" Kate asked Amy, Fatima, and Sharaf. "Preferably one that's low and easily concealed."

"Over here, love," Fatima called from the cage stocked with French weaponry. "I think I see one behind the rack."

Nick and Jake joined her with flashlights, the UPS unit, and the pouch. There was enough space to nestle the UPS on the ground between the rack of gear and the wall. Jake inserted a European plug converter into the outlet and powered on the unit. Nick handed him a wireless-signal extender from the pouch and he plugged it into the UPS.

"Did you get the WIFI network name and password?" Kate asked Charlie.

"Emmanuel gave it to me. Told him I wanted to post a shot of me and the 'Welcome to Timbuktu' sign on Instagram. Analysts are so gullible."

Kate pulled her iPhone from her backpack and found the base's wireless network. She typed in the password and the phone connected, although the signal was weak in the armory.

"You up and running?" Kate called to Nick and Jake.

"UPS and extender are operational."

"Time for George to work her magic." Kate sent a WhatsApp message to George with the network information. The hacker replied immediately and, within minutes, had remotely connected the extender to the base's WIFI, giving them a full-strength signal in the armory. "Okay, got the camera?"

Nick joined her with a tiny black surveillance camera in the palm of his hand. Kate took it from him; it was barely the size of her thumb pad. She marveled at it.

"Same thing we used in Istanbul?" Amy asked.

"Exact same." Kate turned to Nick. "Give me a boost?"

Nick sank to his knees and Kate climbed atop his shoulders. He stood and walked toward the door. Kate positioned the camera well above the door frame, facing straight down the walkway between the cages, and adhered it to the wall. Still on Nick's shoulders, Kate called George.

"Camera is mounted."

"I see you and the gang, and what look like cages full of weapons and stuff?"

"You have an unobstructed view of the second cage on the right?"

"Yeah. Blocks of something. And a chain and padlock on the door."

Kate motioned to Fatima to turn off the lights. The armory went dark. "What about now?"

"I can still see movement, although not as clearly."

"Okay. Make sure you keep a record of everything."

"It's already storing to the Cloud. I'll check the feed regularly."

Kate dismounted from Nick's shoulders and surveyed her handiwork from the ground. The tiny camera was unnoticeable. Nick motioned everyone toward the money cage. He pointed to the chain and padlock.

"You see this? Chain wrapped clockwise, three free links. We do it like this every time."

"All right," Kate said. "Let's go find some hostages."

4

NICK AND JAKE USED the armory to change into their French Foreign Legion uniforms and don their battle gear. Amy took over the women's bathroom in the main office complex for her transformation. Kate, already wearing lightweight khaki pants and a wicking T-shirt plus sturdy shoes, added a white long-sleeved tunic and a pale green pashmina to her ensemble. Professional and culturally appropriate, but comfortable and durable. She waited with Charlie, Fatima, Sharaf, Fraser, and the three Frenchmen near the Pelican cases. Several armored vehicles that would transport them to the base entrance pulled up beside them.

Nick and Jake emerged first. Kate's heart fluttered. Her husband cut a dashing figure in combat fatigues, even weighed down by body armor, pistol, rifle, ammo, and pack. His muscular frame bore the load effortlessly.

"Hey, Laurent, hope you don't mind, but we snagged a couple of your FAMAS rifles. We only have Kalashnikovs and M4s." He and Jake each brandished a French-made assault rifle, standard-issue to Legionnaires. "It's for cover, of course."

Kate shot him a reproving look. She knew full well that he and Jake just wanted to play with new weaponry. He grinned at her.

Ardouin started to object, but Dubois laid a hand on his shoulder. "Henri, we can spare two rifles. Mr. Cavanaugh, Mr. Gillespie, consider them a gift from *la Légion étrangère et la DGSE.*"

"*Merci beaucoup, mon ami.*" Nick turned to Kate. "We ready?"

"Waiting on Amy."

The doors of the office complex opened and out strode Amy Kowalski. Charlie, in mid-swig from a bottle of water, burst out laughing, soaking the front of his shirt. Fatima slow-clapped and even Sharaf appeared impressed by the transformation. Fraser, accustomed to Amy's antics, wore an expression of equal parts amusement, admonishment, and resignation. The three Frenchmen stared at her with mouths agape.

"Dear Lord, please forgive us," Kate murmured.

Amy wore a boxy, light-gray pantsuit that straddled the line between yuppie fashion of the eighties and North Korean communist leadership haute couture, a white dress shirt fully buttoned to the collar, and a large wooden cross hanging from a nylon cord around her neck. She carried a King James Bible clasped to her stomach. Her stodgy, sensible black shoes complemented the outfit perfectly.

"Good afternoon. I am Pastor Amy Smith of the American Evangelical Association, which seeks the immediate release of the children of the Almighty held hostage by Islamic terrorists. May the one true God dispatch the heathens to hell for all eternity."

Ardouin exploded at Dubois. "How could you agree to this? These lunatics will get our people killed!"

Amy turned to the DGSE officers wearing a beatific smile, but there was cunning in her eyes. She didn't need to speak French in order to understand Ardouin's distress. She focused her steady gaze on the chief of protocol. "You, sir. Have you accepted Jesus Christ as your Lord and savior?"

"I'm dying," Charlie gasped. "She's the Flavor Flav of evangelicals."

Kate took Amy by the elbow and pulled her away from the Frenchmen. "Before we head out, I believe the CIA and the DGSE have some documents for us?"

Fraser removed a yellow envelope from her shoulder bag and opened the clasp. She pulled out three passports, newly created by the CIA's forgers and documents experts. "Amy Smith, United States of America. Dieter König, Federal Republic of Germany. Dmitri Federov, Russian Federation."

Amy, Nick, and Jake handed over their real American passports, which Fraser put in the envelope. They flipped eagerly through their new passports, checking stamps and dates and biographical information in the booklets, made to look beaten and used. Kate faced Dubois and waited. She knew Ardouin was on the verge of a cardiac event.

The DGSE director-general smiled at her and held out a passport. "*Et Katherine Moreau, diplomat de la République française.*"

"Your American passport, please," Ardouin said coldly. He extended a hand.

Kate ignored his hand and gave her passport to Fraser, who tucked it with the others. "I promise I will not bring shame to our republic," she said solemnly in French.

"This will be the end of our careers," Ardouin said to Dubois, before stalking back to the office complex.

"I apologize for Henri," Dubois said. "As difficult as he may be sometimes, he is my most trusted adviser. He is simply trying to protect our interests."

"We know how this looks," Kate replied. "A fake sheikh, a fake evangelical pastor, a fake French diplomat, and two fake Legionnaires. Trust us, we know how this looks."

"It looks rather like suicide," Fatima remarked. "It will be epic, as I believe you Americans say."

Ω

Nick and Jake, with help from French military personnel, loaded the trucks that would transport them to the base's back entrance, where they would meet their escorts for the ride to their compound in Timbuktu city. As the group exchanged last words with Fraser, Dubois, and Giraud, a French armored personnel carrier rumbled toward them and stopped near the armory. Two men, clad in combat gear, hopped out and approached them.

"Kate Devlin!"

Kate turned, surprised by a familiar voice she hadn't heard in years. Before she could react, one of the men embraced her and lifted her off the ground, swinging her around before setting her down and giving her a kiss on the cheek.

"I heard you were joining the team! Wow, it's good to see you! Somehow you look even better now than last time we were together."

Kate smoothed her tunic and adjusted the green scarf around her neck, trying to smile through her grimace. She felt Nick's towering, glowering presence behind her, sensed the curious looks from her companions, and knew that Amy would be unable or unwilling to conceal her displeasure over this unexpected development.

"Hi, Chad. It's been a long time." She hoped the emphasis on *long time* was as obvious to the man behind her as to the man in front of her.

"It'll be like old times, us working side by side. Remember Iraq? Man, we had some fun."

He stepped forward to embrace her again, but Kate leaned back into Nick, whose left arm wrapped around her and whose right arm extended into Chad's chest.

"Whoa, bro, take it easy," Chad said.

"Chad, this is Nick. My husband."

Chad's eyes widened. "I heard a rumor you got married, but I didn't believe it. I mean, you passed on this stud from DEVGRU. Nowhere to go but down, am I right?"

Kate heard Amy's muttered "for fuck's sake" and Jake's derisive snicker, but she was more concerned about keeping her combat-hardened Marine with caveman tendencies from killing the former Navy SEAL she had briefly dated years ago. She pulled Nick's right arm away from Chad and firmly grasped his hand.

"We have to get going, but we'll see you later."

"Blake and I are the paramilitary officers attached to the Sahel Department for this evolution. We're usually out reconning and meeting sources, working multiple lines of effort to the hostages. We're also the main liaison to USMIL elements in Africa. You need anything, let us know. Six has got your six." He winked at Kate and slapped Blake, his companion, on the back. They turned and headed for the armory.

Nick spun Kate and held her by the shoulders. "You dated a SEAL named Chad? *Chad?*"

"Not just any SEAL. Team Six," Jake added with a devious grin.

Kate shot him a dirty look and then patted her husband's armored chest plate. "I did. But I married a Marine. Don't make me regret my decision."

Nick sighed and released her. The team piled into the trucks. Fraser slid to Nick's side and squeezed his arm.

"I can't tell you how much I plan to enjoy this," she said.

Ω

The team reached the gates of the base and found French forces in a standoff with a massive convoy of Toyota Hiluxes and technicals outfitted with .50-caliber machine guns. At least a hundred rifle-toting, desert fatigue-clad Tuaregs wearing indigo turbans milled about the grounds, waiting. Two Tuaregs in loose indigo robes and white turbans approached Sandstorm's small convoy. They pulled away the strip of fabric that covered their faces, exposing weathered skin and dark eyes. The taller of the two Tuaregs welcomed them in Tamashek, French, and English. Kate offered her hand and introduced the team.

"I am Cherif ag Salla," he said in clear English. "My men and I are at your service."

"This is awesome," Jake whispered to Nick.

"I can't believe she dated a SEAL," Nick grumbled.

Kate ensured that Cherif and his cousin and deputy, Mokhtar ag Elwafil, understood that the team wanted this movement to the compound in the heart of Timbuktu city to be a spectacle. Cherif and Mokhtar smiled.

"*C'est compris*, Madame Kate. *C'est bien compris.*"

♌

The compound was owned by a prominent Arab who was known to support the Islamic Emirate of the Maghreb. The Arab was happy to host such an esteemed guest as Sheikh Sharaf al-Yemeni, and he headed for his compound to the south in Bamako, where he would continue his agitations against the central government on behalf of the country's Arab minority.

Their Tuareg militia rolled into town at full strength and sent the locals scurrying for cover as the soldier-laden pickups and technicals hogged the roads and established a wide perimeter around the two trucks at the heart of the convoy that transported the Sandstorm team. Nick and Jake had taken control of one Hilux; Jake drove with Nick up front and Sharaf and a fully veiled Fatima in the back. Cherif drove Kate, Amy, and Charlie. Kate gave the Tuaregs credit; they knew how to put on a spectacle.

After a late dinner that Sharaf whipped up from the prepositioned stores of food in the house, they all retreated to their rooms, jetlagged and exhausted. Their militia guarded the compound and patrolled the city, although that hadn't stopped Nick and Jake from placing one of the CIA's machine guns at the top of the stairs, a belt of ammo already loaded, just in case Mali's jihadi hordes breached the walls.

As Kate unpacked her luggage, organized her go-bag, and got ready for bed, Nick paced through the bedroom muttering snark about a certain CIA paramilitary officer and former SEAL of Kate's acquaintance.

"Let me guess, he was on the raid that killed Bin Laden."

"He was with the Agency by then. He wasn't a SEAL for long."

"Is that supposed to make me feel better?"

"About the last thing I intend to do is make you feel better about this."

Nick made a face at her and stripped to his boxer briefs, taking care to fold his uniform neatly and position his weapons and gear for easy access during the night. She watched him, nibbling at her bottom lip. He looked good in a uniform, but he looked even better out of one.

"Do plan to be an overprotective alpha caveman the entire time we're here?"

Nick covered the distance between them and loomed over her. "Absolutely."

Kate smiled and trailed a finger down his bare chest. "Just checking." Then she slid into bed. He remained standing. She raised her eyebrows. "Yes?"

"Can we have sex during this operation?"

"Why on earth would we not have sex?"

"You get some crazy ideas in your head when we're on the job."

"There were very specific reasons, crucial to the success of the operation, for why I declined your amorous advances in Turkey. It was as painful for me as it was for you."

Nick harrumphed. "I seriously doubt that."

"Perhaps it was a different type of pain. If you'd like to join me, I'd be happy to make it up to you." She patted his side of the bed.

He flopped down beside her. "At least I'm taller than he is."

"You do have several inches on him."

Nick narrowed his eyes. Kate kept her expression neutral.

"Are you saying that—"

"I agreed that you are taller."

He harrumphed again, but then was quiet for a moment. "But seriously, am I—"

"You really do talk too much. Now do your caveman best."

Ω

The next morning after breakfast, they retreated to the living room with coffee and tea, spreading out over couches, chairs, and divans. Kate tossed a folder of documents on the coffee table and dropped next to Nick on the sofa. She rapped the table with her knuckles to get everyone's attention.

"*Bienvenue au Mali, tout le monde. Opération Tempête de Sable* has officially commenced with an end date of thirty days from today. The CIA and the DGSE hired us to obtain locational data on five known hostages, two Americans and three French nationals, in hopes of facilitating a military rescue. I want to emphasize that this is an intelligence-collection operation." She looked pointedly at Nick and Jake. "We gather information, and we pass it to Charlie and Fraser and Dubois."

"I don't know, babe, if Double D sees an opportunity to steal glory from the SEALs…"

"Then your dry spell in Timbuktu will make your dry spell in Istanbul seem like a blip in time."

The group snickered. Sharaf turned questioningly to Fatima. "No sex," she whispered in Arabic. He snorted.

Nick saluted. "*Jawohl, mein Frau.*"

"Now, communication will be critical for the duration of this exercise. I don't want to put the kibosh on improvisation, given how well it's worked for us in the past, but whatever we do individually must fit logically within the greater framework of the scenario. Does that make sense?"

"Sure," Amy said. "No outlandish subplots for the sake of outlandish subplots. What about red herrings and double crosses?"

"They may have their utility, depending on the circumstances." Kate paused and waited for Fatima, who was interpreting for Sharaf. He nodded his understanding. "Okay, now that we've got the guardrails in place, let's go over our roles. Flavor Flav, you're up."

Amy, though dressed in shorts and a T-shirt and flip-flops, wore the massive cross and held the King James Bible. Her face, framed by unruly blond curls, had gone beatifically trancelike again. Kate wondered how long it had taken her to get that blissfully vapid look just right in the mirror. Her best friend might be unhinged, but in the best possible way.

"I am Pastor Amy Smith, representing the longstanding and eminent yet totally fictitious American Evangelical Association on behalf of the family of the abducted missionaries. The AEA has deep pockets and shadowy donors, and much sway in Washington. I have the full authority of the association to negotiate for the hostages' release."

"Stuart and Bess Abbott are Pentecostals," Kate said. "I trust you're conversant on that particular form of evangelical Christianity?"

"Bring me a snake and that serpent and I will converse in tongues. The power of Christ compels me!"

Charlie laughed. "You're such a nutter-butter."

"Pastor Amy is representing the U.S. side of negotiations for the Abbotts, and I, Katherine Moreau, will represent the French government. Dubois, much to Ardouin's dismay, has provided me a French diplomatic passport and a letter signed by the French minister of foreign affairs herself attesting to my covert mission on behalf of the government to negotiate for the release of the French hostages, the two sisters Mathilde and Marianne Fournier and the businessman Gilles Lefèvre. The goal is to ensure the hostages stay together."

"So, no playing you two off each other," Fatima said.

"No. Amy and I will present a united front for an updated proof of life, that sort of thing. Assuming we get an audience with anyone of prominence in Khalifa's network."

"That letter is a work of art," Fatima said. "It will garner a response."

"Maybe," Kate replied. "Or we run into the same problems everyone else has had."

"Love, you've never doubted yourself. Don't let that horrible man with the roadkill on his face make you start now."

Nick squeezed Kate's knee. "Concur."

"We'll see. Okay, let's talk about Sharaf's role. He's our in to wherever we get in. Tribal sheikh from Al Jawf Governorate in Yemen, but based in Mukalla, where he operates an import-export business. Has provided financial and material assistance to al-Qaeda in Yemen and Syria. Ideological, but keen to protect his lucrative business interests and not draw too much attention from the authorities.

"In our scenario, Sharaf is the middleman, the broker, the courier. He comes to Mali bearing letters and historical communications, some of it real, some of it not, between himself and core al-Qaeda leaders, who have ostensibly dispatched him on this mission of utmost importance to make contact with IEM and Khalifa and facilitate a ransom payment. Tight compartmentation within AQ and their preference for use of couriers over electronic comms means that it's extremely unlikely that Khalifa would have advanced notice of Sharaf's mission to Mali, and the letters and electronic backstopping on his phone will help deflect suspicion. Given massive losses to the franchise in Syria in particular and a decline in prestige, courtesy of the rise of the Islamic State, al-Qaeda needs an infusion of capital, and quickly."

"Ransoms," Charlie said.

"Exactly. The Islamic Emirate of the Maghreb has been a moneymaker for big AQ over the years by securing major ransom payments for Europeans and other Western hostages, largely thanks to Khalifa. Big AQ has doled out those funds to needy branches. The asking price for the Abbotts, the Fourniers, and Lefèvre is north of nineteen million dollars at the current exchange rate. That'll fund a lot of operations."

"Will you try to talk them down?" Charlie asked.

"Not a priority. Doesn't matter how much they ask for. We can't pay a ransom with the government's money. But we can make them think we're willing to pay, and the more they think they can get, the keener they'll be to keep negotiations going. Movements can be picked up and followed, activity and preparations can be tracked. The goal is information." Kate looked at Sharaf and spoke in Arabic. "If you're not comfortable with any of this, we need to know now."

The tribesman from Al Jawf stroked his white beard. "I have lived many years, seen many things. War and terrorism drove me from my homeland. I detest these people, but I know them. I will speak the words they understand."

"Fatima?"

"I've decided to reprise a character near and dear to my heart. I am Umm Ali al-Yemeni, Sharaf's first and favored wife. I'm educated and act as his translator should English or French be necessary for communication."

"Her Maghrebi Arabic is better than mine," Sharaf added. "I've been studying, but I may need help if our contacts do not speak a dialect with which I am more familiar."

"Otherwise, I'll leave the men to their business and make the acquaintance of any women who may be present."

Charlie nodded enthusiastically. "I've long advocated for pursuing more female sources in the CT arena. Women always know more than we think they do."

"If we find ourselves in a situation where Katherine Moreau is unwelcome, I'll try to present as Sharaf's second wife, Aisha al-Souri, a Syrian. I'll be fully veiled and gloved, not even eyes visible, but as there are lighter-skinned, lighter-eyed Syrians, that will account for my complexion should any flesh make an appearance."

"Aisha will be subordinate to Umm Ali," Fatima said with a devilish grin. "You know how first wives can be."

"That leaves our Legionnaires. Double D," Kate said.

"*Guten tag*," Nick said. "I'm Dieter König, German national and former captain in the French Foreign Legion. I fought in Mali as part of Operation Serval, then left to pursue more profitable work capitalizing on my military skills. I have the heart of a mercenary, love the sandboxes, and found a sheikh who will fund my early retirement to the Bavarian countryside."

"And I thought I'd bring back an old favorite. I'm Dmitri Federov, Russian national and former sergeant in the French Foreign Legion. Dieter was my company commander during Operation Serval and he convinced me to abandon the Legion for the good life. We coordinate Sharaf's travels and provide security," Jake said.

"We'll always be with Sharaf," Nick emphasized, mostly for Fatima's benefit. "Communication won't be ideal, but I have the Arabic and our different nationalities mean that Jake and I use English as our common language."

"Plus, we're really hoping we don't have to speak much in any bad guys' presence beyond military lingo. We're just the help," Jake added.

"And Jake will have his medical gear at all times," Kate said. "Everyone comfortable?"

"Wait, what about me?" Charlie asked.

"What do you mean?"

"I'm seconded to you for the duration of this operation. Can't I play, too?"

"You're here to sort out any intel we stumble across, not be a party to our crimes. Remember?" Kate said.

"Well," Amy began.

Kate sighed.

"Hear me out. I was thinking he could be my assistant. You know that if what we think might happen actually happens, the clown posse won't believe us. But they might believe him."

"Fraser will literally kill us if anything happens to him."

"Then we have to make sure nothing happens to him."

Kate looked at Nick and Jake. "Your call."

"Amy has a point," Nick said. "But let's see what kind of response we get first. That work?"

Amy and Charlie nodded. Kate pulled a sheet of paper from the folder on the coffee table and read it one last time. Had she captured the essence of al-Qaeda in this missive, written in her third language?

"Are we doing this?" she asked the group.

"Hell yes."

♌

Kate summoned Cherif to the house with a call to his mobile phone. He was with several truckloads of his men, tooling around the city and making it known to all that Timbuktu had a guest of great importance. He entered the compound and met Kate, Nick, Fatima, and Sharaf at the door of the screened front porch. They ushered him inside and out of the midday heat, offering water or tea. He loosened the turban and uncovered his face, taking a few sips of water.

He was tall and lean, maybe forty years old. He carried his AK-47 with the same ease that he wore a straight, double-edged, meter-long ceremonial takuba sword from the belt at his waist, situated just below his desert-colored tactical vest that held magazines of rifle ammunition. He was a study in contrasts, an indigo-clad nomad in a modern world, a descendant of generations of warriors who once fought with traditional arms yet now embraced the ubiquitous assault rifle to protect his people and his way of life.

According to the Malian in the employ of the U.S. Embassy, Cherif ag Salla was the first-born son of the chief of the dominant Tuareg clan confederation in Timbuktu region. The clan's support to the Azawad separatist movement that continued to roil the north of the country was crucial, and Cherif's father had an outsized role in occasional but always unproductive peace talks. Kate knew that Fraser and Dubois had done the math and realized that CIA and DGSE—but mostly CIA—funds had been used to hire a militia supplied by one of Mali's warring factions that was intent on overthrowing the government, but they had posed no objections. Fraser would eventually answer to the Agency's legion of lawyers, but her willingness to let it slide spoke volumes about the priority placed on the hostages' return.

"Your arrival has attracted much attention," he said in English. "The Arabs are intrigued."

"We need to get a message to some Arabs," Kate said. "We want to pass this to Khalifa al-Ghazawi. Not to a broker, or a middleman, or some low-level courier. Khalifa himself needs to get it." She held an envelope toward him.

Cherif raised an eyebrow, but accepted the envelope. "You are a bold woman, Madame Kate."

"Can you do it?"

"My confederation has long had a nonaggression pact with Khalifa and his men. It is done." Cherif recovered his face with the turban, bowed slightly, and departed the compound.

"What's next, love?" Fatima asked Kate.

"We wait."

5

THE CALL CAME THE next day, as Sharaf grilled chicken over charcoal for the group's dinner. Nick burst into the kitchen yelling for Kate and Fatima, and they followed him out to the porch, where Sharaf held his ringing Samsung.

"On speaker," Kate said.

Sharaf nodded and took a deep breath. Then he answered. A terse voice offered traditional Arabic greetings, which Sharaf returned in a polite but disinterested tone.

"Brother Sharaf, I represent Brother Khalifa. He received your correspondence and wishes to discuss further. I invite you to join us for tea so we may get to know each other."

"It would be my honor."

"Leave the Westerners behind. We are not yet ready to engage them."

"I will bring only my security men and my wives."

"*Inshallah*, we will meet you in two days' time at the wells two hours north of the city. Cherif will know the way."

"May God the most merciful keep you safe."

"And you, Brother Sharaf."

Sharaf ended the call and looked to Kate for approval. She exhaled the breath she had been holding and squeezed Nick's arm in excitement.

"That was perfect," she said. "I'll call Cherif."

Ω

"Good news," Jake said, reading a message on his phone. "Colonel Patterson arrives tomorrow morning at zero ten hundred."

Nick took a swig of beer. "Thank goodness. I wasn't keen on a meet in the middle of the desert without him on standby."

"Let's hit the base first thing. We'll get him up to speed and see if any info comes back on that number."

"I sent it to Diana," Charlie said. "She put Lacey on it."

"Who?" Nick said.

"Lacey. Crotch Face's PowerPoint minion," Kate said.

He guzzled his beer. "Whatever. It's probably a burner phone, anyway."

"Probably," Charlie agreed. "But it's more than we had a couple hours ago."

"How much are we sharing with the putz parade?" Amy asked.

"We have no reason not to share what we have so far. Which is slightly more than nothing," Kate replied.

"Really? I can think of two reasons to keep our cards close."

Kate sighed. "Look, we have to put personal feelings aside. We took their money—a lot of their money—and while we may not find the hostages, we do owe it to them to be professional."

"We stick to the facts," Nick suggested. "Some dude called us and wants to meet in the desert two hours north of here. That's literally all we have. Even I don't see the harm in sharing that."

"Fine," Amy muttered. "But I want my objections noted for the record. Professionalism is highly overrated."

Ω

"I'm not sure what's cooler," Nick yelled to Jake over the roar of the helicopter's rotors. "Our Tuareg militia or this Huey."

The UH-1 Iroquois, the U.S. military's ubiquitous troop transport and medevac helicopter of the Vietnam War, touched down at the French base's helipad. This Huey was a former medevac, now retrofitted with modern equipment, its red medic's crosses on white squares standing in stark contrast to the dark metal body. As the rotors slowed and the pilot's door opened, Nick and Jake approached a man they hadn't seen since he commanded a Marine Corps attack-helicopter squadron in Anbar Province, Iraq, during the height of the surge. He pulled off his helmet, revealing salt-and-pepper hair in a standard Marine Corps cut. The three men exchanged greetings and hearty handshakes, and then Nick and Jake led him to the welcoming party at the edge of the helipad.

"Gang, this is Colonel Patterson, a Marine Corps helo pilot that Jake and I served with in Iraq. The colonel has agreed to hang out here and be on standby in case we need assistance."

"Retired colonel," Patterson corrected. "Call me Tom."

As Nick made the introductions, Patterson's eyes lingered on Fatima, whose hijab was wrapped loosely around her neck. He smiled and touched his fist to his chest. She returned the smile and offered her hand. Nick and Kate glanced at each other, and Nick saw a hint of amusement in his wife's eyes. Sharaf, though, took a step closer to Fatima and regarded the colonel with overt suspicion.

"Let's load your gear and get you briefed up," Nick said.

ↀ

The CIA contingent was unimpressed with Sandstorm's progress, and made clear that tomorrow's meeting in the desert with unnamed individuals was an unnecessary risk and a complete waste of time. The phone that had been used to contact Sharaf was indeed a burner, according to Lacey Simms's research; the CIA had no information on the number, nor did the French.

"The caller said that Khalifa had received our letter," Kate said.

Neil Weiss rolled his eyes and leaned back jauntily in his chair, resting one hiking boot-clad foot on the opposite cargo pant-clad knee. "Do you know how many times we've thought the same thing? That letter could have ended up in anyone's hands."

"It's possible. But we're here to pursue leads. This is one."

"You could be walking into an ambush," said Stan Van Pelt.

Kate shrugged. "Could be."

"You don't even know where the meeting is," Weiss added.

"We'd like Chad and Blake to accompany you. For your safety, of course," Van Pelt said.

"Absolutely not," Nick said.

"Bro, this is what we do," Chad said.

"And still, the answer is no."

"I served five years with DEVGRU, but this fucking poser thinks he knows what's up," Chad muttered to Blake, but loudly enough for everyone to hear.

"No hard feelings," Jake interjected, "but we can't roll up to this meet with two more white guys. We already visited the market, put ourselves out there for a look. Plus, the Tuaregs have spread the news about the visitors to anyone who will listen."

"And that is possibly the most reckless thing you could have done," Weiss said. "You pigeonholed yourself into a situation that you have no business being in."

"No business being in?" Nick repeated.

"Mr. Weiss is correct, Mr. Cavanaugh. Mr. Yorke and Mr. Doyle are highly trained special operators whereas, if I understand your background correctly, you and Mr. Gillespie were mere infantrymen. Not to mention, they are highly trained case officers, and the point of your endeavors is intelligence collection.

Surely you see the challenges and how we can help you navigate them." Van Pelt
offered what he no doubt thought was an apologetic smile.

"You're right about one thing. Jake and I were just 'mere infantrymen.' But
last time I checked, we have two highly trained case officers running the show."

"Perhaps I should have been clearer. Mr. Yorke and Mr. Doyle are highly
trained case officers with our full trust." Van Pelt kept his eyes on Nick, avoiding
Kate and Amy.

"Enough," Fraser said. "We gave them full operational control."

"No, *you* gave them full operational control," Weiss said.

"And you have our confidence," Fraser said to the Sandstorm team. "The
biggest concern I have is the ambiguous location of the meeting. Two hours
north of the city could put you literally anywhere. Should you need help..."

"We know," Kate said. "It's a risk. But a calculated risk."

"As long as you're comfortable, go forth and conquer. We look forward to
your report."

"Anything else?" Kate asked.

"Can we have a copy of what you sent to Khalifa?" Lacey asked.

"Yes," Kate replied, noting the eager leans forward from her, Weiss, Van Pelt,
Giraud, and Ardouin. "But after the operation concludes. You'll hear from us
once we're back."

"*Bonne chance,*" Dubois said.

Ω

The bland desert scenery never changed as the convoy headed due north toward
an unnamed grouping of wells two hours outside Timbuktu city. Only nomads
and their herds of sheep and goats and camels broke the panorama of sand and
scrub brush, stretching as far as the eye could see.

Their white double-cab Toyota Hilux, driven by Jake, was nestled in the
middle of the Tuareg convoy, which was led by Cherif, who professed to know

exactly where to find the wells. The ride was over rough terrain, mottled, hard-scrabble desert tracks that crisscrossed the region, leading to villages, nomadic encampments, and the wells critical to a people's survival in the Sahel, the semi-arid band of land south of the Sahara Desert that spanned the width of the continent, from Mauritania in the west to Sudan in the east.

Nick, up front beside Jake, murmured a "copy" into his radio, which connected him and Jake to Cherif and Mokhtar. Then he twisted for a look at the three passengers. "Cherif says we're five minutes out."

"And now for my disappearing act," Kate said, flipping a niqab with a sheer eye window over her face. "*Et voilà!*"

"Be seen and not heard, woman," Nick said.

She looked at Sharaf, who absently fingered a set of simple wooden prayer beads. "Are you ready, Sheikh?"

He smiled at her. "I am ready."

"We've got company," Nick said. He pressed the butt of his AK-47 more firmly into his shoulder, the muzzle resting on the dashboard. "Ten motorcycles, two riders each, on our flanks."

Kate peered first around Sharaf, then around Fatima. The motorcycles had thick tires and heavy shocks, designed for harsh ground and nothing like the ubiquitous, lightweight, Chinese-made motos favored by city dwellers needing transportation on the cheap. The riders wore mismatched military fatigues, likely taken off killed or captured Malian soldiers, and black balaclavas to protect their faces from the elements, and had rifles slung across their chests. They kept pace with the convoy, but made no threatening maneuvers.

Moments later, the convoy slowed and the lead vehicle stopped near a grouping of tan trucks, more motorcycles, and an array of tarps and sheepskin tents pitched near a cluster of low trees and scrub brush. Jake eased up beside the lead vehicle.

"Cherif says to wait here," Nick said.

He and Jake gave their gear a quick onceover, covered their faces with olive-drab balaclavas, and situated their sunglasses. Cherif dismounted from his Hilux and approached three men who waited near the encampment. The Tuareg touched his chest in greeting and spoke with the man in the center of the trio. After the exchange, Cherif touched his chest again and walked to Sandstorm's vehicle. Nick lowered his window.

"Please, come with me."

Jake opened the door for Sharaf and Nick for Fatima. Kate slid out after Fatima.

"No shooting anyone unless absolutely necessary," she murmured to Nick.

"No promises," he replied.

Sharaf, flanked by Nick and Jake, strolled purposefully toward the three waiting Arabs. Kate and Fatima trailed at a respectful distance, but close enough to hear.

The middle Arab stepped forward and clasped Sharaf's hand. His armed sidekicks watched Nick and Jake warily.

"Greetings, Brother Sharaf. I am Yunis, son of Khalifa."

ṇ

After more *salaams* and wishes for good health and the casual but fervent praising of Allah, after Nick and Jake reached an unspoken agreement with Yunis's lieutenants, and after Sharaf sent his "wives" to make nice with the encampment's women, who were preparing tea and the midday meal, Nick permitted Cherif and his men to retreat to the outer edges of the camp as a sign of trust and respect. But he and Jake stayed at Sharaf's side as the group moved to a secluded shady area under some low trees. The Arabs sat on mats, but Nick and Jake stood sentry, with Nick positioned to hear the ensuing conversation. He had to be Kate's ears.

"Your men," Yunis said, gesturing to Nick and Jake, "they are Legionnaires?"

"Former Legionnaires. I pay better than the French. And I have far fewer rules."

Yunis smiled. "The French do not object to their foreign sons engaging with a man such as yourself?"

Sharaf shrugged. "Dieter and Dmitri make their own choices. I do not presume to speak for the French government on such matters."

"Do you speak for the French government on any matters, Brother Sharaf?"

"I am but an emissary between the two sides. I was asked to assist by our most senior brothers, and I am here to answer that call. I negotiated a promise of safe passage with the French government, and in return I promised to keep their representative—and the American representative—safe. But I do not speak for either the French government or the American organization."

Yunis stroked his beard. "You say that you were asked by the shura to facilitate negotiations for the hostages, yes?"

"Correct."

"Interesting. I have never heard of you, Brother Sharaf."

"And I have never heard of you, Brother Yunis," Sharaf replied pointedly. "I answer to the shura, and only the shura. If you doubt my veracity, I will report back your personal concerns to Abu Hamza. I'm sure he would be happy to allay your fears."

The not-so-subtle threat of becoming a subject of interest to al-Qaeda's security emir had its intended effect. Yunis shook his head vehemently.

"No, Sheikh, no, I have no concerns. Based on your letter, the shura seems keen to reach an agreement quickly." Yunis tilted his head. "Is the situation truly that dire?"

Nick's hands tightened around his rifle. Though he had to concentrate on the conversation to ensure he followed everything, Yunis spoke clear, educated Arabic. Sharaf, for Nick's benefit, always spoke grammatically, knowing that Nick's command of dialect and slang and idiomatic speech was still a work in progress. This line of questioning was a test, one that he and Kate and

Charlie and Fatima had done their best to prepare Sharaf for, but Yunis was an unknown. How much did he know about al-Qaeda operations outside the Sahel and the group's recent struggles? For that matter, was he truly the son of Khalifa al-Ghazawi?

Sharaf's green eyes drifted away from their hosts and swept over the barren sands and scrub. "I envy you, Brother Yunis. These lands, once home to ancient kingdoms and learned men of wisdom, now shelter their inhabitants from the tragedies and treacheries of the outside world. Is the situation truly that dire?" He laughed hollowly. "In Syria, *Daesh* is the preeminent power. Our brothers are outgunned and outnumbered, hunkered down in their slice of land in the northwest. I traveled there six months ago on behalf of the shura to assess their needs. 'They need everything, as much as we can spare,' I told them."

Sharaf leaned forward. "The problem, Brother Yunis, is that we have nothing to spare. Because while they are bombarded on all fronts in Syria, our brothers in Yemen, my homeland, are even more outgunned and outnumbered by the Houthis and their Iranian patrons, the Saudis and Emiratis and what remains of the internationally recognized Yemeni government, and the Americans and their drones. That is the long answer to your question. The short answer is yes, the situation is that dire. The shura needs money. A lot of money. Ransoms paid for the hostages you hold will help turn the tide in Syria and Yemen. And, of course, the shura wishes it known that your esteemed group here in the lands of the Islamic Maghreb will benefit handsomely from any payments you negotiate."

Yunis stroked his black beard. "We have heard of setbacks on other fronts," he admitted. "My father has expressed concern, especially with the dearth of contact from the shura in recent months. Sometimes we wonder if we are forgotten. But as you say, we are isolated here, often without connectivity to the world." He held up a Samsung smartphone. "A blessing and a curse. We yearn for that bond with likeminded souls, but our anonymity keeps us safe from French and American strikes."

"Then you are among the lucky, Brother Yunis. It seems no one is safe from the Americans and their drones."

"Perhaps eventually, the drones come for us all. Let us break bread and discuss how we may support our glorious cause."

�

Upon being dismissed by Sharaf, Fatima marched toward the makeshift tent providing reprieve from the midday sun to the women of the camp. Kate followed demurely like a subordinate younger wife, which allowed her time to study the camp and its layout. Nick and Jake carried Thuraya satellite phones on their person for emergencies, but they had left smartphones in the trucks and made no attempt to photograph the camp or its occupants upon their approach. They would huddle around Nick and his sketchpad and charcoal pencil later to assist him in rendering the camp and its key personalities on paper.

A fire burned in a shallow pit outside the sheepskin tent, under which Fatima ducked in a swirl of black fabric and offered warm greetings in North African Arabic, French, and even basic Tamashek, courtesy of Cherif. Four women, fully covered save niqabs that had been flipped back while safe from the oppressive male gaze, looked up in surprise.

Their ages ranged from mid-teens to mid-twenties, and Kate knew Fatima was already scheming to rescue the youngest girls. The Yemeni, once a child bride herself, took a dim view of the practice and was a prolific if shadowy liberator in her homeland, even as the violence worsened.

"*As-salaam alaikum!*" she said brightly, flipping back her own niqab to put them at ease.

"*Wa alaikum as-salaam,*" they mumbled in response, still staring at her.

"I am Umm Ali, wife of Sharaf, who visits Yunis in peace."

The oldest girl stood and wiped flour from her hands with a rag. "I am Ahlam, wife of Yunis. Please, join us and be welcome."

Kate slid inside the tent but kept her niqab and gloves in place. The girls paid her little attention, returning to their lunch preparations. Fatima struck up casual conversation about the weather, the wonders of the desert, the uniqueness of the local people and culture.

The girls, all Arabs, were Yunis's wives. Ahlam was from Yunis's native Libya. The second wife was from Algeria, and the third and fourth, both teenagers, were Malians from Timbuktu region, given to Yunis as a peace offering by local tribes.

"We shall be here for a few weeks, at least," Fatima said. "We must exchange mobile numbers and meet in the city. Where is your compound? Ours has a lovely view of the river."

"We do not have phones, and we do not go into the cities or villages," Ahlam said. "We live in camps such as this. Sometimes for weeks, sometimes for hours. We move with our families and their herds. Yunis's men come for us when he wants to see one of us."

"My goodness, such a difficult life!"

Ahlam shrugged. She motioned the three younger wives toward the cooking fire and the iron pot, in which a stew simmered. "The meal is ready. We must serve the men."

"Aisha will help. Go," Fatima said to Kate.

Kate accepted a clay bowl filled with stew and followed the others to the men's gathering. The three younger wives handed bowls to Yunis and his two lieutenants and set a heaping plate of flatbread on the mat. Kate offered her bowl to Sharaf.

"We slaughtered a sheep in your honor, Brother Sharaf," Yunis said as he scooped stew with bread.

Sharaf chewed thoughtfully. "A powerful array of spices. You will learn to make this," he said to Kate.

She bowed her head.

"Your wives are Yemeni?" Yunis asked.

"The first one is. This one, though, is an acquisition from Syria. Her father gifted her to me as thanks for a shipment of antitank missiles."

"Who got the better end of that deal?" Yunis asked with a laugh.

"Her father, certainly. Missiles and one less mouth to feed."

"Should you be in the market for a Malian wife, take my advice and stick to Arabs. The Tuareg women are a handful." He shook his head and slurped stew from the bowl. "My father's first wife is a Tuareg from western Libya, from his home village. They are a matrilineal people, you know. The women inherit livestock and other property, and often think they are entitled to an education. It is madness."

"Your mother is Arab?"

"Yes, although my father is half Tuareg, so I do carry the blood. But I will never marry a Tuareg. My wives know their place, and my property will pass to my sons."

Sharaf raised his tea glass. "As it should be."

Ω

It was dusk when Sharaf and Yunis concluded their business. Kate knew Nick would have preferred to head back hours ago, during daylight, but he had spent enough time in the Arab world to understand the importance of social bonds. Sharaf had been a charming, thoughtful interlocutor, probing unobtrusively into the younger man's background and letting him hold the floor. He had even devised a way to ensure that Kate remained close, insisting that she man the tea station and keep their small cups full. Yunis forgot about the petite, black-clad figure sitting behind Sharaf and spoke at length of his service in the Libyan military as a helicopter pilot under the Khaddafi regime and then joining his father when Khalifa returned to Africa to take command of the Islamic Emirate of the Maghreb.

"I will confer with my father and you will have his decision soon, Brother Sharaf. He will be happy to hear of your assurances that the French and the Americans are ready to negotiate for their people. They become burdens when we must care for them for so long, always hiding from prying eyes. My father has been eager to be rid of them for some time."

"Then we were destined to find each other, Brother Yunis. I await your instructions."

Nick and Jake escorted Sharaf, Kate, and Fatima back to the truck, and the convoy rumbled south toward Timbuktu. Kate flipped back her niqab and rooted around in the small pack at her feet for a pen, notepad, and headlamp so she could jot down details in the descending darkness. As she poised her pen over paper, she looked at Sharaf, who again absently fingered his prayer beads.

"You're a natural," she said.

He smiled.

6

CHARLIE SPENT THE NEXT morning debriefing everyone and hammering out multiple intelligence reports on his secure laptop. Nick sat opposite him at the dining table with his sketchpad and charcoal pencil and took input from Kate, Fatima, Jake, and Sharaf on the camp's layout, orientation, and size. The portraits of Yunis and Yunis's two lieutenants, though, he did from his own memory.

"You have a thing for faces," Kate said as she massaged his tight trapezius muscles after hours hunched over the table.

Nick stretched his neck and squeezed one of her hands as he examined the portrait of Yunis. "Did I nail his ugly mug?"

"Down to the crooked nose and off-kilter eyes."

"Well, odds are good that his parents are cousins."

Charlie transmitted the reports to Fraser, who responded within the hour. *Get your asses over here*, she texted Kate.

"Not even a 'please.' So typical," Amy muttered. But she waited impatiently by the door for everyone else.

"Make sure you have your phone," Kate told Sharaf. He showed her the Samsung.

Thirty minutes later, they joined the crowded conference room on the DGSE side of base. The reception to their meeting with Yunis was both incredulous and hostile, at least from the usual suspects.

"We're not aware of any of Khalifa's sons having joined him in Mali," Weiss declared.

Kate, Amy, and Charlie all lunged for the one remaining sandwich on the platter in the center of the table. Kate won and tore at the cold croque monsieur like a woman who hadn't already eaten two breakfasts.

Amy snapped her fingers in Ardouin's direction. "*Garçon!* More sandwiches, *s'il vous plaît.*"

Dubois laid a calming hand on Ardouin's shoulder and made a quick call. "Lunch is on the way."

"As Mr. Weiss noted, this information is suspect," Van Pelt said.

"No, the information is new, not suspect," Kate replied. She turned to Nick. "Perhaps some visual imagery would be helpful?"

Nick pulled his sketches from his backpack and handed them to Fraser. She and Dubois studied the camp and the portraits of Yunis and his men.

"Can we make copies?" Fraser asked.

"Of course."

Giraud ran the sketches to the copier outside, then distributed sets to each person. The CIA crew huddled over their copies, talking in low voices and making notes.

"Pull up the photo of Khalifa," Fraser told Lacey Simms.

The grainy photo of Khalifa al-Ghazawi filled the television screen. The turbaned IEM leader was fifteen years younger, but one characteristic was evident: off-kilter eyes, an unfortunate genetic quirk that he had passed down to his son.

"This information now seems less suspect, Monsieur Weiss," Dubois noted with some satisfaction.

"Fine, perhaps Khalifa has a son flitting about," Weiss said dismissively. "This still gets us nowhere. We have no coordinates for the camp."

"It was a temporary camp," Nick said. "I guarantee they cleared out five minutes after we left."

"We should have had eyes on you. We could have tracked them to the next bed-down location, maybe even to Khalifa."

"Sure, that would have gone well. 'You can totally trust us, Yunis. Don't mind the American drone hovering overhead.'" Amy shook her head and muttered "idiots" under her breath.

"Again, we're here to find the hostages," Kate said. "Khalifa's whereabouts are important only in that context."

A member of the kitchen staff knocked on the door and the group paused conversation while he delivered fresh sandwiches. Kate snagged another croque monsieur, this one warm with gooey cheese. Ardouin watched in fascination, or possibly revulsion, as the smallest person in the room worked her way through multiple high-calorie sandwiches and then looked around for anything resembling dessert. Preferably something sweet after all that savory, Kate thought. Nick read her mind and fished a packet of peanut M&Ms from his pack for her, his dimples making a quick appearance.

Chad waved his copy of Yunis's portrait. "Let's say for the sake of argument that Yunis is Khalifa's son. Are you confident that he's high enough in the hierarchy to influence events?"

Kate considered this. "Good question. I don't think we can answer that yet. We spent a few hours with the guy and let him get to know Sharaf. I'm confident he'll report on his meeting with us to Khalifa. But without better insight into Khalifa's inner circle, we don't know where Yunis ranks."

Weiss bristled. "We run only the highest-quality operations designed to find, fix, and finish. It takes time to penetrate an emir's inner circle safely and effectively."

"You haven't found, fixed, or finished shit," Nick said. He brandished his original sketches. "So you're welcome."

"I still have my doubts that Yunis is Khalifa's son. And furthermore—"

The shrill ring of Sharaf's Samsung interrupted Weiss's rant. Nick jumped up and pulled Sharaf out of the conference room, followed closely by Kate and

Fatima. Fraser and Dubois got tangled in their chairs in their haste to join them. Fraser ordered everyone in the room to stay put. Kate put a finger to her lips to shush the semicircle of onlookers. Then she nodded to Sharaf.

A familiar voice greeted Brother Sharaf, and the two men again engaged in drawn out well-wishes. Kate tapped the toe of her trail shoe quietly but impatiently.

"Sheikh, we wish to engage in the business that was discussed, with the visitors. Two days from now, drive north in the lands of Azawad along the road to Taoudenni. *Inshallah*, we will find each other."

"*Inshallah*, brother. May God the most merciful keep you safe." Sharaf disconnected and slipped the phone into the pocket of his thobe. He clasped his hands and waited.

"What happened?" Fraser asked.

Kate, Nick, and Fatima grinned. "Either we're going to die at the hands of terrorists, or we're going to negotiate for hostages," Kate said.

Ω

The call to Sharaf had been made from the same burner phone as before. The road to Taoudenni, a village located in the very north of Mali near the Algerian border, was hundreds of miles long and cut straight through the country's badlands, the so-called Azawad Republic, populated and controlled by breakaway factions of Tuaregs waging a violent rebellion against the central government.

After the initial euphoria wore off, the doubts wormed their way to the front of Kate's mind. Nick and Jake were quiet, each mulling over the ramifications of this new development. Ardouin, at their request, had sent a DGSE officer to retrieve Tom Patterson from the flight line and bring him to the conference room. He needed to familiarize himself with the likely operating area and start making calculations for fuel and weight. He took a seat beside Fatima, much to Sharaf's displeasure, and opened his small notepad.

76

"I'm sensing some tension," he whispered to her.

Fatima smiled. "You Americans are more like Arabs than you care to admit. All this yelling."

Kate found some merit to her observation. *Drive north on the road to Taoudenni* had been received with derision, and Chad, with Blake nodding soberly, had felt the need to lecture Nick and Jake on best practices for traveling safely and securely to a meet that the two paramilitary officers were sure would never happen.

"Thanks. Good advice," her suffering husband had growled through gritted teeth.

Patterson, studying the map on the table, looked to Kate, Nick, and Jake in concern. "The Huey will never reach Taoudenni. And even if it did, we'd never make it back."

"I don't think we're going to Taoudenni," Kate said. "My bet is that we don't get anywhere near Taoudenni."

"But the caller said the road to Taoudenni," Lacey said.

"He said, '*Inshallah*, we will find each other *along* the road to Taoudenni.' That could mean ten minutes outside Timbuktu for all we know."

"Still, bro, roll heavy," Chad said to Nick. "Blake and I got this. We can trail behind at a discreet distance and—"

"No, Chad, please stay on base," Kate said. "We're building trust with Khalifa's men. The slightest anomaly will undercut it and cost the mission, and potentially our lives. You wouldn't want anything to happen to me, would you?" She smiled coquettishly at her ex-boyfriend, ignoring Nick's barely controlled fury and Amy's muffled gag.

Chad grinned. "Of course not. Your safety is our priority. We'll be ready to go if you need us."

"Thank you. That means everything to me, knowing you'll be there to save us."

Chad winked at her and shot Nick a smug look. To stave off bloodshed, Kate sent Nick and Jake to the armory for supplies while she wrapped up business in the conference room. An hour later, as the early-evening call to prayer rang out in the city, the team returned to their compound.

Ω

Nick had been giving Kate the silent treatment since they left base. He ate dinner in silence, drank a couple of local beers on the porch in silence, contemplated the view of their compound walls in silence, and then retreated to their bedroom in silence. Kate padded up the stairs after him. He went to the windows and pulled the curtains shut, leaving only a slit out through which he gazed on their Tuareg force milling about the surrounding streets.

Kate snagged a couple of clothing items from her dresser drawers and one from his, and disappeared into the bathroom. When she reemerged, he still peered through the window.

"You have terrible taste in men," he said without turning.

"So I've been told." She knew without seeing that he rolled his eyes.

Then he turned. She had wrapped one of his Legionnaire uniform shirts around her body, and he was left to guess what might or might not be underneath. His pupils dilated and he cleared his throat.

"I was thinking maybe I'd give Stacey—"

"Who?"

"That chick. Stacey."

"Lacey."

"Whatever. I was thinking I'd give her a call. She seems kinda into me."

"She does," Kate agreed. Lacey's lack of empowerment to speak substantively while in the presence of eminent blowhards like Weiss and Van Pelt gave her ample opportunity to drool over Nick while she manned the PowerPoint presentations. Kate couldn't blame her.

"Great. Then you can run back into Chad's tattooed but surprisingly scrawny arms."

"All women dream of being swept off their feet by a Navy SEAL." Nick received the same coquettish smile that she had earlier directed at Chad.

"Let's get one thing straight: I would sooner sacrifice all of us to terrorist savages than accept a rescue from that prick."

"And here I was, worried that we didn't have our priorities in order." She tsked. "Silly me."

Nick gave his face a violent rub with both hands and snatched a book off the bedside table. "I'm going to read downstairs. Good night."

As he rounded the bed, Kate let the Legionnaire shirt slide off her shoulders and pool at her feet. The scraps of black lace she wore concealed nothing. She stretched and yawned.

"Good night."

The book hit the floor with a thud and Nick swept Kate into his decidedly not-scrawny arms. She giggled as he tossed her onto the bed and tore at his own clothing. Seconds later, he loomed over her. One finger traced the lace of the thong.

"Oh, Chad," she murmured.

He growled and pinned her hands over her head. "You're going to pay for that," he said, nibbling at her ear.

She intertwined her fingers with his and found his lips with hers. "I should hope so."

Ω

The next day, Kate invited Fraser and Dubois to the house for lunch and an afternoon strategy session. After a meal of chicken and beef kebabs, Amy, Charlie, and Jake asked Cherif to take them to the banks of the Niger River for a tour—and for Amy to find a snake, much to Fraser's chagrin—while Kate,

Nick, and Fatima sat with Fraser and Dubois on the porch with cold drinks and the remaining mezza from lunch.

"Your Sharaf is a chef extraordinaire," Dubois commented. "That meal would put the Lebanese to shame."

"You should taste his French desserts," Fatima said. "Sending him to pastry school was perhaps the best money I've ever spent."

"I believe I've heard a little something about his French desserts."

"Ah, yes...all part of the game. Speaking of, how is your daughter? I think of her often."

"Camille is doing well. Some days she struggles, but we do our best to be there for her. I talk to her every evening while I'm traveling. This trip caused some angst, until I hinted that I may be seeing old friends of hers. I'm under strict orders to confirm that Madame Cavanaugh is being treated with the utmost love and respect."

"Camille should be a lot more concerned about how *I'm* treated in this marriage," Nick said.

"I have some complaints," Kate said.

Dubois smiled into his glass of water. "I will be sure to take note of them."

"Our troubled union can wait. I need a crash course in how to be a French diplomat. I once had a career pretending to be an American diplomat, but I'm out of practice."

"And never terribly diplomatic," Nick said.

"Says the pot to the kettle," Fraser commented.

"This is a much better conversation for you to have with Henri. He began his career in the Ministry of Foreign Affairs. Diplomacy, as you know, is about everything being just so. Being 'just so' is Henri's forte."

"I need to be a diplomat who wants to get shit done."

"Ah, that is another matter entirely. As you well know, French is the language of diplomacy. One can express any nuance, any shade of meaning, in French."

"Here's the thing," Kate said. "We have no information indicating that Khalifa speaks French. As a Libyan, why would he? I'll communicate in Arabic. I'm less concerned about the words a real French diplomat would use and a lot more interested in how she might behave. We don't have time to quibble over the size and shape of the negotiating table, so to speak."

Dubois swirled the dregs of his water around the bottom of his glass. "No, I suppose you don't."

"I know you don't want to talk about this, but when you negotiated for the release of other hostages, how did you do it?"

"Those decisions were made before my time as director-general. As I understand, we simply made clear we would pay. And we paid. Our negotiations were always done through middlemen, though, and they had to receive their cut as well. I don't believe our diplomats have ever met with a member of the Islamic Emirate of the Maghreb. That would be poorly received by the Ministry of Foreign Affairs, the presidency, and the general public, I fear."

"Did you try to bargain a lower price?"

"Yes, but we weren't terribly successful. Maybe we shaved a few hundred thousand euros off, but it was a token gesture on the terrorists' part. Once they were confident that we were serious, they had us and they knew it. Had we pushed hard for a lower ransom, they would have walked and announced to the world that we had put a price on our own citizens' lives. Domestic support for our activities in Mali and the region has waned in recent months. A good-news story such as the rescue of our hostages would help secure Parliament's support for aggressive counterterrorism operations."

"Were any of your prior negotiators women?"

"No, men only. I suspect you will be a surprise, but I hope that the paperwork that we've provided, and the fact that you speak fluent Arabic, will be enough to dispel any concerns." He paused. "How your interlocutors might react to your friend, on the other hand…"

Kate laughed. "They'll tell stories about her around the terrorist campfire for generations to come."

"Had I not heard firsthand how convincing she is in the personas she adopts, I would share Henri's rather strident concerns. Tell me, though, is she of that religious persuasion?"

Kate laughed again. "Goodness, no. She's a proud atheist. But when she goes in, she goes all in."

Just then, the compound gates swung open and Jake, Charlie, and the proud atheist ambled toward the porch. Amy carried a white bucket and wore a wide grin.

"Do I need to shoot whatever is in that bucket?" Nick asked.

Amy set it down and reached inside, pulling forth a small black snake that she held at the base of its jaws and thrust toward them. "Look! I found a serpent!"

Fraser, seated closest to Amy's outstretched arm, nearly fell out of her chair in her haste to put distance between them. "Jesus, Amy!"

Kate took a closer look at the creature, likely a juvenile. "Is it poisonous?"

"Cherif says it's not."

"Maybe let's not find out the hard way, okay?"

Amy turned her hand so she could stare into the snake's eyes. Her face relaxed into her practiced beatific gaze. Then she began to shout. "Ogay ackbay otay ellhay, atansay!"

Nick, Jake, and Charlie snickered. Fraser shook her head and sighed. Dubois and Fatima looked confused.

"I know many languages," Fatima said. "But I do not know that one."

"It's Pig Latin," Kate said.

"One fake pastor's Pig Latin is another man's glossolalia," Amy said. She set the snake back in the bucket and cooed at it.

"I'm relieved that Henri is not here to see this. I would surely be taken straight to the guillotine," Dubois said.

"Let them eat cake," Amy declared.

♌

That night, Kate brought beers out to the driveway, where Nick and Jake loaded two Hiluxes with Pelican cases and crates of survival gear, extra rifles, and ammo. Outside the gate, Cherif and his men made similar preparations. Kate handed each man a lager and then hauled herself into the bed of the truck where they worked to lash the supplies to the Hilux's roll bar with ropes and bungee cords.

Nick kissed her forehead and chugged half the beer. "It's damn hot in this country."

"We ready?"

"Camping gear, seven days of supplies, guns and ammo."

"I programmed everyone's numbers into the Thurayas. Fraser, Dubois, Ardouin, Colonel Patterson."

"And Chad?"

Kate paused. "And Chad."

Nick nodded. "Good."

"I'm on the hook to make that call," Jake said, winking at Kate as he rolled three flag poles bearing American, French, and Malian flags into a black tarp that he slid along the side of the bed.

"We need to make a decision on Charlie," Kate said.

"Your call," Nick said. "But I think Amy's argument has merit."

"He only has his real documents. He can't carry those."

"So we say he forgot his passport if they ask for paperwork. He's got the excitable puppy thing going for him; he can sell being a space cadet. And if he's Amy assistant, who cares? The rest of us have convincing proof of identity, and Sharaf can vouch for him."

"It would be nice to have another set of eyes and ears," Kate admitted. Then she grinned. "And we'll make him do all the writing."

"Let's call it a night. We need to be on the road no later than six tomorrow morning."

As they hopped down from the bed, the heavy compound doors slid open and a tall, indigo-clad figure stepped into the courtyard. A dog trotted in after him and circled the Americans, nose up in the air.

"Well, hello," Kate said, moving slowly toward the dog.

Nick caught her by her rear belt loop and held her in place. "We do not need a case of rabies on top of everything else."

The dog approached, nose in overdrive. It sniffed their shoes, spending extra time on Kate and Nick. Shadow's scent undoubtedly had traveled to Mali with them.

"She is an Azawakh," Cherif said, taking note of Kate's curious expression. "Bred by the Tuareg people across the Sahel."

"She's beautiful."

Kate watched the dog explore the yard as the men ironed out the last of the details for the morning's departure. Short-haired and fawn-colored, she looked like a smaller, stockier greyhound. A chorus of barks rose in the distance; the Azawakh scampered out the open gate and into the night.

Nick and Jake shook hands with Cherif. He offered Kate a slight bow. "*À demain*, Madame Kate." Then, like the Azawakh, he melted away.

7

KHALIFA'S MEN INTERCEPTED THE Sandstorm convoy three hours north of Timbuktu. Several technicals and a fleet of motorcycles flanked them. A motorcycle pulled up beside Cherif's Hilux and the passenger indicated that the convoy should follow.

The lead technical veered off the road, heading west. Charlie, up front with Cherif, took note of the kilometers traveled from Timbuktu. They drove for two more hours, yet only another sixty kilometers over rough, inhospitable terrain. Human activity materialized on the horizon, and they entered the outer security zone that surrounded a camp, this one larger than that at which their previous meeting took place.

Yunis and his two lieutenants approached the vehicles and welcomed Sharaf with handshakes and smiles. Nick trotted to Kate's vehicle and motioned for them. Kate draped her pale green scarf over her head and slung her backpack over her shoulder. Then she, Amy, and Charlie followed Nick and Cherif to Sharaf, Fatima, and Yunis. Eyes hidden under her Ray-Bans, Kate took a quick look around camp; a large sheepskin tent near several small trees, guarded by four men, caught her attention.

"Brother Yunis, I present the French and American negotiators. Katherine Moreau of the French Ministry of Foreign Affairs and Pastor Amy Smith of the American Evangelical Association," Sharaf said in Arabic.

Yunis touched a fist to his chest and bowed his head to each woman. "I am Yunis, son of Khalifa. Welcome to the lands of the Islamic Maghreb."

Fatima, fully veiled, translated Yunis's Arabic into English. Amy nodded curtly. Kate offered her own formal greetings in Arabic and thanked Yunis for his hospitality.

The Libyan started. "I did not anticipate an Arabic speaker." He peered at her face and looked to Sharaf. "She is not one of us."

Sharaf shrugged. "She is a diplomat. I have met many who speak our language."

"And the American? She also speaks Arabic?"

"English only. My wife will translate for us."

Yunis led them to a spread of mats and blankets in the shade, not far from the large sheepskin tent. Everyone took a seat; Kate, Amy, and Charlie faced Yunis, and Fatima and Sharaf sat offset, between the two sides. Nick and Jake stood with Yunis's two lieutenants.

Yunis's wives appeared and served everyone tea in what Kate hoped were clean glasses. To refuse any offering of food or drink would be a grave insult. Jake had preemptively started everyone on a course of Cipro in anticipation of less-than-sanitary offerings from their hosts.

As was customary, they engaged in polite small talk with Yunis, who held court and lectured them on the shortsightedness and brutality of their countries' foreign policies toward Muslim lands. Kate plastered a smile to her face and Amy's features relaxed into her beatific gaze. Only Charlie hung on Fatima's every translated word. He was under strict instructions not to write anything down unless given permission. Nevertheless, he'd get a few intel reports out of Yunis's ramblings.

Finally, Yunis ran out of steam on the foreign policy front. He stroked his fist-length beard, studying his guests. "You have come a long way."

"I hope our presence demonstrates the seriousness of our mission to recover our respective citizens and the trust we place in you," Kate said.

"Your government has always used intermediaries in the past. Why did you seek direct contact this time?"

"My government has always sought direct contact. Finally, we found the right intermediary. Or, perhaps I should say, the right intermediary found us." She gestured to Sharaf.

"There are many enterprising Arabs and Tuaregs in these lands," Yunis acknowledged with a smirk. "Some more enterprising than others. The Americans in particular are clueless in how they go about negotiating for their people."

"It's easier to have the weight of a government behind you," Kate said. "For the Americans, often it's up to the families to hire negotiators who have no experience in this part of the world. They're easily fooled by your clever compatriots. Not to mention that families generally can't afford to pay millions of dollars to get their loved ones back."

"But this family can?"

"No," Amy said. "The family cannot. But my organization can."

"I have never heard of this association of yours."

"Why would you? You're not an evangelical Christian."

Yunis continued to stroke his beard. "We did not expect women."

"And we expected Khalifa," Kate said.

Yunis's eyes hardened as he stared at her. "If your country wanted an audience with Khalifa, perhaps they should have sent your foreign minister to pay his respects."

"*She* doesn't negotiate with terrorists," Kate said, holding Yunis's stare. She cocked her head. "Tell me, Brother Yunis, do you speak for Khalifa?"

"I sit at my father's right hand."

"That's not what I asked. Do you have Khalifa's authority to negotiate for the hostages in your custody?"

Fatima quietly translated for Amy and Charlie. Sharaf sat impassively, thumbing his prayer beads. In her peripheral vision, Kate saw Nick finger the safety bar on his AK-47. The silence persisted.

"I take that as a no," Kate said. She turned to Sharaf. "Sheikh, as you know, my government will negotiate only with Khalifa al-Ghazawi or his fully empowered representative. I'm not permitted to engage in discussions with anyone else." She stood and Amy and Charlie followed. "Thank you for your hospitality. Should Khalifa wish to negotiate in good faith, please contact us through the sheikh."

As Kate headed for the team's trucks, a figure emerged from the sheepskin tent. He wore a black turban, a gray djellaba, and black sandals. He had a white beard, at least two fists long, and off-kilter eyes that watched Kate.

"Khalifa wishes to negotiate," he said.

Kate approached the pot-bellied Arab, Amy and Charlie in tow. Charlie, at her left shoulder, vibrated in excitement.

"Khalifa al-Ghazawi?"

The man inclined his head in the affirmative.

"Katherine Moreau, counselor to the French Republic's minister of foreign affairs." She introduced herself in both French and Arabic, and presented her letter signed and embossed by the real French minister of foreign affairs. Then she extended her hand for him to shake.

The U.S. government's eighth-most-wanted terrorist—or third-most-wanted, depending on whom one asked—looked at her hand. A touch of amusement reached the off-kilter eyes. He accepted her hand. His grip was tentative, but she squeezed firmly.

"Please, let us adjourn to the shade," he said. "We have much to discuss."

Yunis's wives reappeared with more tea, small glasses of milk, piles of warm flatbread, and an iron pot full of meat sauce. Khalifa gestured to the food.

"A traditional Tuareg meal to welcome you to our lands. Taguella, sheep stew, camel milk, and tea. Let us break bread in peace."

The guests helped themselves. Amy crossed herself and muttered a prayer to a God she didn't believe in before taking a tentative sip of the camel milk.

Khalifa lounged against some pillows that the wives arrayed around him. "Your Arabic is quite good," he said to Kate.

"Thank you. It's one of the reasons the minister sent me."

"But the Americans, they speak no Arabic?"

Sharaf cut in. "Brother Khalifa, if you do not object, my wife will translate. She speaks Arabic, French, and English. She will ensure that your message is relayed accurately to the Westerners."

"An educated wife, Brother Sharaf!"

"She has proven herself a most helpful partner in many of my business ventures. It pains me to admit it, but I would be lost without Umm Ali."

"A sentiment you share, Khalifa," said a woman's voice.

Yunis sneered into his tiny glass of tea as the woman appeared from Khalifa's tent. She was younger than Khalifa but likely in her fifties, tall and dignified. She wore loose-fitting green robes and no veil, and a prominent Agadez Cross on a chain around her neck.

"Ratma," Khalifa said with a resigned sigh.

The woman greeted them in her native Tamashek, Arabic, French, and English that she had clearly been practicing.

"This is Ratma, my first wife."

"Favorite wife," she corrected.

"Never marry a Tuareg," Yunis whispered to Sharaf. "Never."

"Favorite wife, yes. My partner over the course of this most extraordinary life."

"I don't mean to impose, husband, but your guests intrigue me," she said in Arabic. She took a seat beside Khalifa.

"We may finally be rid of our foreign burdens, *inshallah*."

Ratma threw up her hands. "*Alhamdulillah!* Other men of stature control trade and smuggling routes and build their wives palaces in the cities. But you, you kidnap white people and hope their governments don't find you with drones or attack helicopters. I bounce from camp to camp, living no better than my ancestors."

"Ratma..."

"Don't misunderstand me," she said to Kate and Amy in rapid-fire Arabic, "I've enjoyed the exposure to new cultures, my French has come back to me, and I've even learned some English. But I yearn for the days of Khalifa's youth, when he was nothing more than a devout Muslim cigarette smuggler between Libya, Algeria, and Niger."

"Enough, wife, or you shall no longer be my favorite."

She rolled her eyes.

Khalifa's gaze settled on Amy's enormous cross and the King James Bible on her lap. "You are a holy woman?"

"I'm a spiritual adviser within the American Christian evangelical community. I visit churches throughout my country as a guest pastor, and I accept special assignments on behalf of our umbrella organization, the American Evangelical Association."

"Special assignments?"

"Here. There. Wherever I'm needed to minister or to protect our flock."

Yunis cackled around a mouthful of taguella. "She is a CIA agent."

As Fatima finished the translation, Amy turned her beatific gaze on the son. "The CIA would not waste its time on you."

Ratma snickered, and even Khalifa grunted in amusement. Yunis made a face at Amy. Kate slowly exhaled the breath that had caught somewhere between diaphragm and throat at the mention of the Central Intelligence Agency.

"And this eager young man?" Khalifa said, gesturing to Charlie, whose eyes widened.

"My assistant, Charles. He's a pastor-in-training."

"Definitely not CIA," Khalifa said with a hearty laugh.

Charlie shook his head adamantly.

"Tell me, my American friends, are you breaking your laws with this special assignment of yours?"

"U.S. law was changed in the aftermath of the gruesome deaths of several American hostages in Syria at the hands of the Islamic State. Families and private organizations are now permitted to negotiate with, and pay ransom to, terrorist groups should they choose," Amy responded. "But the U.S. government will never negotiate or pay a ransom."

"Did you meet with your government before coming to Mali?"

Amy studied Khalifa. "Indeed, I have supped at the American government's banquet of buffoonery, and been left wanting."

Fatima looked at Kate. Kate looked at Amy, who sighed and toned down the crazy. "A so-called counterterrorism expert briefed us."

"What did he tell you about me?"

"That you're the U.S. government's eighth-most-wanted terrorist, but he personally would rank you third-most-wanted."

"Do you hear that, Ratma? Third-most-wanted terrorist! And you want me to smuggle cigarettes."

Amy smiled benignly. "You know what they say: You can't spell 'special' without CIA."

Charlie choked on his camel milk and Kate cleared her throat. Fatima translated made-up platitudes instead. The conversation, both meandering and substantive, continued for hours; they stopped only for afternoon prayers. But Khalifa made no further mention of the hostages, and Kate and Amy followed his lead.

As dusk fell on the camp, Yunis's phone played a tinny call to prayer. Khalifa rose from the blankets and clasped Sharaf's hand.

"Sheikh, *inshallah* we will continue our dialogue tomorrow."

"*Inshallah*, Brother Khalifa. We trust that you will find us."

"*Maktub*. It is written."

Ω

They departed Khalifa's camp and drove thirty minutes north to a campsite already scouted and occupied by some of Cherif's men. The Tuaregs set a wide perimeter and attempted to give the Sandstorm crew some privacy.

Fatima sat heavily in one of the folding camp chairs that Nick and Jake had placed around the fire, which burned brightly in a pit dug by the Tuaregs.

"My brain hurts," she murmured in Arabic.

Kate sat beside her. "They like to talk, that's for sure."

"It seems they relish a new audience."

"Especially an audience of attractive women," Nick said as he added more kindling to the fire. "That wife of his is something else."

"We need to get Fatima alone with her. I bet she spills all kinds of secrets," Amy said.

"Speaking of secrets," Charlie said, situating himself in a chair and setting his secure laptop on his knees, "I need to send the highlights to Fraser."

"I'll set up the satellite link," Jake said.

"She's going to lose her mind," Amy said.

Kate sighed. Amy was right; Fraser would absolutely lose her mind, and not in the good way.

Nick passed out U.S. military-issue MREs to everyone and helped Fatima and Sharaf sort through and decipher the rations. The tribesman and chef extraordinaire sniffed at his main course.

"Is this edible?" he asked Nick.

"According to the low standards set by the United States government, yes," he replied.

Amy raised her own entrée in salute. "Here's to not shitting for a month."

One of the Thuraya satellite phones rang as the group sipped beers around the fire, discussing the long day with Khalifa. Kate steeled herself before answering, and immediately had to yank the phone from her ear else lose hearing.

"I did not give you permission to bring Charlie anywhere outside Timbuktu city! What were you thinking?"

Kate allowed Diana to rant. After a moment of silence, she asked, "Are you done?"

Fraser harrumphed. "Yes."

"Charlie is a critical member of the team. Today's highlights are the tip of the iceberg. He hasn't stopped writing since we left the camp. You'll get reams of reporting."

"You and Amy easily could have written those intels," Fraser muttered.

Kate laughed. "You want us to write reports, the price goes up. He's a lot cheaper than we are."

"Please, *please* keep him safe."

"Diana, Charlie is my friend. Trust us, okay?"

"I do." She paused. "Weiss spun up like a sugar-addled toddler on amphetamines over the fact that you met with the top dog. One minute you're all lying liars telling lies, the next you're lying liars telling lies who *actually* met with an HVT."

"This particular high-value target is thrilled to be so well regarded by Weiss and his ilk."

"The good-idea fairy is making the rounds back here. Every plan seems designed to get you killed."

"I'd expect nothing less."

"When do you think you'll return?"

"Not sure. We'll see how tomorrow goes."

"Be safe."

As Kate ended the call with Fraser, the other Thuraya rang. Nick answered and passed the phone to Kate.

"George," he said.

"You guys are suddenly very popular online," she said to Kate. "We got some activity on the American Evangelical Association website, your sheikh's website—the Arabic side—and your official Facebook profile linked to the French MFA. He loitered on your page and hit every page on the AEA site."

"Any idea who might be visiting?"

"I tracked the IP address to Timbuktu. Looks like he's on a mobile device."

"Okay, keep records of anyone who visits our sites."

"Roger."

"They're doing their due diligence," Kate told the group.

"What's the plan for tomorrow?" Amy asked.

"Unfortunately, this will move at Khalifa's pace, and he's got all the time in the world."

"You guys should hit the sack," Nick said. "We're in for some long days."

Ω

Kate listened to the sounds of the desert from inside the quick-pitch tent. She heard the occasional movement of their Tuaregs and the crunch of booted feet over the hard sand, but not much else. The vastness and its accompanying silence were disconcerting. Like the ocean, the desert made a person feel small and insignificant. And like the ocean, this desert teemed with unseen dangers.

Nick unzipped the flap and crawled in, leaving his boots just outside. He stretched out on the second sleeping bag atop a thin pad. Kate, in her own sleeping bag, scooted closer and laid a hand on his chest, pulling playfully at his T-shirt.

"Stay a while. Get comfortable."

"Jake has the first watch. I'll relieve him at two a.m."

"Plenty of time for a little fun." Her hand traveled south.

He caught the hand. "You're a menace."

Kate nestled her head in the hollow of his shoulder and watched the rise and fall of his chest in the dark.

"A penny for your thoughts," he whispered.

"I'm worried about the son. I'm not sure how much control Khalifa actually has over him."

"You think Khalifa wants out of the game?"

"I do. He's old. He's been on the run for much of his adult life. Maybe it's time to step aside after one last score."

"Will the empire go to Yunis?"

"Absent other information, he seems like a likely candidate. For all Weiss's bluster, Khalifa's inner circle seems to be a complete mystery to those allegedly in the know."

"We may smoke out another heir. Especially if we get to the point of discussing money."

Kate nodded. "We still have the same problem, though. We can't pay a ransom and we have no idea where the hostages are, or how to track them."

Nick kissed her forehead. "One step at a time. You should get some sleep. We're nothing without that big brain of yours."

She allowed him to extricate his arm so he could lie on his side and face her. As he searched for comfort, she toyed with his belt buckle. "Are you sure you don't want to relax?"

"I can't be caught with my pants down if the bad guys come for us."

"Jake would probably be annoyed," she conceded. "Okay, counteroffer: We make out with heavy petting."

"Counter counteroffer: We make out and you keep your hands above my waist, but my hands have free rein to go anywhere."

"That doesn't seem fair."

He grinned, his teeth flashing white in the darkness. "Those are my terms, Pixie. Take them or leave them."

"Don't tell Khalifa I'm such a pushover in negotiations."

8

DAY TWO BEGAN MUCH like day one. The team rose with the sun, Sharaf prayed with the Tuaregs, they forced down MREs, packed up camp, and loaded the trucks. Cherif set them in the direction of yesterday's meeting site, but Khalifa's men intercepted them within minutes and led them northwest, to a different location.

"We'll never geolocate these camps," Charlie muttered. "Not without slapping a beacon on Khalifa's truck."

"Which we will not do," Kate said.

"I know. But it's an inevitable request."

"It's not about him. It's about the hostages."

"Would we consider slipping something to a hostage?"

"If we had access to a hostage? Sure, but I think their security practices are too tight."

"I draw the line at being the reason a hostage gets beheaded," Amy said.

"Fair," Charlie said.

"I'd settle for an updated proof of life," Kate said. "We need to know what we're working with."

A camp materialized on the horizon, and more motorcyclists flanked them. Kate squinted into the morning sun. It appeared to be laid out similarly to yesterday's camp, the same number of tents, wisps of smoke rising from multiple cooking fires.

"I don't think we're meeting any hostages today," she said.

"Do you think they'll serve us more camel milk?" Amy asked. "It wasn't bad."

"I like you Americans. A brave people," Cherif said.

"Or just nuts," Amy replied.

Cherif glanced in the mirror at Kate, seated behind him, who provided a translation in French. "Crazy."

The Tuareg smiled.

ᛦ

"Tell me, Madame Moreau, how did you become so proficient in my language?" Khalifa asked.

Kate sipped her scalding tea. She had left all the camel milk to Amy. "I've been speaking it since I was young. My father was a military attaché posted to various Middle Eastern countries. I then studied it at university and joined the Ministry of Foreign Affairs, where I've sought assignments to the region."

"Had I not laid eyes on you, I might have mistaken you for a native speaker. Even your dialect is quite good. What other languages do you speak?"

"English, of course. A bit of Spanish and Italian."

"I once spoke some Italian as well. But that was a long time ago, back during my youth in Libya."

"No French?"

Khalifa waved his hand. "In these parts, one has no need of the occupier's tongue. Many older Malian Tuareg learned it in school, as it was required in those days, but here we conduct our business in our mother tongues. It's a surprising pleasure to speak Arabic with someone so obviously an outsider."

Kate raised her tiny tea glass in salute.

"Your career path intrigues me."

"Oh?"

He studied her. "You are a counselor to the minister herself, you said."

"Yes. I hold primacy on the counterterrorism portfolio."

"You are...young for such an esteemed role in your government, perhaps?"

Kate raised an eyebrow. "How old do you suppose I am?"

Khalifa shrugged. "Twenty-seven? Twenty-eight?"

Kate smiled. "Though a woman always enjoys being told how young she looks, I should tell you that appearances can be deceiving. I'm thirty-eight." Concerned over this very perception in light of her alleged stature within the MFA, she had chosen to increase her ostensible age by five years over her actual age.

"No! I don't believe it. Ratma, do you believe it?"

"The French set the standard for beauty products, Khalifa. A good moisturizer will do wonders for one's appearance. I wouldn't know, as I live in this godforsaken land under this brutal sun."

Kate fished through her backpack and found her French diplomatic passport, which she handed to Khalifa. After last night's traffic to the various websites, and the loitering on her online presence in particular, she had suspected that her passport may need to make an appearance. Katherine Moreau's Facebook profile was detailed enough to look legitimate, but vague enough to allow her some flexibility under interrogation.

Khalifa paged through the passport, filled with stamps from worldwide travel, and handed it to Yunis, who examined it more carefully. The son studied her, slapping the passport against the palm of one hand.

"Explain how you came to know Brother Sharaf and to enter into this partnership."

"I served in Yemen and—"

"When?"

"January 2012 to March 2015." The dates of her CIA tour in Yemen.

Yunis searched out entry and exit cachets in the passport. Finally, he nodded. "Continue."

"I first met Umm Ali at a reception in Sanaa for Yemen's business leaders. She and the sheikh had traveled from Mukalla to attend. Umm Ali and I stayed in touch; I often visited her home when she was in the capital. She introduced me to the sheikh, of course, who was a most welcoming and gracious host, but my relationship was with her. Shortly after the war began, my country closed its embassy and all staff evacuated, and I accepted a new assignment as the minister's adviser. I was pleasantly surprised to receive Umm Ali's well wishes several months ago. She asked me to visit her in Dubai to discuss a sensitive matter of great importance to the French government."

"You got on a plane believing this woman was about to provide details on a sensitive matter of great importance to the French government?" Yunis said.

Fatima's posture, always excellent, became impeccable from her seated position. Her dark eyes hardened as they watched Yunis, who was oblivious to her ire.

"I haven't known Umm Ali to be prone to hyperbole. And I believed that she contacted me at the behest of her husband, who is a powerful man with a wide reach. The minister agreed that it was worth a quick trip to Dubai. It was there, over dinner in their villa, that the sheikh told me he might be able to assist the French government in its efforts to free our citizens held in Mali."

"It didn't give you pause, consorting with a man of Brother Sharaf's reputation?" Khalifa asked.

"On the contrary. It was an opportunity we couldn't refuse. The sheikh is a well-known and successful businessman, but we weren't interested in legitimate business contacts. The sheikh promised to cut through al-Qaeda's red tape, as it were."

Khalifa smiled at that.

"We've been trying for years to secure the release of the Fournier sisters and now also Monsieur Lefèvre. We had gotten nowhere with middlemen and brokers all promising access to you or those who speak for you. The sheikh, upon receipt of written promises from my government not to seek legal or military action against him, shared the broad strokes of his connections to senior leadership within al-Qaeda and described how he could assist our efforts in the search for our citizens. At his urging, we contacted our American counterparts. Though the U.S. government cannot and will not pay for the return of their citizens, they did put us in touch with the American Evangelical Association and Pastor Smith, who has long sought avenues to find and recover the Abbotts. We agreed to work together, with Sheikh Sharaf as our intermediary, to negotiate for the release of our people. And that's how we come to find ourselves here."

Khalifa turned to Yunis. "Satisfied?"

Yunis regarded his father imperiously. "I am your chief of security. This is my job. And you are too trusting, father."

"I hardly think the French government sent this single, rather small woman to assassinate me."

"Are you forgetting the presence of two Legionnaires?"

"Former Legionnaires," Kate said coldly, before Khalifa could respond. "These men are a disgrace to those uniforms and the country that gave them a chance at honorable service."

Nick, standing just outside the tent, pulled off his Oakley sunglasses. He glowered at Kate. "I have never met a people more arrogant and self-absorbed than the French," he said in Arabic.

Ratma tittered. "*Il est très beau, d'accord?*" she said conspiratorially to Kate.

"*La bête ne sait même pas parler français,*" she muttered. The beast can't even speak French.

"My men are loyal to me," Sharaf assured Khalifa. "They pose no danger to you, your people, or your operations."

"I worry not, my brother. I believe you come in peace, in good faith, as do our guests. It's about time the French and the Americans came to their senses."

"Your kindness and hospitality have been overwhelming, but our willingness to negotiate has an expiration date," Kate said.

Yunis shot to his feet, spilling tea everywhere. "How dare you speak to Khalifa in such a tone!" He took one step forward, right hand raised.

Nick grabbed Yunis's shoulder and body-slammed him to the ground. The terrorist's breath left in a whoosh and he cried out in pain. Nick put a booted foot atop Yunis's chest and trained his AK-47 at his head. Jake held Yunis's two lieutenants at bay with his own rifle. Nearby, Khalifa's small army roused themselves from their afternoon lethargy and scrambled for weapons.

"*Khalas!*" Khalifa roared. "*Khalas!*"

His men, still in varying states of disarray, froze. Yunis's lieutenants looked between the barrel of Jake's rifle and their prone leader. Khalifa seethed, his face turning a worrisome shade of puce. Ratma regarded Yunis with disdain.

Kate's heart thudded in her chest. Beside her, Amy took a deep breath and laid a hand on Charlie's shoulder. Sharaf had tossed himself in front of Fatima and now disengaged, adjusting his kaffiyeh.

"As I was saying," Kate said calmly to Khalifa, "if we're to proceed, we must start making substantive progress. Words are merely words at a certain point." She ignored Yunis, still pinned by Nick.

"And we have reached that point, Madame Moreau?"

"We have, sir. I'm serious about these negotiations—we are serious," she said, gesturing to Amy and Charlie. "Your son's concerns about our intentions, while valid, mirror our own about yours. We've put ourselves at tremendous risk coming here to speak with you. And this behavior"—she waved at Yunis—"only reinforces those concerns."

"I apologize for my son. You are in no danger here."

The group spent several long seconds in silence. Kate and Khalifa regarded each other impassively, a former CIA operative and a senior al-Qaeda leader sitting mere feet from each other in one of the most dangerous regions in the world. Kate sincerely hoped the lives of five hostages were worth this aggravation. She wondered if she could retroactively increase Sandstorm's fee.

Her eyes flicked to Nick. Sharaf took his cue. "Dieter, release him."

Nick's foot bore down harder on Yunis's chest, provoking another violent exhalation, but then the faux Legionnaire relented. Yunis sat up and rubbed his sternum. His black headscarf had been knocked loose in the ruckus, and he rewrapped it around his head. Nick remained near; he had lowered his rifle, but the muzzle still covered Yunis. His finger rested on the trigger.

"Thank you, Brother Sharaf. And thank you, Legionnaire, for your restraint." Khalifa touched a fist to his chest and gave a slight bow toward Nick. "Son, you are welcome here as long as you control that temper of yours."

"Why you deign to negotiate directly with these...these *women* is a mystery. We have people for this. You put everything we've built at risk by exposing yourself in such a manner."

"Everything *we* have built? Son, I remind you that this is *my* empire in the lands of the Islamic Maghreb. My blood, my sweat, my tears. The shura trusted *me* to carry out this most vital of missions, and so I shall in support of our brothers and our glorious cause. I will not be questioned."

Yunis slouched and sulked. Kate refilled everyone's tea glasses with hands that she managed to keep from shaking. Ratma smiled and raised her glass to Kate and Amy.

"To brave women everywhere."

"*Salut*," Kate responded.

"And now, these actions you speak of. What is it you seek?" Khalifa asked.

"Proof of life," Kate said.

"We have sent your government and family representatives proof of life."

"Months or years old. We need something far more recent."

"No more than one week old," Amy added. "Preferably video of them talking and moving. We need to evaluate their health and well-being."

Khalifa sucked in a breath. "Within the last week?"

"We're not authorized to continue negotiations, much less pay any money, without knowing each is alive," Kate said.

"My word is not enough?"

"I'm sorry, but no."

Khalifa flipped his prayer beads. "How soon must you have this proof?"

"By tomorrow."

He laughed.

"Those are the terms at this stage of the negotiation," Kate said. "Should you provide what we deem suitable proof by *Asr* prayers tomorrow, discussions can continue. If not, we'll report back to our superiors that we have no path forward."

The terrorist continued to flip his beads in his hand, watching her, assessing her. Kate couldn't pull off Pastor Amy's beatific vapidity, but she could channel Ardouin's French aloofness.

Yunis's phone played the call to prayer. Time for today's *Asr* prayers and for the Sandstorm team to retreat to the open desert. They stood and thanked their hosts.

"Tomorrow, *inshallah*," Kate said.

Khalifa inclined his head. "*Inshallah*."

Ω

Khalifa's men found them quickly the next day and led them north into the heart of Timbuktu's vastness. Even nomads and their flocks were few and far between, mere specks on the horizon. Charlie slipped an unmarked CD into the Hilux's player and the desert blues of Tinariwen, a band of Tuareg rebels, filled the cab.

Cherif nodded approvingly. "Excellent choice."

"What are the odds that we get a proof of life?" Amy asked quietly.

"Probably not good," Kate replied. "But if we don't get one today, there's no tomorrow. They're either serious about this, or they're not."

"Will we accept proof from more than a week ago?"

"Depends. If they're holding a newspaper from two weeks ago, or even a month ago, we have to give a little. It may be all we get."

"It'll still be far more than the armada of asshats had. Let's be real, Fraser and Dubois *think* the hostages are alive, but that's based on some pretty flimsy reporting."

"But we'd be no closer to actually finding anyone. Unless they were dumb enough to include geographic features in the photo."

"What did we learn during the course of our illustrious CIA careers?"

"It can always get worse?"

Amy smirked. "That, and to never underestimate the stupidity of terrorists."

There was certainly some truth to that, Kate reflected as she squinted into the blinding desert sun, but plenty of terrorists had lived long and fruitful lives despite the U.S. government's keen interest in ending those lives. Khalifa al-Ghazawi was one such terrorist. Kate couldn't be sure if that was due to Khalifa's intelligence and cunning or the U.S. government's inability to direct a Hellfire missile up his ass; probably some combination of the two, she decided. Khalifa was a worthy foe, Kate knew without doubt, but there was no way she'd let Weiss off the hook for fifteen years of failure.

As soon as the camp materialized though the dust and harsh late-morning glare, Kate knew something was different. This site had an aura of permanence, even if perhaps its occupants moved routinely. This was an oasis to which they always returned.

Khalifa himself led the welcoming committee, flanked by Yunis's two lieutenants and trailed by the son, and he ushered them under a large, open-air sheepskin tent. The ground was covered with mats and blankets, and pillows ringed the rectangular meeting space. This was an august venue reserved for shuras and war councils. Ratma shooed away Yunis's young wives, who had arranged a spread of food and drink in the center area.

"Camel milk!" Amy whispered excitedly to Kate.

"Please sit, be comfortable," Ratma urged.

"Thank you, Brother Khalifa," said Sharaf as he accepted a small cup of tea from Fatima. "Today's journey was long. These are not easy lands for a man of my age to traverse."

Khalifa laughed heartily. "I say that every time we move."

"Every time," Ratma chimed in. "Yet he persists in this madness he calls his duty."

"Do not mock my devotion to our Lord and his Prophet, peace be upon him, wife."

"I mock not your religious devotion but your silly belief that you can outrun the fate that befalls all men of your stature in this business."

Amy seized the moment at the end of Fatima's murmured translation of Ratma's acidic yet poignant assertion.

"Those beset by doubts will never understand the iron-clad faith of true believers. One needs nothing to survive and thrive save faith in the one true God's divine plan," she said, her face slackening into that disconcerting gaze that fell heavily upon Khalifa, Ratma, and Yunis. She kissed the King James Bible in her hands for good measure.

Khalifa studied Amy, stroking his long beard. "I will admit that the one thing that sets Americans apart from their European brethren is a proud and measurable devotion to their beliefs. Although our Muslim and Christian faiths have long been at odds, Christianity is still a religion I respect. Even if your particular brand of Christianity is somewhat perplexing."

Amy cocked her head. "Perplexing?"

"This denomination, Pentecostalism, it is uniquely American?"

"No," Amy replied as beside her Charlie shook his head vigorously, good evangelical pastor-in-training that he was. "Our faith has spread far and wide across the globe. While many of our oldest, strongest, and most influential congregations are found in the southern United States, the so-called Bible Belt, we've worked hard to export our message. Many scholars believe that Pentecostalism is the fastest-growing religious movement in the world. The global

South has been fertile ground for evangelical Protestant denominations, winning millions of converts to the faith."

"Do you encourage your evangelical Crusaders to proselytize in Muslim lands?"

Amy pursed her lips. "No."

Khalifa nodded slowly. "Then can you explain how your citizens found themselves in my emirate, which has been Muslim for many centuries?"

She fingered her cross. "I talked extensively with their children. They said their parents were divinely called to Niger. A higher power compelled them to seek the poorest of the poor in a most desolate land to offer what little succor and solace they could. The American Evangelical Association, and I in particular, would have cautioned them against taking such a risk, but at the end of the day, we all must do what we believe to be right and good. I can educate and counsel, but I never try to dissuade any of our flock against following their calling from God, no matter where it might lead them."

"And the sisters Fournier, Madame Moreau. Does the French government sanction the actions of their Catholic Crusader citizens?"

"Much like the Abbotts, the Fourniers, who are *not* missionaries, were free to travel to Mali and offer their assistance to vulnerable populations, which they did successfully for years via charities."

"They were warned many times to leave Timbuktu city. It is difficult to abide Christian proselytizers, be they Catholic or Protestant, in these sacred Muslim lands."

"I know how to make you people think twice before bringing your heretical beliefs into our world," Yunis said with a sneer. "Maybe I send you back with their heads."

"*Khalas*," said Khalifa.

The real Amy Kowalski spoke. "They were just trying to help. The Abbotts, the Fourniers, all they wanted to do was help people. Not convert Muslims. Just help the people who needed it most."

Yunis spat to the side. "White people always think they know best. They came to Muslim lands to steal and oppress and mock and—"

"No. The Abbotts taught more effective farming techniques and helped women market and sell their wares so they could support their families. The Fourniers trained teachers and helped rebuild schools that warring parties had burned down. It was their Christian duty to help anyone who needed it. Not to convert. To help. That's all."

Khalifa brandished his prayer beads and rolled them through his fingers. "Whatever their true aims, perhaps known only to Allah, they found themselves guests of my emirate. Perhaps your message to your respective flocks should be to confine their questionable activities to traditionally Christian lands, lest they suffer a similar fate."

"The problem with free societies is that people are *free*," Amy said.

Khalifa sighed. "Americans and their freedom."

Kate caught Sharaf's eye and subtly tapped her watch. It was early afternoon; they needed to move things along.

"Brother Khalifa, the time approaches *Dhuhr* prayers. If we are not to see a proof of life before *Asr* prayers, as Madame Moreau and Pastor Smith requested, we must soon depart. I gave my word to the French government that I would not unnecessarily prolong our time outside the city."

"Very well, Brother Sharaf. Ladies, our great distance from anything approaching civilization posed a challenge to obtain photos or videos of the nature you requested."

"We understand," Kate said. "We'll pass along your assurances to the families that their loved ones are still alive. However, this marks the conclusion of our negotiations."

Khalifa stood and the rest followed suit. "Allow me to finish, Madame Moreau. We have no photos or video, but I believe we found a solution. If you'll follow me."

Kate and Amy and Charlie shared a glance. Then they, along with Fatima and Sharaf, fell in behind Khalifa and Ratma and Yunis. Nick and Jake walked with them, keeping the group tight. Nick's rifle, partially at the ready, was pointed at Yunis's back.

They wound through camp to a grouping of three large tents, flaps open for ventilation. Armed guards ringed the tents, but kept their distance. Khalifa stopped in the common area between the tents and turned to his wife.

"They await your summons."

Ratma clapped her hands and called out in both French and English, "Ladies and gentlemen, please join us outside."

For a moment, nothing happened. A light breeze ruffled the sides of the tents. Ratma clapped her hands again. Then, one by one, seven tired, disheveled people emerged from the three tents, squinting into the afternoon sun.

"Holy shit," Amy whispered.

9

KATE ECHOED THAT SENTIMENT. Holy shit, indeed. She immediately recognized five of the individuals from the photos that the CIA and the DGSE
had shared: Stuart and Bess Abbott, the Americans; Mathilde and Marianne
Fournier, the French sisters; and Gilles Lefèvre, the French businessman. But
who were the two young men looking especially disoriented?

"Madame Moreau, Pastor Smith, your proof of life," said Khalifa.

"Thank you, sir," Kate replied. "May we?"

Khalifa gestured toward the hostages, and he and Ratma retreated a few steps
to stand with Sharaf and Fatima. The ladies struck up a quiet conversation.
Yunis, however, remained close, with Nick on the edge of his personal space.
Instinct pulled her toward the American couple, but then she remembered that
she was a French diplomat. Amy and Charlie strode toward the Abbotts; Kate
approached the sisters and the businessman.

"Mesdames Fournier, Monsieur Lefèvre, my name is Katherine Moreau and
I represent the Ministry of Foreign Affairs. The minister herself dispatched me
on this assignment to seek your release."

"It's about time," Mathilde snapped. "We've been prisoners of these animals
for years."

"I know, ma'am, and I'm very sorry for all you've suffered. But it's taken us
some time to find you, and—"

109

Mathilde, her eyes red and ringed by dark circles, looked more closely at Kate. "The minister sent *you* to save us? You are but a child."

"Mathilde!" Marianne whispered, glancing worriedly at Kate. "Please don't insult her. She is here to help us."

"Ma'am, I promise, I just look young. I need to ask you a few questions while we have time together. It's very important that—"

Mathilde grabbed her sister and dragged her past Kate toward Nick and Jake. "*La Légion étrangère* has come for us. We will go with them."

Nick and Jake said nothing, only standing impassively as the two women stationed themselves at their sides. The sisters were both dressed in long, flowing blue skirts and loose white tunics, discolored by dirt and dust and sweat; each held a worn woven sack, likely their only possessions that accompanied them from terrorist camp to terrorist camp.

"Mesdames, please listen to me. We don't have much time and I really need to speak with you," Kate said.

Mathilde looked up at Nick and spoke to him in French, directing him to take them home. Nick's eyes were invisible behind his sunglasses, but Kate knew they were on her. She nodded almost imperceptibly. Nick gave Mathilde a push; a gentle push, but not a friendly push. She stumbled a few steps and stared at him in shock. Then she walloped him in the torso with her sack. Yunis cackled.

"He's not a Legionnaire. Not anymore," Kate said. "He's the bodyguard of the Arab who brokered this contact. He's not here to save you. Now, please come over here."

The sisters meekly rejoined Kate and Lefèvre, who had remained sullen and silent with his arms crossed over his chest. Kate asked each of the French citizens to state their full names, their date and place of birth, and their national identification number. She dutifully wrote down the information; it was for show, as she knew they had an interested audience. A few feet away, Amy and Charlie did the same with the Abbotts, who looked exhausted beyond measure but thrilled to be speaking to fellow Americans, especially ones wearing crosses and holding Bibles.

"You will pay for our release," said Lefèvre.

Kate noted that it was a statement, not a question. She spoke carefully. "Now that your hosts have proven that you're well, the negotiations will continue."

The businessman scoffed. "Negotiations? Do you know how long negotiations take in this part of the world? These people have nothing but time."

"I'm aware of the difficulties, but I must ask you to remain patient for just a little while longer."

Lefèvre snorted and kicked at the sand, and Mathilde threw her sack into the ground at her feet. A few toiletry items spilled out. Marianne rushed to gather the items and refill the sack. Mathilde snatched the bag from her sister and slung it over her shoulder.

As Kate queried them on their health, their living conditions, and their treatment at the hands of their captors, her eyes kept wandering to the two young men standing at the opening of their tent. The shorter of the two supported the taller, who struggled to remain upright. He shivered under the sun, his eyes glassy and his face pale. Finally, he collapsed, nearly taking the second man down with him.

Kate, Amy, and Charlie, along with Bess Abbott and Marianne Fournier, ran toward the men. Charlie helped the sick one's friend maneuver him into a sitting position. He breathed heavily, clutching his stomach.

"Noah, ya cunt, the fuck's wrong with you, dropping me like that?" His accent was unmistakably Australian.

"Um, who might you boys be?" Amy asked.

"I'm Noah Shaw. This poor schmuck is Ollie Jones."

"Oh no, I need to shit again," Ollie moaned.

Sharaf's voice carried over the din. "Dmitri, help him."

Jake pushed through the group, hauled Ollie to his feet, and with Noah took him to the pit latrine with an escort from several armed guards.

"They're from Sydney," Bess Abbott said. "Nice boys, but a touch crazy."

"How long have they been with you?" Amy asked.

"I'm not sure. Maybe a few months? We don't have a good sense of time out here."

"How long has he been sick?"

"At least a week. Around the time we were given a meat stew. We all felt a little off the next day, but Ollie ate a lot more than we did. He's been paying for it ever since."

Jake and Noah returned with Ollie between them. They eased him to the ground in the shade. Jake returned to Nick's side and whispered his diagnosis.

"What's the deal, boys?" Amy said. "How'd you end up here?"

"We graduated from uni last year. Wanted to have one last adventure before real life starts, you know? Took our bikes and flew to Senegal. Planned to do our own version of the Dakar Rally, crossing the continent west to east. We had just left Timbuktu and were heading toward Gao when they nabbed us," Noah said.

Kate, Amy, and Charlie stared at him. "Your own version of the Dakar Rally?" Charlie finally asked. "Through the Sahel? Are you insane?"

"I'm not, but this cunt is," Noah said, gesturing to Ollie. "His stupid fucking idea."

"Could we cool it with the c-word?" Amy asked. "It's very distracting."

Ollie snickered in his fevered state. "Can't say that word in front of Americans, mate. Remember those girls in New York who slapped us?"

"When was the last time you talked to anyone who might have reported you missing?" Kate asked.

"We talked to our families when we stayed a few nights in Bamako. But they knew not to expect regular contact."

"So no one knows you're missing?"

"Probably not. They probably just assume we're in the middle of nowhere."

"Full name, date and place of birth, and national ID or social security number, whatever you call it Down Under," Amy said, whipping out her pad.

The boys complied with the fake pastor's orders. They were only twenty-two years old.

"Are you here for us?" Noah asked hopefully.

Kate rubbed her forehead. "Not exactly. We had no idea you'd been taken. But don't worry," she said, seeing his face fall, "we'll contact your government who will get in touch with your families. That's the most we can do right now."

Noah sat beside Ollie and draped an arm over his friend's shoulders. "It really was my stupid fucking idea," Ollie said morosely.

"Chin up, mates," Amy said in a passable Australian accent. "This will be a hell of a story to tell someday."

The boys smiled.

Kate approached Khalifa and Ratma. "Thank you for allowing us this time with our citizens. May we take a few photos for our superiors?"

Khalifa stroked his beard. "You may. In front of the tents. We will approve each photo."

They started with the Abbotts. One shot of just the couple, then Kate took one of them with Amy. They repeated the process with the Fourniers and Lefèvre, including Kate with each. Charlie posed with the Aussies.

Yunis grumbled about the photos, but Khalifa flipped through them on Kate's smartphone and offered no objections.

Sharaf spoke. "Brother Khalifa, Dmitri is a combat medic. He says that the young man is suffering from amoebic dysentery and needs fluids to replenish his electrolytes and medication to kill the parasite. He's quite sick. Dmitri has the necessary items in his kit, if you'll permit us to help the boy."

"*Alhamdulillah*, anything to stop that atrocious diarrhea," Ratma muttered. "He can be heard across camp, all through the night."

"You may help, Legionnaire," Khalifa said.

Jake jogged to their Hilux for medication and several bottles of Gatorade. He made Ollie take metronidazole and start drinking a yellow Gatorade.

"Go slow," he cautioned in his fake Russian accent. "Little by little, get yourself hydrated and start eating again."

"You will contact the Australian government?" Khalifa asked Kate.

"You haven't?"

"Not yet."

"I'm sure their parents will appreciate knowing they're alive," she replied.

"Tell me, Madame Moreau, Pastor Smith, are you satisfied with your proof of life?" Khalifa asked.

"Mr. Abbott is unwell. He needs treatment, at the very least medication," Amy said.

"We did bring some of the medication that Mr. Abbott was on before he became your guest," Sharaf said.

"No," said Khalifa. "Mr. Abbott can wait. He has lasted this long. It seems to be in his best interest to hold on a bit longer."

"We also brought some toiletries for them. Toothbrushes, toothpaste, soap, nail clippers, small necessities that might improve their welfare. May we offer those?"

Khalifa's intelligent eyes lingered on Kate. "Not at this time, Madame Moreau. If it came with you, it must leave with you. I'm sure you understand."

Kate offered a terse nod.

"Do your demands remain the same?" Amy asked.

"Yes. Nine million euros for the French and eight million U.S. dollars for the Americans."

"And the Australians?"

"Three million U.S. dollars."

"We need some time to discuss with our people and secure the funding," Kate said.

"We will contact Brother Sharaf."

"When?"

Khalifa smiled. "When we see fit, Madame Moreau."

Ω

The following day, the convoy returned to Timbuktu and went straight to the French base, again causing angst amongst the army as the Tuareg militia in full force pulled up to the perimeter. Dubois was on hand to calm the situation, and two Hiluxes entered through the gates and followed the DGSE truck to the restricted side of base.

They trooped into the conference room, dirty and disheveled after several days and nights in the desert, and attacked the platters of sandwiches and fruit and pastries that were delivered while Charlie fiddled with Kate's phone and downloaded the photos of the hostages to an Agency computer. Tom Patterson slipped in behind them and welcomed them back, his face breaking into a wide smile when Fatima turned her attention his way. As the conference room filled with CIA and DGSE officers, Kate felt none of the same elation that the rest of her crew exhibited, talking and laughing amongst themselves, equally thrilled to have found both hostages and a high-value target, and survived said encounter. All they had done was prove that the hostages were alive.

Nick reached for her hand under the table. "Are you okay? You've barely touched any food."

"Just preoccupied," she said.

A week ago, she had eaten her body weight in croque monsieur sandwiches. She noticed Ardouin watching her and she took a bite of the sandwich. It should have been heavenly after days of MREs, but she tasted little. She didn't let go of Nick's hand.

"Sandstorm, welcome back," Fraser said. "Your initial reports—thank you, Charlie—have been very well received."

"You actually met with Khalifa al-Ghazawi himself?" Weiss asked. He pointed to the television screen, filled by a closeup of Khalifa's grainy face. "This man right here?"

Kate nodded. "For three days at three different camps. And before you ask, we kept track of mileage and direction via compass, but we were off the grid and had no GPS capabilities. We'll pass you everything we have, and we can even ask our lead Tuareg to identify on a map where he thinks the camps were. Two were most definitely temporary camps. The third, however, seems like it gets some regular usage. Maybe not by Khalifa himself, but certainly by his men."

Van Pelt and Weiss looked at Chad and Blake. The two paramilitary officers conferred. Chad spoke for the group.

"That's potentially really helpful. We may be able to start triangulating their common travel routes and follow them to a camp once we can get ISR birds back up."

"More importantly," Fraser said, "the hostages?"

"I think showing is better than telling," Kate said. "Charlie?"

Charlie loaded four photos to the television screen: Kate with the Fourniers, Kate with Lefèvre, Amy with the Abbotts, and Charlie with the Australians. A collective gasp rose from the assembled intelligence officers.

"As you can see, everyone is alive as of yesterday afternoon."

"Who are the two with Charlie?" Fraser asked.

"Oliver Jones and Noah Shaw, Australian adventure travelers. Got snagged probably a few months ago between Timbuktu and Gao. Khalifa said they hadn't yet contacted the Australian government, so you might want to make that call."

"Good Lord," Fraser muttered.

"Are the hostages in good health?" Dubois asked. "That Australian boy looks rather ill."

"That's Ollie," Jake said. "He's got amoebic dysentery. Khalifa allowed us to give him a course of medication and some Gatorades. As long as he takes the meds and rehydrates, he'll start to feel better in a few days."

"As for the French," Kate said, "they're struggling. The Fourniers are haggard, too thin, weak. Lefèvre appeared physically okay, but he's younger and hasn't been held nearly as long as the sisters."

"Stu Abbott doesn't look good," Amy said. "Bess seems to focus her energy on taking care of him, and that gets her through the day. Emotionally, they're holding up as best they can. Everything happens for a reason, it's all part of God's plan, et cetera. If Stu takes a turn for the worse, though, or passes, God forbid, I'm not sure Bess will be able to handle it. Not without support from the others, and it seems like there's some tension between the hostages."

"How so?" Ardouin asked.

"Mentally, they're all in bad places. There's a lot of anger and resentment, at least among the French, that no one has come for them yet. Ollie and Noah are a couple of dumb kids who made catastrophic errors in judgment, and their presence has upended the natural order of things in camp, disrupted long-established routines. And I don't think the French contingent shares the Abbotts' belief that everything happens for a reason," Kate said. She gestured to Fatima to continue.

"Ratma, Khalifa's wife, typically moves with the hostages. She knows enough French to communicate with them, and is learning English from the Abbotts. In the beginning the Abbotts and the Fourniers were close, bonding over their shared plight. But it seems Mathilde's mental health has deteriorated in recent months. She's abusive toward the other hostages and antagonistic toward the guards. Her sister tries to keep her calm, but Mathilde is certainly the alpha in that relationship and doesn't hesitate to lash out, even physically."

"That tracks with the behavior we saw," Kate said.

"And then Lefèvre arrived and announced that the French government was no longer paying ransoms. The downward spiral accelerated. Ratma said she tried to assure the French that their government would pay for their release, but Lefèvre, who knew of the sisters' situation before he himself was captured, told them that their brother's exhortations fell on deaf ears within the Elysée Palace. The Americans, of course, know full well that their government will not pay. In some ways, they may be better off for it. They have faith rather than hope."

"Amy's right about Stu Abbott," Jake said. "He has signs of congestive heart failure. His abdomen looked swollen, probably from the fluid buildup, and he had a wheezing cough, not to mention he was struggling simply to stand. I don't think he has much time left without treatment."

"Shit," Fraser said.

"Are you sure we can't pay a ransom? We have all that money just sitting there, waiting to be spent," Amy said.

"Absolutely not. Every dime of that is the U.S. government's money. It cannot be used to pay a ransom," Fraser said.

"Does the DGSE position remain the same?" Kate asked.

Dubois sighed. Ardouin leaned close and spoke quietly in French, too quietly for Kate to hear. Giraud watched them pensively.

"We must contact Paris," Dubois said. "This is a decision that will be taken at the highest levels of government. What is the next step?"

"We wait for Khalifa's call. If it doesn't come within the week, then they're onto us."

"A distinct possibility," Weiss said. "A fake sheikh and even faker connections to al-Qaeda leadership. A fake French diplomat. A fake pastor. Fake Legionnaires. It's shocking that Khalifa didn't execute you all on the spot."

"Khalifa suspects nothing," Fatima said. "He is acting with caution, of course, as is his nature after decades of outrunning your governments, but he does not behave like a man threatened by his interlocutors."

Weiss turned to Van Pelt. "Who is she again?"

"Just a translator."

"Oh damn," Amy murmured.

Despite sleeping at the same desert-wasteland campsites, consuming the same inedible MREs, and suffering the same tremendous stress meeting with the same brutal terrorists, Fatima looked as though she had done nothing more than take a weekend trip to the countryside. She cocked her head, her glossy hair uncovered by the black hijab that was wrapped loosely around her neck, and regarded Weiss curiously.

"After all this, you still do not trust us? Your former colleagues, even?"

"No," Weiss said without hesitation.

"A shame. However this endeavor ends, you will regret your words and actions."

Weiss laughed. "I don't think so."

Fatima smiled placidly, but her dark, soulful eyes were alert and cunning. Umm Ali lurked in their depths. "*Maktub, habibi.* I fear it is written."

Weiss stroked his muj beard. Kate didn't miss Tom Patterson's look of reverent awe that fell upon the woman whose strength never failed to impress. Sharaf directed a crude remark at Weiss that no one translated into English.

Van Pelt cleared his throat to break the uncomfortable silence. "Mr. Weiss and his team wish to debrief you thoroughly on Khalifa and his inner circle."

Kate stood, and the rest of Sandstorm stood with her. "We're done for today. Maybe tomorrow."

10

OVER THE NEXT TWO days, the team worked with Charlie to generate reams of additional reporting, and Kate, Amy, and Fatima each provided written assessments of Khalifa, Yunis, and Ratma. Kate and Amy, in what both former CIA officers considered a magnanimous gesture, spelled Charlie at the Agency laptop and wrote several intel reports themselves. According to Charlie, the reports had not simply been well-received; they had gone straight to the CIA director and the National Security Council.

"What'll that get you?" Amy asked Charlie. "An exceptional performance award of five hundred bucks, three hundred of which will be taken in taxes?"

"Oh, come on, these reports are worth at least seven-fifty."

Kate smirked as she put the finishing touches on her detailed assessment of Khalifa. Being a CIA case officer had come with a lot of paperwork, and most of it tedious, but occasionally she missed the opportunity indulge her inner armchair psychologist for the entertainment of a wide audience. Even if Weiss and Van Pelt would ensure that her conclusions were summarily dismissed.

Nick had sketched the permanent camp and its environs on his largest pad, something that Lacey Simms had asked for repeatedly before they departed the base after the initial debrief. Cherif had marked a map with the general areas where he thought the three camps were located, and Charlie had added distances and time traveled. Kate knew Weiss was eager to send intelligence, surveillance, and reconnaissance flights—either American or French birds—into areas the team had identified as zones of interest. Fraser and Dubois had put a moratorium on ISR flights and anything beyond routine French helicopter traffic while Sandstorm was in country, but Kate was still wary. Neil Weiss was not known for obeying orders, especially orders from a woman, and his reach extended far and wide after a long career in the CT realm.

They owed their clients an in-person debrief on Khalifa and his circle, which they agreed to do after a couple of days of rest and recuperation at the house. Nick and Jake were exhausted from their extended hypervigilance and night watches, and Kate didn't want her husband anywhere near Chad and Blake in a jumpy, sleep-deprived state.

Khalifa's representative still hadn't called by the time they piled into the Hiluxes for the drive to base and an interrogation at the hands of Van Pelt, Weiss, Lacey, and Emmanuel Giraud. Kate had excused Nick and Jake from the debrief; they wanted to restock on supplies and catch up with Tom Patterson.

They entered the conference room and faced the firing squad. At least Fraser, Dubois, and Ardouin were present and might attempt to keep order. Weiss waved a sheaf of papers, their reports that Charlie had transmitted to Fraser ahead of time.

"I can't disagree strongly enough with your conclusion that Khalifa wants out," he declared.

Kate sighed and Amy made a show of taking a swig of her favorite Irish whiskey from a silver flask. It would be a long afternoon.

ဩ

"We need to replenish our stash of MREs and Kate wants another million for passage to the Tuaregs," Nick said, looking over the list he had made.

"Grab more Cipro, too," Jake replied. "We made a dent in our supply the last few days."

"Thank God no one was shitting their brains out. Except for that poor Aussie kid."

"As long as he takes what I gave him, he'll be okay."

"I'm worried that Yunis took it from him the second we left."

"Not if Ratma had anything to say about it."

"Okay, MREs, Cipro, a million bucks. Anything else?"

"I think that's it. I'll find Colonel Patterson and see if he's up for dinner tonight." Jake cocked his head, mulling something.

"Beers," they said in unison.

"I'll call Cherif and get us a case," Nick said.

Jake departed in one Hilux toward the flight line, and Nick pulled up to the armory. He was halfway through punching the D-Day passcode into the armory's keypad when the power cut out. Every afternoon, it seemed, blackouts hit their compound and the base. They were lucky; their Arab landlord had a generator that powered the entire house during blackouts, and of course the French had attempted to secure their own section of the overtaxed grid.

Nick waited for the generators to kick on and restore power to the security system, then retyped his code and pushed through the door. From deep in the armory, he heard voices whispering in English, then the clank of metal on metal. As Nick's eyes adjusted to the low light, two figures approached from the shadows.

"Hey bro," said Chad Yorke in a friendly tone.

"Hey guys," Nick replied, trying to keep the exhaustion and irritation from his voice.

"Just refreshing on ammo. Went out with French special forces this morning for some target practice. Burned through our stash." Chad patted his rucksack. Blake, also carrying a rucksack, nodded tightly.

Nick's brain fog cleared. He looked at the cages filled with French-owned gear and ammo. Then he looked at the cage holding a pallet on which rested millions of dollars of the U.S. government's money that he and his wife and his best friend were responsible for safeguarding. He felt cold in the stifling heat of the armory. Blake's hand moved to rest on his sidearm, and Chad's posture stiffened.

Nick gestured to the cage of gear and ammo. "Jake and I would love to get in some target practice out here. Not enough opportunities back home. Plus," he added conspiratorially, "we snagged some FAMAS rifles and want to give them a workout. Can you hook us up next time you go out with the French?"

Chad uncoiled and Blake slowly and casually moved his hand off his pistol. "Yeah, bro, of course. The more, the merrier."

"Thanks, man, means the world to us. We'll never be up to Team Six standards, but we like to keep the rifle skills sharp."

"We'll teach you a thing or two on the range. Plus, the French usually let us play with their .50-cals."

"Hell yeah," Nick said. "I'd kill to shoot the shit out of something with a .50-cal. Had to let my enlisted guys have all the fun on the heavy weaponry in Iraq and Afghanistan."

"Let us know when you have some downtime and we'll see what we can do," Chad said.

Nick accepted his bro hug and made sure his body bumped against the rucksack. He slapped Blake on the back and nodded in the direction of the cage holding Sandstorm's gear.

"Gotta replenish the MRE stock. Really thought I was done with those abominations when I left the Corps." He sighed affectedly and patted his stomach.

Chad laughed. "See if you can swipe some French MREs. Those taste a thousand times better. Trust us." He winked. "Later, bro."

"Later, guys. See you around," Nick called to their retreating figures.

As the door clicked shut, Nick rushed to the money cage and stared at the lock and chain securing the cage door. Wrapped counterclockwise, four links free. He swore under his breath, paralyzed by rage and dread.

He looked toward the front of the armory and their tiny camera, invisible in the shadows. Then he tried to channel Kate. What would she do? Probably breathe, he decided. He made fun of her often for her ridiculous breathing exercises, even if that meditative practice helped her remain married to him. He pulled in a deep breath through his nose, holding it for several seconds before letting it out slowly through his mouth. Boston was hardly the cleanest city in the world, but it sure didn't smell like the armpit of a French military base in Timbuktu. He wrinkled his nose but tried it again, and a third time. Clarity of thought returned.

He snapped photos of the lock and chain with his iPhone. After one final yoga breath, he brandished his key and entered the cage. He circled the pallet of money, studying the plastic-wrapped stacks of bills. They had taken five million dollars with them upon their arrival to the base; there should be twenty-five million in the cage.

He pointed the beam of a small halogen flashlight at the mountain of money. As he reached the rear of the stack, he noticed a slit in the plastic wrapping at the lowest level. He knelt and snapped more photos before reaching inside to find emptiness where three million dollars should be. He remembered the feel of a bricklike form in Chad's rucksack where it hit his hip during their bro hug.

Nick pulled a million dollars from the stack, placed it in his own pack, and resecured the cage, wrapping the chain clockwise and leaving three free links. He felt calm, clear-headed. Maybe there was something to be said for meditative breathing after all. He set about finding MREs and Cipro, loaded the truck, and called George.

Ω

Dinner was a raucous affair on the porch, dominated by storytelling Marines. Fatima, seated across from Tom Patterson, looked to be thoroughly enjoying his tales from a career spent flying AH-1 Super Cobra attack helicopters and, now, medevacs as a contractor supporting the military.

"Have you ever crashed?" Fatima asked.

"No such thing as a crash landing," Patterson replied. "Only a hard landing."

Laughing, Jake launched into a story of a platoon led by one First Lieutenant Nick Cavanaugh being dispatched outside of Ramadi to secure the site of a mangled Cobra brought down by a rocket-propelled grenade to the tail rotor. Flying low when they were hit, Patterson and his copilot had managed to land the Cobra and escape grievous injury. Nick and Jake's platoon had then destroyed the Cobra in place and rushed the pilots to the nearest field hospital for treatment.

Kate sipped a glass of white wine—Dubois had insisted they take several bottles from the DGSE's supply—and watched Nick. A consummate storyteller, he had been quiet all evening. He nursed a beer and contemplated something far weightier than crash landings versus hard landings.

He finished his beer and stood. "Who needs another?"

Jake, Amy, Charlie, and Patterson raised their empties. Kate followed Nick to the kitchen unnoticed. He rooted through the refrigerator for the beer, turned with five in his hands, and jumped when he saw her, nearly dropping the bottles onto the tile floor.

"Christ, you are like a cat," he said.

She topped off her glass of sauvignon blanc and leaned against the counter. "You going to tell me what has you so distracted tonight?"

"Distracted? I'm not distracted."

"No? You've hardly spoken since we got back from the base. Your loyal sidekick has carried the conversational load out there." She cocked her head. "In fact, this might be the most I've ever heard Jake talk."

"He deserves a chance to shine once in a while."

"What's going on?"

Nick's pause before he answered was but a beat long. "Nothing."

"Nothing?"

"Nothing." He set the bottles on the counter and quickly checked his phone.

"You've been awfully interested in your phone, too. Expecting a message? Maybe from Lacey?"

"Who?"

Kate shook her head in exasperation. "You're not going to tell me?"

"There's nothing to tell."

"Yes, there is. And you will."

Nick sighed. "You and your CIA ilk have ways of making people talk?"

"No, not people. But I have ways of making *you* talk."

"Do your worst, Pixie."

She smiled and sauntered back toward the porch. "Or my best."

He followed her and passed out fresh beers. As they resettled themselves, their friends launched the ambush. Kate was only surprised that it took them as long as it did, as Amy, Charlie, and Fatima were incorrigible gossips, busybodies, and meddlers. It was Fatima who fired the first salvo.

"Tell us, love, this Chad, how long were you with him?"

"Four months," Amy declared, before Kate could respond. "The worst four months of my life."

Kate rolled her eyes. "Oh please."

"Don't 'oh please' me. He was a giant tool and you knew it."

"You didn't help matters by being blatantly obvious in your hatred of him."

"I was right, wasn't I?"

"Your mistake was assuming he was anything more than a little bit of entertainment post-Iraq."

"I knew you weren't serious about him. I just didn't understand why you bothered."

Kate shrugged. "Why not?"

"Because I think he was really serious about you."

"Couldn't have been that serious. He cheated on me, remember?"

Amy nodded. "Which I said he'd do, if you'll recall. Doesn't change the fact that he was super into you."

"I really don't think he was."

"Actually," Patterson said, "he regards you as the one who got away. Ask anyone who spends more than a few minutes with him."

"Ha! Told you so," Amy said.

"It's Kate this, and Kate that, and Kate said, et cetera. I made the mistake of reminding him that you're married, quite happily from what I hear, and I thought he and that meathead buddy of his were going to shoot me full of holes in the chow hall."

"I'm glad you chose this Marine over that SEAL, love," Fatima said. "If only because your Marine takes orders better." She smiled at Nick.

Tom laughed. "He doesn't understand why you married a Devil Dog, that's for sure."

"*Semper fidelis*. Always fucking faithful," Amy said. "He should try it sometime."

"How are you still so hostile? I haven't thought about him in years."

"What can I say? He has a face I want to punch." She clinked beer bottles with Nick.

"I'm sure he's done just fine without me in his life."

"Actually," Tom said again, "I gather there's been some upheaval lately."

Amy and Charlie leaned forward eagerly. Nick did, too, but not in a way that suggested he intended to gloat over the misfortunes of his wife's ex-boyfriend.

"Do tell," Fatima said.

"His girlfriend is due in a few months. An unplanned pregnancy. They're on the rocks and he thinks she'll fight like hell for as much child support as she can get. His goal is to score every deployment he can, both to be away from her—"

"And his child. What a piece of shit," Amy muttered.

"—and bank as much money as possible to have a cushion when she comes for him. It's a crummy situation."

"One that a condom could have prevented," Amy said.

Nick stared at Patterson as he related Chad's woes. Kate watched his thoughts churn, processing a certain understanding that he refused to share with her. She was baffled, and concerned. Nick's emotions were rarely a mystery to her; if she didn't already know what was on his mind, all she had to do was ask. But tonight, that open book was shut firmly.

Jake seemed to notice Nick's odd reaction, too. He slapped his friend on the back. "Relax, big guy. It's not like he knocked up Kate."

Kate threw him a dirty look, but Nick ignored the comment and continued to watch Patterson intently.

"Sounds like he needs money," he said casually. Too casually. Kate narrowed her eyes.

"Sure sounds like it. Between living beyond his means as a government employee and looming child support payments, his lifestyle is going to take a hit."

"I hope baby mama takes his skinny SEAL ass for a ride," Amy said, raising her beer bottle. "Here's to Chad's spawn. May his or her father step up and be a man."

♫

The Azawakh returned the next morning, slipping through the gate behind Cherif, who was making his rounds. She followed him to the porch and waited near the steps, sitting with a straight-backed, royal bearing, looking down her aquiline nose as she observed the motley crew of humans. Kate beelined for her, this time dodging Nick's outstretched hand that swiped for any limb or article of clothing.

"She is not ill," Cherif said to Nick. "I do not believe she poses a threat."

"That's not what he's worried about," Jake said with a laugh. "Some people have children unexpectedly. Nick winds up with dogs unexpectedly."

"We're not adopting another dog," Nick said as Sharaf appeared bearing a bowl of water and a plate of leftover chicken and rice and vegetables. "Ugh, Sharaf, don't encourage her."

As the dog wolfed down the food and guzzled most of the water, Cherif provided his report on the security situation and developments of interest.

"The city is calm. The French have stayed on their base, leaving only for standard patrols. No offensive raids on any targets in the region since your arrival."

"Any sightings of Khalifa's men?" Jake asked.

"A six-man team under Yunis's command met with a prominent Arab who controls much of the arms' trade in the Timbuktu region. According to my cousin, who shared tea with one of the men yesterday evening, Khalifa is await-ing a shipment of surface-to-air missiles. I believe you call them Stingers? They were very popular during the Afghan jihad against the Soviets."

Kate, now stroking the Azawakh's silky ears, looked back at Charlie.

"Yeah, yeah, I'm on it," he said and reached for his laptop.

"The shipment will be transferred to Khalifa's men in the coming days. Their mission seems to have been solely in pursuit of the missiles. They have not approached your compound or made any inquiries about your activities, as far as we know."

"We haven't heard from Khalifa yet," Kate said. "It's been four days."

"I would not let the idea of time distort your thinking. Time has very different meanings to you and Khalifa. He trusted you enough to show you the hostages. That is all that matters."

"It's not quite so simple," she replied. "Some of those hostages are pretty sick. Time is not on their side."

Cherif nodded. "I understand. But I am certain that Khalifa intends to follow through and make a deal."

Kate stifled a sigh. That wasn't so simple, either. The Americans were des-tined to remain in custody until they were rescued, executed, or succumbed to illness. Dubois had briefed the French president on recent developments, but no decision had been made as to their citizens' fate. The Australian government, alerted by the CIA via the State Department, had notified the two families but proffered no preferred course of action, only requesting updates as they became available.

"There is one other matter of concern," Cherif continued. "A faction of Fulanis, allied with Islamic State elements operating near Gao and the tri-border area, has taken an interest in your group. My men have reported that scouts are in the city."

"What's your confederation's relationship with this faction?" Nick asked.

"Poor. My people seek Tuareg independence and have no interest in establishing an Islamic emirate ruled by Sharia law in our lands. Moussa Diallo, this group's leader, adheres to strict Islamic codes and terrorizes the people of Gao and southern Mopti. My units have engaged his men several times over the last year, resulting in loss of life on both sides. He has been hesitant to enter Timbuktu or Kidal, where we are strongest. It appears, however, that this is an opportunity he cannot resist."

"What's his goal? Engaging us or targeting us?" Kate asked.

Cherif held out his hands. "I do not know. Their kidnappings thus far have been only local government officials, resulting in small ransoms. Moussa's men build wealth by stealing livestock and property, and heavily taxing locals under their control."

"Land pirates," Amy said.

Cherif considered this assessment. "If I am to trust my English, I believe Pastor Amy is correct. Moussa and his men maim and plunder. Like pirates. On land." He looked proud of himself, then returned to his original point. "It is possible he sees you as an opportunity, a way to establish ties with a prominent sheikh and businessman from outside the region. Or he sees you as potential bargaining chips, a way to secure a ransom windfall of his own."

"New SOP. If the situation calls for us to be split, those not operational will remain on the French base until we can reunite. No one stays in this compound without Jake and me present, and Cherif's full force in the city."

"As you wish, Capitaine."

"Give us regular updates on Moussa and the activities of his men, especially those in the city," Kate said.

"I will also assign three more technicals to guard your compound and increase the size of patrols in the city."

Cherif bowed to the team and left the porch, pausing beside Kate and the Azawakh. He held his hand toward the dog, who sniffed his fingers and gave a tentative lick.

"She needs a name," he said.

"She does *not* need a name," Nick called.

"Something befitting her heritage," Kate said. "Any suggestions?"

"Kate, do not name that dog!"

"Tin Hanan, our fourth-century queen, was thought to be the 'mother of us all.' She had a daughter named Kella."

Kate looked at the fine-featured Azawakh with her soulful eyes and her impeccable posture. "Kella. I like it."

"Congrats on the new addition to your family," Jake told Nick.

"Cherif, who's the ranking officer here?"

Cherif smiled and responded in French. "*Vous êtes le capitaine, c'est vrai, mais Madame Kate, elle est le général.*" He touched his chest and departed the compound.

Kella trotted into the porch after Kate and sat beside Nick. He regarded her suspiciously; she stared at him with unblinking eyes. Finally, he reached a hand toward her and she leaned into his touch as he rubbed her chest.

"By the way, do you need a translation of Cherif's parting thought?" Kate asked.

"No, General Devlin, I do not."

♌

George's email hit Nick's inbox after dinner. He ran upstairs to the privacy of his and Kate's bedroom, Kella on his heels, and opened the message from the blue-haired hacker.

Best I could do. Semper fi.

Nick tapped the video attachment and his screen filled with security-camera footage from the armory. Two figures, grainy in the low light, came into view and hurried toward the money cage. One—Chad, based on the build—dropped to his knees before the padlock and inserted a metal file of some kind into the keyhole. It took him approximately one minute to pick the lock.

They entered the cage, examined the pallet and wrapped bundles, and Chad motioned Blake toward the back of the pile. Again, Chad knelt, and the angle of the camera and placement of the pallet meant only a partial view of his actions. Nick swore, but then Chad stood, holding bricks of money in one hand and opening his pack with the other.

"Gotcha," he whispered as Chad stuffed the money into his rucksack.

The former SEALs resecured the cage, gave the lock and chain a tug, and turned toward the entrance. Seconds later, Nick came into view.

Nick stopped the video, darkened his screen, did a few deep-breathing exercises, and returned to the living room, where everyone was settled with phones, tablets, and a soccer match on French satellite television. Kella jumped onto the couch and curled up beside Kate.

"I was thinking, we ought to station one of the machine guns on the roof. Want to help?" he said to Jake.

"Dude, game's on." He and Sharaf were engrossed in the match.

"No worries. Just trying to avoid another Fallujah."

Jake rose and followed Nick up two flights of stairs to the door leading onto the roof. Nick walked west toward the setting sun and crossed his arms over his chest. Jake joined him.

"Lay it on me, big guy."

Another Fallujah had been their code for over a decade to indicate the need for a private conversation, posthaste. Neither had used the term since their last tour in Iraq.

"We have a problem."

"You'll need to be more specific."

Nick cued up the video and handed his phone to Jake.

"Holy fuck. How much did they take?"

"Three million."

"Goddamn. This is definitely a problem. I can tell you knew immediately."

"They were overly talkative, overly friendly. And then I saw the cage. They rewrapped the chain counterclockwise and left four free links."

"Our boy Blake looked jumpy. Another new SOP: No one goes into that armory without backup."

"Agreed. And the rest of them don't go in without us."

Jake returned Nick's phone. "What's the plan?"

"I don't know."

"Kate always has a plan. What did she say?"

Nick cringed. "I haven't told her yet."

Jake stared at him. "Why not?"

He sighed. "I've been such a dick about Chad. I wasn't sure she'd believe me without proof. And this isn't high-quality proof."

"It's definitely them. And yes, you've been a dick about her ex-boyfriend, but she knows you'd never lie about something of this magnitude. You need to tell her."

"I know."

"And then we need to tell Fraser."

Nick nodded.

"You think they'll make another go at it?"

"Guess that depends how far in the hole Chad is. Even if they split the take, one-point-five mil under the table will give him a decent cushion when he loses a chunk of his declared income to child support."

The doting father of three children shook his head. "What a disgrace."

"Twenty-five million temptations just sitting there. Hard for a lot of people to ignore that siren call. Especially if you've got lock-picking skills and no knowledge that there's a covert security system in place."

"Don't defend him."

"That's the last thing I'd do."

They watched the sun disappear behind the horizon. The city's muezzins began the call to prayer, one after another.

"You really want to put a rig up here?" Jake asked.

"Nah."

Jake slapped him on the back. "I'll tell everyone it was a dumb idea and I talked you out of it."

11

THE CALL CAME NOT long after morning prayers, as the compound came alive. Kate and Nick entered the kitchen as Sharaf answered his Samsung on speakerphone; Fatima waved to get their attention and shush their conversation, in particular Nick's animated assertion that Kella needed a bath if she wanted access to their bedroom.

"Sheikh, Brother Khalifa wishes to meet with you. In two days' time, you will find his men at the northern outskirts of the city. You will escort them to our camp. Leave the Westerners behind."

"I will bring only my security and my wives."

"No wives. Just you and your Legionnaires."

Sharaf looked at Kate. Kate looked at Nick. He grimaced but nodded.

"As you wish. In two days, *inshallah*."

☊

That afternoon, Fraser arrived with Tom Patterson, the French contingent, and several more bottles of the finest wine that Operation Barkhane had to offer, in advance of a dinner of fresh-caught, grilled capitaine fish from the river. Sharaf had insisted on paying the fishmonger at the market, who wanted to gift the catch to the sheikh for the kindness he had shown the locals. Sharaf had then harangued Cherif for his overzealous patrols of the city, in full view of everyone at the market, much to Cherif's chagrin.

As the charcoal heated in the grill and the wine and beer flowed freely on the porch, Dubois relayed his conversation with the French president regarding the fate of their hostages.

"The bottom line is that our president did not approve a ransom payment at this time. He would like to see whether you are able to obtain locational data that may facilitate a rescue before we resort to paying millions more to this group that will turn around and kidnap more of our citizens."

"I know we've said this before, but we still haven't figured out how we might do that," Kate said. "This next week or two may provide the only opportunity you have to get those people back."

"We explained that. And he also understands that the sisters are struggling both physically and mentally. But your progress gives us tremendous hope, far more than we thought possible, that we may end this without further funding terrorism."

"No pressure or anything," Amy said to Kate. The she turned to the Frenchmen. "I commend your president on a brave decision. Would have been easy to hand over a truckload of euros and call it a day. While the Americans and Aussies continue to suffer, of course."

Dubois smiled wryly. "Our president is also attuned to those particular optics, yes."

"Ratma is the one constant, or semi-constant," Kate said. "She's the only one, so far as we know, who spends considerable time with the hostages. It's too dangerous for Khalifa, and Yunis probably avoids them to the extent possible."

"A gift to Ratma?" Fraser suggested.

Kate turned to Fatima, Tom Patterson at her side. "She wears Tuareg jewelry. A prominent Agadez Cross. Several rings."

"A belt? A watch?" Fraser asked.

Fatima shook her head. "Traditional Tuareg robes. Simple sandals. She's been uncovered in our presence, but I would assume that at times she does veil."

"She must have some personal items in her tent at these camps, but the only one who has a realistic shot at seeing the inside of her tent is Fatima," Kate said.

"Ideally, I could offer her a gift, but it would have to be privately, away from the watchful gaze of the men," Fatima said. "Khalifa is rightfully paranoid."

"If we knew what we were working with, we might have some options for you," Fraser said.

"The upcoming rendezvous seems to be men only. We may be able to string them along for another couple of meetings, but then it'll be time to put up or shut up," Kate said.

"Or end up as guests of the Islamic Emirate of the Maghreb ourselves," Amy said.

"We definitely won't pay for you," Fraser said.

"Sharaf has made clear that he doesn't speak for Kate and Amy," Nick said. "I don't think this will be the last encounter. I think this is an opportunity for Khalifa to get a little inside baseball on the infidels' strategy."

"And get his Stingers," Jake added.

"If he only knew who was providing that escort," Nick said.

"Hey, we can't go to jail for this, can we?" Jake asked Fraser.

She tilted her head. "I haven't decided."

Ardouin sipped his wine in silence, but Kate noticed that his eyes kept flicking in her direction. His overt hostility had diminished since seeing their initial efforts bear fruit, but she knew their collective crazy was anathema to his rigid professional upbringing within the French foreign ministry and the DGSE. Anyone who rose to the rank of chief of protocol in a European intelligence service was bound to react poorly to Sandstorm schemes.

"What's on your mind?" Kate asked him in French.

"I'm simply enjoying the evening."

"Are you sure? You look like you want to say something."

He eyed her over the rim of his wineglass. She saw his discomfort, his lingering doubts, the newfound and unexpected hope he tried to hide beneath a cold and haughty exterior. Then he nodded toward the door. "Who is your friend?"

Kella sat outside the porch, looking simultaneously supercilious and insulted by her exclusion. Nick opened the door and herded her inside the house toward the kitchen, where Sharaf waited with her dinner. Then she returned to the porch and sniffed at each individual before taking a seat beside Ardouin. Kate moved to shoo her away from the Frenchman, but he was already gazing into her soulful eyes and caressing her head. Kate sank back into her chair and watched their comfortable interaction with a touch of bemusement. Frankly, she had assumed Ardouin was a cat person. And that Kella had better taste.

"Beauty products," Kate said suddenly.

Conversation halted. "Babe, you're gorgeous no matter what you slop on your face," Nick said.

Kate rolled her eyes. "No, for Ratma. High-end French beauty products. A gift she would love. And that maybe would pass Khalifa and Yunis's scrutiny."

"I'm certain I could find a way to discreetly slip her some creams," Fatima said.

Fraser looked thoughtful. "How...?"

"Tiniest beacon you have, shoved down to the bottom of the bottle or the tub. Protect it from the liquid however you need to. If we pass her something in opaque plastic as opposed to clear glass, no one will ever see it until it's too late," Kate said.

"Or they'll dump the bottle and find it immediately," Nick said.

"Or that," she conceded. "Operationally, I think it's doable, though. It rests on a couple of key factors: First, we have another meeting with Ratma present and Fatima can make the pass. Second, we're long gone before anyone decides to dump the bottle."

Both Fatima and Diana shuddered at the idea of French beauty products spilled ignominiously onto Sahelian sands to burn under the brutal sun.

"It might be possible," Fraser said. "I'll need to check with the geeks back at Langley. And, of course, Laurent needs to be on board, given the risks to the hostages."

Dubois looked at Ardouin, who said nothing. "We do not object. A support flight is due in tomorrow. We can ensure that beauty products make it onto that plane."

Fatima already had her phone out and perused her favorite French websites. Patterson looked over her shoulder in interest. "I'll give you a list before you leave tonight."

A thrill shot through Kate's stomach. She poured herself more wine and for the first time felt like maybe, just maybe, they had a chance.

☊

The next day, Mokhtar, Cherif's cousin and deputy, called Kate to alert her that Sandstorm had visitors. Kate and Nick, locked in a battle royale with Kella, a hose, and shampoo, paused to discuss the unexpected arrival of Chad Yorke and Blake Doyle, stopped at a Tuareg checkpoint at the outer ring of the compound's security perimeter.

"I'll turn the hose on that horndog if he so much as looks at you," Nick grumbled.

"Or, we can rinse her, dry her off, and you can take her inside while I promise to pass along all their cool-guy tactical advice."

Nick looked like he was about to say something, something serious. She looked curiously at him as Kella struggled to wriggle free from their grasp.

"What?"

A cloud crossed his face. "Nothing."

"Sticking to that line, huh?"

"Maybe your best has been lacking."

She smirked and told Mokhtar to allow Chad and Blake entry to the compound. Nick's jaw muscles twitched as he rinsed Kella with the hose.

The gate opened and the paramilitary officers sauntered toward them. Both men wore body armor and Tuareg-style scarves, and they carried rifles. Blake seemed skittish; his eyes darted between Kate and Nick, though they lingered on the much greater perceived threat. Chad was all smiles and hearty greetings.

"Just wanted to swing by and make sure you were set for tomorrow's meet, bro," he said.

"We're good," Nick replied. He barely looked up from Kella.

"No doubt, no doubt. You guys have made amazing progress, for sure. Even Weiss thinks so. I'm curious, though. Why do you think Khalifa wants to meet just your sheikh?"

The information regarding the Stinger missiles was known only to Fraser, Dubois, and Ardouin. Charlie's report was in Diana's possession, where it would stay until the French were able to resume normal combat operations in the region. There was no mention that Sandstorm was the security guarantor for the transportation of the missiles.

Kate shrugged. "Hard to say. It may be just to confirm our intentions. Or maybe Khalifa wants to talk business with someone he believes can be useful to him."

Chad nodded sagely. "Makes sense. No indications it's a trap, right?"

"None. I think a trap is more likely to involve all of us. Only Amy and I have any real potential value in this scenario."

"Unless they want to cut the heads off two white guys and slap it on the internet."

"Two white guys, not Americans, who are loyal to an Arab supporting al-Qaeda. Anything is possible, but that doesn't seem likely."

"So you'll definitely be at the base tomorrow?"

"The convoy will drop us off before they head north."

"Bro, while you're out in the badlands, you have to get us some intel on Khalifa's pattern of life." Chad held up his hands defensively as Kate gave him a reproving look. "Hey, had to say it. Technically we work for Weiss these days. His shop, his priorities, and he's up my ass about this."

"I understand. We'll do everything we can to help you," Kate said.

"It's an impossible mission," Blake muttered.

"Perhaps so, but we know the hostages are alive, and we've had direct contact with an HVT. That's something, right?" Kate tried to keep her tone light. She had never crossed paths with Blake Doyle prior to their arrival in Mali, but Tom Patterson's assessment was on point. The man was a meathead, and seemed to act on Chad's orders without thought.

The meathead offered an unintelligible grunt, preferring to study the inside of their compound walls. Kate handed towels to Nick, who wrapped Kella before she shook and soaked everyone in her radius.

Chad smirked. "You and strays. Always there for anything that needed a home. She especially likes the broken ones." He looked pointedly at Nick.

Kate took hold of Nick's arm and steered him and Kella toward the house. "Let's get her inside. I'll be right back," she said to Chad and Blake.

"Hey, grab Rodriguez. We have a question from Lacey for him."

"Did he just call me broken?" Nick asked once they were inside.

"That's what it sounded like."

Nick set Kella down and unswaddled her from the towel cocoon. Her shake merely misted them. She trotted into the kitchen to keep Sharaf company.

"I'm not some stray you took in, am I? Some fixer-upper?"

"Every man, by definition, is a fixer-upper. But you're the strongest man I know." She looped her arms around his neck and pulled him down for a kiss on the cheek. "Give me five minutes to get rid of them and then we'll powwow to review tomorrow's plan."

She headed back outside, Charlie in tow, and found Chad and Blake loitering by Nick and Jake's Hilux, already packed with gear. Blake leaned casually against a rear wheel well. Chad patted the hood of the white truck.

"Looks like your boys are well stocked."

Kate forced a smile. "What's the question for Charlie?"

"Lacey wanted to clarify that you started tracking mileage from the city gates, not from the house."

"Correct."

"Cool."

"That's it?"

"That's it. Looking forward to spending tomorrow with you." Chad grinned and squeezed her shoulder, then he and Blake left.

Charlie returned to the house, muttering obscenities under his breath about the two former SEALs. Kate remained in place, her eyes resting on the closed gate. She reached a hand toward the dusty Hilux, leaving the outline of four fingers and a thumb in the coating of Mali's red dirt. Then she joined her friends inside.

ष

Kate's best was more than enough for her husband. Sometimes too much. Tonight proved to be no exception; sprawled beside her, his eyes half-closed, his chest heaving, he was putty her in hands. And her hands weren't about to let him rest long. She wanted him to sleep like the dead tonight, but she also wanted answers.

"You're trying to kill me, aren't you?" he murmured.

"It wouldn't be the worst way to go, would it?"

"I always thought I'd leave this mortal coil in a blaze of glory, but this would be better. Although the obituary might be awkward."

"I think your mother would stop speaking to me."

He smiled drowsily. One of her hands rested on his chest; he covered it with his. "About tomorrow…"

"We've spent the last two days prepping Sharaf for almost any conceivable question that Khalifa could ask about us. He just needs to make Khalifa believe that we're serious about an exchange and secure another meeting. With any luck, the nerds at Langley will give us some tracking options."

"It's not about Sharaf. I have confidence in Sharaf."

"Then what?"

"When you're at the base…just please be careful."

"The terrorists are unlikely to storm a massive base heavily guarded by thousands of professional soldiers."

He shook his head and tightened his grip on her hand. "No. It's not that. You need to stay with the group. And the group needs to stay with Fraser, with Dubois, with Colonel Patterson, even Ardouin and Giraud."

"Is this about Chad?"

His jaws muscles worked. He nodded once.

"Sweetie, Chad is many things, but he's not that kind of guy. A relentless flirt, to be sure, but he knows that no means no."

"He and Blake…"

"Look, I know you don't like them and I understand why, but—"

"They stole money." He reached toward the bedside table for his phone and handed it to her. "There's a video in the most recent email from George."

Kate stared at him, then unlocked his phone and found the email. She watched the entire clip in silence. He regarded her pensively. She returned his phone.

"I couldn't help but notice the date on that video."

"I wanted to tell you. I just didn't know how."

"I'm not sure whether I'm more impressed that you kept this from me or that you kept George from telling me."

He smiled ruefully. "I had to beg her to let me break the bad news. Your personal connections to one of the perpetrators and all."

"How much did they take?"

"Three million."

She sighed. "Shit."

"I think they think I suspect something."

"Blake did seem jumpier than normal."

"I know we have to tell Fraser, but I want to be here for it. Can we wait until after this meet?"

"Yes. The priority is the op. We have to focus on that. The fact that they stole money we were never going to use is unfortunate, but it means we can wait to ruin Fraser's life. I assume George is checking the feed regularly?"

Nick nodded. "She reviews every minute of it. They haven't been back."

"Not yet."

"Jake and I want everyone to avoid the armory unless we're with you."

She raised an eyebrow playfully. "You told our work husband before you told me?"

"Our work husband agreed that I'd been somewhat dickish about the whole Chad thing, and that I was rightfully worried about your reaction when I accused him of grand theft."

"For the record, I'd have been more upset if you weren't a dick toward my ex-boyfriend. My efforts to tame your caveman charms are purely an act for polite company. And besides, not liking my ex is a far cry from baselessly accusing him of a crime."

"Would you have believed me if we didn't have video?"

"Without question. I know you would never lie about something like that." She squeezed his hand. "Do you feel better?"

"Yeah. But I'm still going to worry about you tomorrow."

"I promise we'll stay with the group." She held up her hand and extended her pinkie finger. He hooked it with his.

"Thank you." He checked the time on his phone, then turned back to her with a sly smile. "The night is still young. Now it's time for my best."

"If you insist."

12

NICK, JAKE, CHERIF, AND a gaggle of Cherif's men delivered Kate, Amy, Fatima, and Charlie to the French base before the sun rose. Chad and Blake hadn't been among the welcoming party, much to Nick's relief. Then they returned to the house to collect Sharaf and the rest of the Tuareg army, and met Khalifa's men at the northern gates of the city. Cherif and Mokhtar, in the lead Hilux, greeted the small convoy of Arabs who waited for them. The weight in three truck beds strained shocks; the trucks carried not just Stinger missiles, but also drums of diesel fuel and water.

"I sure hope those missiles are disarmed," Jake murmured he pulled forward and moved out with the convoy. "If they hit any of the bomb crater-sized potholes around here, we might all go boom."

"I'm sure it's fine," Nick said. Jake looked askance at him. "Obviously, it's not fine. These assholes have Stinger missiles."

"And we'll be complicit in the future deaths of French helicopter pilots."

Nick sighed. "Fraser and Dubois know the risks."

"How are we okay with this?"

"Which part? The fact that bureaucrats have effectively decided that the lives of soldiers matter less than the lives of civilians who never should have been here in the first place, or the fact that we've become pawns in the Great Game?"

Jake smirked. "I thought Kate had gone overboard with some of the language in that contract, but now that we're committing a crime, I'm awfully glad she included it."

"Know thine enemy. Especially if that enemy is your ex-employer."

Jake was silent for a moment. "You tell her about Chad?"

"Last night. She promised she'd keep the group together and with everyone else. No one will go near the armory. We'll tell Fraser when we get back."

"I almost feel bad for Chad. I would not want to be the target of that woman's wrath."

Nick's gaze wandered to the side window, from which he saw the outlines of a distant village through the clouds of dust kicked up by the line of Hiluxes. His service in the Marine Corps had taken him to the worst of the sandboxes, but he still remained baffled by how anyone managed to survive in such inhospitable conditions.

He spoke to the window. "Kate once told me that CIA case officers had to have a streak of larceny in their hearts to do what they do. Convince people to betray their country or terrorist brothers, steal secrets, put bad guys on the X."

"And occasionally some of them commit actual larceny. Think he'll spend time in jail?"

Nick shrugged. "You know the Agency. They have their own way of doing things."

Sharaf leaned forward and tapped Nick on the shoulder. He spoke in English. "I do not understand this music."

Nick's iPhone, connected to the Hilux's stereo, played a mix of classic rock. He gave his full attention to the song. "What's the problem?"

Sharaf gave him a bewildered look. "What is this 'rock the casbah'?"

LYNN MASON

The men—Charlie, Dubois, Ardouin, Giraud, Van Pelt, Weiss, and Patterson—looked positively gobsmacked by the overwhelming array of French beauty products that the supply flight had delivered and that now dominated the long table in the conference room. Fatima had bought out most of the *parfumeries* and pharmacies in Paris. She, Kate, Amy, Fraser, and Lacey opened bottles, sniffed, sampled, and discussed the merits of various creams, lotions, and gels.

The smattering of light sun freckles that appeared each summer across Kate's nose and cheeks drove her nuts—no matter how cute Nick thought they were—so she extolled anything with SPF. Fatima and Fraser, if they had smile lines or worry lines or lines of any kind marring their forty-something-year-old skin, which of course they didn't, would highly recommend the overnight firming lotion. Lacey dabbed at a thick cream and smoothed it over her young cheeks. Amy bored quickly of the girly nonsense and kicked back with a cup of Irish whiskey-spiked coffee and a croissant.

"What do you think Ratma would appreciate most?" Kate asked Fatima.

Fatima touched a finger to her lips. "Something that will last all day." She reached for a tub of thick moisturizer with the fresh scent of aloe.

Kate liked the choice because the white plastic tub would hide whatever the nerds fashioned to place into it. It was also large enough to give them a bit of elbow room, or beacon room, as it were. She looked questioningly at Fraser.

"We'll get the specs to Langley right away. They've got someone on standby to hop a flight to Bamako once they know what they're working with."

"Idiotic," Weiss muttered into his coffee. Van Pelt nodded in agreement.

Kate ignored them. "Let's pick a couple of backup options just in case."

"What happens to the rest of the goop?" Amy asked around a mouthful of croissant, waving her arm over the bottles and tubs. "You trash it? That's what we'd do. Let no man—or woman—benefit from overspending taxpayer dollars."

Fatima gasped and put a hand over her heart. Lacey held her chosen product to her chest. Even Fraser, a longtime employee of the U.S. government, looked shaken by the notion.

Dubois smiled. "*Un cadeau de la DGSE, mesdames.*"

♌

Sharaf and Khalifa embraced under the watchful eyes of Nick, Jake, and Yunis and his men. The camp, northwest of Timbuktu, wasn't far from the Mauritanian border, according to Cherif's calculations. As Khalifa ushered Sharaf toward the open-sided sheepskin tent under which they would confer, Yunis ordered the men who had transported the Stingers to reveal their cargo for his inspection. Nick counted six long cases, two in the bed of each truck. Jake groaned softly.

The tea was poured, the bread brought, and the meeting between men began in earnest. Yunis ordered his fighters to begin assembling the Stinger units.

"Brother Sharaf, I am in your debt. Without you, my cargo may not have made it out of Timbuktu. The French have spies everywhere."

"Kismet," Sharaf replied. "Allah meant for you to have these missiles, and so he sent me. It is an honor to play the tiniest of roles in his glorious plan."

Khalifa raised his tiny tea glass. "*Allahu akbar.*"

"Umm Ali sends her warmest regards to your wife. She has become quite fond of her."

Khalifa laughed. "Ratma feels the same. I know she would be much happier if she had a woman of similar breeding and intellect with whom she could pass her days. That is why she moves with the hostages. She finds their company far more stimulating than that of my other wives or the children that Yunis insists on marrying."

"You don't worry for her safety?"

"I have given up trying to control Ratma. What is written is written, and so it will be her fate. But if you ask whether I am concerned that the French or the Americans will find the hostages, then no, that is not a concern. We have held hostages consistently for many years, and not once have these powerful countries come close to tracking us."

"And should you come to an agreement with the Westerners? What then?"

"We take their money, we support our brothers and our cause, and we identify and take our next target. The cycle begins anew."

Sharaf sipped his tea, his green eyes on Khalifa. "I thought you might retire."

Khalifa's laugh sounded like a bark, with a hint of Kella's shrillness when she was agitated. "Would the shura let me retire?"

"Have you asked them?"

"No," Khalifa admitted. "It is a topic I am reticent to address given our current struggles. Al-Qaeda has not been the same since 2011."

"We lost much that year," Sharaf agreed. "But you cannot be expected to carry the weight of this worldwide endeavor. You have done your duty as a good soldier. Others must rise to the challenge, assume the mantle of leadership."

"You sound like Ratma."

"The women are not always wrong. I would never tell Umm Ali, but she is right more often than not. I suspect much the same of Ratma."

A smile pulled at a corner of Khalifa's mouth. "She must never hear such words uttered."

Sharaf raised his glass in understanding.

"But speaking of women...the Westerners."

Sharaf poured more tea for both himself and Khalifa. "They are interesting characters, those two."

"I understand my experience with the West has been limited, but is this what our enemies have become? Reliant on such youth and inexperience?"

Sharaf blew across the top of his tea. Nick watched the wheels turn in his brain. He had no idea where this conversation was headed. In the background,

Yunis kicked at the ground and swore at several of his men. Jake turned to watch. Nick focused on their imposter sheikh.

"As you know, my wife speaks fluent English and French. This allows her to communicate with the visitors, but it also allows her to hear things that would otherwise go unheard. Private conversations, phone calls."

Khalifa leaned forward. Sharaf laughed gently.

"I fear my information will not shock you, my friend. Umm Ali has gleaned that Madame Moreau and Pastor Smith were sent in a final act of desperation by their countries. No one really believed they could ever secure a dialogue with the great Khalifa al-Ghazawi."

"America's third-most-wanted terrorist," he said proudly.

Sharaf smiled. "And because they are considered expendable by their respective organizations."

Nick's hands tightened around his rifle. Khalifa looked surprised.

"Not that their lives are expendable," he added hastily. "But professionally, they are an easy sacrifice. Young women who overshot, and who can be offered up if a scapegoat is necessary."

Khalifa stroked his beard. "Do they truly have the authority to negotiate a deal and see it through?"

"Yes," Sharaf replied without hesitation. "The French government and the American religious organization want their people back. There is no question of that. The funds to pay a ransom are kept on the French base. They are ready and able to pay. And I am here to help both sides as necessary."

"I would like to strike a deal and unload my burdens. Even if retirement is not yet an option, these particular hostages have become tiresome. We did not know the extent of the American man's ill health until you arrived, but we knew he was sick. A dead hostage is of no value to us. And the combative French sister is a problem. Ratma says she continues to deteriorate. The kindest thing we might do is put her out of her misery."

"Or make that deal," Sharaf said. "The window in which to negotiate will not stay open for long. Eventually the women will be recalled to their countries and I will need to return to my businesses in Yemen and the Emirates."

"I'm worried about a double cross."

Sharaf laughed. "From the women? Brother, please, you give them far too much credit. They have been under my protection—effectively my control—since we all arrived. The French military does not take them seriously and the American has no significant connections within her government or military. I'm not sure anyone even believed them that they met with you personally."

"It's a stretch, the elusive Khalifa breaking bread with two Western women."

"Name your price and we will carry out the exchange as you see fit."

Khalifa nodded slowly. "You have given me much to consider, Brother Sharaf. I value your wise counsel."

"I seek only to serve our great and glorious cause."

Yunis stomped over and ducked under the tent, covered in dust and swearing in Arabic. Nick and Jake raised their rifles a few inches. Sharaf held up a hand, not even looking in their direction. Yunis sneered at Nick.

"Son, I hope you bring me news that my money is well spent. These arms dealers were your contacts."

"As far as I can tell, the missiles are operational."

"As far as you can tell?"

Yunis grimaced.

Khalifa sighed. "Son, spending a small fortune on Stingers is a poor use of resources if no one knows how to use them."

"You fought the Soviets. Why don't you know how?"

"My boy, that was thirty years ago, and my role was not to shoot down Hind helicopters. I was a strategist, a planner, a leader. I have never fired a Stinger, or even seen it done. You assured me that you could train our men to operate these systems. You are a pilot!"

"I just need to see it done once. I need to find a tower and watch some videos on the internet."

Nick almost bit through his lip in an effort to keep from laughing. Was there a how-to-fire-a-Stinger video on YouTube? Almost certainly. Was it of some comfort that Yunis needed said video? Yes. And, Nick reminded himself, Yunis was educated and a trained helicopter pilot. The rest of Khalifa's merry band of goat fuckers looked as though they could barely tie their shoes. Plowing a truck full of explosives into a hotel or clacking off in a crowded market was one thing; successfully targeting and downing helicopters with MANPADS was quite another.

Khalifa muttered an expression that loosely translated to, "Kids these days." Nick knew this because he often heard Fatima and Sharaf say the same, in affectionately exasperated tones, about their Sandstorm family.

The leader of the desert emirate flung lukewarm tea over his shoulder and stood. Sharaf immediately joined him. Khalifa approached Nick and Jake, looking up at them with curiosity, as if seeing them for the first time.

"Brother Sharaf, are your Legionnaires trained on Stingers?"

Nick went cold in the heat. Sharaf waited a moment before answering. "They are trained on various weapons systems."

"I would be further in your debt if your men could teach mine to fire these missiles."

Sharaf inclined his head in a gesture of concession. "They are at your disposal."

ῼ

Kate decided that Nick's "stay together at all times" edict didn't extend to bathroom trips. It probably did in his mind—or maybe he just assumed that women in the company of other women always used the ladies' room together—but Kate didn't feel like her death was imminent as she walked alone through the hall, passing only the odd DGSE officer or military liaison to the intelligence service. The DGSE contingent in Mali was large; their equivalent to the CIA's station chief resided in Bamako and directed intelligence operations from their embassy in the capital, with trips to Timbuktu, Gao, and other French military outposts in the country as necessary.

Kate, ever the snoopy spy, may have been guilty of eavesdropping on Dubois's conversations on speakerphone with his Bamako-based chief, who seemed un-enthusiastic about the director-general's presence in Mali, his unwavering faith in their American partners, and an operation into which he had little insight. Fraser and Dubois were genuinely close and in lockstep on counterterrorism issues, but the French were still French and prone to fits of pique.

Lunch was soon to be served, but she had a headache after a morning trapped in a room with the planeload of scented beauty products and so she made a detour to the main entrance and sought fresh air. Air, she corrected herself as she pulled a breath of Mali into her lungs. There was nothing fresh about this country. The air seemed heavier, thicker, browner. It had rained little the past few days, allowing the sand and dust free rein on the currents of the winds. A storm gathered over the desert; the clouds roiled in the distance and the atmosphere crackled with electricity, setting her on edge.

She checked her iPhone for messages, though she knew it was pointless. The men would be far outside the range of cellular towers. The Thuraya satellite phone clipped her to belt remained silent as well. No news might be good news, or it meant Khalifa's men had killed them all. Hard to say.

Just as her stomach growled and she turned to head back inside, she caught a whiff of cigarette smoke and heard the murmur of familiar voices. Chad, Blake, and Weiss, the smoker, stood behind a van that the kitchen staff used for transport. Kate crept closer, staying toward the opposite rear wheel well and pretending to be busy on her phone. The white van was paneled; they couldn't see her through any windows.

"Chief, we need to do this," Chad said.

154

"You know how high the bar is," Weiss replied.

"I have one hundred percent confidence."

"Except I'm the one who has the responsibility of justifying the decision."

"Do you have doubts?"

Weiss grunted, seemingly pained by what he was about to say. "No."

"Then let's shoot our shot. The circumstances are as good as they'll ever get, right? This will probably be our only chance. What harm could there be?"

A cloud of cigarette smoke caught the breeze and passed over Kate's head. She stifled a cough.

Weiss hacked and spat. "I can think of a few problems."

"They seem well worth the risk given what we could gain. What *you* could gain, Chief."

"All right. I'll authorize it."

A hand slapped a back. "Fuck yeah. Let's do this."

The men headed inside, still unaware of her presence. Kate gave them a couple of minutes' head start and then followed, rejoining her friends and wishing she knew what Weiss and the former SEALs were up to.

13

THE FIM-92 STINGER MAN-PORTABLE air-defense system, a surface-to-air missile designed and principally manufactured by American defense companies, gained international notoriety during the Soviet-Afghan War of the 1980s, when the CIA covertly supplied the Afghan mujahideen with hundreds, possibly thousands, of missiles and launchers via Pakistan and its Inter-Services Intelligence organization. Engineer Ghaffar of Hezb-i-Islami was the first fighter to bring down a Soviet Hind helicopter gunship in September of 1986 near Jalalabad.

Nick had read *Charlie Wilson's War*, seen the movie, and deployed three times to Afghanistan as an infantry officer. He also knew that the CIA's effort to buy back unused Stinger missiles, which had made their way out of Afghanistan to other hotspots and rogue regimes around the globe, was only partially successful. He inwardly cursed his wife's former employer.

Nick requested a moment to confer with Jake after explaining to Sharaf and Khalifa that it had been a long time since he had seen a Stinger, let alone touched one. This was true. He and Jake had learned how to operate the system over their decade in the Corps, although they had never used it operationally. The only aircraft to shoot down was their own, or that of their NATO allies.

Sharaf dismissed him and Jake with a flick of his fingers, and Nick shepherded Jake outside the tent away from everyone else. Sharaf occupied Khalifa with small talk, but Yunis watched them suspiciously.

"Don't get mad," Nick began.

"I think I know what you're about to say, and it's too late."

"These fuckers don't know how to use the system. Khalifa wants us to teach them, and Sharaf agreed."

"What the hell is wrong with Sharaf?"

"What was he supposed to say?"

"He was supposed to say no!" Jake hissed.

"It would blow the op, and possibly our cover, and you know it."

"Then get us out of it."

"How?"

"I don't know. Aren't you the smart one?"

"The smart one is two hundred klicks away. Look, we just have to teach them the very basics. It'll be a struggle for me in Arabic, and that won't be an act. We mime it out, either they get it or they don't, and we hope for the best."

"We're going straight to Marine Corps hell for this," Jake muttered.

"On the bright side, I bet the company's great." Nick shot Jake a quick grin and then led them back to the group. He spoke in Arabic, addressing Sharaf. "Sheikh, Dmitri and I haven't used Stingers in many years. Our deployed units never carried them. But, if we're permitted a few minutes to inspect the units and reacquaint ourselves with the technology, I think we'll be able to assist. As you know, Arabic is not my first language. I ask for patience from our hosts if my explanations are not as clear as they might hope."

Yunis scoffed, but Khalifa nodded in understanding. "The fact that you speak Arabic as well as you do is a blessing, Legionnaire. We are grateful for any assistance you can provide. Son, allow these men access to our weapons."

Yunis turned on his heel and stalked toward the trucks and the missiles and launchers strewn about the sand. Nick and Jake followed and took stock. These Stingers appeared to be the basic model.

"They need to be careful or they'll wreck the BCUs," Jake murmured.

157

Nick spoke sharply to Yunis, telling him to re-crate the missiles and launchers to prevent damage.

"I don't take orders from you, Legionnaire."

Nick stepped toward Yunis and ripped off his sunglasses, staring down into the Libyan's dark, off-kilter eyes. "You see those battery coolant units you tossed all over the place? Those are sensitive pieces of equipment and critical to the operability of the system. They're not meant to be abused. Pick them up. Now."

Yunis grudgingly nodded to his men, who scurried to gather the equipment and organize missiles, launchers, grip stocks, BCUs, and antennas. Nick and Jake knelt at one crate and took inventory. They inspected each piece of equipment for cracks or other damage.

"Looks okay," Jake said. "They have a legit supplier."

Nick stood and motioned Yunis and his men to gather. Kate, perhaps jokingly, perhaps not, liked to refer to his teaching style as pedantic, usually when he was explaining how they would tackle a home-improvement project. If there was ever a time to channel his inner humorless, Teutonic pedant, it was now.

"Stinger MANPADS can be shoulder-fired by a single operator, but all professional militaries consider it a two-man system. That's how we'll teach you today. Split up into groups of two. One of you will be the team chief, the other will be the gunner. Then you'll swap places."

The terrorists paired off and stood by each of the six crates. They set aside their rifles and ammunition, and waited expectantly. Nick took a deep breath and launched into his monologue.

"Stingers have a targeting range of four thousand eight hundred meters. That's almost five kilometers. They can engage a low-altitude aerial threat at three thousand eight hundred meters or below. Basically, that means if your target is flying lower than four kilometers above ground, within five kilometers of you, you have a chance to shoot it down." He paused to allow the terrorists to absorb the math, and also to rack his vocabulary for the next portion of the lesson.

One of Yunis's lieutenants raised his hand. "Why does the aircraft's altitude need to be lower than the missile's range?"

"Physics," Nick said imperiously. "If you don't believe me, take a shot at something flying higher than thirty-eight hundred meters. You won't reach it."

"How will we know the target's altitude?"

"Practice. Maybe you have to take a few bad shots before you figure it out."

"But we only have six missiles."

"Then I guess you better get it right the first time."

Yunis cut in. "I am a pilot. I will know if our target is within range."

"Moving on. Altogether, the system—missile, launcher, and accessories—weighs about fifteen kilograms." Nick hefted a unit and set it on his shoulder. "When launched, the missile will accelerate once it's a safe distance away from the operator. It reaches a maximum speed of just over Mach two-point-five."

The Arabs looked impressed.

"What does that mean?"

Now they looked at him blankly.

"It means you never fire with friendlies in front of you. If you're the gunner, where is your team chief?" Nick motioned to Jake. "Your partner is on your non-shooting side, even with you or a step behind. That means when I shoot from my right, Dmitri is on my left. You must always know what's going on around you before you launch. Otherwise, you could put a missile traveling at Mach through your brothers."

A few terrorists snickered and looked toward one of their younger brethren, wide-eyed and dressed in mismatched Malian military fatigues and sandals. The klutz of the group, perhaps.

Yunis waved his hand impatiently. "Yes, yes, safety, what else?"

Nick spared him a baleful glance. "Safety is everything. If you can't be safe, what's the point of these weapons?"

159

"We will sacrifice ourselves for Allah in our quest to bring down every French helicopter and fighter jet and cargo plane that dares violate the airspace of our holy emirate. And we shall save a Stinger to shoot down an Air France flight departing Bamako." Yunis tilted his head. "Yes, an American Stinger missile used to shoot down a passenger plane with hundreds aboard, fired by Allah's holy warriors, who learned from two former French Legionnaires. Dieter and Dmitri, is it? German and Russian? I will ensure that you spend life on the run from the French government, the American government, and your own governments."

Nick dumped the Stinger back into the crate. "Then fucking figure it out yourself, you cock-eyed pussy bitch," he said in English.

Jake raised his AK-47 and covered Yunis. Sharaf and Khalifa rushed to the group, stepping between the opposing sides.

"Dieter?" Sharaf asked.

"Sheikh, I will not be threatened or disrespected. Perhaps the internet would be a better teacher after all."

"Dieter, we are guests of Brother Khalifa," Sharaf said gently. "I know Brother Yunis can be difficult, but we stand to benefit greatly from their friendship. All of us," he emphasized. "I would ask that you set aside personal differences and maintain your impeccable professionality. You are the bigger man."

Something in Sharaf's eyes told him that he needed to obey. He drew himself up to his full height, taller than any man at the camp, and gave the white-bearded Yemeni a curt nod.

"As you wish, Sheikh."

ʊ

"May I join you?" asked a voice from her side, in French.

Kate turned to see Ardouin holding his lunch. She gestured to the seat across from her at a small table in the DGSE's cozy cafeteria. She had secluded herself from her team so as to have a semi-private phone call with their blue-haired hacker, whose relief was evident that Nick had finally told her about the heist. George assured her that she was monitoring the feed, had motion alerts set up on all her devices, and would contact them the second she saw any suspicious activity. Then she had gotten wrapped up in emails from their Sandstorm employees, overseeing an array of jobs across the globe in the partners' absence. She set her phone face down on the table as Ardouin sat with a plate of grilled fish, rice, and vegetables.

"I hope I'm not interrupting."

"Not at all. Just checking in with the office."

"I imagine there's no shortage of potential clients in this day and age. The threats are endless. Physical, technical, political. But security consulting is a crowded field, is it not?"

"Yes. Lots of competition."

"I was surprised when Director-General Dubois said that he wanted to consider using a private security company to find the hostages. Much like your agency, the DGSE doesn't generally outsource its operations, especially its most sensitive matters. I expected him to propose a well-known French or British or American firm, one with far reach and myriad personnel and resources. I was stunned when he and Madame Fraser insisted on your company."

"You don't say," Kate replied, her tone gently sarcastic.

Ardouin smiled. "I could find nothing on you or your partners. At least nothing that you don't want the world to know. This concerned me. But it was of no concern to the director-general. He took Madame Fraser at her word that you and Messieurs Cavanaugh and Gillespie had what it took to get the job done."

"Job's not done yet. We may prove you right after all."

He pushed rice around on his plate. "I understand now why they believed you were the best—the only—choice for this operation. What I still don't understand, though, is why you accepted the job."

"I'm in it for the money. Nick and Jake wanted a Tuareg militia." She shrugged. "Boys will be boys."

He appraised her with interest. "I believe without question that your husband and Monsieur Gillespie wanted their Tuareg militia, and perhaps to embrace a romantic, if somewhat rose-colored, history of *la Légion étrangère*. But I do not believe for a moment that you chose to come here and put your life, and the lives of those you love most, at risk for money."

Kate's eyes wandered around the cafeteria, to Amy and Charlie laughing with Giraud, to Fatima talking quietly with Tom Patterson, to Fraser and Dubois deep in conversation. In her mind she saw a desert camp, two uniformed soldiers, and a white-bearded tribesman bonding with one of the most-wanted terrorists in the world. It was impossible to put a price on that.

"But here you are," he continued, perhaps knowing that an answer was not forthcoming.

"Here we are."

"I trust that you have your reasons, and that they are good ones. But I'm curious: Do you believe the lives of the hostages are worth the millions that the terrorists demand?"

Kate was startled by the directness of the question from the chief of protocol, a man paid for his circumspection. "At the end of the day, money is just money, and if it's a government's money, it's a drop in the ocean."

"Should your government pay ransoms?"

"No. If you pay for one, you have to pay for all, and then it's open season on Americans. It's *already* open season on Americans in some parts of the world."

"So, they die in captivity?"

"I'm a big believer in free will. The Abbotts made a choice to travel to backwoods Niger. Maybe they made that choice knowing the dangers that awaited them, maybe not, but either way, they made a choice. The Fourniers chose to set up shop in Timbuktu—they were even warned by Khalifa's men to leave. They chose to stay. Lefèvre, the Aussie kids, every other Western hostage in Syria,

Somalia, Afghanistan, Pakistan, Yemen, the Philippines, pick a country, made a choice. And choices have consequences, sometimes tragic. If they didn't know what could befall them, then shame on them. Everyone thinks it can't happen to them...until it happens to them." She felt herself becoming strident and stopped talking. As Dubois had said, French was a language renowned for its nuance, the language of diplomacy, but she had left little doubt as to her feelings on the matter.

He wiped his mouth with a cloth napkin. "I don't disagree with you. I wish no harm to my countrymen or yours, or the boys. I hope to see them liberated."

"But you don't object to paying a ransom?"

"Both our governments seem to have decided that these particular hostages are more valuable than other hostages. They are older, they are infirm—"

"They're evangelical Christians," Kate said.

"There does seem to be a political element at work in your government's cal- culations," Ardouin acknowledged with a slight smile. "But as to your question, whether I object to a ransom, I do not. Not anymore. Not after I did my own math and realized that the lives of these people, who made choices, are not worth the lives of those who would be sent to rescue them. Or the lives of you and your friends, who did what no one else could and found them."

Kate's phone dinged and she snatched at it, but it was only a text message from Margaret, their office manager. "Sorry," she mumbled, placing the phone back on the table.

"Given the circumstances, I would be offended on your husband's behalf if you ignored a notification."

"It's too early for them to be back in range," she said.

He glanced at his watch. "If you'll excuse me, the director-general and I have a call scheduled with Paris. A pleasure, Madame Cavanaugh."

Ω

Nick's attempts to articulate the intricacies of the Stinger's battery coolant unit in Arabic were laughable. He didn't have a clue how to explain the cryogenic cooling properties of the high-pressure gaseous argon that the BCU injected into the missile seeker once the unit was inserted into the grip stock. He could tell them that each BCU provided forty-five seconds of power and cooling once inserted, and once that short timeframe had elapsed, they needed to replace the unit in order to fire. This caused Yunis great consternation.

"Forty-five seconds? That's it? We paid a lot of money for these!"

"These are American weapons meant to be used by a professional army. What did you expect?" Nick asked.

"But forty-five seconds!"

"Do you have any idea how long a real army trains on these systems before a single missile ever gets fired? That's why forty-five seconds is forever to someone who knows what he's doing. Because he's done it a hundred times in training."

"I just thought—"

"You thought you could treat them like your Kalashnikovs. Drag them around in the sand, never clean them, fire at will with a decent chance of hitting your target, I get it. But that's not how this works."

"How do we get more of these...cooling units?" Yunis pointed to the unit in Nick's hand.

Nick laughed. "Not a clue. I don't traffic in weapons."

Yunis turned to his lieutenants. "We will call Abu Hussain."

Nick filed away the name Abu Hussain for future reference. He snapped his fingers at Yunis and gestured to the Stingers. "Time to practice. Get comfortable holding the unit. Take turns. And remember, don't insert the BCUs."

He retreated with Jake a few paces while the terrorists worked in pairs. Without fail, they pointed loaded tubes at each other, at their trucks, at Sharaf and Khalifa.

"They really need a sergeant," Jake muttered.

"If you spoke terrorist, I'd have delegated this to you."

"Thank God I'm just the dumb Russian."

They turned their faces from a gust of wind that swirled sand and dust in small tornados through the camp. Both situated clear goggles, secured to their helmets, over their eyes and squinted into the oncoming storm. A wall of brown, at least a couple of kilometers high, bore down on their position, moving westward through Timbuktu and toward Mauritania.

"How long until that hits us?" Nick asked.

"Fifteen minutes? Maybe thirty?"

"Thought we left dust storms behind us in Iraq."

"At least we'll be able to wrap up this training if we can't see a thing."

Nick glanced behind them at Sharaf and Khalifa, deep in conversation. "I hate that I have no idea what's going on."

"Kate's probably going to rip you a new one for that," Jake said with a smirk. "That, and teaching terrorists to use Stingers."

"Will you be my cellmate in federal prison?"

"Only if I get the top bunk."

"Deal."

The gusts of sand and dust intensified as the storm enveloped them. The Arabs dropped the Stingers into the crates and pulled scarves over their faces. Nick spat, feeling the sand grind between his teeth. He and Jake trotted to Sharaf, who huddled with Khalifa under the tent, his kaffiyeh covering his entire face save his squinting eyes.

"Sheikh, let's wait in our truck. Brother Khalifa is welcome to join us."

"*Shukran*, Legionnaire."

As they left the tent and felt their way toward the white Hilux parked at the outer edge of the camp, Nick heard a strange hum under the whipping wind and the occasional shout in Arabic. He looked up and around, straining to see anything more than an arm's length in front of him.

"Do you hear that?" he yelled to Jake.

"Hear what?"

"I don't know. A buzzing. A rumble. It's hard to tell."

"Probably the storm."

"Probably."

♌

"What the hell?" Amy said, jiggling the doorknob of the locked door preventing their entrance to the conference room. "Are we persona non grata?"

Everyone turned to Emmanuel Giraud, who had spent the hour after lunch with them finalizing their top three choices of French beauty products for possible beaconing. Fraser now wanted to brief the beacon shop at Langley via the secure video teleconference system in the conference room. The young analyst looked mystified as he joined Amy and rapped on the door.

"We lock this only when we depart for the night." He called out in French a request to enter. Silence.

"Don't you have the code?" Kate asked, gesturing to the keypad.

"The security system isn't engaged. It's locked by deadbolt," he replied. "Someone is in there."

"Didn't Dubois and Ardouin have a call with Paris?" Fraser asked.

"Yes, but they took the call in the director-general's office." Giraud used his fist to knock louder.

Kate looked around. Amy, Charlie, Fraser, Fatima, and Tom Patterson were clustered behind them. Familiar voices approached from the connecting hallway: Dubois and Ardouin, their call finished and eager to join the discussion with Langley on the beacon options.

"It's Weiss," she said, as a sense of foreboding settled over her.

"Weiss?" Fraser asked.

"We need to get in that room. Now."

They all stared at her a moment. Then Fraser whipped out her phone and started calling Weiss, Van Pelt, and the two paramilitary officers. Amy and Charlie pounded on the door while Giraud ran toward Dubois and Ardouin.

"Damn it," Kate muttered, her heart now beating so hard that it hurt her chest.

Fatima wrapped an arm around her shoulders and pulled her a few feet away. "I'm sure it's nothing, love."

"No, it's something."

"What?"

"I...I don't know. But it's not good."

"Emmanuel, find the chief of security and get the key for the bolt," Dubois ordered.

"No one is answering their phones," Fraser said.

Giraud returned a moment later with a keyring and inserted the marked key into the door. The deadbolt slid back and everyone rushed in to find Weiss, Van Pelt, Chad, Blake, and Lacey clustered around the flatscreen television, online with a uniformed military officer wearing a headset over his buzzcut.

Weiss never looked back. "Cleared to engage the target," he said.

Ω

Nick heard the first missile an instant before it impacted the main tent in the center of camp. The explosion knocked everyone off their feet, but their white Hilux shielded them from shrapnel. Nick and Jake covered Sharaf and made themselves small behind the wheel well. Khalifa, stunned, lay sprawled to their right.

"Who the fuck is shooting at us?" Jake yelled.

A second missile hit a row of tents and tarps, spewing debris and setting off hidden stores of grenades and ammunition. Cherif, connected to Nick and Jake by radio, shouted something that Nick didn't understand.

167

"Stay back, stay back," he told the Tuareg.

Nick choked on swirling sand and strained to see through the wall of brown. He heard the noise again, rising in pitch, and saw the ominous outline of an aircraft banking through the dust, heading back toward them. Yunis, wedged under another Hilux, screamed at his men in unintelligible Arabic. Nick reached out and grabbed Khalifa by his gray djellaba, dragging the pot-bellied terrorist behind the Hilux.

"It's a fucking Reaper!" Jake said.

The MQ-9 Reaper unmanned aerial vehicle fired a third missile, hitting multiple Hiluxes on the opposite side of camp, near the obliterated tents. Men howled and flames licked skyward.

"We gotta scram!" Jake yelled in Nick's ear.

"We'll never outrun it. It's searching for movement!" he yelled back. He rose to a crouch and shouldered his rifle, knowing it was futile. A few rounds from an AK-47 would never bring down the drone.

Sharaf grabbed him by the arm. "Shoot it down!"

"What?"

Sharaf shook him hard and pointed to a nearby Stinger. "Shoot it down!"

Nick and Jake scrambled toward the half-crated Stinger, abandoned by Yunis's men when the storm hit. Nick hefted the launcher and settled it on his shoulder while Jake confirmed that the missile was loaded properly. Then he handed Nick the battery coolant unit.

"Where is it?" Nick asked, his free hand poised to insert the BCU into the grip stock and activate the Stinger system.

Jake pointed Nick to the east, where the Reaper was just visible through the sand and making a wide turn on its way back toward the camp. Reapers carried up to eight Hellfire missiles; this Reaper had shot three. It could also carry multiple five-hundred-pound bombs that would turn the camp into a smoldering crater. It had to fly low because of the storm, but the extremely sensitive sensors and cameras could still penetrate the sand and dust. There was little hope of its operators missing their targets.

As the Reaper reacquired the camp, Nick rammed the BCU into the grip stock and sighted the UAV. He took a second to close his eyes and breathe; then he fired.

14

EVERYONE SHOUTED AT ONCE. Fraser yelled at the man on the television screen to abort whatever operational act was in progress; Weiss yelled louder that the target should be destroyed. The young airman seemed oblivious to the chaos in the conference room, and focused on his array of screens and communications conduits.

"What did you shoot at? What the fuck did you shoot at?" Fraser screamed at Weiss.

Weiss crossed his arms over his chest and ignored her, but Kate already knew. Chad and Blake's visit; the casual loitering near the Hilux while Kate and Nick were inside. They had slapped a tracking beacon on the truck and now an Air Force UAV had laid waste to Khalifa's camp and anyone who happened to be present. Kate hung her head and braced herself against the table. The world spun.

"Coming around," said the airman. "Target in sight."

"Abort now! Abort now!" Fraser yelled.

"Ma'am, my orders are to destroy a validated target. Preparing to fire."

"No, no, no! There are friendlies at that site!"

That caught the airman's attention. "Friendlies?" Then he paused and touched a finger to his headset. "We've lost contact with Talon 12."

"Did you destroy the target?" Weiss snapped.

"I can confirm three direct hits, sir, on the given coordinates before contact was lost. The camp appears destroyed."

"Get your commanding officer now!" Fraser roared.

"Ma'am, I—"

"You just blew up two United States Marines!"

The airman visibly paled. His Adam's apple bobbed as he swallowed hard, and he shed his headset to retrieve his commanding officer.

Everyone looked at Kate. Amy and Fatima helped her sit; her legs were rubber, and she fell heavily into the proffered chair. Fraser pulled at her hair, shaking. Charlie crossed himself and murmured a prayer. Patterson rubbed his face. The Frenchmen stared in shock. Van Pelt fiddled with a pen and cleared his throat. Lacey cowered in a corner. Weiss, Chad, and Blake were impassive, arms crossed over their chests.

A new face appeared on screen. "This is Colonel Michael Spaulding, United States Air Force."

"Diana Fraser, the CIA director's senior representative in Mali. Per the director's agreement with the Pentagon, all military elements were ordered to stand down on operations in Mali. You had no authorization to enter Malian airspace and engage kinetically."

"I was aware of no such standdown. Orders came through proper channels."

"Who authorized this strike?"

The colonel looked confused. "Your agency, ma'am, via the Counterterrorism Center's representative to AFRICOM."

"Get that drone off the target and back to Niger. And do not launch a single aircraft into Malian airspace without my approval. You just shot up a camp with friendlies present."

The colonel blinked. "Friendlies?"

"Three. Including two decorated Marines."

The colonel looked like he might vomit. "We had no idea. Once we reestablish contact with Talon 12, we'll clear the area."

"We may need air assets for the recovery mission."

"Yes, ma'am. Standing by for orders."

Fraser cut the feed and turned to Weiss. "You son of a bitch."

"We had to act. It was our only chance to get Khalifa, a high-value target and an existential threat to the United States of America. I stand by my decision."

"You had absolutely no authority to make that call."

"Except I did. I'm the chief of counterterrorism operations in the Sahel tasked with pursuing and eliminating HVTs. And there was an HVT who needed to die."

"You killed my husband," Kate said in a dull voice.

"I triangulated Khalifa to this area based on intel and intimate knowledge of his historical patterns. We had no proof that your husband and partner would meet personally with Khalifa today. If they did, bad timing." He never looked at her as he spoke.

Chad sighed. "I'm sorry, Kate. But it was now or never."

"You piece of shit," Amy snarled.

"Spare me, Kowalski. This needed to be done and you know it."

As the barbs flew through the conference room, Kate's gaze traveled from face to face, from friends to former colleagues to allied intelligence officers. The shock, the horror, the pity, it was all too much for her to bear. She felt nothing, not Fatima's hand rubbing her back, not Amy's hand gripping her right shoulder. She felt nothing except the emptiness, the vacancy, the pointlessness of whatever life remained.

A few feet away, Lacey watched her with glassy eyes. Her laptop sat open to a draft PowerPoint presentation, titled "HVT-8: Removal from the battlefield." Beside the laptop rested a holstered, CIA-issue Glock 19 pistol that she had removed from her belt, her comfort more important than operational readiness or basic firearms safety. Who could blame her? What danger did she face behind a computer, generating PowerPoints for Weiss and Van Pelt? Why did she even have a gun in the first place?

If Kate had seen herself smile at the young targeter, she would have been surprised that it rivaled Pastor Amy's most beatific. Lacey offered a tremulous smile in return. Kate's eyes again fell on the Glock. Fifteen rounds in the magazine, fourteen people in the room, including herself. Everything was so clear. She would kill everyone and then put a bullet through her own brain.

She lunged for the Glock, but Amy was faster and had a longer reach. She snatched the gun and slid it toward Fraser, who caught it before it flew off the table.

"I fully understand and support your desire to murder everyone here, but let me take care of it, okay? I'll do better than you in prison." Amy wrapped her in a hug.

The tears overwhelmed her.

☊

Nick scored a direct hit on the Reaper, which blew apart in midair and threw chunks of fuselage and wings and unexploded ordnance in every direction. He and Jake scurried for cover behind the Hilux, where Sharaf protected Khalifa. Eventually, as the explosions abated and what remained of the Reaper burned in the sand, the survivors of the attack cautiously peeked from behind trucks and scrub trees and berms.

"Fuck me," Jake breathed.

The terrorists, upon seeing the flaming hulk of drone, launched into a heartfelt chorus of *Allahu akbar* and fired celebratory shots from their Kalashnikovs into the air. The heart of the sandstorm had moved over them and now swirled toward Mauritania.

Jake and Sharaf helped Khalifa to his feet and the Marine medic checked the U.S. government's eighth-most-wanted terrorist for injuries. Khalifa and Sharaf had been spared, only scrapes and bruises from the blasts and diving for cover.

Nick jogged toward the Reaper and pulled out his operational Samsung. He snapped a few photos of the bird, including the tail number, and then rejoined Jake. Cherif and his men, who had obeyed Nick's orders and dispersed, converged on the camp. The tall Tuareg and his cousin ran toward them, excited and breathless, chattering in Tamashek until they remembered that Nick and Jake didn't understand them.

"Capitaine, you and the sheikh are unharmed?" Cherif asked.

Nick took a moment to listen to his body. Jake walked around him, giving him a onceover, checking limbs and torso for any bleeding. He'd feel it tomorrow, but today he was in one piece.

"We're good."

Khalifa staggered toward Nick, an expression of wonder on his weathered, bearded face. His off-kilter eyes looked upon him as a father would a favorite son.

"Legionnaire—Dieter—I am forever in your debt. Thank you for saving my life." Khalifa touched a fist to his chest and bowed his head.

"You're welcome, sir." Nick didn't know what else to say to a man he preferred to see dead.

Yunis strode toward them, shouting and gesticulating, spittle shooting from his mouth and catching in his sand-dusted black beard. "Get away from these spies, these traitors!" He fumbled for his AK-47, but Jake wrenched it from his grasp and rammed the butt into his chest. Yunis fell to the ground with a cry, clutching at his sternum.

"How dare you insult my guests!" Khalifa roared. He snatched Yunis's rifle from Jake and pointed it at his son. "I should kill you myself."

"Father, these men brought a drone to our camp and almost killed you! I am your chief of security and—"

"Son, these men are the only reason we're alive. They were in as much danger as we were. Your paranoia has become tiresome."

"But we have never been found before! Then we engage this sheikh and barely survive an attack. I am not paranoid! They are a danger to us."

Khalifa sighed. He held a hand toward his son, helped him stand, and returned his rifle. "My boy, I understand your concerns. Perhaps someone betrayed us, but I don't think it was Brother Sharaf and his men. Or perhaps it was simply our time to be found. I have been running from the Americans and now the French for a very long time. Fate finds us all, in the end."

"But fate has spared you, Brother Khalifa," Sharaf reminded him. "And I remain more committed than ever to our shared cause and our mission in these lands."

"As do I."

"I believe it is time for us to return to the city. It appears we have a few issues to discuss with our French contacts."

Khalifa embraced Sharaf. "*Inshallah*, we shall meet again soon."

"*Inshallah*, my brother."

The Hilux started without trouble and Jake pulled in behind Cherif and Mokhtar, the truck soon swallowed by the Tuareg army. Nick immediately felt for his Thuraya phone, in a pouch clipped to his vest. He pulled it out and dialed Kate's number. The call failed.

"There's still a ton of junk in the air," Jake said. "Probably can't connect with the satellite."

"Do you think she knows we got attacked?"

"Depends who gave the order. Whose bird was that?"

"Almost certain it was ours."

"Fuck the Air Force. Bunch of desk jockeys," Jake muttered. "Talk about bad timing. What are the odds they find Khalifa the day we're meeting with him?"

It all clicked. "Stop the car," Nick said.

Jake honked and flashed his lights to alert Cherif, then rolled to a stop. Nick hopped out, laid on the ground, and peered under the chassis. Nothing. Then he walked to each wheel well, examining the space. At the rear passenger-side well, he saw it. A beacon stuck to the metal, held in place by a heavy-duty magnet and mostly concealed by the tire. He took some photos with his phone, then pried it loose and held it up for Jake to see. Finally, with a roar of rage, he chucked the beacon into the desert.

They drove in silence for a while. Then Jake asked, "Think they'll bill us for the Reaper?"

Nick smirked. "I dare them to try."

Sharaf leaned forward and spoke in English. "This was an exciting day. Did we 'rock the casbah'?"

Nick and Jake looked at each other. Then they broke into gales of helpless laughter.

Ω

They settled Kate in the small cafeteria. Someone set a mug of fragrant mint tea in front of her; she didn't touch it. Like a robot, she used her cell phone and Thuraya to call Nick, over and over. No calls went through. She finally set the phones on the table and forced herself to confront reality.

"We'll keep trying, love. They may just be out of range still."

"You saw the videos. It's hard to imagine anyone survived that." Her voice broke and she covered her face. Fatima pulled her close. The Air Force had sent over the Reaper's feed as it attacked the camp. The sandstorm made it hard to see details, but the explosions of three Hellfires were unmistakable. Direct hits on the heart of the camp. Nick and Jake and Sharaf had still been there. It was their truck that the Reaper tracked to the site, after all. "I'm sorry about Sharaf," she whispered.

"Sharaf lived a long and full life. If he's truly gone, then he died doing something he believed in, with people he loved." But Kate heard the tears in her voice, and it spurred a fresh outpouring of her own.

"I don't know how I'm going to tell Lisa."

"We will be there with you. She and the children will always have what they need. I'll make sure of that."

Amy rejoined them, taking a seat on Kate's other side. She had been the messenger, receiving occasional updates from Fraser, Charlie, and the French. Weiss and his crew had been escorted out of the building and confined to their rooms under French military guard. Their weapons, phones, and Agency-linked computers had been confiscated. Fraser, with Tom Patterson's help, was coordinating options with Colonel Spaulding in Niamey.

"The colonel said they had another Reaper coming online within the hour. They can have it over the camp tonight. They'll keep it up as long as they need to," Amy said.

"Who will do the recovery?" Kate asked.

Amy needed a moment to compose herself. "The French. Dubois briefed the general and they're making plans to deploy a unit to the site first thing tomorrow, once the storms pass. It's too dangerous for their helos to fly in this weather." The sandstorm had blown out, but now gusting winds and rain lashed the base, punctuated by claps of thunder.

Kate nodded.

Amy rested her cheek against Kate's head. "I'm so sorry, Kate."

"This is what we get for thinking we're invincible. It was bound to catch up with us at some point. I just never really thought it would happen, you know?" She laughed sardonically through her tears, remembering her words to Ardouin only hours ago. "It can't happen to you until it happens to you."

"We still don't know for sure..."

"I know. But it's hard to have hope. I'm trying to be thankful for the time I did have with him. It just wasn't enough." She took a deep, shaky breath. "I had plans for us. No matter where life took us, we'd always be together. We'd die in our sleep, painlessly, but I'd live a second longer, because I can't let him win, obviously. Then we'd reunite in heaven, or whatever circle of hell we're destined to be in, for all eternity."

Amy smiled against her head. "Not a bad plan. I know it'll never be the same, but you still have us. For whatever that's worth."

Kate squeezed two hands, Amy's and Fatima's. "It's worth a lot."

Fraser and Dubois and Ardouin appeared, and Fraser motioned to Amy. Charlie took her place at Kate's side. Kate wiped her eyes.

"Langley must be thrilled they got Khalifa," she said.

Charlie pursed his lips. "I'm not sure what Langley thinks. All I know is that a lot of lawyers just got summoned to the office on a Saturday. Same at the Pentagon."

As Amy made her way back to them, a grim look on her face, her phone rang. She answered it and listened, making the occasional "mmhmm" or grunt of comprehension. Then she spoke. "You know, she's got your death planned out. It's super weird. I'm just saying, be careful."

Kate shot up and nearly assaulted Amy, who was now grinning, for her phone. "Nick?"

"Hey babe. Been trying to call you. Bad weather, shitty reception."

"Are you okay?"

"We're fine." He sounded exhausted.

Kate had to sit again; she wasn't sure her legs would hold her. She'd gone boneless in relief. She bit her lip to hold back a wave of emotion. "Where are you?"

"We're at the city gates. We'll swing by and grab you guys."

"No, go straight to the house. Send some of the Tuaregs for us."

"I'll redirect Cherif. He and his guys will be there in ten. Love you."

"Love you, too," she managed to choke out. Then she faced the small crowd that had gathered. "They're alive."

"I knew it!" Patterson said, pumping his fist. "I didn't want to say anything before, but I bet they shot down the drone somehow. This 'lost link' felt a little more permanent."

Fraser shook her head in wonder, while the Frenchmen broke into smiles and murmured "*grâce à Dieu*" under their breaths. Then Dubois was all business.

"Come. We will get you to the gate to meet your ride."

♐

They found Nick and Jake in the dining room and Sharaf in the kitchen, supervised by Kella. Sharaf bustled about heating leftovers on the stove, his once-pristine thobe streaked with dirt and dust and possibly blood. Nick and Jake had shed their gear and fatigue tops, and sat at the table in white T-shirts as dirty as Sharaf's thobe. They were covered head-to-toe in reddish Sahelian sand. They worked their way through heaping piles of kebabs and rice and vegetables like men who hadn't seen food in weeks. Sharaf spooned more onto their plates.

Nick grinned at Kate. "What a day. Can't say I'm too happy with your ex right now, though."

"Or the goddamn Chair Force," Jake mumbled around a mouthful of food.

Kate pressed a hand to her temple and focused on breathing. She saw only minor cuts and scrapes, and reminded herself that Jake was a medic. He would have evaluated everyone for serious injury. Nonetheless, she'd examine him thoroughly upstairs.

Amy and Charlie raided the fridge for beers and passed out fresh bottles. They joined Nick and Jake at the table, laughing and toasting the United States Marine Corps, the French Foreign Legion, the Nation of Azawad, anyone they could think of. Kate remained standing.

"What would you like for dinner?" Sharaf asked her.

"What?" Kate said, her brain still struggling to process the day's events.

"I have salad and couscous for Fatima, and I will deprive Nick and Jake of thirds if you prefer kebabs."

"No, Sharaf, sit, please. I'll take care of everything."

179

Kate moved toward the counter where he prepared salad, but Fatima took hold of her elbow and redirected her toward the table.

"This is how he relaxes, love. Leave him be."

Kate took a seat at the table. Nick reached for her hand. "What's this about you having my death planned out?"

"Maybe she and Chad were in cahoots," Jake said.

Kate remained quiet as everyone laughed and talked over each other. Nick watched her in concern.

"Are you okay?" he whispered.

"Are you finished?"

He looked at his plate and his half-full beer. "I can be."

"Upstairs. Now." She rose and headed for their bedroom.

He joined her a minute later, Kella slipping in behind him just before he closed the door. He stripped to his boxer briefs and dumped his soiled clothing in a corner. She watched him impassively, permitting only a quick kiss to her forehead before she pointed to the bathroom.

"Shower."

He saluted and disappeared. Kate first examined his discarded clothing—minimal blood. Then she shed her own clothes and slipped on one of his T-shirts. She waited, pacing slowly, Kella observing from her perch on the end of the bed.

He finally emerged, wearing a white towel around his waist and rubbing at one of his ears. "I found sand in places I didn't know I had," he said.

Kate held him at arm's length and eyed his chest and torso. Clean, his cuts and scrapes were redder and more pronounced, but only minor. She pressed fingers into his abdomen, over where she thought vital organs might sit. He raised an eyebrow.

"No internal bleeding, right?"

"Um, I don't think so."

"You're *sure* you're okay?"

"I'm fine. Just tired."

"Okay."

"Okay." He looked at her uncertainly.

Without warning she ripped the towel from his waist and pushed him back onto the bed. Kella yelped and toppled to the floor. Kate climbed atop him and pinned his hands over his head. His surprise gave way to a sly smile of understanding.

"I'm not tired anymore," he said.

Kate returned the smile. "I didn't think so." Then she kissed him.

𝔘

Tangled together, they listened to the rain pound the roof. Kella, not a fan of thunder, had cautiously retaken a corner at the foot of the bed, where she was mostly safe from their thrashing. As Nick shifted to take some pressure off a bruised hip, he felt the bedframe give. It had been a headboard-banging night, and this frame hadn't been made to take their gymnastics routine. Kate had insisted on certain moves, guaranteed screamers. She muffled most of her screams with a pillow or his shoulder, except when she didn't. He almost felt bad for the occupant of the bedroom on the other side of that wall; Amy, he thought.

Kate's restless hand traced a path over his chest and abdomen, perhaps searching for phantom internal bleeding.

"Still okay, right?" she murmured. Her head rested in the hollow of his shoulder.

"Couldn't be better. In fact, I think I should get blown up by a drone more often. But I'm a little concerned that you're not okay."

"I didn't think anything could be worse than you with a terrorist's blade to your throat in Sanaa, but today might have surpassed that. I've never felt so helpless."

"It'll take more than a few Hellfires for you to get rid of me."

"I saw that footage. I have no idea how you survived."

"I prefer not to overthink it."

"I just want to get home and put this behind us. Simple jobs. Normal jobs. A vacation."

"Where do you want to go?"

"Take me to an island."

"We could buy an island with what Fraser and Dubois paid us."

"An island with villas on stilts over calm, clear waters. I want privacy. I want to swim and sunbathe naked, and make love to you whenever and wherever I feel like."

Nick hugged her closer. "I've been waiting the entirety of our relationship for you to say that. I already have a list."

"Maybe we should just retire. We could live in a beachfront cabana. Us and the dogs. You could draw. I could teach yoga. We'd be the charming eccentrics with a past we refuse to discuss."

"I wouldn't be opposed to that. Just one question: How do we keep the CIA from finding us?"

"Guile, cunning, deceit, chicanery..."

"Your areas of expertise."

She tweaked his sore hip. He tried to prevent his slight wince, but he knew she felt it.

"Where does it hurt?" she asked.

He blew out a breath. He was too old for getting blown up by drones. "Everywhere."

She rose above him. "Is that so?"

"*Everywhere*," he emphasized, pushing a lock of hair off her face.

"Well, it's a good thing all of your everywheres are so kissable, or we might really have a problem."

15

MUCH TO SHARAF'S CONSTERNATION, everyone missed breakfast, causing him to shift to brunch and throwing off his carefully planned menu. He grumbled at each member of the team as they wandered into the kitchen at various intervals in search of caffeine, but was soon placated by their ravenous demolition of omelets, crepes, and fresh fruit.

Nick joined Jake, Fatima, and Charlie at the table with a heaping plate and a strong coffee. His best friend sipped a latte and looked at him reproachfully.

"What?" Nick asked.

"How do you have the energy to get blown up, shoot down a drone, save a terrorist, and then go at it all night like a honey badger on speed?"

Nick grinned. "I just had to lie back and enjoy it."

"That is *not* what it sounded like." Jake cleared his throat and raised his voice to falsetto level. "Yes, Nicky, just like that!"

Charlie grunted into his own coffee. "Spot on," Fatima murmured.

"Well, it didn't seem fair to let her do all the work."

Kate walked into the kitchen, Kella on her heels, and smacked Jake lightly upside the head. "I don't sound like that."

Nick shrugged at Jake. "A little bit," he whispered with a wink.

A moment later, Kate returned and hugged Jake around the shoulders. She kissed his cheek. "I'm glad you're okay. I'm not cut out to co-parent your three monsters with Lisa."

Jake smiled. "They are monsters for sure."

"You tell her what happened?" Nick asked.

"Hell no. She'd never let me leave the house again if she knew what we got up to on these jobs. I think she sensed something was off, but I blamed it on extreme desert heat and a few too many beers."

"She knows full well what we get up to on these jobs," Kate said, joining them with a plate that held as much food as Nick's.

"Because someone here can't help but tell a story," Jake grumbled.

"A good story is meant to be told," Nick said. "You should have brought her. Then you'd get some action after being blown up by a drone."

"Sure. 'Hey babe, I know you wanted to go to the Caribbean, but how do you feel about Timbuktu?'"

"Sun, sand, practically the same."

Jake rubbed his dirty-blond beard stubble. "I'm definitely going to need a vacation after this."

Amy stomped into the kitchen and made straight for the coffee. "You two are animals!" she said, pointing at Nick and Kate.

"Sorry," Kate said, in a tone that suggested she wasn't sorry—or embarrassed—in the slightest.

Jake leaned forward and rested his elbows on the table. "So, who do we blame for yesterday's goat rope?"

"Crotch Face," Amy said immediately.

Fatima nodded. "He was rather adamant that HVT-8, in your parlance, be killed, no matter who might perish with him."

Kate and Nick exchanged a glance. They hadn't dwelled on it, but it had been a post-coital topic of discussion. Based on the conversation she had overheard, Kate believed that Chad was the driver behind the strike, and had played on Weiss's obsession with Khalifa to eliminate the only witness to his crime in the armory. Nick was inclined to agree. There was no other reason for Chad to advocate for an unauthorized strike on U.S. citizens, especially U.S. citizens in the employ of their government on a covert mission to find high-priority hostages. Over the course of the last couple of weeks, Chad had expressed no strong feelings regarding Khalifa's life or death; Kate commented that in her experience, Chad's strong feelings concerned only Chad.

According to Amy and Charlie, Fraser's plan to limit flights and strike authorization hadn't survived first contact with the enemy: the bureaucracy. Her request had been granted at the highest level of the Agency, but no one had bothered to tell Weiss, the CIA's representative at AFRICOM, or AFRICOM itself. Thus, Weiss was able to set a Reaper upon them, all in the name of national security. Chad may have been the instigator, but Weiss made the call knowing full well that Nick, Jake, and Sharaf would likely die. It was unclear what consequences, if any, he would face.

"I can't wait for you to tell him that Khalifa is still very much alive," Amy continued. "Then I hope he goes to jail for the rest of his worthless life."

"If there's any punishment to be had, which is doubtful, more likely he'll be banished to some silly task force, like Van Pelt and the rest of the misfit toys," Charlie said. "And allowed to retire with a full pension."

"It's good to be a white man," Amy mused.

"Speaking of white men, I do need to get the full story from you," Charlie said to Nick and Jake. "Unsanctioned and illegal drone strike aside, there are many rabid consumers of reporting on Khalifa within the Intelligence Community."

Sharaf leaned close to Fatima and whispered in her ear. "And Sharaf has much to add on Khalifa's mindset," Fatima said. She paused. "At least his mindset before the strike."

As everyone adjourned to the living room and the eclectic array of furniture, Nick knocked back the last of his coffee and made to stand. But Amy placed two hands on his shoulders and pushed him back into his chair. She grabbed a fistful of his T-shirt and leaned forward so their noses practically touched. Nick froze, unsure what havoc Amy would unleash on him.

"Do not ever die," she said.

♙

While Nick and Jake were teaching Yunis and his men how to use Stinger missiles—"Don't write that down," they told Charlie in unison—Sharaf had been deep in conversation with Khalifa al-Ghazawi the man, not HVT-8. Fatima translated for him.

"He solicited my advice on how best to inform al-Qaeda's shura that he intended to step back and turn over day-to-day operational control to a successor. He said he was willing to act as a figurehead for the emirate while the new leader learns his role."

Charlie paused in his typing. "What did you tell him?" he asked with measurable trepidation.

Sharaf shrugged. "To be honest. He is an old man. He wants to live out the remainder of his days in Libya. What can al-Qaeda say to that?"

Charlie snickered and his fingers resumed flying over the keys. "Hard to argue with that logic."

"All right, so Khalifa, *who is very much alive*," Amy emphasized, "wants to retire. Perhaps after one last massive, twenty-million-dollar score?"

"He is eager to settle. The hostages are deteriorating, and dead hostages are of no use to him. But you should know that his group will continue taking Westerners as they are able to. It is too lucrative a practice for them to stop."

"Someone else can find those future hostages," Jake said.

"Who will take over for him?" Kate asked.

Sharaf smiled. It was the question he had been waiting for. "His son."

"Ugh," Amy said. "Yunis is such a shit."

"It's not Yunis, is it?" Kate said.

"It is not. Khalifa has had many wives, many children. Much to his dismay, Ratma bore him only daughters, whom she has aggressively protected from this life. They are relatively educated and living anonymously in urban areas throughout the region. They have not seen their father in many years, although Ratma regularly travels to visit them and her grandchildren. His firstborn son was his favorite, but that son perished in Afghanistan in the early days of the war."

"I didn't kill that son, did I?" Nick asked.

"I believe you are innocent, Dieter. Yunis is his second-born son, and has been chief of security for years. Khalifa does value his formal military training and connections to state-run security institutions in the region. But as you know, Yunis is impetuous, reckless, paranoid. Khalifa does not trust him with control of the emirate. However, he does trust his third-born son, Talha, who has been leading Khalifa's units in Algeria and Tunisia against government forces in the mountains. They are outmanned and outgunned, but according to Khalifa, Talha epitomizes the warrior spirit and has the strategic vision to push this emirate to greater successes in the region, and beyond."

Charlie typed furiously. "Honestly, how did we not know any of this before now?"

"Because Crotch Face runs CT operations in the Sahel. Duh." Amy shook her head at Charlie.

Kate sipped her green tea. "Does Yunis know?"

"Khalifa is waiting for the right time to tell him."

"I don't see that going well," Nick said.

"Khalifa knows this. He is reticent to make changes until the hostage situation has been resolved."

Kate's phone, set to vibrate, buzzed. She looked at it. Fraser. For the fourth time this morning. Dubois had called twice. Seated beside her on the couch, Nick had an arm draped over her shoulders. His fingers caressed her bare skin below the sleeve of her T-shirt.

"Maybe it's time to rip that Band-Aid off," he whispered.

Kate sighed and answered the call. "I'll let Cherif know you're on your way," she said.

"Fraser?" Amy asked. Kate nodded, and Amy clapped her hands gleefully. "Let the fireworks begin!"

♌

Fraser and Dubois arrived thirty minutes later, looking haggard and uncharacteristically unkempt. The only other time Kate had ever seen Fraser so ragged was in the aftermath of the death of one of their colleagues in an attack on the U.S. Embassy in Sanaa, Yemen. Kate felt a sudden pang of guilt; she hadn't been able to prevent R.J. Reed's death, even with a source under deep cover within the terrorist organization that conducted the attack, and she would have been responsible for yesterday's tragic ends, too. It was, after all, her cockamamie plan that had brought them to Mali and put Nick and Jake and Sharaf on the X.

Both chiefs regarded the Reaper targets with relief. Unbidden, Sharaf brought two espressos, which they accepted gratefully. Fraser, the representative of the government that had just attempted to murder its own citizens, stared at the tiny cup resting atop the saucer in her hands. The awkward silence stretched into eternity.

"I'm so sorry," she said. "I just...I'm so sorry."

Kate knew everyone was waiting for her to stay something, but she had nothing. Only growing contempt for the world and the people she had left behind.

Nick's arm tightened around her shoulders. "Shit happens. Wasn't the first friendly-fire incident in history, won't be the last," he said.

"Kind of fitting it was the Air Force. We've said some nasty stuff about those guys over the years," Jake said lightly.

"Still, there's no excuse for what happened yesterday."

"You're right, there isn't," Kate said.

"I know," Fraser said quietly.

"When I think of what I almost lost..." Kate trailed off, unsure if she was about to cry or scream. She took a deep breath. "What we almost lost. Two husbands, a father of three young children, a companion and friend. We trusted you. And all you've got is sorry?"

Fraser reacted like she'd been slapped. Her ice-blue eyes turned glassy. "You have every right to be angry."

"You're goddamn right I do. This was amateur hour from the start. One look inside the conference room the first day, and we should have turned around and gotten back on that plane. But I put my faith in you—the both of you—and only just escaped a lifetime of regretting it."

Now Dubois looked as uncomfortable as Fraser, and Kate turned on him in French. "No heartfelt apology from the DGSE, Monsieur Dubois? No apologies from your military for not property deconflicting air operations and denying clearance to that drone?"

"You are right, Madame Cavanaugh. We also failed in our duties to protect you."

"For all the non-French speakers, we're in agreement that they screwed up," Kate said with false cheeriness.

Charlie broke the even more awkward silence that followed. "Chief, I'm working on some reports. I should have everything to you later this afternoon. The guys did an amazing job. Boatloads of new information."

Fraser nodded, but her heart wasn't in it.

"Consider that intel our parting gift," Kate said.

"You're leaving?" Dubois asked tentatively.

"Of course we're leaving. As soon as possible."

Dubois looked at Fraser. "Is there any way you'd consider staying?" she asked.

Kate stared at her. "Are you kidding?"

"Langley's beacon guy confirmed that he can hide a device in the face cream. He'll arrive tomorrow afternoon."

Kate continued to stare. "No, really, are you fucking kidding me?"

Fraser cringed; Kate rarely lobbed f-bombs. "It's just that you're our only chance of getting that item into the right hands."

"You want us to take possession of another beaconed item, this time willingly, after nearly killing half the team?"

"I know how it sounds, but—"

"Do you? Do you really know how it sounds?"

"We ran Stu Abbott's symptoms past a doctor at Langley, who also reviewed medical records that the family was able to provide. She doesn't think he has much longer."

"Stu and every other hostage should have known better than to come to Mali, or Niger, or Burkina Faso. Choices have consequences."

Fraser's eyes were pleading. "You're the only hope those people have."

"Then you should have thought of that before you tried to kill my husband and my friends. May God have mercy on their souls."

Kate busied herself on her phone and ignored Fraser and Dubois, who looked around the room for help. None came. They quietly excused themselves. As soon as the front door latched shut behind them, Amy laughed maniacally.

"Damn, Kate. Your inner bitch is a sight to behold."

Charlie resumed typing on his laptop. "Fraser looked positively...human. I felt a little bad for her."

Amy leaned forward and rubbed her hands together eagerly. "All right, so how do we get this festival of fuckery back on track?"

Kate looked up from her phone. "What do you mean?"

"What's the plan?"

"The plan is to go home."

"But..." Amy glanced around the room. "Why would we go home?"

"Because those assholes literally tried to kill the guys. Why would we stay?"

"Because...because we're so close. And the hostages..."

"Fuck those people. They can wait for the SEALs."

Amy opened her mouth to respond, but perhaps for the first time in their nearly decade-long friendship found herself speechless. Charlie stopped typing. Jake and Sharaf watched Kate intently.

"I think what Amy is trying to say, love, is that without us, Stu and Bess and Marianne and Mathilde and Gilles and Noah and Ollie will die in Khalifa's lands of the Islamic Maghreb," Fatima said gently. "And though you are angry, rightfully so, we know that is not a fate you would wish on anyone."

Kate looked around the room, at each pensive face hanging on her every word. "I don't understand. You want to stay? All of you?" Cautious nods from everyone, even Sharaf. She spoke in Arabic. "May I remind you that the United States government almost blew you up a day ago?"

"It is a badge of honor for a Yemeni man to be attacked by an American drone," he replied, his green eyes twinkling.

Kate shot up from the couch, dislodging Kella from her perch on the neighboring cushion. "I can't believe this. We just suffered the ultimate betrayal and you want to pretend like it didn't happen?"

"Trust me, no one's going to forget what happened," Jake said. "But you know full well the SEALs aren't coming for those people, not unless we tell them exactly where to go."

"We just need to get the beaconed item into Ratma's hands, love."

"There's no guarantee we ever see Ratma again. There's no guarantee Khalifa wants anything to do with us after yesterday."

"He will call," Sharaf said.

"And even if he does, there's no guarantee he doesn't execute us on the spot. What in God's name is wrong with you all?"

Amy's eyes rolled back in her head and she started chanting in Pig Latin. Charlie snickered.

"Knock it off," Kate snapped.

"Sorry," Amy said meekly.

"Perhaps we should take some time to consider—"

Kate interrupted Fatima. "There's nothing to consider. They're in breach of contract. We've been paid; it's time to leave. No one needs this bullshit." She glowered at each of them in turn. They fiddled with coffee cups, phones, computers, anything to avoid her piercing glare. Then she realized that Nick hadn't said a word. She looked at him. "Even you?"

"I support whatever you want to do," he said quietly.

Kate stared at him. Then she looked at her friends. "Go to hell, all of you."

ת

After Kate had stormed out of the living room, Kella trotting after her and tossing a baleful, judgmental glance over her shoulder at the motley crew of fake mercenaries, evangelicals, and tribal royalty, everyone turned to Nick. Amy brandished her giant wooden cross as if to ward off demons.

"The Lord compels thee, go fix this mess!"

Nick looked at her incredulously. "Me? You bozos couldn't read the room, and now I'm stuck on cleanup duty?"

"She's your wife."

"She's your best friend."

"Happy wife, happy life," Jake reminded him.

"I hate you all," Nick grumbled.

"Don't forget body armor!" Amy called.

Nick sighed and trudged upstairs, pausing for a moment outside the bedroom. From behind the closed door, he heard a commotion, the slamming of dresser drawers and the thud of heavy objects hitting the floor. He sent a quick prayer to Allah and Pastor Amy's evangelical God, anyone who might be listening, hoping some higher power would see fit to save him from the pint-sized tornado of fury laying waste to their temporary domicile.

She turned on him immediately, the green and gold flecks in her hazel eyes blazing, her cheeks reddened from Sahelian sun and rage. "What the fuck, Nick?"

He dodged an armful of clothing that she threw toward an open suitcase on the floor. Most of his socks and underwear missed the suitcase. "Kate, I—"

"Shut up and pack your shit. We're leaving."

"Baby, please." He batted away a pile of his T-shirts. "Let's talk."

She flung shut the armoire doors. Nick winced at the crack of wood on wood. That piece of furniture was about as solid as the bedframe. She faced him, armed crossed over her chest.

"Let's. Whose side are you on?"

Nick sat on the edge of the bed and leaned forward, elbows resting on knees. "I'm on your side."

"Could have fooled me."

"I'm on your side. We'll do whatever you want to do."

"I want to go home."

"Then we'll go home." He reached a hand toward her. She looked at it suspiciously, but finally relented, joining him on the bed. They faced the exploded suitcase. He nudged her shoulder with his own. "I can't help but notice that it's all my clothes on the floor."

"Merely a coincidence."

He looked at her small hand in his, ran his thumb over her knuckles. "I think we should take our vacation to the South Pacific. We'll obviously spend most of our time making love and skinny-dipping, but maybe we can also dive a few of the World War II wrecks."

She shrugged. "Sure."

"There's supposed to be great shark diving and—"

"I'd rather you were honest with me. You want to stay."

"Let me ask you something. Let's say we leave. A month from now, or a year from now, or five years from now, however long it takes, when we see in the news that some or all of the hostages have died, or that their desperate families continue to beg their governments to save their loved ones, and we know firsthand what their conditions are in this hellscape, are you going to be okay with the fact that we walked away? Can you live with yourself if we don't do everything possible to help?"

"Yes."

"If you say so. The Kate Devlin I know would let that eat at her for as long as she lived."

"Maybe you don't know her very well."

Nick smiled. "Maybe."

She offered a small smile of her own in return. "It's just..."

"I know. Believe me, I know."

"I can't lose you."

"And I can't lose you. Can you imagine me without you?"

"I assume there would be leggy, busty blonds."

He laughed. "Once you go petite and brunette, you never go back."

"We'd be playing with everyone's lives if we continued this charade. The hostages' lives, our friends' lives, our own. And at best we get something to Ratma with no guarantees she takes it with her to the hostage camp."

"What if we shot for the moon?"

"What do you mean?"

"What if we got the hostages back ourselves?"

Kate raised an eyebrow. "How would we do that?"

"Not a clue. But I'm sure there's a way. Don't we have a shit-ton of money just waiting to be spent?"

"Have you forgotten that we absolutely cannot use that money to pay a ransom?"

"Who said the bad guys would get to keep the ransom? Wouldn't it be fun to fuck them over?"

Kate shook her head as if to clear it. "Fun to fuck them over? And if our little bait and switch fails and they do get away with twenty million dollars? What then? I might choose death over life in federal prison."

"Why do you think Fraser and Dubois came to us? Over the objections of literally everyone, I might add."

"Because they were desperate."

"Nah, they weren't desperate. I think they chose us because they were certain we wouldn't play by the rules."

Kate narrowed her eyes.

"This is personal, right?" Nick asked.

"Intensely."

"Then let's do what we do best."

"Sex?" Kate said skeptically.

Nick laughed. She smiled. "Let's be us. Let's do it our way. And fuck 'em if they can't take a joke."

Ω

Kate and Kella trailed Nick into the living room. They retook their seats on the couch, Kella trying to wedge herself between them before giving up and draping herself across their laps. Kate stroked the dog's silky ears, listening to the casual conversations between Amy and Jake, Charlie and Fatima and Sharaf. The Yemeni tribesman excused himself to the kitchen and returned moments later with a mug of freshly steeped green tea for Kate. The corners of his eyes crinkled in affectionate amusement as she mumbled her thanks.

"Welcome back." Amy held up her cross protectively. "Kate, does your inner bitch need to get anything else off her chest?"

"I'm good, thanks."

"Then back to the carnival of numbskullery. We need one more meeting, all of us, and a beaconed gift for Ratma. As befitting the fairer sex, we flake out, can't follow through with the deal, and wait for the SEALs to wreck the place."

"What happens if it's all dudes, no Ratma? After yesterday, I can see Khalifa putting a little more stock in Yunis's paranoia and keeping us far away from anyone who matters to him," Jake said.

"In that case, if we discreetly passed the gift to Khalifa himself, I believe it would end up in Ratma's hands," Fatima replied. "Especially if we made known that it came from me."

"You two are quiet," Amy said to Kate and Nick.

Nick glanced at Kate. She gestured for him to proceed. "What if we're thinking too small? What if *we* could get the hostages back?"

Amy leaned forward, clutching the cross to her chest like a baby. "A bait and switch? A double cross? An outlandish sublot for the sake of an outlandish subplot? A veritable sea of red herrings?"

"In a manner of speaking."

Jake looked doubtful. "I'm all for saving those people, but how would we do it without getting anyone killed or committing a massive crime?"

"Good questions. I don't know. But—"

Charlie's phone rang. "Hold that thought. It's Fraser." He answered and listened, his face turning ashen. He disconnected and swallowed hard. "Langley decided that in light of yesterday's unsavory events, no one will be held accountable but everyone will be blamed."

"What the hell does that mean?" Amy asked.

"It means that Fraser and Weiss are in the penalty box. Van Pelt is in charge."

"May God have mercy on us all."

"I suppose that's the end of our little adventure," Fatima said.

"Not necessarily," Charlie said. "Apparently, he's under strict instructions to facilitate a rescue of the hostages. And for that, he needs you."

196

"Under no circumstances will I take orders or even suggestions from that pathetic excuse for a CIA officer," Amy said.

"Fraser told him that Sandstorm was packing up shop and intending to head home at the earliest opportunity. He became...distressed."

Amy snorted. "I imagine that being chief doofus of this derby would be distressing."

Nick sighed. "Well, this changes the calculus."

"I was never very good at calculus," Kate murmured. That got everyone's attention. She sipped her tea nonchalantly.

"Well?" Amy said. "What's the plan?"

They all waited for Kate. She made a face. "You dummies want to stay, but I have to do all the work?"

"Babe, have you met us? Obviously," Nick said.

Kate harrumphed, shaking her head in self-righteous indignation. She made them wait while she finished her tea, then she set aside the mug. "If we're going to do this, here's how."

16

FATIMA WAS FIRST INTO the conference room, storming through the doorway in a swirl of black abaya, the authoritative click of her stilettos on tile flooring silencing the assembled mass of CIA and DGSE officers, none of whom looked particularly happy to be in each other's presence. She let loose a barrage of profanity in high-volume Arabic, to which Kate felt compelled to respond in English.

"I agreed to this meeting, didn't I?"

"I've seen more cooperative children in the throes of a temper tantrum," Fatima said.

"Just give it a rest, already," Kate muttered.

Fraser and Dubois, still looking exhausted and stressed, exchanged a glance. Ardouin frowned and Tom Patterson narrowed his eyes.

"Chief, we're all here," Charlie said to Van Pelt.

Van Pelt, in a charcoal-gray suit, white shirt, and royal-purple tie, cleared his throat. "Yes, well, thank you for agreeing to meet. Please, be seated."

The group flung themselves into chairs, each of them stony-faced and sullen. Amy pulled a silver flask from her backpack and took a swig. Kate snatched it out of her hand and took a gulp herself.

"As I'm sure Mr. Rodriguez mentioned, DCIA himself has named me his senior representative in Mali for the remainder of this operation. The director also asked me to convey his deepest apologies for the misunderstanding with the Reaper."

Kate laughed incredulously. "Misunderstanding? That's quite the euphemism, Stan."

"Leave it alone, Kate. Time to move on," Nick said.

"Move on? *Move on?*"

"You weren't even there. You were safe here, gabbing with the girls and playing with beauty products while I nearly lost my life."

Kate gaped at him. She saw confusion on faces, even a tinge of satisfaction on Weiss's.

"Yes, well, as I said, the director offered his apologies and expressed his desire for you to continue your efforts to pinpoint the location of the hostages. He's very impressed with your progress thus far," Van Pelt said.

"No."

"Kate, you don't get to speak for—"

"No. Absolutely not." She turned to Nick. "Not another word. We're done."

"I don't think that's a good idea."

"I don't give a damn what you think, darling."

"For God's sake, Kate. We can't just walk away from this."

"We can, and we will. Enough is enough."

"I really think we need to reconsider," Amy said. "The hostages need us."

"How many times do I have to say it? We're not responsible for the plight of the hostages."

"But we can help!"

"They made their choices, and they'll live with those choices. Or die by them." Kate shrugged.

"You are the most self-righteous, sanctimonious bitch I've ever met."

"And you're an unhinged sociopath who was too far gone even for the CIA."

Amy laughed hysterically, her eyes as wild as her mop of curly blond hair. "Worst decision I ever made was standing by your side in Yemen. I lost everything for you. My reputation, my career, my goddamn will to live." She took another swig of Irish whiskey.

"We voted, Kate. You lost," Nick said. "We're staying."

"You can't do this without me, and you know it. I'm the brains behind the operation, you're the mouth-breather with a gun. We're leaving, and that's final."

Nick set his jaw and shook his head. "How did I lose my company to you?"

"Our company," Jake said coldly.

"You're the one who wanted to make her a partner."

"We were about to fold. It was a calculated risk."

"And boy, are you bad at math."

"Sandstorm was nothing, *nothing*, before I got my hands on it," Kate said.

"Sure, now we're something," Jake said sarcastically. "Nick and I babysit you and your little friends during dangerous operations that you have no business being part of, while the rest of the industry has a laugh at our expense. We're a joke. A complete and total joke."

"Her little friends?" Amy and Fatima said in unison.

"Guys, come on," Charlie pleaded. "We need to discuss—"

"Shut up, reports monkey!" Kate and Amy shouted at him.

Charlie shrank into his chair and Van Pelt tried desperately to get them focused on the operation. "If you could just talk us through—"

"If you don't need us, then why do you keep paying us? Huh?" Amy challenged Nick and Jake.

Nick tossed up his hands. "To get Napoleon here off my back, obviously."

"Napoleon?" Kate snarled. "Real funny, caveman. Real fucking funny."

"Chicks love an alpha. You know I have a line of women just waiting for me to come to my senses."

"You think I don't know about your wandering eye?"

"I haven't made it a secret, sweet pea. Know why? Because dudes don't like arrogant, domineering women."

"For once I agree with him," Amy said. "Next time you beg me to help out on one of your insane plans to save the world, the answer is gonna be a big middle finger."

"Fine, you want out, then you're out. I knew you needed money so I threw some work your way. Sorry for being a friend. And God knows we need to help this one fund her shopping habit," Kate said, jerking a thumb at Fatima, who bristled.

"Fuck you, Kate Devlin," Amy said.

Van Pelt looked to Fraser in despair, silently begging her to step in and restore order. But she watched the spectacle with an open mouth.

Kate pointed a finger at Nick. "There are going to be some big changes coming. First off, I make the decisions. None of this 'three equal voices' shit. Secondly—"

Jake's bellow drowned her out. "Brother, you need to get your woman under control."

The commotion ceased. Everyone stared at them, frozen in surprise. Kate shot up from her chair, hands curling into fists. She seethed with rage.

"What did you just say?" she asked in a low voice.

"You heard me."

She turned to Nick. "Are you going to let him talk to me like that?"

Nick stood and towered over her. "I don't care how he talks to you. This isn't working. We're done."

Kate sprang forward and slapped Nick across the face. He never saw it coming. She hit him with such force that he fell backwards, sprawling on the table and knocking over several open bottles of Perrier. The carbonated water sloshed over papers and maps and crept toward Lacey's computer, but she, like everyone else, was too shocked to react.

Then Amy Kowalski burst into tears. Fraser's eyebrows shot skyward. Van Pelt loosened his tie and rotated his neck. His eyes darted between the members of a family torn asunder.

"If we may take just a few minutes to review your most recent reporting…"

"It's over, Stan," Kate said dully. "We have nothing more to give."

One by one, the Sandstorm team filed out of the conference room.

Ω

That night, after dinner, Fraser called Kate and asked if she and Dubois could come by the house. Kate hemmed and hawed, relenting only when Fraser, who sounded on the verge of tears, resorted to a barely audible plea. Her former boss, one of the most formidable women that Kate had ever met, had taken some brutal body blows over the last couple of days, and Kate didn't have the heart to prolong her agony.

Kate, camped out on the sofa in the living room, heard Fraser and Dubois enter via the porch, stopping short as they confronted the serene scene of Amy, Jake, Fatima, Charlie, and Sharaf playing poker at the table.

"Where's your fearless leader?" Fraser asked dryly.

"I believe you will find her canoodling on the couch," Amy responded.

Fraser and Dubois walked through to the living room. Kate, curled against Nick with Kella sprawled over their laps, watched a video of Shadow that one of her brothers, their dog-sitter, had sent. Shadow's frisbee-catching skills were rapidly improving under Jason Devlin's tutelage.

Dubois turned to Fraser in ecstasy, jabbing a finger dangerously close to her face. "I knew it! I knew it!"

"Knew what?" Kate asked innocently.

"That it was all an act, a charade, a ruse. But Diana didn't believe me. Ha! *J'avais raison et tu avais tort!*" Dubois gloated.

"I thought you'd see right through us," Kate said to Fraser.

"I wasn't sure until the very end."

"What convinced you?"

She smiled crookedly. "Amy crying."

"That was a nice touch," Kate said. "But more importantly, did everyone else buy it?"

Fraser laughed. "They've talked of nothing else since you walked out. Van Pelt is wallowing in self-pity knowing he can't succeed without you, Weiss is in a rage over all the questions he has that only you can answer, and Chad is scheming to get you back."

Nick growled. Kate patted his thigh and Kella lifted her head to shoot a bemused look in their direction.

Dubois regarded them with interest and hope. "This subterfuge...to what end? You made quite clear that your role in this operation had ended."

"I really did get outvoted."

"I wasn't aware this was a democracy," Fraser said.

Kate shrugged. "Even the tin-pottiest of dictators needs to give the people what they want on occasion."

A sparkle of life returned to Fraser's pale blue eyes. "So..."

"Even though my own government nearly killed my husband and two friends, even though it's a travesty of justice that Weiss remains a free man, even though it's criminal that Van Pelt was put in charge, and even though you really are in breach of nearly every clause in our contract, we take our commitments seriously. We said we'd give you thirty days, and that's what we'll do."

Fraser exhaled her held breath and placed a hand on Dubois's shoulder to steady herself. Dubois grinned so widely that Kate thought his face might crack.

"There's still absolutely no guarantee we'll succeed," she reminded them. "But we'll do our best to put you in a position to finish the job."

"We can't ask for more than that," Fraser said. "What do you need from us?"

"It would help if the Gulfstream developed sudden mechanical problems."

"Those problems will take many days to fix. As many days as you need," Dubois said.

"And you have to play along with everything, even if you don't understand what's happening."

"You'll be in good company. Most of the time, we don't understand what's happening, either," Nick said.

"Remember when you first arrived in Sanaa and you had serious doubts about Amy and me?" Kate said to Fraser.

"They were minor doubts at worst."

"Skinny bitch!" Amy yelled from the porch.

Kate smirked. "Just be the Diana Fraser the world fears. You know the one."

"I most certainly do not," Fraser huffed. But her lips twitched in a smile. Then she asked, "Do you have a plan?"

"Sort of," Kate replied. "But it all depends on Khalifa."

"It's hard to imagine him being keen to meet again."

"The thought of twenty million dollars might make consorting with the likes of a snooty French diplomat and a wackadoodle American pastor worth the risk," Nick said.

Kate nodded. "Maybe he calls, maybe he doesn't. But have the face cream ready."

"I'll make sure things stay on track from our side."

"I would make one request," Dubois said hesitantly. "May I inform Henri that this was all a deceit in furtherance of your operation? He is distraught over what he believes to be the implosion of your marriage and the unraveling of cherished friendships."

Kate blinked. "Henri? Henri Ardouin? Your chief of protocol who disdains who we are and all we stand for? *That* Henri is distraught over the implosion of our marriage and the unraveling of cherished friendships?"

Dubois smiled ruefully. "He has become rather fond of you and your friends. And as the father of two daughters, he confided that he hopes they one day find a love as strong as yours."

"If he only knew the abuse I take," Nick muttered.

Kate threw an elbow into his ribs. "Go take the dog out."

Nick mock saluted and ushered Kella into the yard. Fraser waited until he was out of earshot before turning to Kate with a hint of uncertainty.

"Everything is okay, right?"

"What do you mean? We agreed to stay. Everything's fine."

"No, I mean with him, with them"—she jerked a thumb over her shoulder—"with Sandstorm."

"Your concern is touching. And your generous compensation means we can retire early." Kate winked at her former boss. Fraser still looked unsure. "Trust me, we're good."

"I told you," Dubois reminded Fraser.

"And you may tell Henri of our deception."

"*Merci.*"

Nick returned and stood before Kate. "Come on, let's go have make-up sex."

Kate raised an eyebrow. "You do know it was a fake fight, right?"

Nick adjusted his jaw with his hand and regarded her skeptically. "That slap felt awfully real."

"You deserved it."

"I *deserved* it?"

"You took their side." Kate nodded her head toward the poker game.

"Flatly untrue. I was on your side from the start."

"Liar. You wanted to stay. And because I recognize that marriage is a compromise, I have magnanimously agreed to direct my talents toward the hostages' liberation. Plus, I can't possibly leave a knuckle-dragger like you in charge of this operation."

"You really are the only woman I know with a Napoleon complex."

"Keep it up, caveman, and you'll sleep down here."

Nick glowered at her. Then he broke into a grin. "Excellent! We're fighting. Come on, make-up sex."

Against her protestations, he pulled her up and tossed her over his shoulder, caveman-style. "I'll be in touch," she called to Fraser and Dubois. "Remember, play along!"

"Animals!" Amy yelled as they headed to the staircase.

"Wear earplugs!" Kate yelled back.

Ω

The next morning, Kate joined Fatima on the porch with a mug of green tea. The Yemeni smiled at her phone before darkening the screen and greeting her in Arabic. The only other activity in the compound was that of Sharaf, who was in the yard, facing Mecca, finishing *Fajr* prayers as the sun peeked over the horizon and bathed the small city in a dusty, golden haze.

Kate had left Nick sleeping soundly and decided to use the quiet of the dawn to think through what may be required of the team in the coming days. Collectively, they had all consented to give Fraser and Dubois the contractually agreed-upon thirty days, but no one advocated for continued efforts much beyond that month-long period. It had been one of Kate's redlines, discussed privately with Nick and Jake, and both men concurred that Sandstorm had gone above and beyond already, with little to be gained from prolonging their absence from pressing matters at home.

She hadn't expected to find Fatima up so early. Her Arabic teacher's hair fell in silky waves about her shoulders, and her face, makeup free, glowed with her smile.

"How are you, love?"

"Hanging in there."

"It's been quite the couple of weeks, hasn't it?"

"That's one way to put it." She gestured toward Fatima's phone. "How's Tom?"

Fatima blushed. "He was just checking in. He was concerned after yesterday."

Kate sipped her tea and studied Fatima, who couldn't hide the glimmer of shy pleasure in her dark eyes. "What did you tell him?"

"That true love and friendship always find a way."

"We plan to read him into the op."

"He'll appreciate that."

"Nick and Jake think the world of him."

"He seems like a good man."

"You could certainly do worse." Kate watched a pensive expression come over her face, and she wondered if she had overstepped. She and Fatima were close, but Fatima's romantic entanglements, if any following her escape from her abusive husband, were unknown to Kate. "He seems worth a chance," she said tentatively.

Fatima waited a moment to speak. "It's not so simple. The past is...the past is always there."

"Maybe the past would be easier to bear if you had someone to share it with."

"It has been my experience that even those who should care most about your trauma would prefer if you simply kept it to yourself," she said, a hint of bitterness creeping into her voice.

Kate knew this was a reference to her family, the people who had sacrificed her to a monster to bolster their own social standing and secure their financial future. The dowry that Rashid al-Jaburi, then a rising star in Yemen's brutal and corrupt Republican Guard, had paid for a beautiful but strong-willed teenager whom he had seen on the street one day lifted the Maqdisi family from poverty and linked them to a prominent Sanaa clan. And then Fatima had the temerity to disgrace them by saving herself and forging a most compelling life out of utter bleakness. Through it all, she still tried to do right by the people who had abandoned and then shunned her.

"You can choose your family," she reminded her gently.

"I can, and I believe I have. But perhaps some secrets should remain buried, for everyone's sake."

Kate said nothing, merely watched her.

Fatima tilted her head, her hair catching a ray of sunlight slicing through the porch. "You disagree."

"It's not for me to decide which secrets should be kept and which should be shared. Talking about it can help, though. I happen to know a macho Marine who would agree."

"Talking about it simply isn't done in my culture."

Kate sipped her tea. "You know what else isn't done in your culture? Having the courage to save yourself from an abusive marriage. Growing into the woman who saves countless girls from abusive marriages."

"Isn't strange how much easier it is to risk one's life than to risk one's sense of self? Who would I be without these secrets?"

"You'd still be you. Just lighter."

"Perhaps."

Sharaf, carrying his rolled prayer rug, entered the porch and greeted them. He set the rug in a corner, took Kate's empty mug, and briefly narrowed his eyes at Fatima, whose face still betrayed conflicting emotions.

"I will bring you coffee," he said to her. "And more tea for you, Kate."

"*Shukran*, Sheikh." Kate glanced at Fatima. "You really sent him to pastry school?"

She laughed. "He asked, I obliged. My parties are can't-miss events for the desserts alone. I think his tortes have doubled my fundraising intake in recent months."

"My waistline hates you. But little girls throughout the Middle East owe you everything."

17

Kate was glad that Khalifa's representative hadn't yet called Sharaf. The team still had work to do, both planning for the next meeting with angry terrorists and ensuring that their other enemies, the CIA's brigade of boneheads, remained distracted by the deception playing out in their midst. They intended to make a return to the base in varying states of disarray and emotional turmoil; each had a particular target, which was causing some consternation in the master suite.

"I forbid you from spending time with him," Nick said as he shaved over the sink in the bathroom.

"You forbid me? Well, that changes everything."

Nick made a face at her in the mirror and flung a blob of lathered gel, speckled with dark stubble, into the basin from the end of his razor. Kate also made a face.

"Clean that up. And please dress in the outfit I've laid out on the bed."

"What?" He turned to look at her, half-shaven, but she had retreated into the bedroom.

She pointed to the bed when he joined her. He looked at a pair of army-green pants and a navy-blue T-shirt. The shirt, made of wicking material, was snug-fitting and something he tended to wear during workouts or under a heavier layer. The pants were his "nice" tactical trousers for the trip to Mali, in case he needed to look presentable.

"I don't understand."

"You don't understand what? How to get dressed?"

"Why this?"

"You need to look your best for Lacey?"

"Who?"

Kate rolled her eyes. "Your not-so-secret admirer."

"I still don't understand."

She heaved a sigh. "It's a good thing you're cute, because sometimes your brains are AWOL." She pressed her hands together as if in prayer. "I need you to use your caveman charms on Lacey."

"I'm really, really not following."

"Flirt with her."

"Flirt with her?"

"Yes, flirt with her. Lacey seems to have insight into what Weiss and Van Pelt are up to. She's invisible to them. Just sits at the table creating her PowerPoints and hearing everything. If we're serious about doing this, we need information. And I need you to collect it."

"Why can't you be friends with her?"

"You want me to be friends with someone who is blatantly lusting after my husband?"

"You're the expert manipulator, sweet pea."

"And I have it on good authority that you were once an incorrigible flirt."

"That was Nick P.K. Pre-Kate. That era of my life is long over."

"I need you to reach back into the past and find that old Nick. I don't see what the problem is."

"She...she makes me uncomfortable. She undresses me with her eyes."

Kate laughed, perhaps harder than she should have. "Sorry, sweetie. I don't mean to make light of your discomfort. I know how oppressive the female gaze can be." She choked back another peal of laughter. "I'm sorry, I'm sorry. Look, all you have to do is reciprocate a little, pay attention to her. Most people want to talk and be heard. Just listen."

"You or Amy, or even Fatima, would be better."

"She's not going to let anything slip to me, and Amy would just beat it out of her. And I have a different mission for Fatima. But you, with your pretty blue eyes and adorable dimples and sexy muscles and cute tush, are perfect for this job."

He pulled on the outfit. "I feel like a piece of meat."

"I'll make a deal with you. If you do this for me, I promise I'll become very jealous."

He narrowed his eyes, clearly intrigued. "What does that mean, exactly?"

"We'll see."

He pointed a finger at her. "I want jealousy of epic proportions."

"It'll rival your jealousy over my alone time with Chad."

He growled, and again Kella shot him a bemused look. Then he shook his head, sighing. "These people better be worth it."

Ω

Amy let loose a feral, appreciative meow when Kate and Nick joined everyone for breakfast. "Don't you two clean up nice? And we'll take five tickets to the gun show, please."

Nick flexed his biceps. "Why can't Jake flirt with Tracey?"

"Who?" Charlie whispered to Amy.

"I'm a happily married man," Jake said.

"So am I, but apparently that's not a disqualifying factor."

"You wanted to stay," Kate reminded him. "We could have been en route to our deserted island."

"The things I do for my country," he muttered.

"Don't worry," Kate said brightly, grinning at the team gathered around the table with food, phones, and tablets. "Misery loves company."

"Oh no," Amy whispered. "No, please..."

211

"You *all* wanted to stay. And now you're about to pay for it."

Kate knew she had Napoleonic tendencies; this was not some shocking revelation. Nick's teasing aside, it was a trait that had served her well over the years, especially in the male-dominated world of espionage. If one were a petite female with a youthful appearance, in danger of being overshadowed by the boisterous alphas and, worse, alpha wannabes in the room, one had better be willing to grab those alphas and alpha wannabes by the balls, figuratively or otherwise, and make them listen to reason.

She now had her team by the balls, and she relished their discomfort. Some experiences brought her an inordinate amount of joy; this was one of them, and she decided not to feel bad about it. To quote her husband, "Fuck 'em if they can't take a joke." Indeed, she thought with a thrilling hint of deviousness. Fuck 'em indeed.

Judging from the reactions around the table, Kate could be forgiven for thinking she had asked them to commit crimes against humanity. She expressed as much.

"This *is* a crime against humanity," Amy screeched.

"All I'm asking you to do is be nice."

There was much moaning and groaning and rending of garments. The massive cross was clutched and kissed and prayed upon. Kate sipped her tea and waited as certain individuals cycled through the five stages of grief at warp speed. Amy's grand finale was a keening wail to Pentecostal Jesus to smite Kate.

"Are you done?" asked the target of the Lord's wrath. Amy glared at her in response. "I will remind you yet *again* that you all wanted to stay."

"You really do need to get your woman under control," Amy told Nick.

Jake, seated beside Kate, turned and clasped her hands in his. "Please don't ever tell Lisa I said that."

"I seem to recall writing that line for you."

"Trust me, that won't matter."

"Then you better do exactly as I say." She smiled sweetly at her work husband, who grimaced.

"I, for one, relish the challenge," Fatima said. "I do not appreciate being referred to as 'just the translator.'"

"Suck up," Amy muttered.

"Look, I'm not excited about this either. But we need to be the maestros of this three-ringed circus. They've proven they can't be trusted. Shame on us if we make that mistake again. It may be a mistake we don't survive," Kate said.

They considered this. "I'm down to clown," Amy said finally. "But only because I don't want to die."

Ω

On paper, they were simple assignments. In practice, they were anything but. All Kate had asked them to do was be pleasant, be helpful, be accommodating. To carry on their canard of the dissolution of friendships, business partnerships, a marriage, all in the name of intelligence collection to protect themselves and the hostages.

They had gleefully embraced yesterday's pyrotechnics. Kate estimated that half of Timbuktu heard their howls of laughter as they prepared for the blowout fight. The fact that they had almost fooled Fraser was testament to their acting abilities and their willingness to highlight their less-pleasing personality quirks.

But they had to see it through. And that meant uncomfortable interactions that would test their limits of self-control.

Amy and Charlie were probably the angriest about their task. They, together with Fatima and Sharaf, were to make nice with Weiss and Van Pelt, answering all questions and obtaining further insight into Weiss's operational priorities and the resources at his disposal. If an opportunity presented itself, Fatima would use her feminine wiles on Van Pelt, who had once taken an awkward interest in her when Fatima had assisted the CIA station in Sanaa as an interpreter.

Jake was on the hook to bond with Blake Doyle, the beta to Chad Yorke's alpha. He could sympathize, the laidback beta to Nick's domineering alpha, the no-nonsense sergeant keeping the captain in line, doing all the work and receiving none of the credit. Or so he said to Nick, a huge grin on his face.

As Nick knew, his goal was to get Lacey Simms alone, but Kate, worried that he didn't fully understand the nuances of his mission, had pulled him aside for a quick lesson in the fine art of CIA case officering. Lacey might have hitched her wagon to the wrong star in Neil Weiss, but she wasn't stupid. She would bask in Nick's spotlight, but she might also see right through it.

"I thought I was supposed to flirt with her," Nick said, growing exasperated.

"You are. But at the same time, you need to project vulnerability, not scare her with your me-Tarzan-you-Jane routine. She needs to let down her guard and trust you enough to spill secrets."

"I'm better at the I-want-to-get-in-your-pants type of flirting."

"Charming."

"Worked on you, didn't it?"

"Just be subtle, please."

"Babe, come on. Subtlety is my middle name."

Kate had sighed. She loved Nick Cavanaugh more than anything in the world, but he had all the subtlety of a meat cleaver.

And then there was her own job, separating Chad from the pack. The Navy SEAL gazelle to her CIA case officer lion. No subtlety necessary. That gazelle would go willingly to his own death and enjoy every minute of it. For the lion, though, it was akin to eating rancid meat.

They had agreed to Van Pelt's plaintive plea to discuss the intelligence reports that Charlie had furnished after the Reaper attack, and they trooped into the conference room like petulant children and took their seats. Van Pelt stood at the head of the table, again wearing a suit and tie, again looking wildly out of place in his surroundings. Even the Frenchmen wore business-casual attire, trending more toward the casual at this point in the operation. Weiss's bushy muj beard looked particularly unkempt, and Kate wouldn't have been surprised to learn that he slept in his clothing, if he slept at all. He seemed like a nocturnal creature, happiest in a dark room staring at the feed from a drone on the hunt.

"Thank you for coming," Van Pelt began.

Kate interrupted him, turning her attention to Fraser and Dubois. "Is the Gulfstream ready?"

Dubois responded. "The Gulfstream is offline. It underwent routine inspection and the flight crew discovered that some parts were due to be replaced. We've ordered the necessary items from Paris, but it's unclear when they will arrive."

"You've got to be kidding me," Kate said.

"I'm sorry, Madame Cavanaugh. We're working the issue, but we cannot fly the plane at this time."

Ardouin turned to Dubois, but spoke in English. "The president's advisers have given an ultimatum. We must cease our involvement in this lunacy."

"Henri, not in front of our guests."

"I knew these people were trouble from the start, Laurent, and I made that clear to the Palace. There will be consequences."

A muscle in Dubois's jaw twitched, and for a second Kate wondered if this was Ardouin playing along or if he was expressing his true sentiments. Insults in French lacked the same wallop as insults in English or Arabic, in her opinion—the language was just too pretty—but she could have her fun.

"It's amazing you can walk, Henri, with that self-righteous protocol pole shoved so far up your ass."

Ardouin regarded her scornfully. "How mature."

"Angling for director-general, I presume." She turned to Fraser and offered a sympathetic look. "Have fun trying to keep the relationship on track with this one in charge. Yikes."

"Madame Cavanaugh—"

"Devlin," Kate said icily. Nick flinched. Chad smirked.

Ardouin smiled thinly. "Madame Devlin, we have much to discuss with your colleagues. Is it too much to ask that you control yourself?"

Kate shoved back from the table and stood. "I want no part of this lunacy, either."

"Can we take ten minutes?" Nick asked with a sigh. "Maybe get some coffee?"

"Of course," Dubois said. "We shall reconvene shortly."

♊

Nick slipped out of the conference room and followed Ardouin to the men's room. The chief of protocol had just settled himself at a urinal when Nick joined him. Ardouin's initial glance became a double take as Nick checked each stall for company and then stood with his back against the main door, arms crossed over his chest, facing Ardouin's profile.

"Ah, Monsieur Cavanaugh, is there something you need?"

"Yes."

"And you need it here?"

"Just do your business and I'll explain."

"It is somewhat difficult to...do my business under your watchful gaze."

Nick smirked. "Stage fright, Henri?" He turned and faced the same direction as Ardouin, leaning a shoulder against the door. "Better?"

Ardouin finished, washed his hands, and then waited, a hint of wariness dueling with curiosity in his eyes.

Nick studied him. "You're playing along, right?"

"*Oui.* Am I failing to convince?"

"No, you're a little *too* convincing."

He smirked. "I did know you were trouble."

"I need a favor."

Self-satisfaction pushed aside the wariness in his eyes. "Oh?"

216

Nick debated the wisdom of what he was about to ask one last time. In the end, concern overtook common sense.

"Kate intends to spend some time with Chad. Alone," he said through gritted teeth. "Except I don't want them alone. I want you to...to chaperone. Wherever they wander off to, I want you to be near enough to see everything."

Ardouin raised his eyebrows. "You don't trust your wife, Monsieur Cavanaugh?"

"I don't trust Chad."

"Perhaps I should rephrase. You don't trust your wife to take care of herself? After all, she nearly decapitated you with that slap." A smile tugged at the corner of his mouth.

"How do you think Chad would react if she slapped him?"

Ardouin frowned.

"She promised she'd stay in open, public areas. The cafeteria, the patio, places like that. You just need to loiter nearby. But make it look natural. And call me if he does anything, and I mean *anything*, inappropriate."

"That she would consider inappropriate or that you would consider inappropriate?" Ardouin laughed, not unkindly, at Nick's consternation. "Does Madame Cavanaugh know that you have cornered me *à la toilette* to ask this favor?"

"She does not. And I would prefer it stay that way. I'm not keen to get slapped again."

"You are most lucky that I have university-aged daughters. I have perfected my discreet loitering over the last few years. It would be my pleasure to assist."

The tension in Nick's shoulders eased ever so slightly. "Thank you."

ʊ

Sans Kate, they reconvened in the conference room ten minutes later, all carrying froufrou European coffees or potent espressos in delicate demitasses, and heaping plates of croissants and pastries. The cafeteria staff remained in awe of their ability to pack down various forms of carbohydrates in quantities meant to serve the sizable DSGE contingent wandering about. As everyone resettled themselves, Nick noticed that they were one additional body short. Ardouin noticed, too, and whispered something in Dubois's ear before excusing himself. Nick reminded himself to stay calm and trust both Kate and Ardouin. The prickly chief of protocol was a man of his word; Nick had no doubt of that.

Van Pelt took a sip of his cappuccino and stood to call the meeting to order. "We're most eager to discuss your reporting. Particularly the development concerning Khalifa's Tunisia-based son."

Weiss brandished a much-read and annotated report, the paper crushed in his fist. "What's his name? The son. What's his name?"

Fatima translated the question into Arabic. Sharaf whispered his response. Kate had told him to withhold Talha's name for the time being, a tantalizing detail that would ensure the CIA's continued interest in their activities. "Khalifa didn't offer a name, and Sharaf didn't pry."

"You didn't think to ask a simple question?" Weiss sneered at Sharaf, shaking his head in disdain.

Sharaf, who had his marching orders from Kate, remained calm and composed. Fatima translated. "He's sorry he failed to gather this key piece of information. But he felt it was dangerous to do more than listen. Khalifa is a man who values his privacy, and clearly wants to protect this unnamed son."

"It's more than we had before," Charlie reminded Weiss. Lacey and Giraud nodded their agreement. "We may learn the son's name."

"And how do you expect to do that?" Weiss asked.

"Khalifa could still reach out," Jake said.

Van Pelt cleared his throat. "That does beg a key question. If Khalifa desires another meeting, are you willing to proceed?"

Nick and Jake exchanged a glance. They were on the hook to sell this part of the deception.

"It depends," Nick said cautiously.

"On what?"

He acted like a man chastened. "On Kate."

"Oh, come on," Amy said. "We have the American side willing to negotiate. It can be done without her." She paused, briefly closing her eyes. "With your guidance, Chief, it can be done."

Van Pelt seemed to inflate. He adjusted his tie, straightening the Windsor knot. "With full insight into your actions thus far, I believe I can offer the necessary operational guidance to ensure success as we move forward."

Nick gave Amy tremendous credit for her reaction, or lack thereof, more accurately. Her face relaxed into its beatific gaze, and she stared through Van Pelt and Weiss, a dreamy smile on her lips.

"It's not that we don't trust you," Nick said.

"We always trusted you," Jake added.

"But Kate had the lead on this. The plan, such that it is, is in her head. She shared what was necessary for us to know at each stage of the operation."

"Wow, bro," Blake muttered.

"Look, we're doing our best to get her back on board, just until we can secure another meeting and pass a beaconed object to Khalifa."

Weiss and Van Pelt shared a glance. "We're very happy to hear that," Van Pelt said.

"But after that, this ends. We need to get home and put our affairs in order before she sics the lawyers on me."

"We understand, Mr. Cavanaugh. And we're sorry to see things end so badly amongst you," Van Pelt said, almost managing to sound sympathetic.

"*C'est la vie*, right?" Nick said, shrugging. He shot a quick smile at Lacey, who bit her lip and blushed.

Weiss slapped the table. "Enough of the touchy-feely bullshit. Let's talk ops."

♌

Kate hugged herself despite the strength of the sun. She heard footsteps and a hand touched her back, lingering. She resisted the urge to pull away. Instead, she half-turned and offered a tremulous smile.

"Want to sit?" Chad asked.

Kate nodded, and he led her toward the cluster of tables under an awning outside the small cafeteria. He pulled out a chair for her and then drew his close, sitting so that their shoulders nearly touched. The hand returned to her back, hot through the thin cotton of her shirt.

"Is it really over?" he asked.

"I think so."

"I'm sorry."

"It's for the best. It's just hard, you know? Didn't even make it two years."

Chad was silent for a moment. "You always told me you weren't the marrying type."

"I always thought I wasn't. Then I stupidly married a man who *definitely* wasn't the marrying type."

"I was shocked when I heard about everything. About what happened in Yemen, you leaving the Agency, marrying some grunt." He spoke calmly, but Kate heard the hurt in his voice.

"It all happened so quickly. We got caught up in the stress, the excitement, the danger. We barely knew each other when he proposed, but I thought he was everything I wanted. I thought I could change the parts of him I didn't like. But you men are hard to train."

Chad smiled.

"It was such a whirlwind. Then, once the headiness passed, the honeymoon was over, literally and figuratively. Old habits die hard. For him, being faithful."

"How did you find out?"

"I searched his phone. The texts, the photos." She shuddered.

He shifted uncomfortably, and Kate was glad she had no idea what was on Chad's phone.

"Everyone has secrets," he mumbled.

Kate went through Nick's phone all the time, usually to remove racy photos of herself that either he had taken or she had sent. He was allowed to store them on an old computer unconnected to the internet; she insisted that his iPhone camera roll be PG-rated before they traveled internationally, especially to or through countries that were less forgiving of possession of explicit material. In the world in which they operated, that seemed to be most countries. She also had to pretend to be him when his parents, especially his father, got on his nerves. Approximately half of the text messages he had exchanged with them over the last couple of years came from her, thus preserving some semblance of civility in their oftentimes contentious relationship. Nick Cavanaugh had no secrets, at least not from her. Of that she was certain.

"Perhaps."

As Chad's fingers caressed her back, she saw movement in the cafeteria. Someone sat at a table near the windows, occupied with his phone and a sheaf of papers. Ardouin. He glanced her way, expressionless, and then returned to his work.

"You loved him, though?"

"I did. Maybe I still do. It's hard to explain. There's something about him."

"If I hadn't..." He frowned, looking from her to the table. "If I hadn't..."

"If you hadn't cheated on me?" she prompted.

He set his jaw, but nodded once. "Do you think we would have made it?"

"It's possible," she said, but her tone was noncommittal.

"I really messed up."

"So did your hookup, by leaving her underwear behind."

"You just walked out and never looked back. I never got a chance to explain." She raised an eyebrow.

"To apologize. Nothing was ever the same after you left."

What Chad didn't know was that she had already intended to dump him before she came home from a training course in advance of her posting to

Yemen, swung by his apartment to clear out her one small drawer of clothes and toiletries, and found a lacy red thong on the floor, half under the bed. A lacy red thong that was most definitely not her own. She had always appreciated that woman's mistake; it had saved her from explaining to Chad that she just wasn't that into him.

"I heard you have big news," she said, trying to redirect the conversation. "When's the due date?"

He finally withdrew his hand from her back. "Early December."

"You don't seem too excited. I always thought you wanted kids."

"I wanted them with you," he said quietly.

Kate was at a loss for words. "Oh."

"You were so careful." He shook his head, smiling ruefully. "And I should have been more careful."

"Are you going to marry her?"

He shrugged. "I know I should." He glanced at her. "But marriage is a big step."

"Is she keen to be Mrs. Yorke?"

"Yeah. And if I don't make her Mrs. Yorke, I'm going to pay. I'll pay either way, I guess."

"Sounds like you have some big decisions to make."

He nodded stiffly.

"Take it from me, if you don't really love her, don't get—"

"You took his name," he blurted out.

Kate started. "What?"

"You took his name. You told me you'd never take a man's name if you got married."

"I did," she acknowledged. "But like the marriage, it just sort of happened."

No one had been more surprised than Nick, not even Kate herself, that she decided to take his name. She didn't think it had ever occurred to him that she would take it. She was a staunch feminist, openly committed to smashing the patriarchy, and for most of her life she had been critical of the institution of marriage and what she believed to be its effective subjugation of women and the erasure of their identities.

It was Amy Kowalski of all people, her sister in patriarchy-smashing shenanigans, who had framed the issue in a way that Kate had never considered. During a pre-wedding girls' night, tipsy on tequila around the fire pit in Kate and Nick's backyard, Kate had opened up about her internal struggle and how she felt like a sellout for even considering changing her name. She had always been Kate Devlin. Amy had listened to Kate's self-pitying mewling, knocked back a shot, and slammed the tiny glass bearing the CIA's seal onto the small table holding their top-shelf tequila, lime wedges, and salt.

"Do you belong to your father?" she had asked.

Kate, gravely insulted, had sputtered a negative.

"The way the world sees it, you belong to Papa Devlin or to Nick Cavanaugh. The way *I* see it is that you get to choose who belongs to you."

Kate's tequila-soaked brain had attempted to process this line of logic. "You mean...?"

"I mean you can stay Kate Devlin, daughter of a woman who took a man's name because that's what society expects, or you can take Nick's name and own that shit like the proud feminazi you are. Kate Cavanaugh is Nick's, but Nick Cavanaugh is Kate's."

Kate had mulled this over, warming to the idea. "That makes no sense, but at the same time, all the sense in the world."

Amy had looked at the bottle of tequila. "Some people get their best ideas in the shower. I get mine with a buzz on. That sexy hunk of man belongs to you."

"Goddamn right he does."

And so the decision had been made, and Kate hadn't had a moment of regret. Her alpha caveman knew who wore the pants, knew which Cavanaugh was in charge, and didn't hesitate to let anyone else know it, either.

"Kate Cavanaugh had a nice ring to it. I'm a sucker for alliteration," she told Chad.

"What's next?"

"Becoming Kate Devlin again. An older, hopefully wiser Kate Devlin. And then...I don't know. We'll see."

She slid him a look that could be interpreted in a number of ways. He smiled.

"I'll really enjoy getting to know that older, wiser Kate Devlin."

♌

To separate his gazelle from the pack, Nick didn't have to do anything but grin, exposing his crater-like dimples, and nod toward the door.

"Want to look over my sketches with me?" he asked.

Lacey Simms nearly tripped over Charlie in her rush to his side. "Chief, I'm going to review Nick's sketches," she said to Weiss.

He grunted, absorbed in his questioning of Sharaf, who, via Fatima, was recounting his private conversation with Khalifa on the day of the drone strike for the third time. Diana Fraser shot Nick a warning look as he touched the small of Lacey's back to guide her through the door. He winked, and she shook her head in resignation.

"Damn, that room starts to feel small with all those personalities," he said as they headed toward the cafeteria.

"I thought I was the only one."

"That boss of yours is an interesting fellow." Nick led her to a table in the corner, opposite from where Ardouin was camped out near the windows. "Very single-minded in his focus."

"That's a polite way to describe it."

"How would you describe it?"

Lacey pursed her lips. "I think he can be a little bit obsessive."

"Maybe sometimes misses the bigger picture? Runs roughshod over his subordinates?"

She shrugged. "We all know how important the mission is. That's what we're here for."

"Still, wouldn't it be nice to be treated with respect? Recognized for your contributions?"

"It's all about the mission," she repeated.

Nick flipped open his sketchpad and pulled a charcoal pencil from the top spiral. The first page was his rendering of the Reaper attack. The moment the drone appeared through the swirling sand had been burned into his memory, and he immortalized it on paper.

"That must have been terrifying," Lacey said.

"I'm used to people shooting at me, but this was a first."

"Khalifa isn't worth your lives," she said quietly.

"Not everyone seems to agree."

"It shouldn't have happened." She reached over to flip the page, turning to a portrait of Kella. "Your dog?"

"Just some stray that Kate wants to adopt. Her problem, not mine."

Her eyes flicked to his. She was young, probably in her late twenties, and often wore a contemplative expression when she wasn't staring at him with unbridled interest in the conference room. He felt bad for her; she probably did have a lot to contribute, but Weiss clearly didn't want to hear it, not unless it was a straight shot to Khalifa, for which he would invariably take credit.

"You both seemed happy when you arrived," she said.

"Anyone can fake it." He flipped back to the Reaper scene, studying it. "It's amazing what a near-death experience will do to clear the mind and reset your priorities."

"She seemed genuinely upset when she thought you had been killed."

"She's *really* good at faking it. Come to find out the next day that she planned to run back to Chad. He's her ex, you know."

"Trust me, we all know."

Nick muted his reflexive growl and focused on the task at hand. "Looks like a Navy SEAL is more her speed than some dumb jarhead."

She tentatively touched his forearm. "I don't think you're a dumb jarhead."

His dimples made another appearance, and she returned the smile. He paged to a fresh sheet in the sketchbook and began an outline, the charcoal pencil making a pleasing scratching sound atop the thick paper.

"What are you drawing?"

"You."

"Me?"

"Sure. I like to draw pretty things."

Lacey blushed a deep red. As the outline of her hair and face took shape, Nick couldn't wait to show Kate. This would be sure to spur that jealousy toward his goal of epic proportions. Then his hand faltered. Would this push Kate over the edge from playful jealousy to actual anger? Kate was the only woman he had ever drawn, outside of purely operational situations. His portrait of Ratma, which Kate had insisted he do, didn't count. But this, this felt like a betrayal.

Lacey noticed the faltering. She touched his forearm again. "Are you okay?"

What had Kate said? Be vulnerable, be unthreatening, and collect intelligence. "It's just that I used to draw Kate a lot. Back when we were happy."

"You don't have to..."

"But I want to." He resumed rendering her hair on the page. From the corner of his eye, he saw how pleased she was.

"You're so talented. Somehow, I think your drawings are realer than a photograph."

"A photograph captures a moment in time. A drawing captures truth."

She nodded, rapt as her portrait took shape on the page. He could almost hear her thoughts. What was her truth?

"Tell me, how did Weiss find us? Is he really that good?"

She tensed. He continued drawing, occasionally glancing at her. She avoided eye contact.

"I ask only because it seems much too coincidental that he triangulated Khalifa's position on the very day of our meeting, and the Reaper was able to find us, despite a severe storm that limited visibility, without...assistance."

Her eyes welled with tears. "It was me," she whispered.

"You? I find that hard to believe." His pencil worked on her cheekbones, deliberately raising them just a smidge. "Now, if you told me that it was Chad..." He grinned, but it was a struggle.

She looked torn. "It...it..."

"What?" he said gently, giving her his full attention. "You can tell me anything. I won't get upset."

"It was all of us," she said in a barely audible voice. "Chad and Blake put a beacon on your truck and I gave the Air Force the sheikh's phone number. The Reaper had it loaded on its collection platform. We couldn't get a bird over Timbuktu early enough to track you from the city using the beacon. Then it took hours of searching the region to find the phone, and by then the storm had blown in." She gripped his arm. "I'm so, so sorry. I never should have said anything about the phone number."

Nick cocked his head. "How did you even know his number?"

"I did the research on the emissary's number. We had call logs from French collection platforms and local cellular providers, but no identifying information. It was easy to determine which was the sheikh's, based on date and time. Like the time the emissary called when we were all meeting together."

"Ah. That's actually really impressive. I'm sorry Weiss took credit for your idea."

"Maybe he was trying to protect me."

"Do you really think that's the case?"

She spoke to the table. "No."

He resumed drawing. "If we're able to get another meeting with Khalifa and pass a beaconed item, can we trust Weiss and Van Pelt to let us clear the area before they strike?"

"I don't think so," she replied cautiously. "Weiss...well, he's determined to get Khalifa. He's expressed no remorse over what happened with the Reaper, and he's bullying Van Pelt to convince the director to lift the standdown. They don't think there's any real hope of rescuing the hostages because there's no way Khalifa will be anywhere near them, but maybe they have a shot at Khalifa if he agrees to meet you again. I'm worried the director will agree, and they'll strike immediately so as not to lose him."

"I'd be a lot more willing to take one last meeting with Khalifa if I knew they'd let us get off the X."

"Maybe I could help you. Protect you."

Nick nodded slowly, still drawing. Channeling Kate, he said nothing. People hated silence, she always said. Would Lacey fill the silence?

"I'll give you a Faraday bag for the beaconed item. And I'll remove the sheikh's number from the system. Switch it for another. That way, if another drone deploys, it won't find the target, not right away. You'd have a chance to get clear."

"You'd do that for me?"

She blushed again. "Yes."

He smiled. "I would be eternally grateful."

18

THEY TOOK TOM PATTERSON back to the house for dinner, much to Sharaf's irritation. The Yemeni tribesman, unquestionably in control in the kitchen, doled out tasks in terse Arabic and brooked no questions or dissent about his planned menu of kofta, couscous, and tabouleh. Kate and Nick were instructed to wash and chop vegetables, but Nick was distracted by the sketchpad in his backpack. Could Kate hear the guilt calling from its pages?

"Are you going to chop those onions, or just stand there staring at them?" she asked.

He looked at her cutting board, on which a tall pile of chopped parsley rested beside sliced tomatoes. The red onions on his on board were still whole. She took one and began peeling it.

"What's on your mind? And don't you dare say nothing."

He braced his arms against the counter and hung his head. "I betrayed you."

"Oh?"

"I drew Kacey."

"Lacey."

"I told her she's pretty and started a rough sketch."

"She is pretty."

"But I *drew* her."

"Was she naked or something...?"

Nick looked at her. "I've never drawn anyone but you."

"Really?"

"You didn't know that?"

"You never told me. I assumed 'stunning portraits in charcoal' was part of your incorrigible-flirt, get-in-a-girl's-pants routine." She cut into the onion, lopping off the ends.

"No. Only you."

She sniffled and dabbed at her eyes with the back of her left hand.

"I'm sorry."

"Sweetie, it's the onions."

"Oh."

As she returned her focus to the vegetables, a soft smile tugged at her lips. "To be clear, though, I'm very, *very* jealous."

Ω

Dinner ran long on kofta and conversation. Tom Patterson expressed his amazement that the two hardcore infantry Marines he knew from Iraq, men who had little time or tolerance for drama, histrionics, or really emotions of any kind, were willing and talented participants in drama and histrionics, and did have emotions running the full spectrum of the human experience that they were willing to put on graphic display.

"We just work here," Nick said with a shrug.

"You had that entire room of intelligence officers, with their allegedly superior bullshit detectors, eating from the palm of your hand. I loved it."

"Did we fool you?" Fatima asked.

Patterson smiled. "If I said no, would you believe me?"

"We need you to play along, of course," Fatima continued.

"It would be my pleasure to have a little fun at the CIA's expense."

Fatima tucked a lock of silky hair behind her ear. "It's rather astounding what people will believe when they are desperate to believe."

"Like Van Pelt believing that a beautiful, intelligent woman has the slightest bit of interest in him?"

The sounds of supper abruptly fell silent. Sharaf, whose command of English had improved considerably but who still struggled with the pace of their conversations, narrowed his eyes as he watched everyone's reactions. Patterson looked down at his plate, his cheeks reddening. Fatima turned to Kate, her cheeks even redder, and begged with her eyes to restart conversation.

Jake beat Kate to it. "I got a hell of an intel dump from Doyle while you two were off flirting with Chad and Lacey," he said, waving a hand in Kate and Nick's direction. "As always, the loyal sergeant doing all the work."

Nick smirked. "I should have busted you down to private when I had the chance."

"Apparently that was one of Chad's favorite plays."

"To be fair," Patterson said, the fire on his cheeks having faded to a warm pink, "some of those SEALs are out of control and could use a heavy hand."

"I agree," Jake said, "but according to Doyle, Chad went after guys he perceived were stealing his thunder, standing out. He had a reputation within the teams as a spotlight ranger."

Fatima raised an eyebrow. "A spotlight ranger?"

"You know, a buddy fucker," Amy offered, then laughed at the confusion on Fatima's face.

"Someone who isn't a team player," Patterson said. "A guy who only leads or performs when senior officers are watching, who takes all the credit."

"You Americans and your slang," she murmured. "It's very...descriptive."

"Doyle said they basically ran him out after a few years. No one wanted to operate with him."

Nick turned to Kate. "You dated that."

Kate ignored him. "Then what's Blake deal?"

"He got injured during an op in Afghanistan, wasn't going to be cleared for the fun stuff, and decided to take a medical discharge. Had some trouble in the aftermath readjusting to civilian life. Chad had left the previous year and gotten hired on by the Agency's paramilitary division. He pulled Blake into the fold and helped him get back on his feet. Blake feels like he owes Chad."

"Explains a lot," Kate said casually.

Amy pounced. "What?"

"Nothing. Just an observation."

"That was a weighted 'explains a lot.' You're holding out on us."

"If we ever did anything like that, which we never would, it would be for your own good."

"Liar, liar, pants on fire."

"It's not important."

Amy arched an eyebrow, but let the matter drop. "Weiss and Van Pelt are desperate to sacrifice us in their quest for Khalifa and hostage glory."

"I would expect nothing less."

"What's-her-name—"

"Lacey," they all said.

"—admitted that Chad beaconed the truck and they loaded Sharaf's phone number onto the Reaper's collection platform. Very thorough, you spies. She thinks we'd be subject to another strike if we take a beaconed item to the next meeting, the assumption being that the hostages won't be present and therefore not at risk," Nick said.

"Bad assumption," Amy said. "If I'm Khalifa, I'm using those hostages as human shields."

"I can't believe I didn't consider the implications of them knowing Sharaf's number," Kate said.

"None of us did," Nick reminded her. "However, fear not, in Stacey's quest to get into *my* pants, she said she'd give us a Faraday bag for the beacon and switch out that number for some other random number. She controls the details, not Weiss and Van Pelt. They'll never know and we'll be off the grid."

"Forgive me if I'm reluctant to trust a young officer who knew exactly what she was doing when she loaded that number in the first place. She knew they would strike. She could have told Fraser and stopped it, but she sat there and watched that entire travesty play out." Kate took a deep breath to tamp down raw emotion. "No. We can't trust them."

"What are we going to do if Khalifa calls and they hand us that tub of girl goop?" Jake asked.

"We have our own Faraday bags to block signals, but Sharaf needs his phone. It has too much valuable backstopping on it to leave behind," Kate replied. "Everyone's phones go into airplane mode and the bags, only to make an appearance if mission critical, and we search every vehicle before we head out."

"I'm starting to think that Khalifa won't call," Charlie said. "I'm worried that they executed the hostages and we'll find the video on the internet."

"If that does happen, it's solidly on Weiss," Kate said.

"Will that help you sleep at night?"

"Look, they're recovering from a traumatic incident the same way we are, taking stock of security protocols, maybe engaging in a spy hunt or two given Yunis's paranoia."

"Why so glum, chum?" Amy asked him. "You're usually our ray of sunshine."

"Dunno. I guess I know deep down that no matter what we do, we probably can't save the hostages."

"The job was only to find them, which we did," Kate reminded him gently.

"But..." He looked at her imploringly, clearly remembering their post-drone attack discussion. *What if we're thinking too small? What if* we *could get the hostages back?*

She sighed. "We can't do much if Khalifa doesn't call."

He rubbed his face. "I think about them all the time, wondering what they're going through. And now, after the drone strike, it's hard to believe that things didn't get worse."

Amy squeezed his shoulder. "Keep the faith, Junior Pastor Charlie. We're not done yet."

Sharaf stood. "Dessert," he said in English. He motioned to Kate and Nick. "You will help."

They followed him to the kitchen, where he cut into a large baking pan of namoura, a traditional Arabic dessert. Once it was sliced, he handed the pan to Nick and a pile of small plates to Kate. Then he stood chest to chest with Nick, a spatula held menacingly close to Nick's nose. The tribesman's green eyes were bright and lively.

"This Tom, you will speak to him," he told Nick in Arabic.

"About what?" Nick asked, leaning back to avoid the spatula.

"I do not like him."

Kate bit her lower lip to keep from smiling. Nick considered his response. "Why?" he finally asked.

"He should not be pursuing her."

"He's not pursuing her. They're just talking."

"His interest is not pure."

"They're really just talking," Nick said. "He's a nice guy, that's all."

"She says he is divorced, with children. He must be a bad husband and father. A bad man. I do not want him talking to her."

"Sharaf…"

"Do not argue with me. He does not understand us or our ways." The Yemeni's eyes flashed as he stared into Nick's. "He does not understand," he repeated emphatically. "You will speak to him."

Nick looked at Kate.

"You have your orders, Marine."

Nick allowed a soft groan to escape. Sharaf glowered at him, but withdrew the spatula to a safe distance and pointed it toward the porch.

"Dessert," he said.

Ω

After they polished off most of the namoura and chatted over coffee and tea, Kate called Cherif to ask for a ride back to the base for Tom Patterson. Then she leaned toward Nick and whispered in his ear that he had five minutes until Cherif's mobile unit arrived.

Nick stood and motioned Patterson toward the door. "It's a nice evening. Let's wait outside."

Patterson looked like he was about to object, but Fatima had disappeared into the house with everyone else, all carrying dishes to the kitchen. He nodded once and joined Nick in the front yard, Kella at their side. It was a pleasant night by Timbuktu standards, less humid than it had been the last few weeks, the mosquitoes kept at bay by a light breeze. Nick looked up at the night sky; the stars were obscured by a light cloud cover, although the half-moon made an occasional appearance. He felt Patterson watching him.

"You've done well for yourself, Nick."

"Thank you, sir."

The retired colonel smiled. "You don't need to call me 'sir' anymore, you know."

"Yes, sir."

"It's hard enough leaving the Corps and reentering the real world, but to build a successful business from scratch in a field teeming with flag officers and the spec-ops community? Truly impressive. I'll talk you up wherever I can."

"You can't talk about anything you see or hear during this operation."

"Then I'll settle for vouching that you and Jake and Kate are top-notch talent."

"That's kind of you, sir."

"It's nice to see the good guys do well. Remember that major from the—"

"Look, about Fatima," Nick interrupted.

"What about her?"

"It's a complicated situation."

"Divorces often are," Patterson said dryly.

"The divorce was the least complicated part of that situation."

Patterson knitted his eyebrows. "What are you saying?"

"I'm not saying anything. Her story is hers to tell. I hope you'll respect her wishes, whatever they may be."

He drew back, insulted. "Of course. I would never—"

"I know. I'm only saying that it's complicated. Just listen to what she says." Nick paused. "Or doesn't say."

Nick heard the sounds of three trucks arriving, Cherif's mobile unit, and the Tamashek greetings exchanged with their static security element. The guard force commander rapped on the heavy gate before entering the compound, offering a casual salute. In Arabic, he told Nick to take his time, and then he rejoined his unit.

"Look, I've enjoyed chatting with her. It's entirely up to her if it goes any further."

Nick clapped the colonel on the shoulder and walked him to the gate. "I'm glad to hear that. Otherwise, I'll have to kill you. And I really don't want to kill you."

Patterson stared at him, a multitude of questions in his eyes. Then he nodded, shook Nick's hand, and left with the Tuaregs.

Ω

The call came the next evening, from the same burner phone as the other calls. Sharaf and the emissary exchanged traditional greetings, offered well-wishes, and praised Allah before turning the focus to business. The familiar voice on the line was controlled, but a hint of rage simmered under the calm.

"Brother Khalifa is displeased, Sheikh."

Sharaf tried to match the caller's tone. "As am I."

"Brother Khalifa was disrespected, his property destroyed, his men injured. Our trust was betrayed."

"A grave injustice," Sharaf said.

"Those responsible must be held accountable."

Kate, Nick, and Fatima, gathered around Sharaf, exchanged worried looks. Sharaf chose his words carefully.

"I have spent much time with the French and American representatives. I believe they are blameless."

"That is for Brother Khalifa to decide," the voice said.

"I must have your word that no harm will come to the Frenchwoman or the Americans," Sharaf said, more forcefully. He ignored Kate's mouthed warning to throttle back.

"Brother Khalifa has no intention of harming the Westerners. He wishes to continue discussions." The caller paused. "He wishes to educate."

"As long as they will be safe, I believe they will agree to meet."

"They will be safe."

"Then we are ready to proceed."

"In two days' time, at first light, drive east toward Gourma-Rharous. *Inshallah* we shall find each other along the banks of the river."

"*Inshallah*, brother."

"May God keep you safe, Sheikh Sharaf." The caller disconnected.

"I'm not sure I've ever heard a more ominous conversation," Nick said, as Kate motioned Jake, Amy, and Charlie back into the room.

"Think Fraser will convince them to give us stars on the Memorial Wall if we die?" Amy asked.

"Only I get a star," Charlie said. "You all will be nothing but an internal investigation and shoddy coverup."

"The goal is no stars on any wall," Kate reminded them. "Especially a star for Charlie. Because if he dies, Fraser will kill us, and then kill us again for good measure."

"That is absolutely true," Charlie said. "But I trust you have a plan to keep us alive?"

Kate shrugged. "*On verra*. We'll see."

Amy raised the giant cross and kissed it. "The Lord is my shepherd; I shall not want. Into the lands of the Islamic Maghreb go I."

♌

Van Pelt's excitement caused nonstop jiggling in multiple extremities. He made several attempts to lift and sip his cappuccino before his right hand cooperated, and even so he dribbled some on his charcoal suit. Amy slipped into her beatific trance to avoid verbalizing her thoughts while Lacey discreetly slid him a napkin. He dabbed at his lapel and then uncapped his expensive pen, poising his hand over his legal pad. He nodded to Weiss.

"You must get the beaconed item into Khalifa's possession," Weiss declared.

"Oh, is that all?" Kate asked.

Weiss ignored her and spoke to Nick and Jake. "By any means necessary. Khalifa must take that item."

"He definitely seems super into women's beauty products," Kate said with an acidic laugh. "So good luck with that."

Van Pelt's nerves again got the better of him. He made illegible notes on his pad, and when he spoke to Kate, he did so while looking past her into the middle distance. Shades of Yemen, Kate thought. He could barely look at her then, too.

"You won't be accompanying your team, Ms. Devlin?"

"Are you kidding? This is a suicide mission."

"You don't need her," Weiss said.

"Here's the problem," Nick said. "The caller made clear that Khalifa expects to meet the Westerners, both French and American. His bullshit antenna will be way up already, and if the French rep doesn't show, I'm worried what that means for the rest of us."

"And the hostages," Jake added.

"And the hostages." Nick paused. "This is still about the hostages, right?"

"Of course, of course," Van Pelt said hurriedly, adjusting his tie. "The hostages are our top priority. Mr. Weiss?"

"Top priority," Weiss said in a tone clearly meant to humor Van Pelt. Lacey, her eyes fixed on Nick, shifted uncomfortably.

"Glad to hear it," Nick said. "Now, as we said before, we stand by our commitments and—"

Kate scoffed. "That's a good one."

"Kate, could we please keep our personal life out of our professional engagements?" he asked quietly.

"Are you doing this or what?" Weiss asked impatiently. "You really don't need her."

Van Pelt looked less sure of that assertion. Nick's jaw muscles twitched in time with the muscles in his forearms as he squeezed his hands together atop the table.

Kate smiled and used a taunting tone. "What do you say, sweetheart? Do you need me?"

"We need you," he said, looking straight ahead.

"Oh, darling, that's not what I asked. Do *you* need me?"

His biceps joined the twitch-fest. "I need you," he choked out.

"For the love of Christ, this is brutal," Weiss muttered. "So are you in?" he asked Kate.

She laughed. "Absolutely not."

Weiss let loose a barrage of profanity under his breath and stood, shoving his wheeled chair against the wall. He ran a hand over his bushy hair and paced behind Van Pelt.

Van Pelt rotated his neck. His hands trembled. "I...I've been given..."

"Spit it out, Stan," Kate said.

"The director has given me the authority to increase your fee for your continued participation in this operation."

Kate raised an eyebrow and avoided glancing at Nick and Jake. This was an unexpected development. "How much?"

Van Pelt wrote a number on a sheet of paper, folded it, and passed it down the table. Kate opened it and stared at the figure, doing some quick calculations that involved division by seven. She pulled a pen from her backpack, crossed out Van Pelt's number, and replaced it with one of her own. She refolded the paper and sent it back to the director's senior representative in Mali. He opened it, visibly paled, and nodded once.

"I want proof that the transfer has been initiated by tonight, close of business Washington time. We'll hold the equivalent agreed-upon sum in cash, taken from operational funds. The cash will be returned upon electronic receipt of payment. Additionally, you *and* DCIA will sign a revised contract that will be made public, along with our original contract, should any kinetic action be launched against us. The terms are nonnegotiable, and will cover only this upcoming meeting with Khalifa. Any further efforts will require additional payments and separate contracts."

Fraser, Dubois, and Ardouin shared a three-way glance. Fraser seemed to be enjoying herself. Van Pelt was, on his best days, a mediocre manager, barely capable of making routine decisions without assistance. He didn't have a leadership bone in his body. And here, in the heart of Mali, facing off against his former subordinate, he had brought a knife to a gunfight. To his credit, he seemed to know it.

"Agreed," he said.

"Then I'm in," Kate said. "Give us the beaconed item, we'll get the cash, and then we'll be on our way. A pleasure doing business with you."

19

LATER THAT NIGHT, IN the wee hours, as the minutes ticked by to a pre-dawn departure from the compound into the Sahelian unknown, Nick massaged Kate's back. His thumbs bumped over knots formed by an interruption to her daily yoga routine, contact with despised former colleagues, and the anxiety inherent in face-to-face meetings with terrorists. The knot inside her right scapula was stubborn. She winced under the pressure.

"Sorry," he murmured, easing up. "But you're really tight."

"Can't imagine why."

"Are you worried about losing me to Macey?"

"Am I that transparent?"

"You'll be fine. You'll have Chad and all your future children."

"Ugh, kids."

"Plus, you'll be a stepmom."

"I do hope someone in future Baby Yorke's life has his or her best interests at heart."

"Maybe Chad will use those millions he stole to provide the best possible life for his child." Nick's hands moved south, finding more knots where her lower lats met the crest of her glutes. She yelped into her pillow, and he immediately relented.

"Don't stop."

241

He changed from thumbs to fingers, diffusing the pressure over the tender areas. She relaxed. "Speaking of stolen millions…"

"We need to tell Fraser, I know. But not yet. He hasn't been back."

A fact they had confirmed with their visit to the armory, where they had taken a quick count of the remaining money. After verifying that Van Pelt had not been given a key to the padlock securing their cage, Kate had told Fraser, Dubois, and Ardouin that they had no intention of taking cash, which would sit in a lightly guarded house while the team was in the hinterlands. Still, they had pretended to load the agreed-upon sum into a Hilux, and Amy had stood in the bed of the truck and mimed making it rain, nightclub-style.

Diana Fraser, seemingly done with it all, had made clear that Van Pelt was responsible for any and all consequences moving forward, to include the loss of millions of dollars. Kate reminded her that shit rolled downhill, but Fraser had waved away the concern.

"After this I'm going to enjoy my last year in Paris, then maybe retire."

"You're not old enough to retire. At least not with a full pension."

"Details, details," said Paris's station chief. "You're a lot happier on the outside. I'd like to be happy, too."

Nick, watching Kate's interaction with her former boss, saw that the remark had packed an unexpected emotional punch, hitting his wife in a place that still harbored warm feelings for the CIA, or at least Fraser, whom she grudgingly admired. He thought Kate might give Fraser a hug, but Fraser didn't like displays of emotion. Especially her own. So Kate had settled for a squeeze of her arm and the team had departed with an empty crate. Margaret confirmed that the transfer was in progress as it neared five p.m. on the East Coast, and she had a copy of the contract signed by Stan Van Pelt and the director of the Central Intelligence Agency committing to a standdown on all military action in Mali until Sandstorm's return to Timbuktu city.

"Is it weird that I feel a little larcenous over this new payment?" he asked.

"They offered, we accepted. We're buying our island with that money."

Nick smiled. "Well then, there's something to be said for larceny."

The Sandstorm partners had agreed that the newly transferred sum would be split evenly amongst the three of them and their motley crew, a bonus on top of what they'd already been paid as independent contractors for their work on this operation. Amy wanted to consult her accountant before receiving any money, as she was about to find herself in a new tax bracket. Fatima and Sharaf were unconcerned about the expectations of Emirati financial authorities, but they tried to refuse the payment; Fatima had more than she could ever spend, and Sharaf wanted for nothing in Fatima's employ, caring only that he be allowed to continue his culinary exploits in her chef's kitchen in Dubai. Charlie was the challenge; he had no idea he would receive significant compensation for his work as an honorary Sandstorm "consultant" while also earning his CIA salary. His share would be put into an interest-bearing account until they figured out how to skirt CIA regulations.

"We're going to earn every penny of it," Kate said. "We *have* earned every penny of it."

"I know."

"And it's the government's money. This isn't costing the families a dime."

"I'm convinced. I was just worried it had the stench of *eau de* Chad."

Kate rolled over and sat up. She placed a hand against his cheek, the one she had slapped without warning, her thumb scraping over his beard stubble. "You couldn't be more unlike Chad if you tried."

He pulled her onto his lap, taking her weight on his thighs as she wrapped her legs around his waist. He breathed in her scent and nuzzled her chest and neck, feeling her pulse beneath his lips. He finally asked the question that had been on his mind since the call came.

"Tomorrow?"

"I think it's going to be bad. I don't know how, but we have to be ready for anything. And we may have to let things happen."

"Meaning I have to let things happen."

She ran her hands over the heavy muscles in his back. He had knots in the same places she did. "I know it goes against every fiber of your being, but you have to recognize the difference between what's necessary far and too far."

"You sure you won't consider sitting this out?"

"Oh, Nicky," she whispered, smiling against his ear. "You need me, remember?"

ᚸ

They weren't more than an hour outside of Timbuktu, heading east toward Gourma-Rharous, when Khalifa's men intercepted their convoy. Turbaned motorcyclists swarmed around and between vehicles, the passengers brandishing assault rifles. Far more aggressive than their escorts had been in the past, these fighters were more than hired help, more than the black Africans that the Arabs of the Islamic Emirate of the Maghreb used as cannon fodder in engagements with French and Malian forces.

"It would appear that Khalifa is upset," said a veiled Fatima from behind Nick.

"Tallyho," Jake said with a nod to the north, where a group of trucks tore across the desert, making straight for the heart of their convoy.

"Shit," Nick said, as Cherif's voice filled his ear over the radio.

"Capitaine, your orders?"

The Tuareg's voice was tight. Even though Cherif's men outnumbered the IEM force headed their way, a gun battle would result in mass casualties on both sides. Their vehicles were unarmored, there was no cover in sight, and it was unclear how the Tuaregs would fight. He and Jake couldn't save everyone.

His earpiece crackled again. "Capitaine?"

He heard Kate's voice in his head. *We may have to let things happen. You have to recognize the difference between what's necessary far and too far.*

He pushed the transmit button and spoke. "Let them come. Comply with their orders. No aggressive moves."

Jake glanced at him and raised an eyebrow. "Where is Captain Cavanaugh and what have you done to him?"

"Cherif?"

"As you wish, Capitaine."

"I hope I don't regret this," Nick muttered.

Jake laughed. "Brother, the USS *Regret* has long since set sail."

Orders had been given and the terrorists were upon them, and Nick had to own what came next. Jake stopped the truck.

⏏

Armed men clawed at their doors before Cherif had even braked to a complete stop. One balaclava-clad terrorist smashed the butt of his rifle into Kate's window. Still belted in, she dove across the seat toward Amy and covered her head against an anticipated shower of glass. Cracks formed in the shape of a spider's web, but the glass held.

Cherif shouted in Arabic at their attackers. He held his hands off the steering wheel, showing he was unarmed. Ahead of them, Nick and Jake were out of their Hilux, held at gunpoint by at least ten men. Sharaf and Fatima remained in the cab, unmolested by the angry terrorists.

As Kate's attacker wound up for another strike against the window, she released her seatbelt and threw open the door, surprising the Arab as she tore into him in his native tongue. Praise Allah that Fatima had been her teacher; Kate could make even hardened terrorists blush with insults she had learned from the Yemeni.

The terrorist's eyes, the only part of his face that was visible, widened in shock as her diatribe encompassed his father's inbreeding, his mother's ugliness, and his own sexual dalliances with farm animals.

"This one has a mouth on her," said Yunis, striding to his man with his two lieutenants in tow. "I should slap her senseless."

"Touch me and you'll cost your father and his emirate twenty million dollars."

Yunis entered her personal space, but Kate refused to budge. He ripped off his cheap sunglasses and stared into her eyes.

"Apologize for your offense."

Kate peered around him to address the insulted terrorist. "I'm sorry you fuck sheep."

"You foul-mouthed bitch!" Yunis snarled.

Sharaf's calm voice carried over the commotion. "Brother Yunis, if I may suggest that cooler heads prevail?"

"But this...this *woman* thinks she has the right to speak to me in such a manner!"

"My brother, she speaks only words, easy enough to ignore. We have too much to lose by alienating those who can pay, don't you agree? I know your father wants to see you rise above her childish insults."

"She's still a foul-mouthed bitch," Yunis muttered.

"Be that as it may, you must not let her antagonize you so. Now, what is the meaning of this? I was assured that our interlocutors would be safe."

Yunis spread his hands innocently. "Sheikh, everyone is safe."

Sharaf fixed him with piercing green eyes. "Young man, I do not stand for insults, either. This is not what we agreed to."

"I agreed to nothing."

"Your father—"

"I am my father's security chief. My orders are to safeguard him and our emirate."

"And this is how you protect him? By bullying women?"

"Had these women"—he nearly spat the word—"not brought death and destruction to our lands, perhaps I would be more convinced that their continued existence is beneficial to our glorious cause."

Sharaf stood tall. "You will not harm them."

Yunis smiled, exposing yellowed teeth. "On my father's orders, I will not hurt them. But they will experience the full glory of the lands of the Islamic Maghreb."

Kate's stomach sank, but she knew what was coming was a so-called necessary far.

"They will join us at camp," Yunis continued. "But they will walk."

Sharaf looked at Kate, who had been joined by Amy and Charlie and Cherif. Kate met the Yemeni's eyes.

"As you wish, Brother Yunis." He turned to walk back toward his Hilux, but stopped and snapped at the Libyan. "Release my Legionnaires. Now."

Yunis smirked. "Of course, Brother Sharaf. Please forgive me. My men can be overeager sometimes."

ᘒ

"Goddamn, it is hot. Like hotter than however many circles of hell Dante claimed there were," Amy said.

"Nine," Charlie interjected.

"Maybe even hotter than all nine circles combined."

"It's definitely more humid. A hundred and thirty degrees is toasty, but it's the humidity that gets you."

"I bet it's at least a hundred and forty degrees. What do you think?" Amy asked Kate.

"I think you two talk a lot."

They had been walking for three hours, trudging over barren desert, the convoy a distant metallic glint across the wasteland, an elusive oasis of shade and air-conditioned trucks and as much water as they could drink. Yunis's motorcycle-borne fighters occasionally zipped past, hot-dogging their way through the sands and scrub brush, spewing dust and exhaust in their faces. The target of Kate's ire screamed graphic insults at her from the back of a motorcycle, and Kate was glad that Nick had complied with Sharaf's orders to remain with him and Fatima. This trek across the moonscape, under the brutal sun, was their cross to bear. Or so said Pentecostal Pastor Amy, rather dramatically, when confronted with Yunis's edict.

They each carried a single small bottle of water, not nearly sufficient hydration for their odyssey through the bush. Kate had already sweat out at least a gallon of fluid, she was certain. Her wicking T-shirt was soaked through, and sweat stains had appeared on the front, back, and underarms of the long-sleeved, khaki-colored hiking shirt that she wore over the T-shirt. Her sage-colored pants caught drops of sweat that plunged off her nose, spotting her thighs and shins. She adjusted her white headscarf, now dingy from dust and sweat, to cover her face save her eyes, protected by Ray-Bans. At least Yunis has not thought to confiscate their layers and sunglasses, sparing them lobster-red skin and scorched corneas.

Kate did feel bad for Amy, though. There was no way her staid gray polyester-blend suit breathed well. And mile after mile in those awful shoes? She looked the part of an uptight evangelical, but devotion to detail came at a price.

"White Tuareg needs water," Amy panted, fumbling for her bottle.

"Make it last," Kate said. "The closer we get to the convoy, the farther away it moves. We have no idea where this camp is."

"I was just gonna knock you down and steal yours, small fry. After all, this is your fault."

"Um, who wanted to stay?"

"We did," Amy and Charlie said in contrite unison.

Kate waited for the motorcyclists to pass again, closing her eyes and covering her nose and mouth against the kicked-up sand. The sun neared its zenith in the cloudless sky, a blinding white orb in the gauzy blue expanse. The convoy remained motionless on the horizon.

"One foot in front of the other," she said.

Ⴥ

They reached the camp late that afternoon. The three trekkers had long since halted conversation, conserving what little energy the sun and its brutal, unrelenting heat hadn't sapped from their worn bodies. Kate had stopped sweating hours ago, a sign of dehydration. She looked at her friends and saw that exhaustion had dulled their eyes and aridity had cracked their lips. Kate had no idea where they were, but she was confident they had traveled north, away from Gourma-Rharous and the Niger River, farther into the vast region of Timbuktu.

Yunis met them at the outskirts of the camp, surrounded by his two lieutenants and a phalanx of fighters. Other armed Arabs trained their rifles on Nick and Jake, who had been relieved of their own weapons and looked tense and furious. Sharaf and Fatima appeared from under a sheepskin tent, where an array of tiny tea glasses and plates dotted the red blanket placed over the sand. Fatima's face was hidden by her niqab, but Sharaf's expression was dark and displeased.

Kate controlled her desire to tell Yunis exactly where to shove it, and instead offered a polite greeting in Arabic. He looked surprised and perhaps disappointed, but recovered and gestured grandly.

"Welcome to camp, Madame Moreau and Pastor Smith." He then looked at Charlie. "And you, the one who is not a CIA agent, welcome to you as well."

Fatima translated, and again Charlie paled at the mention of the CIA. But Yunis had moved on and was commenting on their weary bodies and weathered faces, laughing with his men. Kate licked her bone-dry lips and watched the sands shift beneath her feet. Or, more accurately, the illusion of sands shifting beneath her feet. She hoped the dizziness would pass with some water. If they were permitted water.

"Brother Yunis, you've had your fun. I must insist that our guests be given water and shade," Sharaf said.

Yunis peered at Kate's face. She met his stare, matching his hostility with her own. "Have I had *enough* fun, Brother Sharaf?"

"This has gone too far. If they die of dehydration, no one will pay your ransom. And their drones will take to the skies like these infernal flies." He swatted at a black fly orbiting his kaffiyeh-wrapped head.

"You seem to have a soft spot for these Westerners. Has the good life in Dubai colored your views?"

"Never question my devotion to our shared cause. My interest in their well-being is purely economic. I did not travel this distance, and at great personal risk, to lose my cut of a large ransom because you felt the need to showboat. Now show our guests some compassion and, for the last time, order your men to unhand my Legionnaires."

"Your Legionnaires—"

"Are no threat to you."

"The big one looks angry."

"The big one always looks angry. Return their weapons and allow Dmitri to treat the Westerners. They are clearly dehydrated."

Yunis waved a hand and his men dispersed their semi-circle around Nick and Jake. The Americans rearmed themselves and hurried toward Kate and the others, Jake a step behind after retrieving his medical pack from the Hilux. Nick handed bottles of water to everyone.

Kate snatched hers from his hand and stepped a few paces away, fixing him with a look that she hoped conveyed the need for him to act like a mercenary in the employ of a terrorist-adjacent businessman and not a concerned husband. He looked confused, but then Fatima whispered to him in English, a barely audible murmur under her veil.

"Dieter, you must remember who you are."

Understanding registered in his stormy blue eyes before he slipped on his sunglasses and moved to stand near Sharaf, the sheikh's security paramount.

"Careful with the water," Jake advised. "Don't drink too fast."

Too late. Amy and Charlie had already finished their bottles, and Kate was nearly done with hers. They all accepted another, cracking them open and guzzling.

"I'll get you Gatorade and MREs."

"I don't think we should take a meal without an invitation," Kate said.

"You need some calories. At least an energy bar."

She nodded her assent. Jake went to the truck and returned with Gatorades and high-calorie energy bars, then led them to the sheepskin tent where Sharaf, Fatima, and Yunis had retreated from the late-afternoon sun. They gingerly eased themselves to the dirty red blanket. Yunis bellowed in Arabic and an abaya-clad figure materialized from a neighboring tent bearing more tea. It appeared to be one of his teenaged wives. She served them silently and disappeared. Fatima watched her.

"Is she with child, Brother Yunis?"

"You have a good eye, Umm Ali."

"She's very young," Fatima commented in a neutral tone.

"She's old enough."

Fatima was almost certainly plotting Yunis's demise, but the niqab offered one the ability to hide murderous intentions.

"After evening prayers, she will serve us dinner," he continued. "I'm sure our guests are hungry after all that exercise."

"Where is your father?" Kate asked through parched lips.

"My father's whereabouts are none of your concern."

"We're eager to speak with him."

"And he is eager to speak with you. In particular he would like to know at whose feet to lay the blame for that drone attack."

"We'll be happy to address that with him."

Yunis's right eye sat a smidgen higher than his left. He raised that eyebrow, furthering the cockeyed look. "Is it normal in Western culture that the smallest among you is also the bravest?"

Kate chose to consider that a rhetorical question. "How are the hostages?"

Yunis sipped his tea. "They are alive."

"We need to see them again."

"You will."

His phone trilled a tinny call to prayer. The hour of sunset was upon them. Dusk blanketed the camp in long shadows and the hint of cooler air. Kate felt a chill, and caught Jake's concerned expression as a shiver racked her body. She drank more Gatorade. Beside her, Amy and Charlie sat catatonic with exhaustion.

Yunis rose and spoke to his lieutenants. "Guard the Westerners. And if the Legionnaires give you any trouble, shoot them."

"*Aiwa.*"

"Sheikh, shall we pray?"

"Lead the way, Brother Yunis."

♌

The slop that Yunis's teenaged wife served after prayers was barely edible, at least for the three desert trekkers, whose systems were on the fritz. Kate suspected that Ahlam, the first wife, was the mastermind in the makeshift kitchens of Yunis's network of camps. She nibbled at some dusty-tasting flatbread and, after accepting a small helping, avoided the communal pot of stew, which tasted of rancid camel. She wanted only to get through dinner, retreat to their own camp, and crawl into a fluffy down sleeping bag with a big Legionnaire at her side.

Kate knew that Nick would want to address in greater detail what constituted *too far*. He had shown remarkable restraint thus far; restraint was not one of his defining characteristics when it came to direct dealings with terrorists.

"Brother Yunis, thank you for your hospitality. I believe it is time for us to take our leave," Sharaf said as he placed his empty tea glass on the tray that the young wife held toward him.

"There is no need to go, Sheikh."

"I think our guests require some rest. We shall make our own camp and leave you in peace."

"No, you will stay."

"I don't understand, brother."

Yunis swirled the dregs of his tea in his tiny glass. "I have been made aware of an expression in English that I think applies well to the situation in which we find ourselves."

"Oh?"

"It is said that one should keep one's friends nearby, but one should not let one's enemies out of one's sight." Yunis looked at Fatima, who properly translated the adage for Amy and Charlie. "Did I get that right?"

"Yes, Brother Yunis, well done."

"You will stay," Yunis said. "I will not let my enemies out of my sight. Should your drones come for me, they will come for us all."

"As you wish, Brother Yunis," Sharaf said, after a pause during which no one objected. "My men will situate the women's tents in an appropriate area of camp."

"The women will sleep here. Under this tent."

"But brother, the sides are open. The women—"

"They are French and American. Women of neither nationality are known for modesty."

"It's fine," Kate said. "We'll make do. Thank you for hosting us."

Yunis smiled without humor. "Stay warm. Nights bring a chill."

20

THE NIGHT PASSED IN a haze of discomfort and confusion, exacerbated by the disruptive movements of restless men and the lingering symptoms of dehydration. Kate finally fell asleep against her will, and awoke with a crushing headache and a screaming back as Yunis's phone blared the call to dawn prayers from across camp. She and Amy had ended up pressed together to conserve warmth, as the night had quickly cooled.

Kate disentangled herself from Amy's embrace and sat up, brushing sand from her hair and face and reaching for what was left of her Gatorade. She didn't have a drop of spit in her mouth, which tasted like the remnants of the rancid camel stew and the charred flatbread. As she sipped, she peeked out of the tent and saw Nick seated in the bed of the Hilux, the only Sandstorm vehicle permitted to remain in camp. His watchful eyes swept the grounds, but returned often to the open tent. Jake was in the cab, reclined in the passenger seat.

Amy groaned. "Did we cuddle last night?"

"You were the big spoon. I couldn't escape."

"Vegas rules? What happens in a terrorist camp stays in a terrorist camp?"

"Agreed."

"What does today bring?"

"Hopefully eyes on the hostages."

"But?"

Kate looked at her. "But you know. It can always get worse."

"Yeah, I was afraid of that."

Fatima appeared and ducked under the tent. She had been given a closed tent of her own in which to pass the night, but when she flipped back her niqab, she exposed drawn features and dark circles under her eyes.

"You look like you slept as well as we did," Kate commented.

"Yunis paid a visit to his wife's tent last night. It should come as no surprise that he is not a tender and thoughtful lover."

Kate squeezed Fatima's arm. "Did they search the truck?"

"They rummaged around and took some food and those French rifles that the boys were so excited about. But they left my possessions alone."

The beaconed face cream was secured in a signal-blocking Faraday bag, disguised to look like an ordinary black pouch, and hidden amongst Fatima's belongings in her Louis Vuitton overnight bag. With any luck, Weiss was beside himself that the signal hadn't come online. The poor geek from Langley's beacon shop was in for a haranguing.

"Any idea what's on today's docket?"

"I gather we will move as soon as prayers are finished."

"Did Yunis let anything useful slip yesterday?"

"Mostly he complained."

"About?"

"You, the hostages, you again, how no one respects his operational prowess, you some more. He's a walking grievance."

"Fantastic," Kate muttered.

She and Amy followed Fatima to the outskirts of camp, where the men were breaking down tents and loading trucks. Cherif joined them in his Hilux and parked beside Nick and Jake's truck. He dismounted and looked at Kate and Amy with some concern. Nick's jaw muscles twitched uncontrollably, but he maintained the air of a bodyguard concerned with the wellbeing of his client.

Kate used one of the Hilux's sideview mirrors to take stock of her appearance. She winced. Dehydration wasn't a good look.

Yunis strode toward them. "You will be permitted your two trucks. The rest of your convoy must not pass the wells. Is that understood?"

"Brother, I must ask you to reconsider. Cherif and his men are in my employ and no threat to you or your father. Surely you know that."

"We have no issue with Cherif and his men. But this is nonnegotiable, Sheikh."

Something in Yunis's tone suggested that this request was far more than bluster, that their agreement was paramount if they ever wanted to see Khalifa and the hostages again.

Sharaf flipped his prayer beads, appraising the younger man. "And I have your word that our guests will be unharmed and treated with respect?"

"You have my word and that of the emir."

Sharaf looked at Nick, who nodded once. "Then the convoy shall not pass the wells."

"Come. The emir awaits."

Ⴖ

The Tuareg convoy broke off an hour's drive north deeper into Timbuktu, surprising a gathering of shepherds and their flocks at the wells. The two Sandstorm Hiluxes stayed with the IEM contingent and traveled another hour over teeth-rattlingly rough terrain. Cherif had placed several MREs in the cab for their consumption, but the bouncing and jarring made eating anything requiring utensils a challenge. They settled for energy bars and rehydrated with Gatorades as the desert continued its abuse of their bodies.

Cherif spoke quietly into his radio, calling for his cousin Mokhtar. He received no response. "We are out of range."

"If this were a movie, I'd be real worried about our intrepid heroes," Charlie said. He peered upward through the dusty windshield. "On the bright side, no drones."

"Yet," Amy said.

"Clear skies. They'll strike from miles away," Kate said. They both looked at her, Charlie twisting in his seat to fix her with tired eyes. "What? It's true. We'll never see it coming. But Fatima said that the beaconed lotion is still secure in the Faraday bag, and Sharaf's phone has been in airplane mode since we left the city."

"Doesn't mean they don't have a fleet up there scouring the ground for camps," Charlie said. "No matter what that contract said, all bets are off."

"The same thing that will make a rescue attempt almost impossible is the same thing that will probably prevent Weiss from finding us without geoloca-tional assistance: the vastness of the space."

"That's both comforting and terrifying."

"Look, we just need to get eyes on the hostages, convince Khalifa we're still legit, pass the cream, and get the hell out of Dodge. After this, we step aside for the door-kickers."

"We're approaching a camp," Cherif said. "What is my role?"

"Same as it's always been. Follow the captain's orders."

"*D'accord*, Madame Kate."

Khalifa himself stood at the head of the well-armed welcoming committee, his gray djellaba fluttering in the light breeze. He regarded them stolidly as they dismounted the Hiluxes, first turning his attention to Sharaf, whom he embraced. He touched a fist to his chest to greet Fatima and then spoke coldly to his guests.

"Madame Moreau, Pastor Smith. Do you come alone, or should my men prepare the Stingers?"

Kate stepped forward. "Sir, on behalf of the president of the Republic of France, I offer our sincerest apologies for the incident."

"My men examined the wreckage of the aircraft and concluded that it was an American drone."

Kate saw little point in evasion. "It appears the French military had a misunderstanding with their American counterparts in Niger. One of their aircraft was erroneously cleared to enter Malian airspace by a junior officer who wasn't privy to our efforts."

"My concern is less a miscommunication and more how that drone found us. We have never been found before."

"I believe the Americans got lucky."

"That's all?"

Kate shrugged. "Wouldn't you agree that luck plays a role in most military and intelligence operations? Even your own?"

Yunis looked poised to snarl his disagreement, but Khalifa raised a finger to silence him. "I prefer to attribute our successes to the divine will of Allah, but I will concede that a touch of luck never hurt." He turned to his son. "The vehicles have been searched?"

"We found no devices, though the sheikh and his Legionnaires have their phones, both mobile and satellite."

"Brother Sharaf and his men are above reproach, and we are nowhere near a tower. They may keep their phones." Then Khalifa peered more closely at Kate and Amy and Charlie. "Why are these three so dirty and disheveled?"

Yunis wore an expression of innocence. Kate answered for the group. "We had some car trouble."

Yunis shot Kate a toothy, mocking grin as his father turned and beckoned them to follow. She ignored him and trudged toward Khalifa's large, open-air tent. The blankets and pillows, arranged artfully under the sheepskin ceiling, looked new, or at least freshly laundered. She doubted it was for their benefit. In a corner of camp, she saw three more large tents with armed guards milling about, and breathed a sigh of relief. Hostages.

"Be seated," Khalifa said.

"Thank you for meeting with us," Kate began. "I know we all desire the same outcome: the ransom and safe return of the hostages."

"Yes, Madame Moreau, but—"

"I thought I heard familiar voices!" Ratma, looking resplendent in indigo robes, joined the group and offered greetings in Arabic, French, and English. "My goodness, what happened to you three? You looked like you walked here." She turned to Khalifa and Yunis. "I see no tea. Where is that poor child wife of yours, Yunis?"

Yunis bellowed for tea, and Ratma settled herself beside Khalifa and made small talk with Fatima. The tea arrived shortly, borne by the pregnant girl.

"As I was saying, we're here to demonstrate our commitment to—"

"Please, Madame Moreau, business can wait. Let us enjoy our tea."

"Of course."

Ratma murmured something to Khalifa in Tamashek. His reply was curt, but they both glanced at Kate and Amy. Kate sipped the strong tea and wondered how to interpret the subtle shift in mood under the tent. Even Yunis looked subdued, drained of his earlier bombast.

"Well," Ratma said brightly. "I heard all about the drone attack. Quite exciting. Sheikh, blessings upon you and your men for saving my husband." She followed her last statement with a pointed look at Yunis.

"*Mashallah*. The will of God was carried out that day."

"I have long wondered if God intended for Khalifa to spend his last years with me, in quiet solitude, tending to grandchildren and village life. Now I have faith in his plan."

"Wife, you are uncharacteristically sentimental. Where is my irascible Ratma?"

She smiled at her husband. "We are so close. We can finally go home again." Her eyelids fluttered shut and her amused expression changed to one of peaceful reminiscence.

"Brother Khalifa, does this mean what I think it means?"

259

"On your advice, Brother Sharaf, I have taken steps to…how did you describe it? Create my own reality?"

Sharaf swallowed, his Adam's apple bobbing. "Did I say that?"

"You did, my friend, and I took it to heart. I have dispatched a courier to the shura with a letter stating my intent to retire and pass this emirate to my chosen successor, effective immediately."

"I thought you intended to wait until the business with the Westerners was concluded."

"That had been my plan, but I was made to see the error of my ways in the aftermath of our enemies' treachery." He swung his gaze to Ratma, who looked pleased with herself. "I am an old man. I do not have much time left. I wish to spend it in peace."

"I understand." Sharaf stroked his well-groomed white beard. "I think that raises some concerns among our guests, however."

Kate worked to keep her tone even. "If you're no longer the emir, with whom do we negotiate?"

"You will negotiate with me," said a quiet voice in Arabic.

Kate swiveled her head, searching for the man who belonged to the voice. Standing sentry behind Sharaf and Fatima, Nick and Jake tensed. A tall figure emerged from a tent to the right of Kate, Amy, and Charlie. Dressed in desert-camouflage fatigues and a black-and-white kaffiyeh, the man walked over the rough ground with barely a crunch, like a biped cat. His full black beard, sans mustache, dominated his face; his eyes were dark and intelligent and curious, and they were fixed on Kate.

"Ladies, I present my son, Talha, the new emir."

"A pleasure to make your acquaintance," Talha said in Arabic, and then repeated the same in French. "And this must be our indomitable Sheikh Sharaf al-Yemeni, to whom we are indebted for saving my father's life."

Sharaf rose to shake Talha's hand and exchange traditional greetings. Talha touched a hand to his chest and nodded toward Fatima, and then folded his lean frame into a sitting position, kitty-corner to Kate. He lounged against the pillows and motioned for tea. Yunis again bellowed for his wife.

Talha's gaze resettled on Kate, a slight smile toying with his lips. She wished for more space between them. He was close enough to touch her if he reached out a long arm.

"I was skeptical when my father told me that he had been negotiating with female emissaries," he said in Arabic. "But you are most certainly female."

Kate wasn't sure how to respond to such an obvious statement, and she hoped Amy had enough sense to keep her snark to herself. Talha was a different breed; the atmosphere under the tent had changed the moment he appeared. Yunis remained silent, and Ratma had drawn closer to Khalifa. The former emir of the Islamic Emirate of the Maghreb seemed content to oversee the proceedings from his perch at the head of the mini desert shura, now relegated to the role of *éminence grise*.

"We've made excellent progress with your father and hope to quickly secure an agreement for the release of our citizens."

"In due time, Madame Moreau."

"As I'm sure you know, several of the hostages are struggling with their physical and mental health. Time is of the essence."

"Time," he mused. "Such a Western construct."

"Is congestive heart failure a Western construct?" Amy asked. "Because if you had it, you'd be a lot more concerned about time."

Talha's eyes remained on Kate. "My brother warned me that you and Pastor Smith had strong ideas and even stronger personalities. My father has always been drawn to strong personalities, always been intrigued by the possibilities inherent in the complementary nature of yin and yang, the hard power of a man matched with the soft power of a woman."

Kate sensed that this was a reference, though not a positive one, to Ratma, whose face was expressionless save a hardening of her eyes.

"Now I understand why he persists with you, despite your betrayal," he continued. "A fascination, a need to explore a forbidden aspect of our world."

"I thought it had a lot more to do with twenty million dollars," Kate replied.

Talha smiled. "That never hurts."

"Then perhaps we should remain focused on our shared priorities."

The son cocked his head. "What does your husband think of your exploits in our lands?"

"I'm not married."

"I should have known. The concept of marriage, of a wife serving her husband, has fallen out of favor in your country. No man I know would ever permit his wife to gad about on secret missions with the express purpose of making contact with enemies of the state. And Pastor Smith? A religious woman such as yourself must be married."

"I'm currently unattached."

"Interesting. Very interesting. Perhaps you are married to your job? I'm told this is a phenomenon now in your countries. Especially for women who are unsuitable for traditional marriage by virtue of their overbearing natures."

Talha stated this matter-of-factly. Behind Sharaf, Nick coughed. Ratma whipped her head around, but the man married to a woman with an overbearing nature clamped his jaws to keep his dimples from making an unwelcome appearance. His eyes were hidden by sunglasses, but Kate could imagine the laughter dancing in the deep blue. The elegant Tuareg fingered the Agadez Cross at her neck and winked at Kate.

Très, très beau, she mouthed.

"Ah, yes, the Legionnaire who speaks Arabic," Talha said. "You are most lucky, Sheikh, to employ a professional Western soldier who speaks our tongue. You must have a knack for languages, Legionnaire, to become fluent in Arabic."

Nick shrugged. "I've spent my entire adult life deployed to the Arabic-speaking world. At some point it becomes hard not to learn."

"But no French, despite your former employer?"

"That was a matter of choice."

Talha laughed and spoke to Kate in French. "The French and the Germans, shackled to the past, *d'accord?*"

"Just because we're allies doesn't mean we're friends."

Talha nodded thoughtfully and transitioned back to Arabic. "An astute sentiment, Madame Moreau. And what say you, Legionnaire? Can the Fatherland ever truly be embraced by its neighbors, or will it always be a wolf among the sheep of Europe?"

Nick removed his Oakleys and used the olive-drab headscarf wrapped loosely around his neck to wipe the Sahel's reddish dust from the lenses. He focused cobalt eyes on Talha. "*Ich bin der Teufelshund des Krieges.*"

Talha clapped delightedly, his long fingers wrapping around his hands as he clasped them to his chest. "German is a wonderfully guttural language, sonorous kin to our mother tongue. What does it mean?"

Nick replaced his sunglasses and reset his hands on his weapon. "It doesn't translate to Arabic."

Nick's ability to speak German consisted of memorized lines and militaristic commands shouted in movies in which evil Nazis figured prominently in the storyline. Kate persisted in pretending to believe that President John F. Kennedy had, in fact, called himself a jelly doughnut during his famous speech in West Berlin at the height of the Cold War; this annoyed Nick beyond reason. Nick persisted in truly believing that the German army had dubbed the United States Marine Corps, their tenacious foes in the 1918 Battle of Belleau Wood, *die Teufelshunde des Krieges*, or the devil dogs of war. Kate never tired of reminding him of the apocryphal nature of this World War I legend, much to his dismay.

Talha stroked his long beard and apprised his guests. "It's been a long time since I've had such stimulating conversation. And with women, no less." He shook his head in mock self-reproach.

Kate stole a glance at her watch, a gesture missed by no one. She smiled patiently at Talha. "We're glad you enjoy our company. It must be lonely in the mountains."

He raised an eyebrow.

"The Atlas Mountains, of course, where your group has sought refuge to escape the Tunisian security services. Your force is down to what, maybe a couple dozen men? But you persist in the face of overwhelming odds, scoring the occasional victory against small army patrols using guerrilla tactics. No doubt your father sees some of himself in you, what with his background fighting the Soviets and then the Americans in Afghanistan."

Talha looked at his father, who held out his hands in defense. "I said nothing, son."

"I'm the foreign minister's special adviser on counterterrorism issues. It's my job. And you speak French with a Tunisian accent."

"Since we know each other so well now, perhaps it's time that I got to know my hostages." Talha stood, and Kate, Amy, and Charlie jumped to their feet. "Brother, would you lead us?"

Yunis choked on the last of his tea. "Me?"

"You are my security chief, correct?"

Yunis scrambled to stand, snatching at his AK-47 and prompting quick reactions from Nick and Jake. He ignored the rifles trained on him and shouted for his two lieutenants, who appeared from under a tan tarp.

"Our new emir will view the hostages. Gather the men."

Talha walked beside Yunis, abbreviating his stride so as not to outpace his shorter brother. They stopped in the clearing near the three tents. "We shall do this your way, Yunis."

"My way?"

"Yes, your way. You have preferred methods, do you not?"

Yunis glanced uncertainly at Khalifa, who waited with Ratma, Sharaf, and Fatima, flanked by Nick and Jake.

"Look at me, brother. Who is the emir?"

"You are."

"Then let us bring our emirate the glory it deserves. Let us show the *kuffar* who we are."

A slow, sneering smile contorted Yunis's face. "*Aiwa*, brother. It is a pleasure to serve." He motioned to his lieutenants. "Start with the men."

Six of his soldiers burst into the tent on the far right, provoking shouts and thrashing limbs. The sheepskin structure, held aloft by rickety poles staked in the sand, collapsed atop the melee. Outnumbered and weakened from months in captivity, Gilles Lefèvre, Ollie Jones, and Noah Shaw were no match for the energized IEM fighters. Yunis's men dragged the three hostages from the tent and threw them to the ground.

Ollie's forehead smashed a partially unearthed rock, splitting skin and unleashing a deluge of blood. He swung at the nearest terrorist's legs, his fist catching a kneecap. "Oi, you fucking cunt!"

The terrorist kicked the young Australian in the side. Ollie heaved, blood pouring from his face into the sand.

"Hey, come on!" Amy said, moving toward him.

Yunis aimed his rifle at her head. She stopped and held up her hands. Nick and Jake, rifles raised, fanned out and inched nearer to the mass of terrorists and hostages.

"Pastor Smith, you are a guest. I ask that you control yourself," Talha said via Fatima, who had moved to stand with Kate and Amy.

"He's hurt."

"It's not life-threatening. Please, step back."

Amy stared at him for a moment, then retreated to Kate's side. Kate grabbed her arm and held tightly, willing her to remain calm. Her own heart pounded her chest hard enough to reverberate in her ears. Movement in the shadows of the left tent caught her eye; the Abbotts peered out, fear paling their tanned, wrinkled faces.

The middle tent's flaps flung open and Mathilde Fournier rushed out, oblivious to the grasping hands of her sister attempting to keep her inside. The Frenchwoman made straight for Yunis and slapped him across the face. Yunis put a hand to his wounded cheek and looked at his brother in shock.

Talha made a gesture of invitation. "Your way."

Yunis backhanded Mathilde, snapping her head sideways and sending her sprawling to the sand. Marianne cried out and ran to her sister. Mathilde screamed and thrashed, and tears streamed down Marianne's cheeks as she tried to calm her.

"Yunis!" Ratma snapped. "Enough!" She turned to Khalifa and ranted at him in Tamashek. He leaned close and whispered in her ear. She hissed a response and crossed her arms over her chest. Yunis made a show of examining his knuckles.

Talha languidly circled the bedraggled hostages. Marianne held her sister, whispering soothing words. Ollie's face still bled. Noah tried to stanch the flow with a dirty headscarf. Talha bent at the waist and peered at Lefèvre, on his knees and staring at the ground.

"*Qui êtes-vous?*"

"Gilles Lefèvre," he muttered.

"Yes, of course, Monsieur Lefèvre. Our Burkinabe brothers made your acquaintance when you were visiting one of your mining ventures in the north. I'm told the conditions in that mine are horrific, no different than slavery. And you use children!" Talha tsked.

"I had no idea—"

Talha kicked Lefèvre in the gut. The Frenchman yowled and keeled over, holding his midsection.

"I don't like liars, Monsieur Lefèvre."

"The conditions at that mine really are horrific," Khalifa murmured to Sharaf.

"Your company rapes and pillages these lands and their people. Tell me why I should not kill you on the spot, monsieur."

"Please," Lefèvre gasped. "Please, I can pay. My company is very successful. They will pay whatever you ask to get me back."

"Perhaps you should tell him the bad news, brother."

Yunis snapped his fingers at Fatima. "Translate." He continued in Arabic. "The first thing we did was make contact with your company, *L'Or d'Afrique*. We spoke to a man called Pierre. Pierre Lefèvre. A relation, perhaps?"

Lefèvre gaped at Yunis. "My younger brother."

"He said that the company couldn't afford our asking price of two million euros."

The Frenchman sputtered. "But that is simply not the case!"

Yunis shrugged. "We were forced to lump you in with your countrywomen, whose family also cannot pay, and seek a ransom from the French government. Happily, we could raise the price for your head, as the government does not appear to have the same liquidity issues as your company. That was how your brother described it. A liquidity issue."

"He would not betray me like that!"

Talha laughed and patted Lefèvre on the back. The man flinched. "You must watch out for those younger brothers," he said in French, shooting Kate a wink, proud of his role of usurper within IEM.

"If we could get back to the matter at hand," Kate began.

Talha ignored her and turned his attention to the two Aussies. "I'm told you boys set the standard for stupidity. Cycling, of all pursuits? When the people of this land struggle for even scraps, you arrive with your toys and make a mockery of their plight. We sold your bicycles to some Russians in Algeria and used the proceeds to put food in hungry mouths."

"You fuckin' sold our bikes?" Ollie said. "How the fuck are we gonna finish our trek, then?"

"Ollie!" Noah hissed.

"No, I'm serious. We committed to our rally, and we're gonna fucking finish it one way or another."

Ollie flung blood from his hand and launched himself toward Talha's knees, but the tall Arab lithely evaded the lunge and chopped a hand down on the back of the young Australian's neck. Ollie fell face down and went limp. Noah crawled toward him, shaking his shoulder and whispering urgently.

"Is this necessary?" Kate asked.

"He attacked me, Madame Moreau. Don't I have a right to defend myself?"

Kate set her jaw. Ollie was still unconscious. She glanced at Jake, but he offered no indication as to the severity of the situation.

Talha turned and motioned to the Abbotts. "Please join us."

Bess wrapped her arm around Stu's waist to steady him. He leaned heavily on her as they shuffled to join the others. His skin was ashy, his eyes ringed by dark circles. His belly looked more distended than the last time they had seen him. He put a hand to his chest and hacked a wet, wheezing cough.

Jake keyed his radio and spoke softly to Nick, but Kate was close enough to hear. "If he's not in heart failure already, he's on the verge."

Talha recoiled from Stu's phlegmy discharge and cast a critical eye at the string of spit hanging from the American's lips. "This must be Mr. Abbott."

Amy stepped forward again, hands out and open. "Please, he's very, very sick."

"I can see that."

"Let us help him. Dmitri is a medic. He can try to stabilize him."

Talha cocked his head and stared deep into Stu's eyes, as if in a trance. "His time is near."

"*Please* let us help him. If he dies—"

Kate interrupted Amy and addressed Talha in Arabic, ensuring no captives would understand. "No one will pay for dead hostages. Not my government, not her organization, not the Australian government. Mr. Abbott is a dead man walking, Madame Fournier is in extreme mental and emotional distress, and the boys are not worth this aggravation. Don't you see that the time is now to come to terms?"

Talha's black gaze captured Kate's. His eyes were dark and foreboding, like empty caverns. She saw little light, little life in their vacant depths.

"What if I'm not interested in money, Madame Moreau?"

"Money is what you asked for and money is what we intend to pay."

"I never asked for money. That was the demand of the former emir."

"Son," Khalifa said, stepping forward, "what is the meaning of this?"

Talha addressed Kate. "What if I'm interested in a statement of a different kind?"

She focused on breathing, trying to mentally prepare herself. "What kind of statement?"

The new emir of the Islamic Emirate of the Maghreb looked to the hazy afternoon sky, perhaps seeking divine inspiration. He clasped his hands at his waist, as if he were about to pray, and regarded both Kate and his father with something akin to pity.

"We are nothing, an afterthought at best. No one takes us seriously."

"Son, I don't understand. I don't disagree that we've had our struggles in recent years, but our contributions have always been critical to our movement's success."

"We are an ATM machine, a hawala, nothing more, for our leaders," Talha said flatly. "We fund small-time operations in corners of this planet long since forgotten by the West and our own despots. We must seize the spotlight again, channel the glory of fallen towers and an imperial military command in flames. A handful of Allah's bravest once brought the most powerful nation on earth to its knees, and not even twenty years later we have made a mockery of their legacy. And that is why God the merciful has chosen me to usher in a new era of our emirate's glory."

269

His audience digested this. A motley crew of intelligence officers, Marines, and Arabs opposed to terrorism in all its forms looked at Khalifa al-Ghazawi, *éminence grise*. The father watched the son with a hint of uncertainty.

"I chose you to stay the course."

Talha laughed incredulously. "To stay the course? Father, look around you. Even our guests know the folly of staying the course. They are here negotiating because the world has changed, and they hope to secure a deal before we come to our senses and change with it."

"If you are suggesting that we will adopt the practices of *Daesh*..."

"It is not a suggestion. We have ceded territory, funding, and prestige from the Levant to our own backyard. *Daesh* adapted to the new media landscape, traditional and otherwise, and captured the attention of a rapt, insatiable audience that was just waiting to be tapped; we did not. They feed the beast with spectacular violence and atrocities; we do not. You are negotiating with women; our *Daesh* brothers would have slaughtered the *kuffar* one by one, ever more creatively and for maximum effect. They could have generated the same twenty million dollars that you seek as each new execution video posted across the internet. All it takes is a click of a button on a website, and the money pours in. No intermediaries, no negotiators, no drones." Talha gazed down at Ollie, just coming to, and Noah. "I cannot think of a better combination than easy money and agonizing death."

Kate looked at Amy and Charlie. Her friends, privy to Fatima's murmured translation, couldn't hide their terror, their revulsion, and the dawning realization that they would not save the Abbotts, the Fourniers, Lefèvre, and Ollie and Noah. Seven individuals, in the wrong place at the wrong time, would now die by blades or firing squad or thirst or immolation or some other barbarity. Khalifa's lands of the Islamic Maghreb would seem an oasis of peace and serenity in the face of Talha's impending reign of terror.

"Pastor Smith?" Kate asked in a tight voice. The priority now was saving her friends.

Amy offered a single nod. She stared at the ground.

Kate inclined her head toward Khalifa in a show of respect, but then addressed Talha, the emir. "It appears we have nothing more to discuss. Should you wish to revisit negotiations, we can be reached through the sheikh."

She turned toward the trucks, fighting for composure, Amy and Charlie in her wake. She couldn't look at the hostages; none of them could. Then Talha's quiet voice stopped her.

"You will stay, Madame Moreau. You will all stay. Only I decide when, and if, you leave these lands alive."

21

"WHAT THE FUCK IS going on?" Amy hissed.

Kate shushed her. Now was no time for a fake evangelical pastor to be overheard dropping obscenities, not in the presence of her flock. Bess Abbott's wide-eyed start suggested she caught the profanity over the din of the tumult building beneath hastily strung tarps near the pit latrines. Amy bowed her head in contrition.

"My apologies, Mrs. Abbott, to you and the Lord, but under the circumstances I think he'll forgive my transgression."

Bess attempted a smile, then turned her attention back to Stu, who lay on his side. Sweat dotted his brow, and his face drooped. She shifted her position to block a shaft of afternoon sunlight that found the gap between sagging tarp panels from reaching him. Stu coughed.

"*Mon Dieu*, it never stops!" Gilles Lefèvre muttered.

He pulled as far away from the Americans as he could without exposing himself to the brutal sun, but the shaded area was much too small for all the bodies crowded into it. It was, Kate thought, very much like an overcrowded prison cell, perhaps Talha's nod to the Islamic State's notorious prisons in Syria and Iraq, where they tortured and disappeared all who opposed them. Stu had to lie prone, taking up valuable space; Ollie's long legs flexed akimbo at the knees, jostling his neighbors; Mathilde swatted at him every time he bumped her, with Marianne offering mumbled apologies. Kate, Amy, and Charlie, herded unceremoniously under the tarps with the hostages, made themselves small while everyone else argued and sniped amongst themselves.

"Really, though, what's going on?" Charlie whispered from behind them.

"I think Talha is making a point," Kate responded in a low voice.

"What point would that be? That the Islamic State does it better?" Amy said.

"Just keep up the act. There's no way he leaves twenty million dollars on the table."

Charlie looked dubious. "We've all been doing this long enough to know that ideologues can't be bought."

"Everyone has a price."

"You! Child!" Mathilde snapped. "What is the meaning of this? Why haven't you secured our release?"

"The negotiations are continuing," Kate replied.

"She's lying," Lefèvre said.

"Excuse me?"

The Frenchman switched to English. "She's lying. The negotiations are over. No agreement."

The Americans and the Australians, perhaps accustomed to French hyperbole after so many months and years in the closest of quarters, looked skeptical.

"Gilles," Bess said gently, "we knew when they arrived that any agreement would take time, and that nothing was guaranteed. But they're still here."

Lefèvre sneered. "She was going to leave us to die. They all were. Isn't that true, Madame Moreau?"

Kate rubbed her temples. "We're doing everything we can to bring you home. But the situation is complicated."

"What is so complicated?" Mathilde challenged in heavily accented English. "Is it the Americans?" She made a dismissive gesture. "Leave them."

"Mathilde!" Marianne said.

"Ouch," Amy murmured, but Bess and Stu said nothing.

"Our goal is to obtain everyone's release. We don't want to see anyone left behind."

"But you are here to save us. Not them. Us," Mathilde insisted. "Everyone knows the Americans will not pay. Why must we suffer a moment longer than necessary?"

"The American government won't pay," Kate explained, "but Pastor Smith's organization can and will. Her organization has even agreed to pay for the release of Ollie and Noah."

The boys brightened. "Yeah?" said Noah. Then he turned serious. "Do I need to convert? I'm Jewish. I don't want my mum to get upset."

Amy bit back a smile. "No conversion necessary. It's on the house."

Noah and Ollie fist-bumped.

"So this organization will pay and our government will pay. What is the problem?" Mathilde asked.

"There is no deal!" Lefèvre snapped. "She spoke in Arabic so we wouldn't understand, but I saw it in her eyes. I see it still."

Kate sighed. "Monsieur Lefèvre..."

"Is the government too cheap to save its own citizens?"

"Like your brother?" Mathilde said, cackling.

Lefèvre responded with a crude insult in French, but Kate stepped in before the spat turned violent. "Enough. Both Pastor Smith and I have agreed to all terms as laid out by the opposing side. That includes the full price they've asked for."

"Then—"

Bess Abbott's quiet voice silenced Mathilde. "It's this new man, isn't it?"

Kate studied her, seeing intelligence and understanding in her tired eyes, and finally nodded.

"He's different than the others," Bess continued. "He...he believes."

One by one, the hostages turned to Kate. She saw confusion, questions, assumptions, accusations on their faces; but she also saw hope, stubborn hope that refused to die despite their dire circumstances. It was not her place to extinguish that light.

"We're doing everything we can," she said.

Ω

"Brother, I must object to these developments."

Khalifa held up a hand to silence Sharaf and spoke to his son. "Talha, Brother Sharaf's concerns are valid. He gave his word that the Westerners would come to no harm if they negotiated in good faith."

"And have they negotiated in good faith?"

"Yes, they have."

"The drone incident suggests otherwise."

"I believe they had nothing to do with it."

Talha touched a finger to his shaved upper lip. "I'm not convinced."

Khalifa sighed. "Son, they are women and civilians."

"Never underestimate a woman's capacity for guile."

Ratma's nostrils flared in irritation, but she remained silent. Khalifa pursed his lips and stroked his beard. Nick heard the distant strains of bickering hostages.

"I don't appreciate being treated like a hostage myself, young man," Sharaf said.

"You and your men are free to leave at any time, Sheikh."

"I cannot leave the Westerners behind. Their governments will find me."

"You could return to Yemen. Our brothers there will protect you."

"Our brothers in Yemen depend on me to provide for them, and for that I need freedom from suspicion, freedom of travel, freedom to conduct legitimate business to hide my activities in support of our movement. You put worldwide operations at risk with this need to grandstand!" Sharaf snarled.

275

Nick's hands already had a death grip on his rifle; his fingers went numb with the force he exerted on the weapon. The tall Arab regarded Sharaf curiously, intrigued by the outburst.

"Our brothers desperately need this ransom," the Yemeni continued. "Twenty million dollars—"

"Minus your cut. What is your cut, brother?"

"One million dollars."

"That is a generous token of our appreciation for your services."

"It is a pittance. I stand to lose everything if this deal falls through and you bring the rage of the American and French governments to my doorstep."

"I'm not convinced that this deal is in our best interest."

"Oh, you're not convinced? The upstart drunk on power?" Sharaf laughed in disbelief. He whipped his phone from the pocket at the front of his white thobe and scrolled through chats on which he, Kate, Nick, and Fatima had collaborated to create with help from Charlie's highly classified intelligence. He held the phone, open to a semi-fictious thread in Telegram, toward Talha. "The shura begs to differ."

Talha accepted the proffered phone, his eyes lingering on Sharaf before turning his attention to the words on the screen. Nick tried not to hyperventilate; if Talha suspected that the chat was a fake, planted on the phone thanks to George's technical prowess, they were all dead. The wait was interminable.

Finally, Talha returned the phone. "I admire Abu Musab's sense of humor. The world burns around him in Yemen, and still he has a quip for the occasion."

"One does not survive Yemen without a sense of humor," Sharaf said dryly.

"It appears I underestimated your influence, Sheikh. I have been in the wild for many years, and admittedly not privy to discussions among our most revered brothers."

"Then we are in agreement that we will reach a resolution with the Westerners?"

Talha looked toward the makeshift tent of tarps. "I will consider it."

"At least permit my men to check on them. I don't trust the more unstable hostages to remain in control."

"Your men will stay with you. Your wife will be permitted to check on the Westerners as often as she likes."

Sharaf flicked his head. Fatima and Ratma scurried toward the tarps.

"Let us pray and take our supper. I look forward to hearing more about the shura from you and my father. It seems I have much to learn."

"As you wish, Emir."

♌

Fatima and Ratma passed the dinner hour with the hostages. Yunis's young wife, with an escort from armed terrorists, delivered a small pot of unidentifiable stew and a plate of flatbread for their consumption. Only Ollie and Noah, elated over the news that the fictitious American Evangelical Association would pay for their release, ate anything, keeping up a running conversation with everyone and no one as they inhaled the food. Ollie's forehead still oozed blood, but he seemed unbothered by the injury.

Mathilde Fournier and Gilles Lefèvre had reached a truce as the sun disappeared behind the horizon, each blissfully silent and lost in his or her own world. Kate encouraged Marianne and Bess to eat, but the sister and the wife had other priorities.

"Your English is excellent," Bess said to Kate as she mopped Stu's brow. "If I didn't know better, I'd think you were American."

"My father was in the French military. I grew up all over the world. And the one thing that unites the world is American television and movies."

Bess smiled. "That's true. No matter how far we go, we can usually find something to remind us of home." The smile faded and she brushed away tears.

Amy rested a hand on her back. "Tell me about home," she said.

Kate ducked under the tarps and joined Fatima and Ratma, who chatted in the dusk. A guard gave her a critical look, but soon lost interest. The tall Tuareg broke off a thought in mid-sentence and addressed Kate in Arabic.

"I didn't know this is what Talha had become. The boy I knew years ago wanted to follow in his father's footsteps, but this is beyond the pale." She wrapped her arms around herself. "Khalifa's Arab wives raised monsters," she muttered.

Fatima's dark eyes encouraged her, but Kate treaded carefully. "Is there any possibility that your husband would delay the transfer of power until we've come to terms?"

"The message is en route to the shura and power passed from father to son the night before you arrived. Talha is the emir, and will be treated as such." Ratma smiled ruefully. "He caught me off guard with the speed of his decision. I pressured him, yes, but I didn't actually expect him to relinquish power so quickly. That drone attack rattled him. I believe it's the closest he's ever come to death, despite his years at war in Afghanistan and Pakistan and Libya."

"I'm happy for you," Kate said, and found a small part of herself meaning it. Ratma was complicit in the hostages' misfortune, but had almost certainly staved off further suffering, to the extent she was able to influence the men around her. "Where will you go?"

"I suppose you are well aware that Khalifa comes from southwestern Libya, as do I. Our tribes often traveled together when we were young. I hope to return to our roots. I joke about an easy life in the cities, but my home is the desert."

Kate watched the temporarily serene scene under the tarp. "I hope they can go home, too."

"How imminent is your departure?" Fatima asked. "Will you continue to move with the hostages?"

Ratma tossed up her hands. "I don't know. Khalifa will have some business to wrap up before we depart, but I cannot imagine that Talha will permit my presence near our guests."

"That's a shame. I believe these people need you."

"I've done my best to protect them from Yunis's excesses, but I fear the situation will become...challenging."

"Anything you can do," Kate said. "Anything at all, we appreciate."

Ratma squeezed her shoulder. "I am on your side, Madame Moreau, and will use whatever remaining leverage I have to assist you."

She snatched her hand away at the sound of approaching voices and retreated a few paces. Fatima flipped her niqab over her face as Amy and Charlie made an appearance beside Kate.

"What fresh hell awaits us?" Amy whispered.

"Sheikh, as you see, no harm has come to our guests. My friends, did you enjoy dinner?" Talha peered under the tarp, where Ollie and Noah polished off the last of the stew with bits of flatbread. "At least some of you did." The Arab straightened and turned to Fatima. "Umm Ali, may I make use of your linguistic abilities?"

Fatima stepped forward, waiting to translate.

"Will you please ask the rest of our guests to join us?"

At Fatima's request in English and French, the hostages roused themselves, moving stiffly after hours on the ground. Charlie and Bess helped Stu rise to his feet.

"Madame Moreau, I see you're wearing a watch. What time is it?"

Kate illuminated the face of the cheap digital watch on her wrist. "Almost nine p.m."

"Your Western construct of time is now of critical importance. In three hours, I will expect you to render a decision."

"A decision on what?"

"Who lives and who dies, of course."

Kate turned to Fatima, praying she had misunderstood Talha's words. The Yemeni's eyes widened, and she stared at him before mumbling a translation for Amy and Charlie, who looked stunned.

"I have decided that a compromise is in order. You will have the opportunity to pay for and repatriate some of the hostages. I will have the opportunity to kill others. A win-win, as they say, yes?"

"You can't be serious."

"I'm quite serious. One American, one Australian, and one French citizen will be permitted to keep his or her life." Talha pointed a long finger at Kate. "And you will render the verdict."

"This is insane."

"Umm Ali, please inform our guests of their fate. I believe they will have opinions on the matter."

Fatima cleared her throat and explained the situation, in spare language, to the assembled hostages. The outcry was immediate and thunderous. Talha turned his back on the group and meandered toward his tent, leaving Khalifa and Sharaf sputtering in his wake. Kate sprang forward to catch the new emir.

"You can't do this. I won't be a participant."

He looked down at her and shrugged. "Either you choose who lives, or they all die."

"But—"

"You have three hours. The executions commence at midnight."

Ɬ

Amy, Charlie, Fatima, and Ratma attempted to help Kate keep order, but the situation deteriorated rapidly. Yunis and his men prevented Nick and Jake from joining the fray, leading to much shouting and insults exchanged in Arabic. Nearby, Sharaf held a heated conversation with Khalifa, who stood with a hand to his bearded cheek as if in shock. Kate couldn't blame him.

In a state of shock herself, she watched as Mathilde Fournier dumped the contents of her sack at her feet, rooted through the hodgepodge of accumulated sundries over years in captivity, and launched a small mirror at Kate's head. She

280

saw the glint of light as it sailed toward her face, and ducked just in time. Yunis howled in laughter and fumbled for his phone, perhaps intending to post a video of the fracas to terrorist YouTube. Marianne tried to pry the next projectile out of her sister's hand, but the used bar of soap glanced off Kate's shoulder.

Ollie and Noah cornered Amy and Charlie dangerously close to the pit latrines, and the two Americans tried to calm Ollie, who gestured wildly and bellowed profanity. Noah vomited into the nearest latrine.

Kate dodged another missile; Mathilde had surprisingly good aim. She stumbled to a safer distance, only to find herself the object of Lefèvre's ire. He screamed unintelligibly, his eyes bulging and his face turning a dangerous shade of maroon. Kate saw Nick shove one of Yunis's men from the corner of her eye; if she didn't get the situation under control, he might, and that would mean the death of them all.

She felt the rage building inside her chest, constricting her throat, pounding in her ears. She was mad at everyone: at the terrorists for being terrorists, at the hostages for being hostages, at her husband for being an overbearing alpha caveman, and, most of all, at herself for misjudging every aspect of this operation and causing the certain deaths of people she was meant to save. The rage blinded her; then it exploded.

"*Assez! Khalas!* Enough!"

Her primal roar in three languages shocked everyone, perhaps most especially those who knew her best. Nick froze, locked in a scuffle with a terrorist, who also turned to stare at her. Amy murmured "holy fuck," and didn't apologize for it.

Kate squared off against Lefèvre. "If you don't get the hell out of my face this instant, you'll be the first to die." The Frenchman backed away and mumbled what might have been an apology. Then Kate strode to Mathilde and smacked a hairbrush from her hand. "Do not throw another piece of junk at me, is that clear?" The older woman snarled a retort about Kate's youthful appearance, but allowed Marianne to clasp her hands. Lastly, Kate turned to the two Australians. "Calm down, both of you." The boys nodded meekly.

Satisfied that she had everyone's attention, she took center stage in the horseshoe of hostages, with a calmer Nick and a quiet Sharaf and Khalifa at her back. Kate had never been one for the spotlight, had always dreaded public speaking. She thought it was one of the reasons she had chosen the CIA over the State Department; the shadows so rarely entailed the limelight.

But here she was, standing on reddish, mottled earth in the heart of the Islamic Emirate of the Maghreb, under an endless black sky, illuminated only by the moon and the stars and a handful of battery-powered lanterns, with a motley crew of good guys, bad guys, and those caught in between awaiting her words. Nothing had prepared her for this. What could she say? What could she possibly say to those who would die?

"Here's the deal: Your captors intend to kill four of you at midnight, and I don't think we can stop it."

"Offer more money," Lefèvre said.

"This isn't about money."

"It's always about money. Just—"

"It's *not* about money," Kate said in a tone that silenced him. "The new emir intends to make an example of you. Your deaths will be recorded and almost certainly posted on the internet and sent to news organizations. Your families and friends may see the footage. It will be…" She couldn't finish her sentence.

Bess tentatively raised a hand. "Why…?"

"Why am I telling you this?" Kate threw up her hands as tears sprang to her eyes, but she kept her voice steady. "Because I want you to focus on what you can control. The terrorists can take your life, but you can face death with dignity, with defiance. Your families can take the smallest bit of solace that you died bravely in the face of unspeakable depravity."

"Easy for you to say," Lefèvre muttered.

"Yes," Kate said. "But this is your reality. In less than three hours, he'll be back and the executions will start. You can die how he wants you to die, a blubbering mess on your knees, or you can stand tall and look that son of a bitch in the eyes before it ends."

Ollie and Noah nodded slowly. Bess and Stu embraced. The Fournier sisters touched foreheads. Only Lefèvre remained belligerent.

"He said you would choose. How will you choose?"

Kate shook her head. "I won't choose. You will. Somehow, you need to come to an agreement by midnight."

☊

They were the longest, most agonizing three hours of Kate's life. She felt like the amateur Jane Goodall of the Sahel, a bumbling interloper intruding on a closed ecosystem, sowing discord in a mini-community already beset by the inherent strife of a much larger one. Had the situation not been so dire, she might have been fascinated by the drama playing out in her midst.

In the face of certain death, how did humans behave? How should they behave? Kate thought she could answer the first question. They behaved as individuals. She had known Bess and Stu and Ollie and Noah and Marianne and Mathilde and Gilles for the briefest moment in time, yet she knew they were acting in character.

Bess and Stu Abbott reached consensus quickly; Stu would make the ultimate sacrifice. He quelled Bess's protestations with a long embrace, and then they asked Amy and Charlie to pray with them. As Kate watched her two friends—one an avowed atheist, one a semi-practicing Catholic—gather with two true believers in their own right, she saw the depths of their humanity as well. Pastor Amy, the over-the-top caricature of an evangelical inspired by too many real over-the-top leaders in the American evangelical community, was

283

nowhere to be seen; she was simply Amy Kowalski, one of the most decent people Kate knew, demonstrating compassion and humility and strength.

The Aussie boys sat in silence outside the tarp, staring up at the night sky. Fraser's Australian counterpart in Paris, whom she'd contacted after the State Department had notified the Australian government of the boys' plight, had passed along some additional background. Ollie and Noah were childhood friends, inseparable since they were in diapers. Ollie was the big personality, the idea guy; Noah was the calming influence, the practical thinker. Kate recognized that dynamic. There was little doubt in her mind how the scenario would play out if Nick and Jake found themselves forced to choose who would live and who would die, and it brought tears to her eyes just thinking about it.

The French had split into two camps—indeed, they had always been two camps, the bonds of shared language and heritage never enough to overcome the challenges posed by Mathilde's deteriorating mental state and Gilles's cynicism and perceived selfishness. Lefèvre paced and threw agitated looks in Kate's direction. She paid him little mind. She was more interested in the sisters. They talked quietly under the tarp, too quietly for her to hear.

According to Dubois, the Fourniers' younger brother described how the sisters had raised him after their death of their mother and how they had devoted their adult lives to teaching and supporting those less fortunate. Mathilde, the oldest, had developed a case of wanderlust in retirement, convincing Marianne to accompany her to Francophone West Africa in search of the adventure they weren't able to have in their younger years. This was the tragic coda to that adventure. Kate knew instinctively that the sisters would choose death. Not to spare Lefèvre, but because of how they did everything: together.

At one minute to midnight, Kate heard the footsteps. She acknowledged no one until Talha materialized at her side.

"It's time, Madame Moreau."

She turned to him and looked up into his eyes, barely visible in the moonlight. "Please don't do this."

"I have no choice. It is the will of God."

"Bullshit."

Talha raised an eyebrow. "Do you pray, Madame Moreau?"

Kate shook her head. "I want nothing to do with a God who sanctions this."

"Funny. We Muslims think the same of your Crusader God and all those who act in his name."

"Let's change the narrative. Let's demonstrate to the world that it doesn't need to be this way."

"*Allahu a'alam.* One does not transgress Allah's divine will. And now I need your answer. Who shall live, and who shall die?"

"They decided."

"Democratic sentiment to the end. How very Western." He smiled without humor. "Come, let us begin. You will translate for me."

Kate followed him to the tent, where seven individuals awaited their fate. He surveyed them wordlessly, his eyes lingering on each. Did he see people? Or did he see a spectacle?

"Americans first," he said to her.

"Mr. and Mrs. Abbott, what have you decided?"

Stu stepped forward. "It will be me."

"No surprise there," Talha said. "Next, the Australians."

"Noah, Ollie?"

Ollie raised his hand. "It was my stupid fucking idea, this mess."

"Interesting," Talha said. "I could have gone either way on that one."

"And I could do without the editorializing," she said to him.

"There is no need to be snippy, Madame Moreau," he said lightly. "Although, if I were in your situation, perhaps I too would find myself a bit churlish. This cannot be good for your career progression, I imagine. And with that, let us move to your countrymen."

"Mesdames, monsieur," Kate said. "The emir needs your decision."

The sisters clasped hands and shuffled forward. "This *connard* deserves to die," Mathilde said, gesturing to Lefèvre with her free hand, "but life is nothing without a sister." Then she pointed a finger at Talha. "And you, young man, I hope you burn in the pits of hell for all eternity."

"Do you need me to translate?" Kate asked Talha.

Her faux innocence provoked a smirk. "My French is good enough. I believe I got the gist." He turned to Yunis and his lieutenants. "I want them on their knees, facing their loved ones."

Yunis snapped off a salute to his brother. He and his two lieutenants first grabbed Stu Abbott and the sisters. Stu and Marianne put up no resistance as they were forced to their knees, but Mathilde made sure to offer Yunis a parting gift, payback for the earlier slap. She lunged and raked her dirty fingernails across the side of his neck, right over his carotid artery. Yunis recoiled and clapped a hand over his slashed skin, then pulled back his fist to punch her.

Kate sprang forward and slipped between them, facing the angry terrorist. "You'll get to kill her. Isn't that enough?"

"Stand down, brother," Talha said before Yunis could respond. "The Australian, please. And Madame Moreau, I prefer if you remain by my side."

Kate rejoined Talha, conscious of Mathilde's eyes on her. The sister gave a single nod and the smallest of smiles.

Ollie went willingly and sank to his knees beside Stu. The older man squeezed the younger's shoulder.

"You're a good friend."

Talha paced slowly before the line of hostages. Bess wept into her hands. Noah's shoulders shook with the effort to contain his emotion. Lefèvre stared stonily into the middle distance.

"This isn't right," Talha said.

Kate's heart leaped into her throat. "Will you reconsider and—"

He faced her, and her heart sank. "This isn't right," he repeated. "This is not my vision. This is not God's will. Yunis!"

The eager chief of security grinned. "Yes, brother?"

"Fix this."

Yunis's small army joined him and his lieutenants, dragging bodies forward and throwing others back. The scrum turned loud and violent as sisters were separated and friends and spouses were exchanged. Talha watched with his arms crossed over his chest, sliding the occasional glance at Kate to gauge her reaction.

He regarded the new lineup of kneeling hostages with evident pleasure. "This is better."

Bess, Mathilde, Lefèvre, and Noah stared up at him, shock etched on their faces. Behind them, restrained by terrorists, Ollie roared his fury and Stu wheezed his objections, begging to take his wife's place. Marianne sobbed her sister's name over and over.

"What are you doing?" Kate asked Talha. "You said they could choose."

"No, I said that *you* could choose, Madame Moreau. You abdicated your duty."

"What does it matter to you who lives or dies?"

He shrugged. "This way, everyone suffers the most. The sick husband who will lose a healthy wife; the boy whose idiocy cost the life of his best friend; the sane sister who will replay this moment for the rest of her years."

"This is barbaric."

"Would you prefer that I kill all seven?"

Kate clenched her jaws, her mind racing for any possible opportunity to talk him down, change his mind. But her eyes met his, and she stared into the abyss.

"It's time. Please step back."

Kate turned to Amy and Charlie, who pleaded for Talha to reconsider. He ignored them, pulling his pistol from its holster and letting the barrel seek its preferred target. He settled on Bess Abbott. Yunis immediately leveled his gun at Mathilde Fournier, and his two lieutenants took aim at Noah Shaw and Gilles Lefèvre. The Frenchman hyperventilated, but the other three squared their shoulders and remained calm.

Kate made one last effort. "Emir, please. Let's continue negotiations."

"Negotiations are over."

Kate looked behind her, suddenly aware of the silence. All eyes were on her. Everyone seemed to be trying to send her a message, even Khalifa. Nick tapped his rifle magazine, seemingly a nervous gesture. But Nick didn't have nervous tics. He could be signaling her in Morse code, but if he was, it was all dots, no dashes. And in any case, she didn't know Morse code. She watched the tapping more closely. Two fingers, deliberate. The magazine. Ammunition. And then she understood.

She grabbed Amy and Charlie and pulled them close to her. "It's over. His mind is made up."

"But—"

"It's over." As they retreated, she whispered, "Ixnay onyay ethay ammoyay!"

"These fucking psychos," Amy muttered.

Talha began the count. Three hours of decisions, three seconds of pure, unadulterated terror. Four men pulled four triggers; four empty pistols dry-fired, their quiet clicks just as shocking as the report of a .45-caliber round.

Talha turned his back on the traumatized hostages and holstered his pistol. He offered a slight bow to Kate. "It is time for *Tahajjud* prayers. *Bonne nuit,* Madame Moreau."

22

KATE, AMY, AND CHARLIE passed the remainder of the night with the hostages, offering what little comfort they could in the aftermath of the mock executions. The hostages were subdued but alert, exhausted but unwilling to close their eyes. They talked of establishing their own sentry schedule, discussed ways they could protect themselves from the scores of armed men crawling about camp. Then they reflected. Everyone had someone, everyone but Gilles Lefèvre, who separated himself from the group. Shoulders slumped and head bowed, he stared at his hands. Kate sat beside him.

"You think I'm weak and pathetic."

"No."

"You think I'm selfish."

"I think you're human."

He smirked. "That's of little comfort coming from a diplomat."

"Do you *want* me to tell you what I really think of you?"

He shook his head. "I know what you think of me. I know what everyone thinks of me. Even my own family doesn't want me back."

"I think you should be careful what you believe from the mouths of terrorists."

"The problem is, it sounds just like something my brother would say."

"Families are complicated. And so is negotiating with terrorists. You have no way of knowing what misinformation your brother received or what decisions he faced."

He looked at her. "Do you think people deserve their fate?"

"Sometimes. But not always."

"I'm worried that I deserve this fate."

"Why?"

Lefèvre used a finger to draw shapes in the sand. A star, a whirlpool, an infinity sign. Then letters. A name.

"Who is Jeanne?" Kate asked.

He erased the name with a swipe his hand. "No one."

"I doubt Jeanne, whoever she is, thinks you deserve this fate."

"I'm not so sure." He smiled wanly. "Much like the terrorists, she didn't approve of my business practices."

"You know what I do believe in? Second chances. But to have yours, you need to ease up on everyone. And ease up on yourself. A little compassion might just get you through this."

She stood and he gazed up at her, as if seeing her for the first time. "Is this your second chance, Madame Moreau?"

She offered a quick smile. "Something like that."

𝔘

The sheikh, his Legionnaires, and their hosts returned for them late morning, striding through camp with purpose.

"It is time for us to depart," Sharaf said. "I believe we are in accordance with our hosts."

"The original terms? Twenty million dollars for the hostages?" Kate asked.

Sharaf nodded. "Brother Talha sees the benefit of such an exchange."

Kate exhaled slowly and felt some her body's tension release. She turned to the hostages, who had immediately scurried to the perceived safety of the tents but who watched them with wide eyes, hanging on every word of a conversation they didn't understand.

"Be patient and be strong. We'll be back for you as soon as possible," she said first in French and then in English.

The hostages broke into smiles and clasped one another in relief.

Talha turned to Kate. "May I speak with you privately?"

Behind her, Nick tensed; she heard the metallic click of his AK-47's safety switch flip from safe to semi-automatic. She regarded the terrorist critically, taking in his easy movements, his hands clasped behind his back, the utility belt around his waist supporting a holstered pistol and a long knife, the beaten Kalashnikov slung over one shoulder.

"As you wish."

"Let's walk."

She followed him as he retreated to an open area beyond some trucks, within sight of the group.

"Your compatriots worry," he said.

"Can you blame them?"

"I like you, Counselor Moreau. You speak your mind."

"Even though it makes me unsuitable for traditional marriage?"

He laughed, seemingly in genuine amusement. "I trust you took no real offense to my earlier commentary on your status as a thoroughly modern woman."

"None. Though I do wonder why you deign to speak to such a woman."

"It's become clear over the course of our brief relationship that you are the brains of this operation. As such, direct dialogue with you is essential to achieving my aims."

"I'm still not clear on your aims, to be honest."

He leaned toward her conspiratorially. "Can you keep a secret?"

"I get paid a sad government salary to do just that."

"Smart and funny. I'm sure you make your minister laugh, though I fear what I will share with you will distress you and your government."

"I doubt you can surprise us."

"Perhaps not. If I'm honest with myself, you've heard it all before. Your country has seen much tragedy in recent years. Many dead, many wounded in your own land at the hands of my brothers. Your military force here has faltered since its first successful foray into this region, and it seems your countrymen tire of the cost. This has become your Afghanistan, I think?"

Kate waited for him to continue, but it was not a rhetorical question. She wanted to direct him to a certain Legionnaire who had strong opinions on this very topic, but instead she marshaled her inner Ardouin. "I defer comments on military matters to my colleagues in the Ministry of Defense. I'm sure you understand," she said.

He nodded sagely. "I would not presume to speak on my brothers' operations in Yemen or Somalia or Syria. Although I do have opinions," he said with a wink.

"You still haven't told me your aims."

"Ah, yes, forgive me. I've enjoyed the opportunity to converse with someone of your obvious intelligence. My intellectual stimulation was lacking in the mountains." He glanced sidelong at her as they walked, his hands cradling his rifle. "You really are a beautiful woman. I see why the big Legionnaire is in love with you."

Kate jerked in surprise. "What?"

He regarded her as if she were dim. "The big Legionnaire, Dieter. Ratma assures us that he is in love with you."

"That's absurd. I don't even know him and he works for a businessman," she said, putting a sarcastic emphasis on *businessman*.

Talha absently stroked the barrel of his Kalashnikov. "Ratma is a ridiculous creature, no doubt, but she is rarely wrong in matters of the heart." He tossed a glance over his shoulder. "He watches you intently."

"I think you've seriously misread this situation. If you just tell me what you want, we can move forward."

Talha stopped. They faced each other an arm's length apart, in full view of the Sandstorm team, the hostages, and their hosts.

"Counselor Moreau, I never misread a situation. And as for what I want, perhaps showing is better than telling."

Talha pivoted and rammed the butt of his rifle into Kate's solar plexus. Her breath left in a whoosh and she doubled over, clutching her ribs. He grabbed her, slapped her face, and flung her sideways. She hit the ground hard, smashing her left shoulder and hip onto the parched earth. She was still gasping for air when he hauled her up by her hair, provoking a cry of pain, and used her as a shield between himself and the angry Americans rushing toward them.

Nick and Jake had their rifles trained on Talha's head, and Nick roared for the terrorist to release her. Talha drew his long knife and placed it against Kate's throat. She ceased her struggle, trying to keep still but unable to control the tremors of pain and fear coursing through her body.

"Not another step, Legionnaire. Lower your weapons, both of you, or I'll bleed her like a sheep." To Kate he whispered, "Now do you believe that he's in love with you?"

Kate could barely breathe, both from the shot to the ribs and Talha's hand yanking her head back awkwardly to keep her throat fully exposed. Bright lights assailed her blurry vision, but she saw Nick and Jake slowly lower their rifles. Amy, Charlie, Fatima, and Sharaf surrounded them, Sharaf grabbing at Khalifa and snarling his displeasure.

"Son, release her."

"Enough, father. Your soft spot for the *kuffar* is clouding your judgment. They have not taken us seriously." He pressed the flat of the blade against Kate's trachea, bumping over the ridges under the thinnest layer of skin. "But now I have their attention. I do have your attention, don't I, Madame Moreau?"

"Yes," Kate gasped.

"Listen carefully. The theater you witnessed last night will be the hostages' reality if my instructions are not followed exactly. All seven will be released into your custody—*your* custody, Madame Moreau, and that of Pastor Smith—following payment. You will bring the money to a location of my choosing on a date of my choosing, and we will make the exchange. The price for their lives is now thirty million U.S. dollars. Is that clear?"

Kate rasped an affirmative. He yanked her hair again, pulling her tighter against his body. The knife's pressure against her throat increased. Then he withdrew the blade and shoved her away. She stumbled and crumpled in a heap, clutching her midsection.

Amy and Charlie sprinted to her side. Sharaf ordered Fatima to assist. Talha meandered toward Yunis and his men, who held Nick and Jake at bay. Nick first hurled orders and insults at the brothers, and then the bodies of their fighters started to fly as he pushed and shoved terrorists from his path.

"Are you okay?" Amy asked, helping her to sit.

Kate's breath came in short, wheezing gasps as her abdominal muscles engaged. The pain was secondary to her concern over Nick's blind rage. "Calm him down or he's going to get us all killed!" she hissed at Fatima.

Fatima returned to Sharaf and spoke loudly enough for Kate to hear. "She will survive. But your Legionnaire embarrasses us."

Kate watched as Sharaf said something to Nick. Her husband paused in mid-scuffle and stared at him. Then he released Yunis's man and retreated to the background. Jake disengaged and joined him.

Amy and Charlie helped Kate to her feet, supporting some of her weight until she found her sea legs. Her steps, initially halting, grew stronger as she made her way to her team and their enemy, whom she faced, shoulders square and chin held high.

Talha gestured to their two dusty Hiluxes; Cherif had returned to the camp and waited by the open door of his truck, his posture tense. "You are free to go."

"We'll await your call."

As the team hurried to the trucks, Talha raised his face to the hazy sky and breathed deeply. "Travel safely. I sense danger in the lands of Azawad."

ϰ

The Hiluxes tore through the desert, bouncing violently over uneven terrain and straining worn shocks. Jake followed Cherif's dusty contrail, trying to stay in the Tuareg's tire tracks that mirrored a semi-permanent path through the Sahelian moonscape.

Nick's head swiveled side to side, front to back, seeking any indication that Talha's men had followed them. They were minutes from the IEM camp, and there was no sign of any human life save their own. Nick keyed his radio and raised Cherif.

"Pull over."

"Capitaine, we must not stop. This is extremely dangerous territory."

"Cherif!"

"Capitaine, we must wait until we have numbers. I will contact my men as soon as we are in range of the wells."

"If you don't—"

Jake pressed the transmit button on his own radio and disrupted Nick's bellow. "I know you're concerned, but he's right. We're way too exposed out here."

Nick's pulse raced and blood pounded in his ears, behind his eyes. This was worse than Fallujah, Ramadi, Kandahar, Helmand, all places he had killed men, seen his own men die. The deaths of and grievous injuries to Marines who had chosen to enlist, chosen to fight, had left lasting scars on his psyche and soul; but the unprovoked attack against his wife, the rag doll in a terrorist's mastiff jaws, broke something inside of him that would never be made whole again.

He took a deep breath from his core to center himself. A calm descended. He knew what must be done.

Nick ripped his pistol from the holster on his thigh and pointed the gun at the side of his best friend's head. "Stop the truck or I'll blow your brains out."

Jake set his jaw and stared straight ahead, but radioed Cherif and asked him to stop. Both trucks rolled to a halt in the open desert. Nick ran to the other Hilux and jerked open the rear passenger-side door.

"Out," he ordered Amy.

She scurried to join Jake in the front of the vacated truck and Nick clambered in beside Kate. Cherif hit the gas and they shot forward.

Nick's hands hovered over Kate. She held tight to the door's armrest, wincing with each bounce as the lighter rear of the vehicle took the brunt of the bumps.

"Kate, are you—"

The front wheel glanced off an unseen pothole, sending the truck skyward and then fishtailing at high speed. Nick, not wearing a seatbelt, smashed his helmeted head into the ceiling. But Kate's cry of pain nearly blinded him in terror.

"For fuck's sake, Cherif!"

"I'm sorry, Capitaine, but we must reach the wells. There is danger."

Nick turned back to Kate. One corner of her upper lip was swollen and her face was covered in dirt and sweat, but her hazel eyes were bright and alert.

"You should have stayed with the sheikh, Legionnaire," she said gently.

"Not a chance. What hurts?"

"I'm fine."

"Nothing about this looks fine."

"He caught my ribs. I'm sure they're just bruised."

Jake's voice filled his ear. "Motorcyclists on the horizon. Approaching from the south."

Nick struggled to see through the rear passenger-side window, damaged days earlier by an angry terrorist. "Talha's men?"

"Moussa Diallo's men. It has reached him that we are separated from my unit and no longer under Khalifa's protection." Cherif increased speed, but the flotilla of motorcycles would soon be within striking distance. He again tried to raise his cousin, but they were still out of range. "They will attack, Capitaine."

"Just keep going." Nick readied his rifle, wishing he had his trusty M4 with the scope and barrel grip instead of the Kalashnikov.

"Should I shoot?"

"Focus on driving. Use the vehicle as a weapon, but *don't* crash. Follow Jake's lead." He keyed his radio. "You got this?"

"You know it, big guy."

"Amy?"

"She's ready to go."

"No spraying and praying. Conserve ammo." Then to Cherif he said, "You see the heart of the convoy? Go straight through it."

"But—"

"We can wreck some of them. Turn when Jake does."

Nick tried to roll down the damaged window; finally, he rammed his elbow into the center of the cracks and the glass shattered. He braced himself as best he could in the tight back seat and nosed the barrel of the AK-47 out of the truck. In range, the cyclists let loose a volley of small-arms fire; most rounds went high and wide, but a few of the passengers got off shots that ripped through the bed.

Jake and Cherif turned suddenly into the wave of motorcycles, catching the drivers off guard. Front wheels locked and threw riders into oncoming bikes; others skidded out and caused crashes. Nick raked those they passed with rifle fire, wounding several men. But the uneven terrain was impossible to anticipate, especially at breakneck speed, and any strikes on attackers were pure luck.

"Coming around," Jake said over the radio.

The mass of motorcycles regrouped behind them, turning to follow and putting safer distance between bikes. They were still at least twenty bikes strong, with double the manpower, and far more maneuverable through the thickening scrub than the Hiluxes. Nick leaned out the shattered window and picked off two more.

"On the left! On the left!" Charlie yelled.

Nick whipped around in time to see a motorcycle zoom up on their flank, the armed passenger lining up a shot at the truck. He dove toward Kate and pulled her down onto the seat, covering her with his body and muffling her cries of pain. Three rifle rounds tore through her window and exited through the roof, narrowly missing Nick's head. Cherif yanked the wheel and careened into the motorcycle.

"Stay down," he told Kate. And to Cherif he said, "Try to keep us steady."

"Nick, don't do anything crazy," Kate said.

But Nick was already slithering out the shattered passenger-side window, one hand grasping the grab handle inside, the other reaching around for the roll bar in the bed. His armored vest and ammo pouches caught, momentarily arresting his progress. He had to stretch backwards, parallel to the ground whizzing underneath him, until his chest cleared the top of the window frame.

Still holding onto the grab handle and the roll bar, he managed to swing one leg out and find the running board with his foot. He was about to pull his second leg from the cab when Cherif clipped some brush, knocking his foot off the running board. He dangled for a few seconds before regaining his footing. He ripped his leg out to stand with two feet on the running board, took a deep breath, and hooked his left leg around the roll bar, which he used to pull himself into the bed. With a clearer view of the battlefield and far more maneuverability, he braced himself amidst their gear and lined up his shots.

The insurgents turned their attention to the visible threat, as Nick knew they would. Rounds tore through the bed and blew through camping gear and crates and Pelican cases. Nick positioned himself between the trailing terrorists and Kate in the cab, his back pressed to the rear window, and picked off terrorists.

"We are in range! We are in range!" Cherif yelled over the radio. "Ten minutes! Ten minutes!"

A lot could happen in ten minutes, Nick knew. In war, ten minutes was a lifetime. He tried to line up a clean shot at a passenger fumbling with a rocket-propelled grenade launcher, but the incessant bouncing caused three straight misses. The Hiluxes picked up a worn path; Nick sighted cleanly and pulled the trigger. The shot went through the driver at center mass and into the passenger. The bike wrecked.

Nick reloaded and pivoted to track a rider racing up their right side. Just as he pulled the trigger, he felt like he had been hit in the back with a sledgehammer. He pitched forward and fell face down into gear, momentarily unable to breathe. The armor plates in his vest, meant to stop a rifle round, did just that. He roared in pain and fury, climbed to his feet, and flipped his rifle to automatic. He went through ninety rounds in seconds, pausing only to reload, but many of the ninety rounds found their mark. The handful of surviving riders peeled off, heading southeast toward the river and friendly Fulani encampments.

Minutes later, Cherif's men appeared on the horizon. Some swallowed the two Hiluxes into a protective cocoon while others chased down the fleeing motorcycles. Nick dropped to his haunches and rapped on the back window. Kate gave him a weak thumbs-up. He slumped against the cab and prayed for an uneventful return to the city.

☊

Charlie reached Diana Fraser and requested that the two Hiluxes be cleared through without delay and escorted to the base hospital.

"Charlie, I'm fine," Kate said.

He ignored her and continued his conversation with Fraser. "Whatever you do, keep Chad away."

That was an excellent idea, Kate thought.

Charlie finished the call and provided instructions to Cherif. Then he called Amy. "Tell Jake to go around to the southwest gate. Fraser and Dubois will meet us there."

Cherif followed Jake, who stuck his arm out the window and waved to the French sentries as they approached. Cherif's militia stopped well clear of the gate. Dubois, Fraser, and Ardouin waited in a truck, which swung around and made straight for the hospital. Nick launched himself out of the bed before Cherif put the truck in park and opened Kate's door, releasing her seatbelt and easing her out.

"Oh my God," Fraser said. "What happened?"

"This way, this way," Dubois said, as Ardouin ran into the hospital to alert the staff of their arrival.

Two nurses met them and tried to take hold of Kate, but Nick refused to release her. An older man approached, gestured to Nick, and spoke to Dubois and Ardouin in French.

"You cannot be armed in here," Dubois said.

"I'm staying with her."

"Yes, you can stay with her. But you must leave your weapons outside."

"Jesus Christ," Nick muttered. He allowed the nurses to support Kate while he handed rifle, pistol, and magazines to Dubois and Ardouin. Then he retook possession of Kate and they followed the nurses to an exam room.

She conversed with them in French, then turned to Nick. "They want to take some X-rays. Wait here and—"

"I'm coming with you."

"Nick, please. Stay here. I'll be back in a few minutes."

When she returned, she found him pacing in the small room. He had shed his armor and the top half of his uniform. His white T-shirt was as brown as the Legion-issue desert fatigues, but she saw no blood or obvious injuries. His cheeks were burned from sun, wind, and sand, and his short hair was matted from sweat and his helmet. Deep blue eyes, normally calm and thoughtful, were stormy and full of emotion, mirroring the tension she saw in his coiled posture. A kiss would pacify him, but just as she reached for him, the doctor and one of the nurses entered the room.

The doctor introduced himself while the nurse hung X-rays films on the wall-mounted light box. He looked inquiringly at Nick; Kate nodded her assent for him to share the diagnosis.

"You have several cracked ribs, with a more significant fracture here," he explained in French, using his pen to point to specific areas of her ribcage visible in the films.

"What's he saying?" Nick asked.

She held up a hand, gesturing for the doctor to continue.

"There isn't much we can do for ribs besides at-home remedies and allowing the breaks time to heal. X-rays of your left shoulder are negative for fracture."

"What's the deal?"

"Hold on."

The doctor regarded Nick warily. "As I was saying, no visible fracture. With luck it's a simple sprain, but if you continue to have pain a month from now, I recommend an MRI to check for a tear."

"Kate!"

"Nick, hush. Just wait."

"If I may ask, how did you sustain these injuries?"

"It's complicated," she said with a tight smile.

"All right," Nick said, rising to his feet in a most menacing fashion, "if this snail-slurper doesn't start explaining himself in English, it'll take surgery to put his ribcage back together."

"Nick!"

The doctor and nurse glanced at each other. The nurse inched toward the door, one hand reaching into her scrub pocket for her phone.

"I'm so sorry," Kate said. She grabbed Nick's arm and squeezed, digging her nails into sensitive skin on the underside of his wrist to get his attention. "Calm down right now."

"But—"

"You're out of control. She's about to call the MPs and I'll let them take you," Kate said, nodding toward the nurse.

Nick scoffed.

"Madame, I don't mean to overstep, but you do need...help?" asked the doctor, his eyes never leaving Nick.

"Sweetie, please sit." She tugged his arm and he finally returned to his seat. She leaned close. "They think you did this to me."

Nick stared at her, then at the doctor and nurse. His shoulders slumped and he took her hand in his, chastened.

"Please forgive my husband. He's had a bad day. To put him at ease, would you mind repeating what you told me, in English if you're comfortable?"

"Of course."

After a thorough explanation and discussion in English, the doctor dispensed bottles of painkillers and muscle relaxants, disinfected cuts and scrapes, and fitted Kate for a soft shoulder brace. He accepted Nick's apology with a smile, shook hands with the imposter Legionnaire, and gave Kate his mobile phone number in case she needed to reach him.

They found the Sandstorm crew milling about the trucks outside, with Fraser, Dubois, and Ardouin pressing them for information on the events that led to Kate's injuries. To Kate's exhausted amusement, the team had deferred all questions to her, driving Fraser mad.

"Well?" Amy said.

"Broken ribs and a sprained shoulder," Jake guessed. "And Nick added insult to injury with literal insults aimed at the French doctor."

Nick sighed. Kate squeezed his hand. "Nailed it."

"What the hell happened?" Fraser asked.

"Got sideways with a terrorist. Then the land pirates attacked. It's a long story."

"But epic," Amy said. "In all the wrong ways, of course."

Fraser, Dubois, and Ardouin stared at them.

"It's a story that can wait. Kate needs to get home and rest," Nick said.

"Absolutely," Fraser said. "But..."

"No. No buts."

"But we appear to have a slight problem brewing. We can handle it," Fraser said hurriedly, "but we need to know how you want us to handle it."

"Is this day really going to get worse?" Amy muttered.

"What kind of slight problem?" Kate asked.

"Weiss and Van Pelt were busy in your absence. They convinced the director to pull the plug on your operation and let them take the lead. Weiss is hellbent on finding Khalifa, and Yorke and Doyle are putting together a plan to rescue the hostages. They're finalizing their briefing now for the director's approval."

"We got paid an awful lot of money to get sidelined," Jake said with some amusement.

"If we were smart, we'd wash our hands of this and laugh all the way to the bank," Nick said, looking at Kate.

"Is there any way to delay the briefing?" Kate asked.

"I don't think so. It's on for five p.m. our time."

Kate checked her watch. The Western construct of time was impossible to escape. They had an hour.

"We're definitely not smart enough to laugh all the way to the bank, so what's the plan?" Amy asked.

"I don't really have one. Just play along."

"Do we still hate each other?"

"More than ever." Kate looked to Fraser. "Get us an audience?"

"They're eager to debrief you."

Nick helped Kate into the rear of Cherif's Hilux. "I really think we should laugh all the way to the bank," he whispered.

She kissed him, her lips lingering against his. "I love you. Please don't forget that."

23

THE BRIEFING ROOM WAS a hive of activity. Maps, intel reports, and laptops littered the long table. A PowerPoint presentation flared to life on the flatscreen television; Weiss barked edits to Lacey, who wrote furiously on her notepad. Van Pelt nodded in agreement, pretending to have a role in the proceedings. Emmanuel Giraud looked shellshocked, as if the centrifugal force of stupidity had plastered him to his chair.

The team filed into the room and took their seats. No one helped Kate, who fell into her chair. Chad looked up from a map, on which he was plotting coordinates, and did a double take.

"Kate! My God, what happened?" He rushed to her side and hovered, his hands clumsily poking and prodding.

She pushed him away, trying to smile to lessen any feelings of rejection, and leaned forward to protect her ribs. He laid a hand on her wrenched shoulder, and she grimaced.

"Don't touch her!"

Chad released Kate and faced Nick, a hand resting on his holstered pistol. Blake Doyle already had his Colt leveled at Nick. Jake went for his own Glock. Fraser and Dubois stepped between the warring parties. Van Pelt used shaking hands to smooth his tie and then cleared his throat nervously. Weiss snorted his derision.

"Chad, no guns," Kate said. "He's upset but he's unarmed. We had a rough trip. Please just be the bigger man."

Chad glowered at Nick, but withdrew his hand and motioned Blake to stand down. "Yeah, yeah, of course. You know I'm always the bigger man." He winked at her.

Amy pantomimed vomiting.

"Shut up, Kowalski."

"She's a bitch, but at least she commands a room," Weiss said to Van Pelt while gesturing to Fraser. "You let this turn into a goddamn soap opera."

"Ladies, gentlemen, perhaps we could all calm down and focus," Van Pelt said, before Fraser could stab Weiss with a pen. "We're eager to hear about your progress with the hostages and brief you on new developments."

"You're out," Weiss said. "Director's orders. This is now a CIA-controlled operation, and you will stand down on all operational activity from this moment forward."

Van Pelt winced at the bluntness. "Mr. Weiss is correct. The director has decided to go a different direction. He has asked that Mr. Weiss pursue HVT-8, Khalifa al-Ghazawi, using any means necessary to remove him from the battlefield. Mr. Yorke has been tasked to develop a rescue plan for the hostages. Time is of the essence, and any additional information you can provide based on your recent activities may prove useful."

"The hostages are dead," Kate said. The Sandstorm team gave nothing away. "IEM executed them last night."

"Khalifa has never executed any hostages under his control," Weiss said.

"Khalifa is no longer the emir of IEM."

"I'm sorry?"

"That drone stunt drove him to retirement. His son, Talha, is now in command. Khalifa's message to the shura to that effect is en route."

"Horseshit. There's no way Khalifa al-Ghazawi would cede control of IEM to yet another son that no one has ever heard of. And there's even less possibility that AQ's shura would permit that passing of power without their explicit approval."

"If you say so."

"I've spent most of my career tracking this man. I know him better than I know the people closest to me."

"That explains a lot," Amy said. "Like why your wife has cheated on you for years." A few people coughed to muffle snickers, and Fraser shot Amy a warning look. "What? Literally everyone knows she's screwing the guy in—"

"Enough," Fraser said, as Weiss's face turned blotchy red. "Neil, you were saying?"

"I'm saying that they're full of shit. Khalifa remains the emir and therefore the target."

"I agree completely," Van Pelt said.

"It's like they're trying to protect him," Weiss muttered. "Just like she tried to protect that source of hers in Yemen, even when everyone knew he was a fabricator."

Kate said nothing. Her "fabricator" source in Yemen had been the reason they were able to take a different HVT off the battlefield. Weiss, in his capacity as chief of the Yemen Task Force at the time, hadn't hesitated to take credit for her work. She had been assured by reliable sources at Langley that her success had led to his last promotion.

Van Pelt leaned close to Weiss. "She's easily manipulated. Multiple sources in Yemen played her. If she hadn't resigned, she'd be on a desk. The streets aren't for her."

It appeared Amy might go for any available gun, but Kate cleared her throat and shook her head slightly.

"Did you pass the beaconed item to Khalifa's wife?" Van Pelt asked.

"Our trucks got ransacked," Kate replied. "Anyone could have it." The beaconed lotion remained secure in a Faraday bag in Fatima's luggage.

Lacey pulled up a tracking program. "It's not online."

"We don't need it. I've narrowed down his bed-down locations to a certain radius. Once the director authorizes flights into the zone, we'll have him in no time," Weiss said.

"Oh," Kate said mildly. Lacey frowned and stared at her computer. Weiss had just taken credit for her work. The likelihood that she had actually determined a radius for his bed-down locations was slim to none, but Kate wasn't about to be the bearer of that bad news. "We have nothing to add. We have no idea where we were the last few days."

"Damn, didn't the Corps teach you boys anything?" Chad asked Nick and Jake. "No map-tracking, no breadcrumbs?"

"Look, you have no idea what it's like, two dudes trying to keep five civilians and seven hostages alive while surrounded by a hundred terrorists," Nick said. "Especially with Napoleon here calling the shots."

"Someone had to do something," Kate snapped. "You just sat back and watched. I acted."

"And now seven people are dead and we're on the sidelines. Thanks for destroying my career, sweet pea."

"Whoa, bro, not cool. We offered to help at every opportunity, but you had to be a tough guy. You were in way over your head from the start," Chad said.

Nick looked at Kate. "Yeah, I suppose I was. From the moment I met you."

Kate felt that like another punch to her ribs. "Don't blame me. You wanted to be a hero. And when push came to shove—literally came to shove—you were nowhere to be found."

Nick recoiled. She begged him with her eyes to remember her last private words to him, but she knew that he was back in the desert, helpless as a terrorist beat her.

"Here we go again," Weiss said. "Jesus Christ, just sign the divorce papers already."

"If you have nothing else to offer, perhaps we can wrap up. We have an audience with the director in thirty minutes," Van Pelt said. He tightened his tie and straightened his pocket square.

"We're outta here. Let's go," Nick said.

Chad bent to Kate. "Stay on base, stay with me."

"I need to go with them. All my stuff is at the house."

"I'll send Blake to get everything. You need some TLC." He pushed a lock of dusty hair behind her ear and smiled. "Let me take care of you."

"Hey, asshole, she said she's coming with us," Nick said.

"She's not going anywhere with you, you fucking animal. Look at her. You let this happen. This is your fault."

"Fine, Kate. Do what you want. You always do anyway." Nick stormed out of the conference room and slammed the door.

"Chad, really, I'm fine."

"This is not a discussion. You're staying."

Kate sighed.

Ardouin cleared his throat. "I am sorry, but that will not be possible."

"What are you talking about?" Chad asked.

"We have no additional space to accommodate her. The base is full."

"No, she'll stay in my room."

"That is not permitted."

"What?"

"This is a military base, and Madame Cavanaugh is a married woman. Like your military, our military prohibits adultery."

"You've got to be kidding me."

Ardouin smiled thinly. "These are the rules. She must leave the base with her team. I'm sure you understand."

Fatima murmured something in Arabic and left the room. Kate closed her eyes and thanked the universe for the peevish chief of protocol.

Ω

"Nicholas."

Nick slowly raised his head from where it rested on his forearms, which rested on the edge of the bullet-riddled Hilux bed. Fatima's voice was understanding, compassionate; he felt like he deserved neither understanding nor compassion. She joined him at the Hilux and wrapped her arms around one of his in an embrace, briefly touching her forehead to his shoulder.

"Kate will be all right. She *is* all right."

He nodded once. He couldn't speak.

"We are safe because of you. Today was a bad day by any objective standard, but we survived. I know you will engage in pointless self-flagellation, but remember how strong your wife is. You know her. You know this will only make her stronger and more determined."

"We can't keep doing this," he managed to choke out. "I can't..."

"You will not lose her." She squeezed his arm. "You will *not* lose her."

"We keep cutting it awfully close."

"What is it you Americans say? Close, but no cigarette?"

Nick laughed in spite of himself. "Cigar. But you knew that." He looked at her. "Do I need to worry about losing her to Chad?"

"Monsieur Ardouin has taken it upon himself to cite French military code prohibiting adulterous liaisons on base. I was not aware the French cared about such indiscretions, but I do not believe there is cause for concern. And in any case, Kate can be counted on to extract herself. Even if that means admitting deceit and ending our little charade."

Nick shook his head. "She didn't want to take this job. I should have listened to her."

"You both would have spent the rest of your lives wondering, 'What if?'" Fatima said.

"Better wondering than regretting."

"But here you are. So close to saving seven people who do not deserve this fate."

"Christ, what is taking so long? She needs to rest."

She gestured to the building. "Here they come."

Kate, walking gingerly but unsupported, led the way to the trucks, Jake just a step behind and ready to catch her. They piled into the Hiluxes in silence and returned to the villa.

ꭥ

Nick helped Kate shower and settle in bed. He measured out doses of painkillers and muscle relaxants, then laid beside her. She looked at him, clean but haggard and exhausted, his gaze focused on the ceiling.

"I'm sorry," she said.

"Try to get some sleep."

She closed her eyes, feeling the prick of tears behind her eyelids, and wished for a reprieve that she was certain she didn't deserve. Then she slept.

She slept all night and most of the next day, waking only for water and a small meal that Nick brought to her. He gave her more pills. The darkness overtook her.

The next evening, Kate found Nick on the roof, overlooking the city as the last vestiges of light clung to the sky. His M4 carbine, slung across his chest, looked at home in his big hands. She closed the door behind her, but not quickly enough to prevent Kella from slipping past and scampering toward a flock of birds perched on the waist-high wall surrounding the roof's perimeter. The birds took flight, squawking their annoyance at this interruption of their quiet dusk.

The distance between them felt greater than it was, and every step hurt her ribs, every step brought with it breathtaking anxiety that this time it had finally gone too far, this time there wouldn't be humor and pathos and forgiveness, this time love wouldn't be enough.

He turned to face her and, in that moment, she saw the man she had met in Sanaa, a man fighting his demons, a man scarred by psychic wounds from battles won and wars lost. She saw the man who had seen the worst of humanity and his own country, and the dark side of himself. She saw the man who had met The One, but couldn't get out of his own way. She hated herself for being the cause of his pain.

They stood side by side in silence, watching their Tuareg guard force rotate personnel. The nightshift commander looked up and raised his hand in greeting. Nick mirrored the gesture, and before he could return the hand to the gun's forward grip, she captured it with her own. His palm, warm and calloused, pressed against hers. Their fingers intertwined automatically, the most natural thing in the world. She used her free hand to touch his ring finger, the tan lines from his wedding band visible on his skin.

A lump formed in her throat, but she forced herself to talk around it. "When you said you were in over your head...did you mean it?"

He looked at their hands, looked at her. "I've been in over my head since the second I spotted you across a crowded room surrounded by admiring sheikhs."

She nodded once, struggling to keep the tears at bay.

"And I've loved every minute of it." He smiled crookedly. "Well, almost every minute of it. I could have done without yesterday."

"Are we...?"

He turned to her, his hand tightening around hers. His other hand left the M4 and caressed her face, his fingers featherlight against her bruised cheek and swollen lip. He finished her thought. "Are we okay?"

She nodded.

"Kate, we will always be okay. Always."

She smiled and tears leaked out, tears that he caught with his thumb. "Promise?"

He held up his pinkie finger and she linked it with hers, giving it a good shake. His cobalt eyes were glassy and full of emotion, but his dimples gave away a hint of a smile.

"All this time I thought I was the only one who worried about our marriage imploding over our inability to be normal people with normal jobs."

"All those other times would have been your fault. This time would have been my fault."

"You mean I finally get to blame you for something?" He adjusted the gun so it rested against his back and drew her close, careful not to squeeze her torso or jostle her sore shoulder. She leaned into him, her back against his chest, and directed his hand to an area of her stomach that was pain-free. "It's a relief to know that you're perfect only most of the time, not all of the time."

"I had hoped you'd never find out."

"I keep thinking about what would have happened if he hadn't attacked you."

"What do you mean?"

"If he hadn't assaulted you, I'd have been in the other Hilux when the land pirates attacked. You and Amy and Charlie would have been defenseless. I'm going to kill Talha, but maybe he saved your lives."

"You saved our lives."

"Only because a terrorist butterfly flapped its wings." His hand, splayed over her stomach, increased pressure, hot through her shirt. "Speaking of the day we met...a butterfly flapped its wings then, too. Jake was supposed to go to that energy conference, but he was laid up with gut rot. First and only time he ate street food." He turned her in his arms and gazed down into her eyes. "I was stuck in a riptide, but you threw me a lifeline."

She placed her hands over his heart. "You just needed to remember you could swim."

"And you need to remember that the shitty things happening here are not your fault. Yesterday was not your fault." He kissed her forehead. "You're going to be the reason we save those people."

"I don't have a plan."

"You will."

"Are you sure you want to stay?"

"I can't be the reason you live with guilt for the rest of your life. Not for some busted ribs." He forced a smile.

"I had to keep up with two older brothers. I've had worse injuries. I'm curious, though. What did Sharaf say to you?"

He smiled ruefully. "One day in Sanaa, Jake and I were sideswiped by a taxi. It was obviously that guy's fault, but you know the deal. Always blame the Westerner. Naturally things escalated, and I was about to haul off and clobber the other driver when a tribesman from the crowd stepped between us. He told me then, 'You are not that man.' He said the same thing yesterday. Had the same effect—stopped me in my tracks."

"At least we know one of us can get you under control."

"Did I blow it with my caveman chivalry?"

She patted his chest. "We'll channel your rage appropriately. I think we can sell that a man with your Attila the Hun tendencies doesn't handle rejection well."

"You're going to ruin my rep with the terrorists. They think I'm getting some."

"Sorry, sweetie. No self-respecting French diplomat would jump into bed with a German mercenary."

"Even though I really like your *derrière*?" He smiled when she smiled, then touched a finger to her neck, where redness from Talha's blade lingered. "I wish I could take the pain away."

She took his hand and pulled him toward the door. "You can. Just be with me."

"Forever."

Ω

Talha himself called Sharaf's ops phone three days later and asked to speak to Counselor Moreau. Kate quieted the gathered team and set the phone on speaker. Amy readied her own phone to record the conversation.

"I hope you're recovering from your injuries," he said solicitously.

"I'm fine, thank you."

"And your companions? You all survived your run-in with your *Daesh* attackers?"

"We were lucky."

"I think you fail to give the big Legionnaire enough credit. The surviving Fulani fighters say he fought like a man possessed." He laughed at her silence, but then his tone turned serious. "That attack was an unfortunate development. It's also the reason I'm calling."

"I hope you're not reneging on our agreement."

"No, merely amending it."

Kate gritted her teeth and stared at the phone resting on her lap. "Oh?"

"It's clear that Moussa Diallo intends to make a play for my thirty million dollars. I would like to ensure that doesn't happen, either before or after I receive the money."

"We're open to ideas," Kate said.

"That's not how this works, Madame Moreau. If you want to see the hostages again, alive, you will devise a plan to keep that money out of Moussa's hands."

"You expect me to protect you *after* the swap has been made?"

"Indeed I do."

"That's impossible."

"I think not. You've come this far. Don't give up now. I'll expect your plan in three days' time. If what you propose fails to meet my approval, the hostages will be executed."

Talha disconnected and Kate tossed the phone on cushion beside her. Nick rubbed her back as she squeezed the bridge of her nose, ruing every choice that had brought her to this moment. Her head hurt, her ribs hurt, her soul hurt. And the question remained: Was Talha serious about conducting an exchange, or was this his bait and switch?

Amy raised her massive cross by its nylon cord and swung it to and fro, as if hypnotizing herself. "I'm losing track of all the double crosses and red herrings. Who's about to fuck whom here?" Then she kissed the cross. "Apologies, Lord."

"I think we're about to take incoming fire from all sides," Kate said.

Fraser's call to them earlier that morning had confirmed the worst: the CIA director had approved Weiss and Yorke's plans to pursue Khalifa using all available resources, including drones, and the team was under physical surveillance. The latter piece of information wasn't news to them; Nick and Jake had spotted Blake Doyle lurking near the compound, even before Cherif had called to tell them the same. It was difficult for a large white man to be inconspicuous in a small city of Arabs and black Africans.

"The CIA is watching our every move," she continued, "and now Talha expects thirty million dollars and safe passage out of hostile lands. Plus, we run the risk that he hands over dead bodies, or kills us all. And that's assuming our own countrymen don't get everyone killed first."

"Sounds like we need to up our game," Amy said.

"As I just told that asshole terrorist a minute ago, I'm open to ideas."

Amy laughed. "Bestie, you know I'm just the hired help, the comedic relief. I have no idea how we're going to outwit surprisingly intelligent terrorists. But I'd bet anything we can outsmart the Agency's best and brightest."

"Of those available," Kate and Charlie added automatically. Nick and Jake smirked.

"Let's say we could protect Talha once we made the exchange. How would we protect ourselves and the hostages?" Kate asked.

"We could ask Cherif to increase the size of his force," Jake suggested. "Make the convoy so overwhelming that we become an extremely unappealing target."

"What if Talha insists that we leave the bulk of the force behind like last time?"

"Or what if he insists that the Tuareg force go with him?" Nick asked.

Kate stood and wandered to the window, Kella at her side. She absently touched her neck; it was impossible to forget the sensation of steel against skin. Sharaf joined her, his green eyes catching the sunlight and narrowing against the glare.

"He must only *believe* that he is protected," said the Yemeni tribesman. "As for reality..." He shrugged. "That is in the hands of Allah."

Kate stared at him. He smiled and motioned her to the kitchen.

"Come. You must eat. You think better with a full stomach."

24

Cherif called the next morning to check on Kate and request an audience. She invited him for lunch and asked Sharaf to make enough for an additional three: Cherif, Mokhtar, and Cherif's father, who desired to meet the team and thank them for their generous contributions to the fight for Azawad independence.

As the three Tuaregs entered the compound and approached the porch, the team gave a collective start.

"Holy shit," Amy said. "Papa looks just like..."

"Khalifa al-Ghazawi," Kate finished.

"The resemblance is uncanny," Charlie agreed. "If he wore a djellaba instead of the indigo, I'd think, not for the first time in recent days, that this was the end of us."

Kate nibbled her bottom lip in thought. She glanced at Nick, whose dimples betrayed his amusement.

"I know that look," Amy said, a grin spreading across her face.

"Call Fraser and get her over here," Kate told Charlie. "And tell her to bring Dubois, Ardouin, and Colonel Patterson. I have an idea."

"Which is?"

She smiled. "They want Khalifa. So we give them Khalifa."

Kate outlined her idea to the most motley of crews assembled on the porch of the villa, pausing only for clarifications in Arabic or French. She felt like a raving lunatic, pacing slowly as the stream of consciousness spewed forth like Old Faithful. The plan came together as she spoke it aloud; she saw each piece of the puzzle in her mind, and how they interlocked to form a tableau of recovered hostages. The trick was making the rest of them understand.

When she finally stopped speaking, out of breath and in pain, Cherif's father offered a thunderous belly laugh, slapping his knee.

"This one, I think she has some Tuareg in her!"

Nick helped her sit and leaned close. "That was quite the plan for someone who didn't have a plan." Then he gave her a quick kiss on the cheek.

Ardouin spoke for the three intelligence officers. "What absolute insanity." He looked at Dubois. "But their insanity has been remarkably effective thus far."

"You're confident you can get the hostages?" Dubois asked.

"Look, nothing is guaranteed. And a lot can go wrong in this scenario. But I believe this has a chance."

"The question is, are you sure you want your people back? Mathilde, oof." Amy shook her head. "How many pieces of junk did that old battle-axe chuck at your head?" she asked Kate. "And Lefèvre, massive douchebag. Even his own brother left him for dead."

Dubois studied Kate, then his eyes moved to each member of the team. He finally nodded. "You have the French government's support."

"Diana? We can't do it without you."

"You know I'm not in charge. I'm as sidelined as you are."

"When has that ever stopped you from getting the job done?"

She pulled a pen and notepad from her shoulder bag. "Tell me again what you need, and when."

"Ten million dollars more, in clean bills, by Friday."

"One of my Farm classmates is an executive assistant up on the seventh floor. He owes me a favor."

"That's one hell of a favor to call in," Charlie said.

"I got him out of one hell of a mess in Uzbekistan. A mess that would have ended his career." She set down her pen and looked at Kate with foreboding. "If they get away with that money, the U.S. government's money…"

"I know."

"Madame Fraser, together we will impress upon the general the importance of ensuring that doesn't happen," Dubois said. "This will fall well within the French military's rules of engagement in this theater. Correct, Henri?"

"Correct."

"If we don't act, Talha will kill every single one of them." The team nodded as Kate spoke. "He takes his inspiration from the worst of the Islamic State."

"Stu might be dead already," Jake said. "The rest are weakening by the day. At some point it'll make more sense to kill them for the propaganda value than waiting for a ransom they may never see."

"A military rescue is a nonstarter," Nick said. "Their movements are too random, their camps too remote, the area too vast. Contrary to popular belief, the Marine Corps did teach us something. That area Weiss thinks Khalifa's in? He's not. That's territory they're using for this specific purpose, in and out with alacrity."

"I agree with *le capitaine*," Cherif added. "Our meetings with Khalifa have been in what we consider disputed territory. Azawad elements and Moussa Diallo's *Daesh* forces are just as active as the Islamic Emirate of the Maghreb, and greatly outnumber the group. Khalifa—now Talha—will stay no longer than necessary."

"I'm not opposed to sending Weiss on a wild goose chase, but why the subterfuge?" Fraser asked.

"I want them fully distracted, as far away from our operating area as we can safely get them. The fact that we've had surveillance is telling. They don't know what they're doing, and they're hoping we'll give them a clue. We can't roll out of here for a meet with them at the base—they'll have Reapers over us before we pass the city gates. If Weiss and Chad are on the hunt somewhere else, they can't be monitoring us," Kate said.

Diana nodded. "The director lifted the standdown on UAV flights. They basically have carte blanche to flood the zone with resources, and DOD is standing by to insert a special-ops team if an ideal situation presents itself."

"Colonel Patterson?" Kate said.

The pilot grinned. "Craziest CONOP I ever heard. I'm in."

Kate spoke to Cherif's father in French. "Sir? Can you help us? We'll do everything we can to ensure your safety."

The elder Tuareg stroked his beard. "My son tells me you are a woman of your word. It would be an honor to assist."

"I guess the real question is whether you guys are on board," Kate said to her friends. "It being your lives and all."

"What a ridiculous question, love," Fatima replied.

"Let's carpe the fucking diem," Amy said, "and rescue some hostages."

♊

Nick jerked awake and sat up in bed. "What in the hell?"

Beside him, Kate stirred, but muscle relaxants and painkillers were more powerful than the commotion that emanated from downstairs. Until two voices, which were once distinct, shouted over each other with increasing intensity.

"It's one a.m.," she murmured. "What are they doing?"

Nick slid out of bed, pulled on a pair of pants, and shoved his feet into flip-flops. "I need to stop an honor killing."

"I'll help," she said, and began the slow process of sitting up and standing.

Nick rushed to her side and put a gentle hand to her uninjured shoulder. "*Au contraire*, Madame Cavanaugh. Stay in bed. I'll handle it."

Then something shattered—a plate, a vase, a window?—and they looked at each other uncertainly.

"Okay, maybe I need backup." Nick helped her up and ensured she didn't take a groggy tumble down the stairs.

Trailed by confused and irritated friends who were desperate to catch up on lost sleep, they followed the sounds of furor and found Fatima and Sharaf lobbing verbal hand grenades at each other in the living room. The ugliest of the Arab homeowner's vases lay shattered between them, at the feet of an abashed Tom Patterson. Nick looked sternly at the retired colonel, who was at home in aerial combat but cowered as Sharaf's Arabic zingers, of which he didn't understand a word, broadsided him.

"Nick, we were just talking. Nothing happened," Patterson said, his eyes pleading with them for a rescue from one irate Yemeni tribesman.

Nick held up his hands and waded into the fray. "Maybe we could just calm down and—"

Sharaf snatched the second-ugliest vase from the wall-mounted shelf behind his head and whipped it to the floor, but away from people. Glass shards skittered across tile.

"*Khalas!*" Fatima snapped. "I am not your property. In fact, I am your employer. If you cannot respect my private affairs, then go back to Yemen. Your backwards, misogynistic brethren in Al Jawf eagerly await your return."

Sharaf ignored both the pointed reminder of his place in Fatima's realm and the insult to his Jawfi heritage. When he and Fatima ramped up in Yemeni dialect, Nick sometimes lost the thread of conversation—or argument, as the case may be. But this line of attack wasn't hard to follow.

"Did he just call the colonel a gold digger?" he whispered to Kate.

"I believe so." Her eyebrows shot skyward. "And a man-whore."

"Come on, Sharaf, enough. The colonel is a good man who—"

Both Fatima and Sharaf turned on him. "Shut up!" they yelled.

"This is between us, Nicholas," Fatima continued. "I do not need or want your help."

"Fine. But don't throw anything else," he told Sharaf. The Yemeni grunted.

LYNN MASON

"I should go," Patterson said, and tried to slink toward the door.

"Stay," Fatima said. The man accustomed to giving orders stood meekly behind her. She returned her attention to Sharaf. "What gives you the right to dictate how I spend my time?"

"I see lust in his eyes."

She rolled her own eyes. "He is a man."

"What would possess you to indulge him?"

She tossed up her hands. "I enjoy his company."

"I do not want to see you hurt. I do not want to..." The tribesman's green eyes filled with emotion.

Fatima's sandals crunched over broken glass. She touched Sharaf's hand and spoke softly. "No matter who is in our lives, we will always be us. We will grow old together."

Sharaf searched her face and finally nodded. Then he peered around her and spoke to Patterson in formal Arabic. "I am sorry I threw a vase at you."

Patterson looked questioningly at Nick and Kate. "You're good, sir," Nick said.

The colonel looked at his watch and groaned softly. He would not be going back to base tonight.

"And you're welcome to the couch," Nick continued. "I don't think he'll try to murder you in your sleep. Not anymore." He grinned. Fatima shot him a look of amused chastisement.

"I will clean up and find a blanket," Sharaf muttered, not keen on having a houseguest but seemingly placated.

Amy, Jake, and Charlie headed back to bed, and Fatima excused herself with a shy smile in Tom's direction. Patterson immediately turned to Nick and Kate.

"I swear, time just got away from us. Nothing happened."

"It will. Just be patient." Nick winked at him, and he and Kate headed upstairs.

322

Ω

Kate stared at the phone on the coffee table beside a map and her handwritten notes, her *Beautiful Mind*-esque vision for the coming days. Step one: Call the emir of the Islamic Emirate of the Maghreb and propose the details of a swap, thirty million dollars for seven lives, all while protecting the life about which he cared most—his own.

Ardouin was right; it was absolute insanity, that which she intended to propose to a terrorist. Desperate times, desperate measures, she reasoned. Fuck 'em all if they couldn't take a joke.

Fraser, true to her word, had secured an additional ten million dollars, which arrived this morning on a support flight from Paris. It was spirited directly into Dubois's office safe; no one went near the armory so as not to raise the antennae of paranoid CIA officers engaged in feverish efforts to prove that they had the inside track on HVTs and the bodies of dead hostages. Reapers scoured the skies over Weiss's preferred coordinates, but no joy, according to Fraser, who provided regular updates.

They had the money, they had the Tuaregs, they had the French general; now they needed Talha. Kate picked up the phone and dialed. The emissary's familiar voice answered on the second ring, offering effusive greetings to Brother Sharaf.

"This is Katherine Moreau of the French Ministry of Foreign Affairs."

"Counselor Moreau, a pleasure. How may I be of service?"

"I'd like to speak with the emir."

"He was not expecting your call until tomorrow. I will pass any messages you have."

"It's imperative that I speak with him. Now." Kate was as certain as she could be that the emissary had her on speaker, with Talha by his side, just as she had him on speaker for the team to hear and record.

Silence greeted her demand. Then a quiet voice spoke. "Madame Moreau, what a pleasant surprise."

"I have a plan."

"I never doubted you. Please, enlighten me."

Kate walked him through her idea, focusing on his personal security. She imagined him stroking his beard with his long fingers, his mind sifting through the pros and cons, making a judgment on whether he could trust her.

"Your plan intrigues me. However, I do not like the idea of meeting so close to Timbuktu."

"The closer we meet, the more distance you can put between us, quickly, once we've made the exchange. We've got a limit of about five hundred kilometers, and I'd prefer that you have the ability to cover that ground. We'll have Cherif and his men."

"We will meet here." He gave her a set of coordinates, which Nick and Jake scribbled down and began plotting. Nick pointed to their map, highlighting a spot to the northeast of Lake Faguibine, which was northwest of Timbuktu and well within range. "Cherif will know the way."

Kate repeated the coordinates, which he confirmed.

"We will rendezvous on Saturday, *inshallah*," he said.

"*Inshallah*."

They ended the call. "We're a go," she said for all the non-Arabic speakers.

"Praise the Lord!" Amy rejoiced with her cross. "Let's give the cavalcade of kooks a taste of their own medicine."

♌

At the team's request, Director-General Dubois summoned Sandstorm to the base to obtain more clarity on the deaths of seven hostages and to articulate his government's extreme displeasure over the events that led to said deaths. Ardouin slapped a veritable tome of documented instances of Sandstorm's incompetence and immaturity on the table before him and treated the exchange like the Nuremberg trials. Van Pelt took copious notes as Ardouin made his case; if nothing else, he planned to sink Fraser alongside the SS *Sandstorm*.

Kate busied herself with a plate of pastries as the chief of protocol enumerated their gaffes, flubs, and faux pas. He had clearly put some thought into his presentation, which she appreciated.

At exactly eleven o'clock, Sharaf's phone rang, disrupting the kangaroo court. He held it up for all to see. "It is Khalifa's emissary," he said in practiced English.

"Answer it," Weiss ordered.

Charlie readied his phone to record, and Lacey Simms did the same, prompting an appreciative nod from Van Pelt. Sharaf answered in Arabic.

"Sheikh, *as-salaam alaikum*."

"*Wa alaikum as-salaam*, my brother," Sharaf replied. "It is a surprise to hear from you, in light of recent events."

"Recent events are the impetus for this call. Brother Khalifa would like to speak to you. Right now."

Fatima whispered a translation, and a low murmur rose from the crowd. Weiss leaned forward intently.

"I am at his disposal."

They heard the fumble of the phone exchanging hands and a boisterous voice greeted Sharaf, bestowing blessings upon him and all those he held dear.

"Brother Khalifa, how may I be of service?"

"Brother Sharaf, what happened mere days ago was a shock to us all, a terrible tragedy and a loss for our great and glorious cause."

"We are in agreement. I had hoped our efforts with the Westerners would bear fruit."

"Those hostages were never supposed to die. My son Talha acted without my consent or the consent of our esteemed brothers on the shura."

"A truly unfortunate turn. But by your hand, he is emir."

"My hand made him thus, but it is his hand I fear."

"How so?"

"I believe Talha means to kill me."

"That is a strong accusation to level against a son."

Khalifa dropped his voice. "You saw what he is capable of. He is consolidating power, but he knows that many remain loyal to me. I am a threat."

"How can I help?"

"I wish to discuss a deal."

"I don't think that will be possible. As you well know, the hostages are dead."

"No, Brother Sharaf, not a deal for hostages." He paused dramatically. "A deal for me."

"I don't understand."

"I wish to surrender."

Fatima's translation provoked a collective gasp. The Khalifa on the line laughed heartily, and Kate imagined him slapping his knee at the hilarity of it all.

"It seems you are not alone, Brother Sharaf."

"No," Sharaf admitted. "The French and the Americans requested one last meeting before Umm Ali and I return to Dubai. They must explain the demise of the hostages to their leaders."

"An unenviable task. But perhaps I can lessen the blow. In exchange for American and French assurances that Ratma and I will not be harmed, I will surrender myself to their custody."

Weiss and Chad gestured wildly to Sharaf. "Brother, stay on the line while I discuss your proposal with the Westerners." He muted the call and leaned back in his chair in satisfaction. Kate took a bite of croissant and winked at him.

"Is that really Khalifa al-fucking-Ghazawi?" Weiss roared.

"Of course," Sharaf replied indignantly to Fatima's creative translation. "Who else would it be?"

Weiss looked to Kate, Nick, and Jake. "Since when does my expertise matter?" Kate asked around the croissant.

"Kate, don't be a…" Nick stopped himself and addressed Weiss. "Yes, that's Khalifa." Jake nodded.

Weiss stood and paced. "Pull up and compare previous voice cuts of Khalifa with this call," he told Lacey.

She ran a search on her laptop. "We have no voice cuts. We've never had coverage on him."

"We need to hear him out," Chad said. He looked at Kate. "You're sure it's him?"

Kate smiled at her ex. "That's definitely him."

Chad sat up straighter and spoke more forcefully. "This is our chance to take HVT-8 off the battlefield and interrogate him on everything he knows. Langley will throw you a fucking parade."

Weiss sat and snapped his fingers at Fatima. "Translate for me. Take him off mute." Sharaf complied. "Khalifa, my name is Neil. I'm a senior CIA officer."

"CIA! The Frenchwoman claimed I was, how do you say, a high-value target? This is true, yes?"

"Yes, you're a very high-value target. I'd like to help you surrender."

"I would be in CIA custody?"

Weiss never looked at Dubois. "Yes."

"I don't want to go to Guantanamo."

"We don't send people there anymore. If you help us, we'll take good care of you."

"And Ratma, my wife."

"Yes, and Ratma. You'd both be safe with us."

"We would have much to discuss, Mr. CIA."

Weiss laughed giddily. "What you'll do is—"

"No, Mr. CIA. You will follow my instructions. On Saturday, as the sun approaches its zenith, you will find me two hundred kilometers due north of Timbuktu. I will wait for you in the desert sands. If you come in peace, as I believe you do, my men will stand down. No one will be harmed."

Chad plotted the distance on his map and shot Weiss a thumbs-up. "I look forward to making your acquaintance," Weiss said.

"*Inshallah*, Mr. CIA."

"Are you sure about this, Brother Khalifa?" Sharaf asked.

"I am an old man, my friend. I'm tired of running."

"Then God be with you."

"And you, Brother Sharaf." The line went dead.

Chad jumped to his feet, scribbling on a pad and muttering to himself. "Okay, we need French air assets for the movement and a company-sized force. Gunships and medevacs should accompany. Weiss, Doyle, and I will make contact with Khalifa. We'll need a translator, too."

"Of course, Mr. Yorke. We'll supply any resources you require. I'll plan to accompany you, given the sensitivities surrounding Khalifa and his role regarding the hostages," Dubois said.

"No, Laurent, it should be me. The director-general cannot take such a risk," Ardouin said. "Emmanuel and I will go and represent the DGSE."

"If that is what protocol dictates."

"It is."

"*D'accord.*"

"Hey guys, if you need a couple extra guns, Jake and I would love to get in on the action," Nick said.

"Bro, this is a legit special operation. No room for strap-hangers."

Nick held up his hands. "I get it. We're here if you need us."

With the CIA crowd distracted, Kate took the opportunity to send a quick text to Fraser. *We need to talk to you. Alone.*

She checked the message and leaned toward Dubois, whispering something in his ear. He nodded and she replied to Kate. *Dubois's office.*

Kate stood. "I could use some tea."

"Yeah, we'll get out of your hair," Nick said. "Jake and I need to pack our gear."

Only Lacey looked up to watch them depart. A minute later, they all slipped into Dubois's office and closed the door. Fraser looked apprehensive as she faced Kate, Nick, and Jake.

"We have some bad news," Kate said.

"How bad?"

"About three million dollars' worth of bad."

♌

As Friday wore on, the team made discreet preparations at the base while the CIA crew was occupied with planning tomorrow's capture of Khalifa al-Ghazawi. Kate, Nick, and Jake had an audience with the French general, who expressed his support but also his skepticism that they had any hope of recovering the hostages. They inspected Tom Patterson's Huey with him and readied the cargo area for its future load, which would be onboarded just prior to his departure. Then they visited the armory for a last look at their cage full of money, short three million dollars.

Fraser visibly lost years off her life as they broke the news. She regained a few years when they showed her the video evidence and connected her via FaceTime with George. The blue-haired hacker explained the technology and assured Fraser that she maintained full control over the original video, which would be turned over to the government at the conclusion of the operation. Kate instructed George that she was to adhere to Fraser's directions regarding the video and associated evidence in the event of the partners' untimely demise at the hands of terrorists.

Then, as they went in search of a late lunch, the CIA planning session reached an intermission. The small cafeteria was a target-rich environment. As gazelles wandered from the safety of the herd, the lions made their move.

♫

Nick, wearing a gray, snug-fitting USMC T-shirt that emphasized his broad, sculpted chest and shoulders, leaned back in his chair and put his hands behind his head, flexing his biceps. She immediately took notice, and he grinned at her, waving her over. She smiled shyly and nodded, then turned back to the cafeteria's lunch offerings.

Panic seized Nick. He whipped out his phone and sent a text message. *Babe...* Kate responded within seconds. *OMG Lacey. Her name is LACEY.*

"Hey, Lacey," he said casually as she approached. He pulled out a chair for her and touched her shoulder as she sat. Fraser, a few tables away with Dubois and Giraud, watched him with obvious exasperation. He smirked at her, knowing his dimples were irresistible, and she rolled her eyes, a smile tugging at her lips. He turned back to the young targeter. "Hell of a day."

"It's so exciting. I never thought I'd ever have an opportunity to see it up close and personal."

"You're going tomorrow, right?"

She poked at grilled chicken with her fork. "I'm not sure. They don't seem to want me there."

"Oh, come on, that's ridiculous. Aren't you the Agency's top targeter of Khalifa?"

"I wish. Weiss is the expert. I mostly take his ideas and do the legwork."

"Don't you have any ideas of your own?"

"Lots. But that's not my role. I'm just trying to learn as much as I can from him. If I'm lucky, maybe he'll let me help with the interrogations."

"It'll take years to sift through all the intel that Khalifa has in his head."

"Do you think he'll talk?"

"To you? Sure. Like all men, he enjoys a pretty face."

She blushed and took a sip of her Perrier.

"Your boss might want to tone down the tough-guy routine, though. That won't impress Khalifa. Or scare him."

"How would you get information from him?"

Nick shrugged. "Talk *to* him. Treat him with respect, like an equal."

"That makes sense, but Weiss will never go for it."

"I'd hate to see you miss out on all that intel because Weiss can't see the forest for the trees. That's why I think you need to be on the op tomorrow. You know what needs to be done. Make yourself indispensable to him."

"How do I do that?"

Nick cocked his head. "My soon-to-be ex-wife used to say something, a CIA truism of sorts. 'If it's not in writing, it didn't happen.' Sound familiar?"

Lacey laughed. "That's exactly what we say."

"Is Weiss a writer? Or does he foist that off on you?"

"I do all his writing."

"And I bet Chad and Blake would love for you to do theirs, too. I mean, let's be real," he said in a low voice, "those two have a combined I.Q. of about seventy."

She giggled and looked around to make sure they weren't overheard. "Chad is a terrible writer. I had to redo his entire briefing for the director."

"Sounds like you need to be there to capture every detail. The details make the story, right? And correct me if I'm wrong, but Weiss and Van Pelt and Yorke and Doyle will want every detail, no matter how insignificant, recorded for posterity. Be the scribe who secures their legacies."

She nodded enthusiastically. "They might go for that."

He smiled and touched her hand. "Good. And when Langley starts handing out medals, I hope you get one, too."

Ω

331

Kate lured Chad out to the patio area again, doing her best to look sad and forlorn as she picked at her second lunch. He beelined for her with his plate of food, a made-to-order hamburger and *frites*. She snagged a fry with a flirty smile and allowed him a squeeze of her forearm where it rested on the table.

"You must be ecstatic about tomorrow."

"Can't wait. It's been forever since I had any excitement." He took a huge bite of his burger and chewed thoughtfully. "Maybe since you and I tore up the town in Baghdad. You were like a bloodhound, always knew where to find the bad guys."

"One of my more puzzling skill sets. Seems to get me in trouble on a regular basis."

"I wish you hadn't left. You could have laid low a couple of years and everyone would have forgotten about Yemen. Maybe it could have been us on this op together."

"I don't think Van Pelt and Weiss would have forgotten. Maybe Van Pelt is right, maybe I belong on a desk, but it would have killed me. Of course, then I go and get seven hostages literally killed." She smiled bitterly.

Chad stared down at his lunch. "That plan was destined for disaster. I wish you had let me help you. I could have prevented this," he said in a gently accusatory tone.

"I'd say I'll know better next time, but there won't be a next time."

"I'll help you while you get back on your feet."

"I can't ask that of you. Not with everything going on in your life."

He waved away the concern. "I've come into some money recently. Turns out I'm in a really good place financially, and I know what I want. I want you, Kate."

She smiled.

"So let me help you. Let me take care of you, and we'll give us another chance. I won't make the same mistake."

"Thank you, Chad."

"Yorke!" Weiss bellowed from the cafeteria entrance. "Conference room, now!"

Chad scarfed down the last of his lunch and stood. Kate stood with him and reached a hand toward his biceps—biceps she had once thought were more impressive.

"I'm glad it's you out there tomorrow. I'll be worried, but I know you're the best man for the job."

He leaned forward, intending to kiss her. She dipped back, her ribs screaming, and forced a smile, moving her hand from arm to chest.

"Not even for good luck?"

"First you get the glory, then you get the girl."

He grinned. Weiss bellowed again. "I'm holding you to that, Kate Devlin."

Kate watched him jog into the building and disappear with Weiss, Van Pelt, Lacey, and Blake. She picked up her phone, which was face down on the table, and stopped the audio recording of their conversation. Fraser would be thrilled to hear about Chad's suddenly improved financial situation. Then she sauntered inside and approached a table with a lone occupant. Ardouin pretended he didn't see her and made a show of scribbling nonsense on his legal pad.

"I hope Nick asked nicely," she said.

"*Pardonnez-moi?*" He pushed his glasses up his nose and regarded her in a most pompous French fashion.

"When Nick asked you to spy on me, babysit me, chaperone me, whatever you're doing, I hope he asked nicely."

"Madame Cavanaugh, I would never stoop to such depths. Especially for your husband, of all people."

"Be sure to report back that his favorite Navy SEAL swept me off my feet and positively ravished me."

"I'll do no such thing. The amount of paperwork would be heinous should a homicide occur on base." He kept a straight face, but the corners of his eyes crinkled in amusement.

Kate smiled. "Be safe tomorrow, Henri."

"And you, Kate. *Bonne chance*."

25

THE FLEET OF HELICOPTER transports and gunships lifted off mid-morning, carrying a motley crew of French Operation Barkhane soldiers, DGSE officers, and CIA officers on their mission to bring America's HVT-8, Khalifa al-Ghazawi, to justice.

Much to the amusement of the French commander of the company that the general had assigned to the capture, Henri Ardouin ceded control of the operation to Stan Van Pelt, who then ceded control to Neil Weiss, who would inevitably look to Chad Yorke, the former Navy SEAL, to ensure both survival and success. The French commander was privy to the ruse; he had been summoned by the general, who was in the company of two senior DGSE officers and a vaguely introduced foreign partner, and given a briefing in flawless French by a petite woman purporting to be from the Ministry of Foreign Affairs, who was flanked by two imposing men wearing *la Légion étrangère's* old Operation Serval uniforms. The commander was not convinced the petite woman was French, despite the perfection of her speech and accent, and he was certain that the Legionnaires were not Legionnaires, but he acknowledged his orders and saluted.

"*C'est le Mali*," he had muttered to himself as he departed the general's office to prepare his men.

Ardouin and Emmanuel Giraud had donned well-worn armored vests, helmets, and sidearms as their American partners had geared up in the latest and greatest battle-rattle that the CIA's money could buy.

"Battle-rattle," Ardouin repeated softly, filing it away for future use. He prided himself on his mastery of formal English, but he secretly enjoyed slang and Americanisms, which he occasionally deployed in juvenile but effective efforts to annoy their British Secret Intelligence Service counterparts.

Beside him on the bench seat of one of the transports, Giraud trembled. Ardouin peered at the young analyst in concern, but then he realized that it was giddy anticipation making him vibrate. Across from them, Yorke and Doyle sat serenely, their eyes closed. Lacey, swimming in protective gear not meant for an average-sized woman, held tight to a pen and stenographer's pad. Weiss tapped his foot and turned often to crane his neck and peer out the open side door where a gunner sat ready. Van Pelt looked most out of place in khakis and a white dress shirt under his armored vest; he had been reluctant to place himself in harm's way, rebuffing Diana Fraser's urging until Ardouin stepped in, insisting that the CIA director's representative must be the one to take Khalifa. Then he had gamely agreed.

The pilots maintained a leisurely speed north, in no hurry to cover the two hundred kilometers. They would circle a few times to get eyes on the force accompanying Khalifa, then set down and make contact. Ardouin leaned toward Giraud and told him to take good notes; he thought this would be an operation that went down in DGSE lore.

𝕫

Once the French force disappeared from sight, the Sandstorm team drove a tarp-covered pallet to the flight line and loaded it into a waiting helicopter under the watchful gazes of Fraser and Dubois. Nick and Jake shook hands with the pilot and wished him a safe flight. Then two Hiluxes departed the base and joined the Tuareg army milling about outside. Cherif turned them west, toward Lake Faguibine. Charlie commandeered the sound system, again choosing Tinariwen as the soundtrack to their final chapter in Mali.

"It feels like we're driving headlong into destiny," Amy said.

"God, I hope not," Kate replied.

�

The helicopters touched down fifty meters from a mass of pickup trucks and armed men. Yorke and Doyle were on their feet immediately, shouting orders. The company commander looked at Ardouin, who discreetly nodded his assent. The transport's rear lift gate lowered and men clambered out. The commander and a trusted sergeant stayed with Yorke and Doyle as the two Americans led the way, rifles raised and clearing a path through tall, lean, balaclava-clad men wearing desert fatigues and carrying Kalashnikovs. The tall men were wary but calm.

"Khalifa al-Ghazawi!" Chad Yorke shouted. "Show yourself!"

The DGSE's interpreter dutifully provided the command in Arabic. Ardouin watched several of the tall men glance at each other. One walked to an idling white Hilux and spoke to an occupant in the passenger seat through the cracked window. The door opened. Yorke and Doyle tensed, training their rifles on the truck. The commander and his sergeant subtly drew their sidearms.

"Khalifa! It's Mr. CIA!" Weiss called. "Come out."

The interpreter looked at Ardouin, who merely sighed and motioned for him to continue. A few of the tall men laughed at the translation.

A figure emerged from the truck, a portly, bearded man in indigo robes and a spotless white turban. A smile creased his weathered face.

"Mr. CIA! I'm so glad you could make it," he said in English.

Weiss squinted at the man, comparing him to a crumpled copy of Nick Cavanaugh's sketch of the wanted terrorist clenched in his fist. "Wait a minute. This isn't Khalifa al-Ghazawi. Who the fuck is this?"

"*Et* Monsieur Ardouin, *comment ça va?*" he continued, offering his hand to the chief of protocol.

Ardouin accepted with a smile and replied, "This day goes better for me than for our American friends, I think."

Cherif's father laughed heartily. "I wish the honorary Tuareg woman were here to see this."

"Where's Khalifa?" Weiss roared.

Yorke and Doyle surged forward, only to face a wall of Tuareg soldiers who closed ranks around their chief. The French commander and his sergeant disarmed the Americans and informed them that they would be restrained if they resisted. Emmanuel Giraud and Lacey Simms, the assigned scribes for their respective intelligence services, alternated between wide-eyed stares at the action and furious note-taking.

"I don't understand," said Van Pelt. "Are we in the wrong location?"

"We are at the precise coordinates given by the man purporting to be Khalifa al-Ghazawi," Ardouin replied.

Van Pelt, Weiss, Yorke, and Doyle stared at him. Lacey recorded his every word.

"Devlin, Kowalski, the Marines, where are they? What are they doing?" Weiss snarled.

Ardouin looked at his watch. "Why, rescuing the hostages, I presume."

♊

Talha's men met them thirty minutes from the coordinates located northeast of Lake Faguibine. Cherif received a call on his satellite phone as they followed their escorts.

"Moussa Diallo's men have left Goundam and are traveling north," he said to Kate. "They are maybe an hour behind us."

Kate called Nick on his Thuraya. "The land pirates are on the move."

"We need to get this done as fast as possible."

"Our cargo?"

"Inbound."

"Cherif's men?"

"They stay with us or we abort."

"Agreed. Looks like we're getting close," Kate said, peering through the dusty windshield.

"I love you."

"Love you more." She disconnected with a smile and found Amy shaking her head. "What?"

"You two make me sick."

"She's just jealous," Charlie said. "She wants a sexy, strapping man of her own."

"I hear Chad is on the market."

Amy heaved.

"Look alive. It's game time."

The convoy rolled to a stop at the outskirts of the camp, where dozens of armed terrorists awaited them. The fighters permitted the two Hiluxes carrying the team to pass the outer perimeter. The Tuareg army arrayed themselves in defensive positions, .50-caliber guns at the ready.

Talha, Yunis, and the latter's two lieutenants greeted them. Talha appraised Kate with a critical eye.

"You appear to be in some pain, Madame Moreau."

"None at all," she lied.

"Then I shall no longer rue my actions during our last encounter."

Khalifa and Ratma emerged from a tent and embraced Sharaf and Fatima. Ratma smiled at Kate, and Khalifa shook his head in wonder.

"This plan, Madame Moreau, it is masterful. All this time, I had no idea the French were so clever."

"It just took the appropriate motivation," Talha said.

"I hope my son has apologized. I thought better of his upbringing."

"No hard feelings. May we see the hostages?"

"My money?" Talha said.

Nick spoke into a handheld radio. The reply was terse. "Inbound. We'll set up the landing zone. With your permission, sir," he said. He was under strict orders not to escalate unless absolutely necessary.

"Yunis will observe," Talha said.

Yunis and his two lieutenants followed Jake, who carried brightly colored panels and stakes, to an area north of camp away from vehicles. While Jake marked the LZ and relayed instructions via radio, Talha led everyone else toward dilapidated tents.

"Your hostages, Madame Moreau, Pastor Smith."

His men threw back sheepskin to reveal seven haggard, underfed people in ragged clothing. They cowered at his appearance. Talha was a less accommodating host than his father had been.

"Five minutes out," Nick said.

Kate and Amy urged everyone out of the tents. Mathilde insisted on bringing her beaten sack of personal items, which she spilled while trying to rise. Charlie and Marianne tossed the sundries back into the sack and helped her to her feet. Then Charlie ran to Stu, who was barely able to stand, and supported him with Amy's assistance. Bess herself struggled to walk.

Amy snapped her fingers at Ollie and Noah, who moved like zombies. "Hey! Help Mrs. Abbott."

"To the trucks," Sharaf ordered.

"No, Sheikh. You and the *kuffar* will stay with me until I am satisfied that all is as it should be. Let us wait with Yunis and your Legionnaire."

Talha strode toward the landing zone while Kate, Amy, Charlie, and Fatima pushed and prodded and cajoled their seven charges to hold on for just a bit longer. Their last week in captivity had sapped their strength and broken whatever spirit they had left.

"Jesus Christ on a cross," Amy muttered as Stu stumbled, nearly taking down both her and Charlie. Then she caught Bess's eye. "I am so sorry, Mrs. Abbott. May the Lord strike me where I stand for such blasphemy."

As they reached the LZ, Kate heard the first faint whapping of rotors. She turned east and found the black speck in the sky, flying low over the earth. Terrorists pointed and readied their rifles; two men stood poised with a Stinger missile.

"That's him," Nick said to Talha. "The helo has no offensive capabilities. No need for the Stinger."

"I'll be the judge of that, Legionnaire." Talha took a pair of binoculars from Yunis and watched the approach. "This is a medical transport?"

"A relic from America's debacle in Vietnam," Nick replied.

The Huey medevac, with red crosses painted onto white squares on sides, nose, and belly, was piloted by Colonel Tom Patterson, retired, who swung around in a lazy arc and angled the helicopter into the light breeze. He touched down and throttled back to an idle. Yunis and his two lieutenants ran to the pilot's door, waving him out. Patterson emerged holding his empty hands aloft. He wore a pistol at his waist, and Kate knew there was an AK-47 and boxes of ammo beside his seat, his protection in the event of a hard landing.

"The pilot doesn't speak Arabic," Sharaf shouted to Talha over the rotors' din. "If Yunis has questions, Umm Ali can translate."

"I want to see the money."

"Of course, Emir, of course."

"Sheikh, Madame Moreau, please accompany me."

Kate, Sharaf, Fatima, and Nick followed, soon joined by Jake, Khalifa, and Ratma. Talha motioned to Yunis's lieutenants, who clambered into the Huey and tore the tarp off the pallet. Blocks of clear, cellophane-wrapped cash were piled high: thirty million U.S. dollars in new, unmarked hundred-dollar bills. They cut into the cellophane and examined random bricks, flipping through the packets like hawaladars. They nodded to Talha, replaced the tarp and secured it, and jumped down.

The group joined Patterson and Yunis. "You sure you know how to fly this thing?" Kate yelled to Yunis. "Or do you need a minute to Google it?"

The former helicopter pilot in Khaddafi's Libyan air force sneered at her. "I can fly any helicopter you put in front of me."

"The transponder has been disabled?" Talha asked.

Patterson nodded as Fatima translated. Yunis said, "It is destroyed. No one can track us."

"Excellent. Then it is time for us to depart." As Yunis hauled himself into the cockpit and fiddled with instruments, familiarizing himself with the layout, Talha backed toward the Huey's open side door, his Kalashnikov cradled in his hands.

Behind Kate, Nick radioed Cherif and ordered him to bring multiple Hiluxes toward the LZ to accommodate the hostages. Yunis's lieutenants faced the team, standing between them and the Huey. Khalifa took Ratma's arm and guided her toward the helicopter.

"Just a moment, father," Talha called. "We need to clear space for you."

Khalifa and Ratma paused, shielding their faces from swirling dirt and dust as Yunis powered up the engines. Talha reached the Huey and took one giant step up, settling himself partially behind the hull.

"Brother Sharaf," he shouted. "Blessings upon you."

Sharaf touched his chest and bowed.

"Madame Moreau, I should like to express my appreciation."

The tension at the LZ was palpable. Kate's eyes never left the tall figure folded inside the Huey, mere feet from thirty million dollars of the United States government's money. Then he grinned.

"Take her!"

Yunis's lieutenants lunged at Kate. Nick moved faster, hurling Kate aside with his left hand and using his right to draw his pistol and shoot each man through the head. The second was dead before the first hit the ground.

Women screamed; Ratma, the Fourniers, Bess Abbott. Gunfire erupted from Tuaregs and terrorists alike. Nick hauled Kate to her feet and threw her behind Cherif's Hilux, which had shot forward and screeched to a stop near them. Yunis, rusty at the yoke, lurched the Huey up and sideways before stabilizing the ascent.

"Son!" Khalifa shouted, waving at the Huey, the skids out of reach.

"Apologies, father! But today you shall die a martyr!" Talha yelled.

Nick and Jake clustered the hostages low behind trucks and picked off confused terrorists, who were leaderless and surrounded by Cherif's force. Mathilde Fournier, wild-eyed and frantic, screeched like a feral cat in heat and made a break for it, dragging her dirty sack behind her. Kate dove toward her, but grasped only a tattered strip of her tunic.

"Mathilde, no!"

A burst of rifle fire from the Huey bit at the Frenchwoman's heels as she exposed herself on open ground, the rounds gaining until one felled her. She collapsed. Beside Kate, Marianne wailed. Nick, covered by Jake and Cherif and a squad of Tuaregs, ran to her and dragged her back toward the trucks.

Bright red blood spurted from the exit wound in her thigh. Nick jammed his knee into her leg close to her groin, cutting off the femoral artery, while simultaneously returning fire. Jake readied a tourniquet and made to join them, but then Stu Abbott, braced against a truck with Bess at his side, keeled over, unconscious.

"Jake, tourniquet!" Kate yelled.

He threw it to her and lunged for Stu, first feeling for a pulse and then ripping open his shirt. Kate worked around Nick's knee to fit the tourniquet high on Mathilde's leg and cranked the plastic windlass as tight as she could.

Jake began chest compressions on Stu, driving hard and fast. "Cardiac arrest!" he shouted to Nick.

"Not good, not good," Nick muttered to himself, rising and taking stock of the situation.

"Nick, stay down!" Kate said.

The Huey receded from view. Tom Patterson had outfitted himself with a rifle and ammo pouches from one of the Hiluxes and was covering a corner of their vehicular nest while the Tuaregs fought off IEM.

"Make the call," Nick said.

Kate, with hands covered in Mathilde's blood, grabbed the Thuraya phone from her belt and punched a pre-programmed number. Fraser answered on the first ring.

Kate had to shout to be heard above the battle. "Exchange made. Is the helo pinging?" In addition to the money, the team had hidden the beacon from Ratma's ungifted French moisturizer in the hold. The Huey's transponder was useless, but the beacon was invisible and online.

"We've got it heading west toward the Mauritanian border."

"Talha and Yunis on board with the cash."

"French attack helos are en route. What the hell is going on?"

"Cardiac arrest and a major gunshot wound."

"Gunships and medevacs from the earlier mission are peeling off toward you."

"We need radio contact before they engage at our position," Kate said.

"Understood."

As Kate disconnected, more Tuareg trucks converged on their location. Mokhtar, standing in the bed of one truck holding tight to the roll bar, yelled to Cherif in Tamashek. Their Tuareg commander grimly turned to them. Before he could speak, Amy, moving from truck to truck and popping up here and there like an evangelical groundhog, broke the bad news at the top of her lungs.

"Land pirates!"

♫

Nick vaulted into the bed of a Hilux for a better vantage point. He rotated the technical's .50-cal toward the threat, a mass of motorcycles appearing on the horizon. IEM fighters paused in skirmishes with Cherif's men and everyone looked to the south. Moussa Diallo, the Islamic State-aligned insurgent leader, had sent hundreds of men into hostile territory in pursuit of riches, high-value hostages, or both.

Jake, still performing chest compressions, looked up at him. "How bad?"

"Fallujah bad."

"Charlie, bud, need your help. Take over compressions," Jake said. "You know 'Stayin' Alive' by the Bee Gees?"

Charlie, who had been shielding Bess Abbott, looked nervously at Stu. "Yeah."

"Compress to the beat of the song. I need my kit."

Nick waited with his finger on the trigger of the .50-cal. As soon as the motorcyclists were in range, he would unleash hell. Jake crawled into the bed of their Hilux and returned to the hostages with his full medical kit, including an automated external defibrillator unit. He set the bright yellow case next to Stu and slapped the pads on the sick man's chest. Then he connected the electrodes.

"Back, back," he said to Charlie and Bess as the unit began assessing Stu's rhythm.

As Jake pressed a button to deliver a shock, Nick unloaded on the motorcycles. Other Tuareg-manned technicals did the same. Bikes went down, but more took their place. The mechanical AED voice instructed them to resume CPR while the unit recharged.

"I got it, I got it," Charlie said.

Jake ran to Kate with his kit. He checked the tourniquet and handed Kate a packet of powder. "This is a clotting agent. Dump it in the wound and then wrap it the best you can."

Nick instructed Cherif to deploy vehicles forward to meet the surge. Cherif passed the order to Mokhtar, who led the charge across the desert, still holding tight to the roll bar with one hand while he fired his AK-47 with the other. Jake ran to each hostage, checking them for injuries. He even checked Khalifa and Ratma, who sheltered with them.

"Where are the helos?" Nick yelled. He took his frustration out on a pack of approaching motos, mowing down several more. Still the tidal wave flowed toward them.

Then he heard it, the crackle of static and an accented voice over the French military radio he wore clipped to his vest. The voice cut in and out; Nick didn't understand a word of what was said.

"English!" he yelled back. "Speak English!"

"Nick! Give me the radio," Kate called.

He handed the radio to Amy, who scurried to Kate. Then Cherif pulled alongside his Hilux in a panic.

"Capitaine! Capitaine! My cousin! He is injured. *Daesh* will take him, Capitaine!"

"Calm down and stay right there," Nick ordered.

"But—"

"Just wait. I'll go with you."

♺

Kate took the radio from Amy and raised the pilots, ascertaining that they were ten minutes out. She confirmed their coordinates. The lead pilot asked for a recognition signal. Kate, perched on her knees over a grievously wounded woman, looked around for anything to differentiate them from the targets. She saw white trucks, tan trucks, balaclava-clad Tuaregs, balaclava-clad Arabs. With their luck, French attack helicopters would aim rockets right into their little circle of Hiluxes, which felt tighter by the minute.

"Kate!" Nick made a *what gives* motion with his left hand.

"Ten minutes out. But they need a sign that it's us."

He grinned. "On it."

Kate told the pilot to wait, then looked at the packet of clotting agent in her hand. Her stomach lurched.

"Want me to do it?" Amy asked.

"No." Kate ripped it open and dumped it in the wound. The blood bubbled as the wound heated, but then a cauterized layer formed over the gaping hole. Kate ripped off her tunic, leaving her clad in a black Kevlar vest over a T-shirt. She tied the tunic tightly around Mathilde's leg to protect the wound.

"USA! USA!" Amy yelled beside Kate.

Kate turned to see what prompted the outburst, and felt the urge to laugh. Nick lashed a six-foot tall pole flying a large American flag to a Hilux's roll bar. The flag caught in the breeze, whipping straight out, prepared to join the charge.

Nick jumped down and ran to Kate, placing a second radio beside her, one that would link her to him and Jake and Cherif. "Cherif's got guys down in no-man's-land. Including his cousin."

She looked into his bright cobalt eyes and reached a blood-smeared hand toward him. "Don't you dare die on me, Nick Cavanaugh."

He linked his pinkie with hers, suddenly pulling her to him and kissing her hard. "Never."

"Put me on the .50-cal. I'll cover you," Amy said.

"Seven minutes, seven minutes," said the voice on the radio. "Do you copy?"

"Copy," Kate replied. "Jake, seven minutes!"

Jake prepared to shock Stu's heart again with the AED. "Colonel! Mind landing those helos, sir?"

Patterson made his way toward the disheveled landing zone. Panels uprooted in the fighting now skittered across the desert. Fatima slipped out of the truck cocoon and followed him, much to Sharaf's dismay.

"What is the signal, over?"

"*Le drapeau américain,*" Kate responded.

"*Le drapeau...américain?*"

"*Mon Dieu,*" Kate muttered to herself, and then she snapped into the radio, "*Le drapeau américain, la bannière étoilée,* goddamn Old Glory herself."

"*Compris.*"

Marianne stroked Mathilde's ashen cheek and looked at Kate, her eyes welling with tears. "Will she live?"

"She'll live." Then Kate said the words she knew better than to utter. "I promise."

⇧

Amy shed her North Korean haute couture and hopped into the bed of the technical behind Nick clad in a tight black T-shirt covered by a black Kevlar vest. The giant cross still hung from her neck. She rubbed her hands eagerly.

"The CIA never let us play with the fun stuff!" she yelled.

"It's not rocket science. Hand grips, butterfly trigger, rack the slide if it jams." He patted the top of the gun. "This will fuck people up."

An unfamiliar expression crossed her face. Nick grabbed her shoulder.

"Hey, look at me. You don't have to shoot anyone. Just get their attention, try to divert them from this position. Anyone with half a brain will think twice before coming near this beast. Got it?"

She nodded.

"This radio connects to Jake and me, and Kate has one, too. We're gonna grab Mokhtar and come right back."

"I will kill you if you die."

"Get in line." Then he jumped from the technical into the bed of Cherif's waiting Hilux.

Two technicals flanked them. The gunners had no qualms about mowing down Moussa Diallo's men in their mismatched uniforms and ill-fitting equipment. Nick focused on the disabled truck in the distance and the several Tuaregs sheltering behind it with bodies at their feet. Cherif screamed into his radio at his men, his Tamashek rising to a crescendo. His fighters responded, intensifying their resistance despite being outnumbered and overwhelmed.

Nick looked to the sky as the first faint rotor beats reached his ringing ears. Attack helicopters low on the horizon, approaching from the east. Nearly in range.

The trucks skidded to a halt and Nick and Cherif dismounted. Multiple wounded. Mokhtar wheezed, his hands clutching his midsection. Nick cut off the Tuareg's ammo rack and sliced through his fatigues to expose his torso. He saw the hole in his chest, bubbling blood with each labored breath. He slapped a hand over the hole, then rooted around in his thigh-mounted medical pack for an occlusive dressing.

"Dry the area," he ordered Cherif.

The Tuareg used his turban to wipe his cousin's chest. Nick adhered the bandage to skin around the wound. Air now escaped his chest through the bandage's vent, but could no longer enter. He checked the other men for serious injuries, but their wounds could wait.

"Load them up."

As Cherif and his able men loaded wounded into the trucks while the technicals laid down covering fire, the attack helicopters swung wide. Nick pulled the pin on a smoke grenade and heaved it. He prayed for just a bit of time.

"Tell them to fire west of the green smoke!" he shouted into the Sandstorm radio.

"Copy," Kate said.

Ω

Kate grabbed the radio connecting her to the French helicopters and relayed Nick's order: engage west of the green smoke.

"*Bien reçu, à l'ouest de la fumée verte.*"

"No, no, no!" Amy screamed. "He's in the kill zone!"

"Abort, abort!"

But it was too late. Multiple helicopters launched a volley of rockets into the zone, incinerating insurgents and their motorcycles. As thunderous explosions rang out and shook the earth, Kate left Mathilde's side and scrambled into the bed of the technical beside Amy, straining to see through the smoke and the sand and the dust. She knew it was useless; no one could have survived that barrage. As she slumped against the cab, Amy grabbed her and pointed, whooping.

Three trucks emerged from the smoke, a tall Marine standing beside a tall Tuareg in the bed of one, both holding the roll bar like the reins of a bucking bronco. They rejoined the team and began unloading men.

Kate looked sternly at Nick.

He grinned. "Sorry."

The lead pilot announced the imminent arrival of medevacs and a transport. Kate coordinated with Fatima and Tom over one radio and relayed instructions to the pilots over the second. Jake took charge of triage, moving the critically injured onto fold-out stretchers. Amy rounded up the mobile hostages and kept them in a tight group. The attack helicopters continued mopping up the battlefield and Cherif's men turned their attention to disarming Khalifa's remaining fighters.

Khalifa, still sheltered with the team, took hold of Ratma and urged her toward one of his abandoned Hiluxes. "We must go!"

Sharaf al-Jawfi, the ostensible sheikh and eminent businessman who lived to serve al-Qaeda, reacted faster than anyone. He snatched a Kalashnikov from the ground and leveled it at Khalifa.

"Brother Sharaf!"

"I am not your brother, Khalifa. And you are coming with us."

Ratma slapped Khalifa on the arm and pointed to the American flag whipping in the rotor wash of descending helicopters. "You foolish man. I knew you could not outrun them forever."

Khalifa's shoulders sagged. He looked at Kate, understanding dawning in his eyes. He inclined his head and touched his chest. "Well done, Madame Moreau."

Covered by Cherif's force, the team approached the LZ and handed off Stu, Mathilde, and Mokhtar to French medics. The medics loaded their patients and set to work as each helicopter lifted off one by one and swung east toward Timbuktu. Soldiers then herded Sandstorm, the remaining hostages, and Khalifa and Ratma toward the large transport. Cherif refused to accompany them; he intended to make the drive back to the base with his men and pick off Moussa's surviving fighters.

As the transport rose, Kate looked from face to face. Exhausted but elated friends, former hostages in a state of disbelief, and one high-value target sitting quietly between two French soldiers. Kate realized she had a death grip on Nick's hand and tried to relax, but her body wasn't ready to obey her mind's commands. In any case, he didn't seem to mind.

Ratma pointed to her and Nick. "I knew it!" she called to them in Arabic.

Kate smiled. Then the radio clipped to her belt let loose a burst of static followed by a most welcome transmission. A French pilot gave a description of a UH-1 Iroquois helicopter traveling northwest toward the Mauritanian border and requested orders. Before anyone could respond, she replied in French.

"Shoot it down and obliterate it. Leave nothing but a crater in the sand."

She recognized the general's voice. "Engage."

"*Compris.*" Then a moment later, "Target is destroyed."

Kate leaned against Nick and breathed a painful sigh of relief. "Two terrorists and thirty million dollars of the U.S. government's money up in flames," she called out for everyone to hear.

Amy held aloft her giant cross. "Raise your fist, evangelist!"

Kate laughed and shook her head. "You're ridiculous."

Her best friend grinned and kissed the cross. "Figured it couldn't hurt. Seemed like we needed all the help we could get."

ᛗ

Medical personnel, soldiers, intelligence officers, and ambassadors and consular officers from the American and French embassies in Bamako met the transport as it touched down. American embassy officials, empowered to act on behalf of the Australian government until one of their regional officers arrived, would represent Ollie and Noah. Stu, Mathilde, and Mokhtar were rushed into the hospital. French military police took Khalifa and Ratma into custody.

Kate and Nick wandered away from the chaos, and Kate watched it all with a detached sense of fascination. Amy and Charlie stood with Fraser, excitedly telling a story with grand hand gestures. Fraser unexpectedly pulled both of them to her in a hug. Jake remained with Bess, who was being tended to by medics. Dubois and Ardouin stood with the general and Gilles Lefèvre, who said something and nodded toward Kate and Nick before medics took him away. The three Frenchmen turned toward them; the general shook his head in wonder, Dubois smiled, and Ardouin studied them, his expression inscrutable.

"You've really outdone yourself, love," Fatima said with a smile. She squeezed Kate's arm as she and Sharaf passed to stand at Tom Patterson's side.

"Hey, Fraser!" Nick yelled. He pointed to Patterson. "You owe him a new helicopter!"

Fraser laughed and shook her head in resignation. A truck pulled up to the outskirts of the mass of people and disgorged five CIA officers, none of whom looked pleased, although some looked more displeased than others. Van Pelt just appeared confused.

Nick draped an arm over Kate's shoulders, taking care not to jostle the injured joint. "Think Chad's figured it out yet?"

She turned to him. "Let's make sure. Kiss me."

He leaned down and pressed a kiss to her forehead.

"What the hell was that?"

He looked confused. "All these people...you don't like PDA, remember?"

"I'm a big fan of it when my idiot ex-boyfriend is watching."

"In that case..." Nick drew her close and kissed her in a way that put to rest any questions over the status of their marriage.

Kate smiled up at him and from the corner of her eye saw Chad turn and kick a tire on the Hilux. Lacey's face fell.

"Much better," she said.

"I'm leaving you for Lacey."

"Who?"

He smiled and kissed her again. "I have a very important question for you. *Voulez-vouz coucher avec moi*?"

"*Ce soir*?"

"*Oui.*"

"*Plus que tous,* Capitaine Cavanaugh. *Plus que tous.*"

EPILOGUE

STU ABBOTT, MATHILDE FOURNIER, and Mokhtar ag Elwafil survived and were expected to make satisfactory recoveries. In the days following the rescue, America's HVT-8, Khalifa al-Ghazawi, refused to talk to anyone except the woman he knew as Katherine Moreau, counselor to the French minister of foreign affairs. Fraser, back in command, received approvals from Langley to permit Kate to debrief Khalifa, with the goal of getting him comfortable with Charlie and others who would spend considerably more time with him over the coming weeks and months and possibly years. Neil Weiss, banished to operational oblivion with Van Pelt, was beside himself over losing the opportunity to interrogate the man he had spent a career chasing, and pleaded his case to the highest levels of the Agency. He was rebuffed.

Following several talkative sessions with Kate and then tense coordination between the French and Algerian governments, Ratma was released into the custody of her eldest daughter, who lived in Tamanrasset. Before Ratma departed on a French military flight to Kidal to make the trip overland into Algeria, Kate arranged a discreet meeting between her and Fatima. A brick of cash changed hands, and Ratma promised to "disappear" the late Yunis's young widows and children to safety. Then the elegant Tuareg turned to Kate.

"This did not end how I had hoped it would, but I believe it ended how it was meant to. Thank you for your mercy."

The U.S.-based Sandstorm team departed Timbuktu ten days after the rescue on the DGSE's Gulfstream, which stopped in Paris only to refuel and allow Kate and Nick to walk and relieve Kella. Before they left, Cherif ag Salla presented his ceremonial takuba sword, passed down to freedom fighters throughout the generations, to the finest warrior he had ever met. Nick Cavanaugh accepted the gift with glistening eyes and embraced the tall Tuareg as a brother.

Then they arrived in Boston and settled back into life, with nary a word to anyone about their recent exploits, and watched the frenzy from afar.

Mathilde Fournier was France's newest media sensation, first holding court from her hospital bed and then from her home in Paris. Her dramatic recounting of her kidnapping, captivity, and eventual rescue beguiled the nation, especially her descriptions of and commentary on two Legionnaires and the youthful, petite counselor to the minister of foreign affairs who had saved them all.

The journalists salivated and set out to find the mystery rescuers. The French Ministry of Foreign Affairs stated they had no counselor to the minister by that name, and referred the matter to the DGSE. The DGSE referred the matter back to the ministry. Reporters tracked down a Katherine Moreau in the employ of the MFA, but she was a sexagenarian secretary on the brink of retirement and amused by the notion that she had personally negotiated with a wanted terrorist in the heart of Mali.

The Ministry of Defense acknowledged only that a French unit based in Timbuktu had participated in the rescue of seven hostages from three nations. The French Foreign Legion professed no knowledge of two Legionnaires, current or former, in the employ of a shadowy Arab businessman who allegedly brokered contact with the emir of the Islamic Emirate of the Maghreb for the French government.

"Two Legionnaires," Mathilde insisted. "One German, one Russian. Both very handsome."

A spokeswoman for the German government, when asked about the activities of a German mercenary believed to be named Dieter, appeared perplexed, but offered lukewarm praise for said mercenary, if indeed he had been responsible for the rescue of hostages from terrorists. A spokeswoman for the Russian government, in contrast, first railed against Western imperialism in Africa and then castigated the French for failing to properly credit a man possibly named Dmitri. She urged the newest hero of the Russian Federation to come forward to be recognized. Several Dmitris did step forward, but they were not the stoic, sandy-haired Legionnaire as described by all seven hostages. And most of them were drunk. The diplomatic brouhaha threatened to escalate into crisis until calls were made from Washington and Paris to Berlin and Moscow, smoothing ruffled feathers and offering assurances that their citizens had neither broken laws nor consorted with terrorists.

Marianne and Lefèvre, when pressed, were more circumspect about their rescuers. "She claimed to be French," Lefèvre said during a group interview, "but I'm not sure."

"You all mentioned an American flag. Was she American?" asked the interviewer.

"Possibly," he conceded, as Marianne nodded.

"Yes, of course, the Americans, always there making a nuisance of themselves," Mathilde said dismissively. "But I say with certainty that Katherine Moreau is not American. She is a French national treasure."

The furor crossed the Atlantic. An American flag flying during a pitched battle between the forces of good and evil in the barren lands of the Sahel? After double- and triple-checking, the Department of Defense, with obvious disappointment, professed no involvement in a rescue operation. The CIA had no comment on the matter. All online content related to the fictitious American Evangelical Association disappeared, and the community was in a tizzy over the actions of apparent Pentecostal interlopers. Nonetheless, evangelical leaders were more than happy to claim credit for the Abbotts' return and generate an influx of donations to their megachurches, much to Amy's dismay.

The Abbotts, who quickly realized their rescuers were red-blooded Americans once the fight began, had promised Diana Fraser that they would keep Sandstorm's secret. They limited their media engagement upon their return to Kansas, where Stu spent weeks in the hospital and underwent further procedures to stabilize his heart, offering only sincerest thanks to the men and women who had brought them home.

Ollie and Noah basked in their celebrity back in Sydney. They had no strong feelings about the true identities of the people who saved them. They just wanted to get laid and plan their next adventure.

Margaret and George, the only Sandstorm employees who had any inkling of the company's involvement, set aside their differences and collaborated on a scrapbook of media highlights for Kate and Nick and Jake, with special attention paid to the most humorous and outlandish stories and conspiracy theories zipping across the internet.

"This is bullshit," Nick said to Kate and Jake one day, as another segment on CNN speculated on their identities and explained Mali to a geographically challenged American audience. "This should be a major motion-picture event, with Hollywood's handsomest Chrises vying to play me."

"Then I would insist on playing myself. Especially for the post-drone attack love scenes," Kate said.

Nick made a face. "I guess there's something to be said for anonymity."

𝄐

Director-General Dubois sent engraved invitations to all of their homes, scattered throughout the United States and the Middle East: a black-tie affair, to be held in December, to reaffirm the partnership between the CIA and the DGSE and to pay quiet tribute to those who had risked everything to save strangers.

Paris was aglow and the Christmas markets bustled on the night of the soirée, and the Palace of Versailles, Dubois's hand-picked venue, positively shimmered as the guests of honor arrived. The receiving line of intelligence officers, ministers, diplomats, and former hostages and their families broke into applause as a motley crew alit from chauffeured luxury vehicles, in awe of their surroundings and shocked at the sight of who awaited them.

"Is this your idea of quiet tribute?" Kate hissed at Fraser.

The CIA station chief grinned. "They've been begging to see you. We took everyone's phones. Just enjoy."

Mathilde, cane in hand, limped forward and crushed Kate in an embrace. Then she held her at arm's length, studying her. "*Je sais que tu es américaine, mais tu resteras à jamais française dans mon cœur.*"

Kate smiled. "*C'est mon honneur.*"

"Come. The minister would like to meet you. She has heard much about you."

Ω

As Kate was engulfed by the crowd of admirers, Nick made for the bar and requested top-shelf scotch. Jake soon joined him, having left his wife Lisa in the company of Amy, Charlie, and the Abbotts, who gushed about his heroics. He ordered the same scotch.

"When you convinced me to leave the Corps, forgo a full pension, and partner with you—just simple, straightforward security consulting, as I recall you saying—this is not what I bargained for," Jake said.

"Yeah, sorry. It's all Kate's fault."

Jake laughed.

"Regrets?"

"Not a one." They clinked tumblers. "Damn, this is good scotch. Can we afford this?"

"No."

"We were made aware that your tastes run to the extravagant. No expense was spared to ensure your satisfaction this evening," said a voice from behind them.

Nick turned. "Henri, a pleasure. What are you drinking? We're buying."

Ardouin spoke in French to the bartender, who poured him a snifter of cognac. He raised his class. "*À la vôtre.*"

"Cheers."

Ardouin swirled his cognac and sipped. He cocked his head. "Would it be wrong of me to think that you had already made Director-General Dubois's acquaintance prior to our trip to Boston?"

Nick laid a friendly but firm hand on Ardouin's shoulder. "Would it be wrong of us to think that you're asking us that question because you know you'll never get anything out of Kate?"

A smile tugged at the corner of Ardouin's mouth.

"If we had ever met Monsieur Dubois, which we hadn't before that day, we would maintain the strictest confidentiality, as we do for all our clients. And as we would do for you should you ever seek our services again for a professional—or personal—matter."

"I appreciate your discretion. As does Director-General Dubois."

Amy, Charlie, and Lisa joined them, and Amy snapped her fingers at Ardouin. "*Garçon! Champagne pour tout le monde, s'il vous plaît.*"

The chief of protocol, in good humor, requested a bottle of their finest champagne and partook in the toast.

"I don't think you're ever getting Kate back," Amy said to Nick. "She's the belle of the ball."

"She deserves the adulation." He looked around the palace ballroom, finally finding Kate surrounded by Fraser, Dubois, Emmanuel Giraud, the minister of foreign affairs, the minister of defense, the general from Timbuktu, the Fourniers, and Lefèvre, who had a woman on his arm. Kate said something and everyone laughed. It was the first time Nick had seen Lefèvre smile. "She deserves very minute of it," he said softly.

"Hey bro."

Amy swore and Nick swallowed a sigh before turning. "Hey Chad."

Fraser had warned them that Chad, Blake, Lacey, and Van Pelt would make an appearance. Dubois, out of respect for protocol, didn't feel as though he could dictate to the CIA director whom he could send. The director wanted the Hostage Task Force represented, and Dubois graciously agreed. Neil Weiss declined the invitation; he was prohibited from official travel following an internal ruling on the illegality of the drone strike he had ordered.

The investigation into Chad and Blake, Fraser explained, was ongoing, and every effort was made to obscure investigators' activities, especially into the men's current spending habits. Therefore, they were encouraged to attend and enjoy their stay in Paris.

"Just wanted to say no hard feelings over that stunt you pulled, sending us after the fake Khalifa. Doyle and I get it—hard to share that kind of glory," Chad said. Blake nodded in agreement.

Nick tried a yoga breath. "Thanks for understanding."

"We saw the video from the French helos. Hell of a battle on the ground, but you held your own. Not bad for a couple of leathernecks."

"To paraphrase General Pershing, 'A Marine and a gun...'"

"'...second to none,'" Jake finished. They fist-bumped.

"Sure, sure. Listen, about Kate..."

Another yoga breath, and still he felt his blood pressure rise. "What about Kate?"

"Just want you to know, we're done."

Nick gritted his teeth. Chad had regularly texted Kate since the summer, begging to see her, venting his frustrations with his pregnant girlfriend, complaining he didn't get enough credit for his role in the rescue and Khalifa's capture. Kate had replied only a handful of times, anodyne responses in hopes he would get the message. Earlier in the month, she had wished him congratulations on the birth of his child.

"Great," he said, conscious of everyone's keen interest in their conversation.

"Not gonna lie, bro. I feel like I dodged a bullet."

Nick blinked. "Dodged a bullet?"

"I mean, I don't know how you do it, letting her run your ops and all. Especially after what happened in Yemen. You know she got a guy killed, right?"

Nick gaped.

"I guess whatever she's doing for you outside the office must be worth it. Am I right?" He gave Nick a friendly shot to the shoulder, while Blake smirked.

Nick turned to Amy. "Mind holding my drink?"

"With pleasure."

He handed her his scotch and in one swift movement decked Chad with a right cross. Chad's head snapped around and he stumbled and fell. Blake moved toward Nick, but Jake slid into his path.

"Not your fight, bud."

The rapid click of heels on marble preceded Kate's appearance at Nick's side. She stepped between him and Chad, who was attempting to rise, dazed, and smacked Nick in the chest.

"What the hell, Nick?"

Nick looked at his fist. "Oops."

"You know the rules. Pick on someone your own size."

Their friends guffawed. Ardouin smiled into his drink. Amy took hold of Chad's arm and helped him stand.

"You poor thing. Are you okay?"

"I'm fine," he said, touching his lip and trying to shrug free of her grasp.

"Good." She pivoted and drove her knee into his groin. He crumpled, howling and cupping himself.

"Amy!"

Fraser, with obvious reluctance, intervened and ordered Chad and Blake to disperse. Kate pushed Nick away from the crowd and backed him against a wall. She was three inches taller in her heels, but he still had nine inches and well over a hundred pounds on her. And yet he was certain that his pixie of a wife, in her mouth-watering little black dress, could kick his ass. He managed to suppress a smile.

"What is wrong with you?"

"It needed to be done."

"During a formal event, at one of the most famous and majestic historical sites in the world, in an opulent ballroom full of dignitaries, you had to slug my ex?"

"Yes."

She stared up at him, hazel eyes flashing. "And not even an apology?"

"I don't know what I'd be apologizing for."

Her stare turned to a glower. She smiled icily and took hold of his hand, but less in the manner of an affectionate lover and more like a marshal controlling a flight risk. "You will not leave my side."

Ω

Kate finally released him hours later, when the CIA contingent made for the exit. Nick settled himself at a table with a fresh scotch. He needed the bottle; hobnobbing with the French was exhausting. He watched Kate, still the center of the universe, and knew she tired of the attention. She glanced his way a few times, probably just to make sure he hadn't followed Chad outside.

As the party wound down after midnight, the ministerial ranks departed and left behind the intelligence officers, the former hostages, and Sandstorm. Jake and Lisa, making the most of a child-free trip, cuddled at a table with their own bottle of champagne. Fatima, resplendent in gold-trimmed white robes, cozied up to Tom Patterson, occasionally resting a hand on his arm as she laughed at his jokes. He looked elated. Sharaf examined the remaining spreads of hors d'oeuvres and desserts, taking mental notes.

The Abbotts were gamely hanging on, but clearly out past their bedtime. Mathilde Fournier, under the supervision of her sister, was the life of the party, a *raconteuse* par excellence. The Aussie boys downed tequila shots with Amy and Charlie at the bar, making a ruckus and embarrassing their parents. Lefèvre departed first, spending a quiet moment with Kate. He clasped one of her hands in both of his, and then offered a wave to Nick from afar. Nick touched his forehead in a casual salute and wondered if he should have another scotch.

Fraser sat beside him. "Quite the place, isn't it? *Louis Quatorze* knew how to live."

Nick grunted.

"If you have time during this trip, I want to introduce you to my British counterpart here. He's got a little problem that I think—"

"Is that how people at the Agency see Kate? They still believe she was responsible for Reed's death?"

Fraser sighed. "The cable in which she took the blame was purged from the system, but people still saw it. Men like Van Pelt and Weiss have large networks and powerful friends. Every few months, Charlie and I instigate a viral release of the correct version of events, especially when Yemen makes news. Unfortunately, the lowest common denominator would prefer to believe their lying eyes."

"She's saved so many people. Hassan, Camille, two embassy communities, these seven people here."

"And you," Fraser reminded him.

"And me. She gave up everything for me."

"She gave up a good thing to gain something better. You know that. And without her operating out here, with you, there's no way Camille, hundreds of embassy employees in Paris, or seven former hostages would be where they are today: alive."

"She deserves for the world to know."

The CIA station chief smiled. "Perhaps someday, the world will know. Until then, those ops will remain some of the Agency's most highly compartmented. Just how she wants it."

Kate caught his eye and jerked her head toward the door. Nick stood and buttoned his jacket. "Off to sleep on the floor tonight."

"Oh, I think you'll manage to recover."

The look on Kate's face suggested otherwise. He joined her as she wrapped up a conversation with Dubois and Ardouin. An attendant fetched their coats and Nick helped Kate into hers.

"Thank you for a wonderful evening, messieurs. I apologize for any...boorish behavior that may have occurred."

Ardouin spoke in French. "*Je ne serais pas trop dur avec lui*, Madame Cavanaugh. *Un coup de poing dans la bouche est parfois tout à fait justifié.*"

Nick looked questioningly at Kate.

"He still thinks you're immature and incompetent," she snapped.

Ardouin shot Nick a sympathetic look. Dubois kissed Kate on the cheek and shook Nick's hand.

"*À la prochaine*," said the director-general with a smile. "Until next time."

Ω

Kate stood before the window in their hotel room, gazing upon Paris. She had been here countless times—as a student, as a tourist, as an intelligence officer—but never like this. She smiled at the Eiffel Tower as she considered the surprise she had for Nick. Dubois and Ardouin had arranged a private tour of World War battlefields across France with an English-speaking historian over the course of the next week. He would be in Marine Corps heaven.

She closed the curtains and faced him. "You can't assault people."

He crossed his arms over his chest and regarded her stonily.

"You going to tell me what he said?"

"It doesn't need to be repeated."

Kate already knew what had been said. A barrage of text messages from Amy, Charlie, Jake, and Lisa had described the exchange in detail. Amy had screamed her recounting of events in all caps.

"Then I'll continue to believe that you were in the wrong."

"If you insist."

"You owe me an apology."

"I'm sorry you dated an asshole."

"Funny."

He shed his suit jacket and tie and moved across the room, entering her personal space. Heat radiated from his body and his deep blue eyes. She itched to place her hands on his broad chest and press herself against him.

"I won't apologize, but I'll make it up to you."

"Impossible."

"Disagree. I'll prove it in just four easy steps. Step one: I kiss you."

Kate allowed a pause. "Fine. Just so you know, I don't intend to kiss you back."

But Nick was an outstanding kisser, and her lips and tongue had minds of their own.

"Step two," he continued when he finally broke the kiss. "I get you out of this most perfect little black dress."

His breath caught as the dress pooled around her heel-clad feet. If he thought the dress was perfect, she wondered how he would describe what she wore under it.

"Holy fuck," he murmured.

"I just bought this lingerie yesterday, and it cost a fortune. Do *not* destroy it."

"I wouldn't dare."

"You would, caveman."

But he treated her special purchase just for him with reverence. His hands caressed her bare skin, and she shivered under his touch.

"Step three: I take you to bed."

"Whatever. I don't intend to enjoy it."

Nick scooped her up and laid her down, threw off her heels, and then undressed himself. He joined her, looking his fill.

"Not even step four? All your favorite things?"

"I have a lot of favorite things. You better get started."

♌

"I hope that was as terrible for you as it was for me," Nick said.

Kate moaned a response. She couldn't move. She had too many favorite things. He drew her close and splayed a hand over her stomach, his fingers tracing her ribs, long since healed. She turned her face to his for a kiss.

"I accept your non-apology," she said.

"He really did deserve it."

"I know."

"Fraser wants us to meet someone. A Brit."

"What did you tell her?"

"To go to hell. We're never taking another job involving the CIA ever again."

"At least until the next time, right?"

He groaned and she laughed.

"You'll be the death of me, Kate Devlin."

"Cavanaugh," she corrected. "I'm yours, but more importantly, you're mine."

He smiled and held out his pinkie finger. "Promise?"

"*Toujours et pour toujours*, Capitaine Cavanaugh. Always and forever."

Enjoy this book?

You can make a big difference. Honest reviews of my books help bring them to the attention of other readers. If you've enjoyed this book, I would be very grateful if you could spend just five minutes leaving a review (it can be as short as you like) on the book's page at your favorite retailer.

Thank you!

THE SANDSTORM SERIES

A spy, a mercenary, and a motley crew of friends. Can they save the world, or will they die trying?

—

CIA operative Kate Devlin and security consultant Nick Cavanaugh get off on the wrong foot. After all, her accidental terrorist had orders to kill him. And if there's one thing Nick can't abide, it's creating terrorists.

But it turns out that Kate's good intentions count for something. She saves his life, in more ways than one. While creating terrorists may not be a good career move, it does lead to a most unexpected outcome: love. Kate's never been in love before, but she thinks this might go the distance.

They were made for each other, this pixie spy and caveman mercenary. Lovers, best friends, and...business partners? Is Sandstorm International big enough for the both of them?

And will they ever be able to escape the CIA? Kate may have quit the Agency, but the Agency just can't quit her. Whenever an impossible problem arises in a foreign land, the CIA calls in Kate, Nick, and their Sandstorm family.

Shenanigans ensue.

Maybe they can't save the world, but they sure can have fun trying.

The Sandstorm Series features Kate, Nick, and their motley crew of friends on rollicking adventures in foreign lands. If you enjoy action, intrigue, humor, and a love that conquers all, you'll love *The Sandstorm Series*.

—

Book 1: *The Stars Refuse to Shine*
Book 1.5: *Sandstorm Rising*, a free novella
(download at www.lynnmason.com)
Book 2: *The Edge of the Night*
Book 3: *A Gathering Storm*

A SUMMER OF WAR

Conflict on the battlefield and in the newsroom. A feisty female journalist and a stoic hero. Can their love survive the tragedy of the Vietnam War?

—

Journalist Chris McKenna would do anything to cover the Vietnam War. If there's anything she knows, it's that she was born to tell this story.

Chris rolls into South Vietnam intent on sniffing out the overlooked stories of America's most unpopular war. Much to the dismay of the military establishment, she hops a Huey to a remote base in the Mekong Delta and hits the motherlode. A mission both tactically and strategically questionable. Inept junior officers more concerned about image than protecting the troops they lead. A platoon of grunts taking fire from all sides. A stoic soldier powerless against the woman keen on breaking through his defenses.

John Rawlins rues the day he met Chris. The last thing he wants is to be a story, but Chris has glory in mind for the quiet, heroic soldier who simply wants to make it home alive. He figures she won't last long. Journalists never do.

He couldn't be more wrong.

Through jungle patrols and firefights, amidst the chaos and the comedy that is the war in Vietnam, Chris earns the respect and affection of a squad of men who have nothing to lose by telling it like it is.

But as the pressure from her editor mounts, as journalistic competition descends on the Delta, as Chris reckons with the consequences of the choices that led her to Vietnam, she discovers how hard it is to separate the story she was born to tell from the story she was born to live.

Pick up *A Summer of War* to follow Chris on her adventures today!

ALSO BY

FREE BOOKS!

Love free books? Sign up for Lynn's newsletter and be the first to know about new releases and freebies! No spam—just the occasional update with links to free or heavily discounted books. Don't miss out!

www.lynnmason.com

ABOUT THE AUTHOR

Lynn Mason likes strong female protagonists with a penchant for getting themselves into trouble all over the world. The only thing more fun than watching a character get into trouble is watching her get out of it.

Lynn believes that the journey of creation will take an author to wild and wonderful places. The artistic wilderness can be daunting, but the creator has a duty to leave footprints in the sand.

When she's not globetrotting in search of her next story, she and her menagerie of furry friends live near Washington, D.C.

Find Lynn at www.lynnmason.com